The Line in the Sand

SOLA ODEMUYIWA

Copyright © 2015 Sola Odemuyiwa
All rights reserved.
ISBN:-10:1517498821
ISBN-13:978-1517498825

All rights reserved.
ISBN:-10:1517498821
ISBN-13:978-1517498825

Cover design: nextgendigitalmedia.com

In memory of my indomitable Dad.

PART ONE

ONE

Dele Verity snapped her sticky eyes wide open in terror, heard Dad's gentle snoring next door and puffed her cheeks out in relief. *Phew, only another bad dream, but the really really sick news is we're still here.* Separated from her parent's bedroom by white plasterboard, and no larger than the shoe cupboard Mum had in Zadunaria, her bedroom opened on to the front room. She sat up, in a bed so tiny Dad called it a crib, leaned away from the sloping ceiling, fetched the two-plug extension with a sleepy foot and stamped. The pilot light flickered on and the standing fan in the corner grumbled into life, lifting grey buds of dust off its rusty cage. But before Dele could settle into the breeze, the wagging tails on the balls of fluff flopped back down and the fan wheezed to a halt.

'Electric people, God will punish you, oh,' she heard a woman shout from the back street. A parrot re-tweeted the woman's cry.

'Shut up you or I'll screw your beak off,' said Dele with a wry chuckle. She knew that it was not yet half past five because Eddy the civil servant's smelly bath suds had not gurgled through the shallow gutter running under her bed. A snort came from next door, then a cough and the sound of Dad's shuffling feet, but Dele didn't want him to come with her today. She was a big girl now.

She put on her dressing gown. Her door creaked as she prised it open. She crept across the front room, eased her new yellow bucket from under the sink and opened the front door. It opened straight on to the street and the rotting rubbish tips gave the cloying morning air a smell like bad breath. In the dim light Dele could just make out the ghostly *muezzin*, in his white gown, with white megaphone in hand, as he rattled open the corrugated doors to the mosque. She knew she had to hurry because the man's calls to his faithful and Pastor Kalistus's plaintive prayers in response would soon get many out of their beds. So, wedging her feet further into her slippers, she leapt off the sandbags Dad had laid against the floods and skipped down the street, using the bricks wedged in the mud as stepping stones. But, to her dismay, Little Mama had beaten her to the standpipe.

Little Mama was said to be fifteen but looked about nine. And she loved a sales patter. Dele turned away and waited out of range, but Little Mama would not be denied. She walked up to Dele. 'Do you want tea, green tea, camomile, iroko, palm wine tea, or a coffee, with cow's milk, tinned milk, do you take sugar?' she said.

'I don't want a drink,' said Dele.

'Then can I offer you our marine selection, fried fish?' said Little Mama, raising a fork to her mouth in pantomime.

'Have you got shark?' said Dele. *That will shut her up.*

Little Mama looked over her shoulder and at the ditch. 'I think so,' she said.

'No, I mean whale,' said Dele.

Little Mama shook her head.

'Don't bother. Maybe tomorrow,' said Dele.

Little Mama looked disappointed to have let down her client. She went quiet and her face dropped. Dele felt guilty. She turned away from Little Mama and watched the bucket fill. When the water shimmered and tinkled to its brim at last, 'it's full,' said Dele and gave Little Mama a gentle nudge.

'Don't worry I'll have whale next time,' said Little Mama. She rolled an old vest into a cushion for her head and, without a slop, heaved the bucket on to the pad and made her jaunty way back up the street.

What's wrong with Little Mama? Relieved that there was no one else in sight, Dele placed her plastic bucket under the trickling tap so that the water did not drum into its base but ran down the sides. The water had barely covered the bottom of the bucket when Sandman's unmistakable silhouette appeared outside his doorway halfway up the street. Most people called him Sandman, but only behind his back. Some said he got the name because his gowns and fez made him look like a desert dweller. Koseri, Dele's new best friend, said it was because the way his head and neck jerked forward when he walked made him look like a chicken pecking at sand. Dele's dad, Wale, said the name suited him because the man was always hatching or laying a plot.

With a short chewing stick hanging from his thin lips and a silver bucket in his left hand, Sandman loomed to within spitting distance of Dele. 'Hey, yinbo girl, your time's up. Some of us have important things to do,' he said. Everything about Sandman, his squeaky voice, long neck, the shifty eyes placed almost on the side of his narrow long face, as if made from a mask too big for him, or as though the eyes could not stand each other, made Dele cringe.

'My five minutes at the tap takes me to this scratch Dad made here with a blade,' she said, tipping the bucket towards Sandman.

Sandman didn't even bother to look. 'Which stupid line? *Shia*, you and your mama think you are the only people on this planet,' he said. He pushed Dele on the shoulder, spinning her round and she slipped on the slimy concrete surround. Sandman laughed, emptied Dele's bucket into his and tossed hers into the bush. Dele seethed with impotent fury. But Mum would go volcanic if she lost that new bucket. So, watching out for broken glass and snakes and rats and careful not to lose her slippers, she squelched into the swamp to look for the bucket. She found it lying, dented, in a pool of stinking water in the hollow of a fallen tree trunk. As she turned for the standpipe who should she see but her dad striding down the street looking like a bare-knuckled prize-fighter? A white shirt billowed behind his bare chest and he had his fist and jaws clenched. Dele flew out of the swamp to meet him.

'I saw that,' said Wale, emptying Sandman's bucket into Dele's.

'Do you know who I am?' said Sandman. 'You think you can dis me? I'll show you that we are not on the same level in this Sankara city,' he said, pounding his chest.

'Go on then, tell me. Those filthy bottles of piss you peddle can cure cancer, diabetes, depression, so how come you live on this Nigeria Street with the rest of us?' said Wale.

Sandman's eyes narrowed to angry slits. He jabbed three fingers in the air, folding each in turn. This is how I will break your family. One by one like matchsticks. You, your *kolo* whore and your bastard child. One…by…one, you watch me, you will see.'

Fear clawed at Dele's chest.

'Don't listen to him,' said Wale, taking his daughter's bucket in one hand and her hand in the other. 'The man is a nonentity. He can't hurt you. Let's get you ready for school.'

TWO

A little boy wobbling bedewed plastic bags in his hands and crying "pure water, pure water, buy one, buy one" squeezed through the crowd. He bumped into Dele, swore and pushed off before she could react. It was Friday, a week after the row with Sandman and, to surprise and cheer up her mum, Dele had gone to collect that week's milk supply from the cash and carry.

Rickety stalls teetering on mounds of stinking refuse lined the narrow dust track and Kubaku's hit song "Sankara of Excellence" boomed from box speakers stacked outside a barber's saloon. Above, a grey bird hopped this way and that on top of a pole and a couple of snagged balloons hung from lank and faded buntings, like rags on a washing line. *Have I gone past the railway line?* thought Dele with a little tick of disquiet in her chest, now sorry for giving Koseri the slip after Maths. And Mum would go off the Richter scale if she was late. She steadied the tray of milk tins on her head with a tentative wobble of her neck and, watching where she put her feet lest she turn her ankle in a pothole, followed the street round a right bend. Here, the crowd thinned out and ahead, a bloated ditch lazed like a sated serpent in the blazing heat. Behind it stood a weather-beaten green train carriage mounted on bricks, the smartest house Dele had seen on the street. A young woman with skin as black as a crow emerged from behind the coach carrying an armful of firewood. She had a ChinAfrican toddler in tow. The child toppled over, brayed, tears and snot running down her orange face on silver tracks laid by forerunners. Distracted by the child, Dele did not see a man swing a red bucket from the coach window until it was too late. A broad arc of fluid slapped into the ditch, hissed, reared up and spewed a smell of night soil and rotten eggs.

'Hey,' said Dele. Pinching her nostrils against the smell, she stamped hot slime off her feet and wedged her mascot back into place.

'Hoy, hoy, milk seller girl, come.'

Dele blinked the searing sweat and smoke from the roadside cooking fires from her eyes, steadied the tray with a tap of the hand, put on her trading smile and turned towards the caller. A man with teeth in such disarray that his lips seemed to have grown out of their way to avoid the chop, stood in front of what looked like a storey-high pile of rusting steel and rubble. Round of shoulder, with long arms and small hands, his T-shirt showed the scary face of Monday Babubacka the General who, with the rest of the world distracted, invaded North Roko the year before, on 9/11.

'How many do you want?' said Dele, batting away a beefy fly.

'I give you sixty,' said the man.

Dele shook her head. A lick of salty sweat slipped between her lips.

'Come on, my fine girl. Original or fake?' the man said. With one giant leap he was upon her, wrapping her in his shadow and his aroma of cooling charcoal. 'Hah, original…import. I give you hundred Roko for all,' he said, pawing a tin.

Dele closed her eyes tight and tried to do a quick sum. A hundred Roko seemed far too much when Mum got them for thirty and sold them for between fifty and sixty Roko. But she'd be over the moon with a hundred. *My mascot's working and this man might even tell me how to get home.* 'Ok,' she said, lifting the tray off her head and lowering it over a shallow pothole. The man's stare down the front of her blouse made her blush.

'The money is inside my house. You want a big man like me to carry tray in this hot sun? You think I am your boy-boy?' said the man, puffing himself up.

The snap in his voice made Dele start back and the thick oily smell of pork roasting on the charcoal-black woman's fire made her retch.

'No, I remember now sir. My mama will not be happy for me to sell at that price. She crossed one hand over the other like a supplicant puppy at a dogs' show. 'Look at me and this my brother,' she said, with a toss of the head at the bundle on her back. 'At that price all my brothers and sisters will die of hungry,' she said, slipping into the demotic that she thought might clinch a sale. 'Hunger,' she whispered to herself in correction as she turned side-on, to show the swaddled bundle.

The man's shoulders dropped further. He hacked his throat and spat. 'What spoiled you like this?' he said, sneering at the rash on the side of Dele's leg. Someone laughed. Dele blushed. Her dad had a rash like that too and she also had his stubby, cocktail-sausage toes. The man lobbed a tin over Dele's head.

'Ah no, please sir,' she said, pushing a clump of damp hair back from her face. As she bent over to stop a tin rolling into the ditch a stabbing pain from the cluster of swollen glands in her groins forced her straight back up. The tray crashed to the ground. Two tins of milk hovered for a few seconds in a grassy dip before they rolled and squelched into the ditch. The bad-toothed man laughed.

'Milk seller, no vex, major is not good. Thank God you are not made to suffer like that girl who passed by yesterday. All her eggs, he broken…one by one,' said a woman in a sweat-streaked blouse. 'Only God can save us in this Sankara,' said another as she hurried past. As Dele stooped to retrieve her wares a fair-faced, curvaceous woman, with a large backside, the ideal Sankara woman, according to Dad, came to help. She handed Dele two battered tins. 'How the pickin?' she said, with a peep round Dele's back. Dele prepared to walk away, but the ideal Sankara woman followed her. 'Can it breathe proper in this hot sun?' she said and thrust her hand down Dele's back. 'Yeah, pah, yeah pah,' she screeched, yanking her hand back as if she had been stabbed. The woman smacked her thunder thighs and hopped around. 'Is your head correct, you white girl? Your brother dies, and it is tins you are chasing inside gutter?' she said, wrestling Dele for the harness. Like chicks attracted to a handful of grain, a crowd soon gathered to watch and before Dele knew it, her harness unravelled, padding dropped off and her mascot, an old Barbie doll, slipped to the ground. Someone gasped. One woman put her hands over her mouth, another over her head in shock. The crowd formed a horse-shoe, backing Dele and the ideal Sankara woman up against a culvert.

'Maybe she's not well. Look at her hair, like Rasta,' said one woman.

'Hundred percent correct and look at her head, like coconut, and her nose like parrot's nose,' said another woman.

'And her thin craw craw legs.'

'Stupid woman, she is not white,' said a man in a bright yellow T-shirt.

'Me. You call me stupid? Ten years I studied in London.'

'That is where they used cricket bat to knock common-sense from your head,' said the man in the T-shirt.

Dele looked round for help. 'Please, it's only my good luck, mascot-'

'No it is juju,' said a woman.

A kick to the back of her knee felled Dele. She caught an elbow on a rock and curled into a ball, tucked her head under her forearms and closed her eyes, convinced by the searing pain in her side that she had a spike in her chest. Then followed another kick, from a child's foot, and another, from its mother perhaps. *What sort of woman are you?* She thought of her own mother, Jane, in her favourite colour, red, her tanned face sculpted by carefree laughter in the days before the Rokopats forced them out of North Roko and into South Roko. She thought of Wale her dad, who tried to keep them all going from a grubby backroom drug store in Sankara after he lost his pharmacy, "Veritreatable", in the Zadunaria riots. Then another kick got through, winding her. Dust puffed up her nose. She sneezed. A clear voice rang out.

'Stop now in the name of all that is still good in your lives in this Sankara.'

The crowd parted and fell silent. Dele peeped through a gap between her fingers as a man pushed towards her, his head haloed by the yellow sun. In one hand he had a furry black book and he had the other hand tucked into his flowing white cassock. His small head and square, but lopsided, shoulders made him look like an awry weighing scale.

'Have we not enough Rokopat *walaha* without flogging our own children. Let her go,' the man said, dragging Dele up by the elbow. 'What's your name?' he said. Dele staggered on to her feet and brushed grit off her brown school skirt.

'My name is Dele Verity,' she said.

'I am Pastor Ambasirika, they call me Ambasi.' He made a jerky sign of a cross on Dele's forehead and waved his arms at the stragglers. 'You touch her; I will turn your guts into barbed wire.'

The curvy woman sidled over. 'Sorry my child,' she whispered. 'I didn't know pastor was your friend. We just finished service in the railway church.' Ambasi looked down at the rim of brown dust on the hem of his robe, frowned and pointed with his eyes at the tins of milk scattered about Dele's tray. The woman picked up the tins and tucked the doll under Dele's arm. 'I'm sorry,' she said again. Dele seethed and kissed her teeth. *Could have got me killed.*

'Where do you live?' said Ambasi.

'Nigeria Street,' said Dele, poking her left ear.

'Not far from me. You want me to come with you…to explain?'

Dele shook her head. 'Show me how to get back over the railway line…I'll be alright.'

'Did you not know?' said Ambasi. 'Vandals stole that stretch two days ago to make scaffolding, woks, car parts and the devil knows what else,' he said.

Dele had heard of Ambasi, the pastor who preached from the church pulpit but also cast juju spells. She imagined him as seven feet tall with large probing eyes, bulging muscles and a magic whisk in bone-crushing hands. The real-life Ambasi was about the height of an average fifteen year old boy. His bald head, with its large vault and pointed chin, looked like a pear. He had a strange sheen to the left side of his face and a smaller, lower, left eye, perhaps the legacy of some sort of surgery or fight. From a mole on his lower lip peeped a thin tuft of grey hair and he had a wrinkled button of a nose that looked like a dried guava. Folds of skin tumbled down his thin neck, yet his straight back, the upright head, smooth swivel on the heels of his shiny ox-blood sandals, and his clear voice hinted of the armed forces.

'Thank you, sir...pastor,' said Dele.

'To me not the gratitude but to the Lord,' said Ambasi, cracking his knuckles. He ran a finger under his bad eye. 'You know Algeria Street...between the minaret on Namib and that useless transformer on Angola Street. That's my area...by the way...what is it with Babubacka and these stupid street names? Come to my table-tennis academy when you need a break from life as a retail magnate.' He laughed. 'Dele Verity, the Traytop Mountain. Traytop Mountain, I like the sound of that.'

***

An hour or so later Dele turned, limping, into her street. Like others in central Sankara, Nigeria Street was like a "devil's golf course," a narrow collection of potholes and bunkers joined by strips of rubble, and lined almost exclusively by ramshackle dwellings - shacks, mud huts, with the odd tarpaulin tent and unrendered brick bungalow dropped in for good measure. Rumour had it that after some let down, personal or otherwise no one knew, an inebriated colonial governor had decreed that the streets in the working class district of Sankara were to be no wider than he could puke.

A faint aroma of fried plantains swept up on a gust of smoke. Mama Taju pointed at the ocean of oil cooling in her wok. No titbits today she signalled with a sad shake of the head. Dele dug up a smile. Mama Taju pointed down the street with her eyes. 'Your mama is waiting,' she said.

Oh no. Jane stood glowering from her perch on top of the sandbags. She had her hands behind her back, like Mrs EsuBiseyu at school just before she gave you six of the best from her crooked white cane. Her gait shortening with cramp and her budding excuses wilting under her mother's piercing glare, Dele stumbled down the street towards her fate.

'I've been scared out of my wits. Where are your school sandals? Been playing football outside the barber's again have you?' said Jane.

'I got lost and-'

'Jesus and what happened to the tins? How many left?'

Dele took the tray off her head, passed a trembling forefinger over each tin like a child learning how to count. She didn't want to tell her mum that she may have crossed into forbidden territory.

'Cat got your tongue?' said Jane. Idiomatic English was a sign that Mum was getting cross. 'Answer me…you can talk can't you?' she said, fingering her silver chain.

Ah, a simple question that I can answer. 'I can talk,' said Dele.

'And what is that?' said Jane, pointing at the doll.

Dele pointed up the street. 'Found it on the road…was going to hand it in,' she said.

'Get in, shower…all that stuff off your feet…I've cleaned out your new bucket. What on earth am I going to do with you, Dele?'

Mum doesn't love me anymore thought Dele as she climbed into bed that night. Teacher had said every little *will* helps. So, with her hands together, a gap between the tips of her middle fingers to let the words go straight up to God, Dele prayed for Dad to get the visa to let him take his family with him back to England. Amen. She prayed for God to make Mum happy and more like Dad. Amen. She prayed to get better at Maths and for more time to draw and paint when she got to England. Amen. She prayed for her nose to stop growing and for more tint in her skin, browner and less pink so that she would look more like Dad and not stand out so much in Sankara (she felt guilty for asking for this). She prayed for Koseri and her mum Asafa and prayed for her old friends in Zadunaria, wherever they may be.

THREE

Loud pips from a car radio outside announced the hour of seven. Dele's mouth burned from the baked beans in a hot pepper stew, the high octane fuel supposed to scramble her brain for that day's sortie with algebra. Sucking air did not help. She looked round for a mug of water.

Jane stormed in to the front room for the fourth time in as many minutes. 'It's hot in there. And why is that contraption making that grating noise?' she said, pointing at the fan by the window. Dele shuffled her chair back a little so that her shirt did not get snagged on the rough table edge. She tried to get Dad's attention, wondering whether to ask him for some more water, but changed her mind because she might get him into trouble with Mum for the implied criticism of her cooking. Oblivious to his daughter's fiery dilemma, Wale swept a fresh white school shirt off the back of the chair and on to a blue bedsheet he had folded over the other half of the table. He switched on the chipped electric iron, pressing it to duty.

'I don't care if it's the end of the week, but you're not going to school in that crumpled shirt,' he said. 'If I can just get the front and collar done,' he said, shuffling from foot to foot like a girl desperate for the bathroom. As he turned his attention to the shirt sleeves, the pilot light on the iron died. Wale let out a long sigh.

'It's only quarter past seven. Thought we'd have power till half past. That'll have to do,' he said, putting the shirt to one side. He turned away and coughed into an elbow.

'Power here flits in and out like a moth...' said Jane, scratching her head.

'That's why electricity to Siroko people is like sunshine to the English...ah it's bright today, a bit overcast, what's tomorrow's forecast, do you think we'll have any next week...this month?' Wale shrugged. 'You have to laugh.'

'Can't Dele iron her own shirt? Thirteen, and still your little girl-girl. Rifiti over the road there already runs a shop,' said Jane.

Why does Mum keep adding years to my age?

'Rifiti's sixteen, and Dele's twelve-'

Jane tossed back her thick sandy hair. She turned to Dele. 'Life's not silk and perfume you know. It's smelly; like a loo. It *is* a loo. And if you go on like this, you'll spend the rest of your life shovelling and cleaning up other people's...mess.'

'I'm getting better,' said Dele. To Dele, twisting numbers into new ugly forms, naming them after a tiny x and asking you to find it, was a form of torture; and should be banned, frowned on or at least optional, like blowing your nose.

'Teachers tell you what you want to hear. But you don't have pretty shades of opinion in maths. Two times two is what...four. It is four in Outer Mongolia. It is four as well in Monrovia. Isn't it Wale?' said Jane.

'We're getting there, aren't we my little girl-girl,' said Wale. He walked round the table to hug Dele round the shoulders. He left the better soap for Dele and Jane and so smelt of cheap, home-made South Roko soap, sometimes like a tomato at other times like a banana. Today he smelt like boiled snail. 'Mum didn't sleep that well...which reminds me, I need to see if we can move the manger from under that damp spot,' he said. Dele fished the beans out of the stew with her fork and fought back a sniffle.

'I wish your Home Office would make up its mind...about these visas,' said Jane. She sat down next to Dele.

'If only we'd applied when I said...anyway water under the bridge of Verity,' Wale said.

Dele looked up. *Did mum not want to go to England?*

'Been through this,' said Jane, running her hand back through her hair.

'They danced in the streets here when Babubacka took over from that thief. In the national interest he said. Shaking his fist full of cast-iron answers...in the national interest, then only cast-iron fists…in the national interest, then he dropped the pretence and simply ruled over us…in the national interest. I told you that smelly flycatcher he calls a mouth was full of a rancid pile of lies…you wouldn't listen,' said Wale.

Jane rolled her eyes and sighed. 'I was making the perfectly legitimate case that because some animists burned down a farmer's hut, didn't mean we should up staves. North Roko was my home, you know, but trust your juggernaut of unique African perspective to sweep my mild dissent before it,' she said.

'This is not about me. 'It's about nabobs and vagabonds in power and…power without steering,' said Wale. He dropped his head, and let his arms hang by his side.

Poor dad. A motorbike revved up outside. It sounded like an aeroplane taking off.

Jane turned the tap. At first nothing happened, then the tap growled and a few brown drops spluttered out. 'Grit. Perhaps we should pan for gold,' said Jane. Wale didn't reply. 'Didn't mean it,' Jane said. She put the jug down and gave Wale a hug. Wale put an arm round her back. 'That's better,' she said.

'Calo, calo,' said Wale, waltzing round with Jane, a grin on his face. They bumped into the table, spilling some of Dele's water.

Dele knew that 'calo' was short for calories or warmth, but she hadn't heard them use the code, or heard them giggle in bed since Babubacka's men forced them out of North Roko. Her mind leapt back a year to North Roko, to Esau their helper, to the cars, one white one blue, to the swimming pool and her green and blue-walled bedroom, to her friends at the Niroko Junior School. She wondered what happened to Amina. Amina, the high jumper, had been her best friend. Now it was Koseri, dark, giggling Koseri. At school they called them the "little tinklers," after ebony and ivory piano keys.

The clang of the sooty kettle on the kerosene stove dragged her back to reality. Jane pointed at Wale's wristwatch. 'Aren't you going to open up? Cleaners will be here soon, and we've got to fix that gap between the corner bricks in the shop,' she said.

'You mean *I've* got to fix the bricks. Told them not to come today, I'm hoping they'll deliver what's left of "Veritreatable." They've taken all the drugs, but at least the ledgers might help me trace old clients…and the debtors. But I haven't heard…and I smell trouble,' he said. He rubbed a greying sideboard and leaned backward to peer through the window slats.

'We could do without this…and your palaver with Sandman,' said Jane.

'I couldn't help it. We haven't seen him for over a week or so, wonder what he's up to,' said Wale, cradling his mug in his hands. He peeped out on to the street again, an anxious look on his face, then turned to see if Dele was watching. Dele looked away and in her muddle, took in too full a fork of spicy beans.

'Stop scoffing your food, and leave your ear alone,' said Jane.

'You asked me to drink lots of water,' said Dele, between gasps of breath.

'Someone has to stand up to that pest. The man is a dick. No; he'd cut *his* off to spite his mistress and he's so ugly she'd be delighted.' Wale laughed. 'Perhaps that's why they deported him from UK…at Her Majesty's pleasure. For indecent exposure.' He spread his arms out like a performer. 'Sandmangate…after the indecent exposure, the merciful cover-up,' he said, putting on the portentous air of a newsreader.

Dele shuffled her feet on the floor.

'Language,' said Jane, but the mirth in her parrot grey eyes betrayed her.

'Sorry,' said Wale, with an exaggerated bow. Dele, saw with a little jolt in her chest, that her father had begun to look like a Siroko man. He had a thinning crown, a deep wrinkle shaped like a wishbone on the back of his neck and the armholes on his shirt dropped almost halfway to his elbows.

'Mum, why does Little Mama talk like that?'

Wale sighed and looked at Jane as though to ask if he should tell. Jane shrugged consent.

'Her mum was in her busy coffee shop…' said Wale. 'A Rokopat general wanted her shop for his friend.'

Jane took up the story. 'But Little Mama's mum wouldn't give it up. So the general took it by force. He shot her. They said it was an accident, that he thought his life was in danger when Little Mama's mum ducked behind the counter,' said Jane.

'Poor Little Mama saw it all,' said Wale.

'Come here,' said Jane. She pulled Dele in. 'Sorry darling. I don't mean to be cross with you. I'll make you a pancake when you get back,' said Jane, patting Dele on the back. *I shouldn't have made fun of Little Mama. I'd die if a soldier shot mum.*

'You're sure you don't want me to come with you?' said Wale. Dele shook her head. 'I'm meeting Koseri at the top of the street,' she said.

'Good, she's more streetwise. I know you were trying to help, but you shouldn't have gone to the depot without her,' said Jane.

'My little girl must have got the gene for getting lost from me. Perhaps that's how I ended up with your mum in North Roko. Stowed away at Heathrow, but got on the wrong flight,' said Wale, with a chuckle.

'Charming, your dad.'

Dele swung her pink plastic satchel over her shoulders and lifted her school stool on to her head. She turned round to wave beside the peanut seller's stall half way up the street. Jane waved from her usual spot in front of their crumbling saloon; with two hands high up in the air, like a teenager at a pop concert. Wale, behind her, taller by half a head, stood with hands on Jane's shoulders. His fixed grin, cocked head, small ears, big round eyes made him look like a sad teddy bear.

FOUR

Three weeks dragged on and her dad still hadn't heard about the visas. Dele gave up football and stole off after school to play table-tennis at Ambasi's academy instead. Then Mum found out. Volcanic does not get close. They made up in the end over a sugary pancake on a Wednesday night two days later.

That same night Dele dreamed not of staghorn-headed soldiers chasing her on the beach, but about Koseri, her best friend who lived up the street. So when she heard a crash she thought it was the sound of Asafa, Koseri's mother, collapsing to the floor in shock at catching the girls inspecting each other's little bits in the dream. Then came an even louder crash. Thinking that it was probably Suba and Aka the "boxing match couple" from across the street at it again, Dele pulled the inviting warm counterpane with its sweet and sour morning smell and the aroma of her first pancake fart of the morning back over her head. Barely had she snuggled back down again when she heard frightened whispers and scurrying feet. Cursing the loss of those last few bonus minutes in bed, Dele crept through the door to peep out of the window in the front room. Her heart thwacked against her throat because a giant, with what looked like a good chunk of the left side of his skull missing, stood a few feet away scratching his ear with a pistol butt.

What is this?

'What number that?' the man said, waving his pistol at a ghostly ruin. *Mr and Mrs Nalukwani and ten children live there.*

'On this street, sir, we do not have yet local government numbers, sir,' said a woman, cowering from the man.

'I am looking for number six, don't hide the people who killed our man,' said the giant.

'They are not here sir,' said one woman, jabbing the ring in the side of her nose. 'We just want to draw water for-'

'Shut up.'

'Sorry, sir,' said the woman.

The big man dipped into his pocket and threw something in the air, it looked like a nut. He caught it in his mouth. A man in a white gown pushed to the front and, in his eagerness, bumped into the big man's elbow. *Sandman.* Dele trembled with terror.

'Look how you make me wet my uniform, what do you want?' the man said, glaring at Sandman.

Sandman tapped his lips with his joined fingertips, bowed and shuffled up to the man. Dele strained to hear what was said.

'Have you forgotten me?' said Sandman. He lowered his voice. Dele thought she heard him say something about their meeting at a netball match.

Sandman? Netball?

The big man threw another nut into the lightening sky, tipped his head back but missed this time. He swore at Sandman. 'So where is this pharmacist man?' he said.

Dad's a pharmacist.

'All of you go,' said the man. He waved the small crowd away and straddled the ditch on Dele's side of the street. Sandman scurried after him. The two men conferred, Sandman's head and red fez jerking, his eyes darting about like a nervous pigeon, while the big man, stooped, his knobbly head held still and with his forefinger over one ear, looked like a teacher listening to the class snitch. The man nodded three times, then, with an air of final comprehension, he raised an arm and pointed straight at Dele's window. Dele fell backwards as if she had been punched. At that, the door creaked behind her and Wale shuffled in, with the little drag of his left foot. He had a tatty green and white loincloth round his waist and a threadbare green towel hung lopsided from his neck.

'What are you doing, darling, wrestling the stool before breakfast?' he said. He turned and coughed into his elbow.

'There's a big...Rokopat man outside,' Dele said, righting the stool and crawling away from the window.

Wale sucked his teeth. 'Have they nothing better to do, but defend us from a few insolent market women?' Dele went back to the window.

'This him?' said the big man, as Wale appeared outside.

Sandman nodded.

'How can I help you?' said Wale. He stepped off the sandbags.

'You are pharmacist?'

'You are sick?' said Wale.

'I charge you for Mulou,' said the big man.

'I think you've got the wrong man...man,' said Wale.

Sandman whispered into the big man's ear. The man nodded. 'Where your woman?' he said.

Mum. Dele dashed into the back room where, Jane, in the grip of a yawn, had her arms stretched out to the ceiling. 'Mum, quick come, it's Dad and Sandman outside and this giant Rokopat soldier with a funny head.'

Jane screeched. 'Oh my God, oh...your dad and that creepy Sandman again, no...disaster...wait here.' She tied a scarf round her hair, pulled a pair of jeans on under her nightshirt, tripped into one slipper and with the other slipper in her left hand, hopped outside. Dele scampered back to the window. Wale had his hands cuffed behind him. He turned to the window and with a blink and an almost imperceptible shake of the head warned Dele to stay out of sight. In that split second and for the first time ever Dele saw fear in her father's eyes. He winced when he saw Jane and moved towards her but a soldier grabbed him by the elbow and dragged him away. Dele saw him stumble. Each staggering step he took away from her stabbed her chest with icicles. A green lorry trundled up. Dele saw the soldier tumble her dad over its tailgate and into the dark. He then rattled a chain through hooks and rings and marched to the front. Doors clanged shut.

Dad. Tears prickled Dele's eyes. Through a blur she saw the big man point at Mum.

'Handcuff her too,' he said. 'Either you are guilty of this offence or you are an enemy combatant. How do you people say it: heads you lose tails you lose, not so? We will take you to Alaga.' A soldier jerked Jane by the elbow. Jane's scarf slipped off and she dropped her slipper. Sandman laughed, pointing at Jane's untidy morning hair. 'Take her,' said the big man. A soldier lifted Jane over his shoulder and threw her into the back of the same lorry.

Mum.

Sandman got in the front of the same lorry with the big man. The lorry lurched up the street. Dele charged through the door, hurdled the ditch, darted between the crumbling green jalopy and dustbin and chased after the van. 'Mum, dad, stop, help.' The lorry slowed down and Dele caught up. Reaching through the hot exhaust fumes, she grabbed the tail-gate by her finger-tips and pulled herself up. Just as she thought she had lift-off she felt Koseri's long arms pull her down. She fell, hands first, into a puddle and stubbed her right toe. 'What are you doing?' she said, scrambling to her feet just as the left brake light blinked twice, and the lorry turned right and out of sight.

Asafa, Koseri's mother, seemed to appear out of nowhere too. She cuffed Dele round the ear.

'They've gone,' said Dele pointing up the street in despair.

'Why do I have to chase you to get ready for school, eh?' said Asafa in her singing voice. 'Get back home now, you stupid girl,' she said, rolling up a blouse sleeve. She leaned over to whisper to Dele. 'What did you think you were doing? You want to die? Do you think the Alaga canton is for small girls?' she said.

Dele shook her head. 'It's Mum and...Dad...taken,' she said. She shook mud and a wriggling worm off a finger.

Asafa wiped Dele's face with a cloth. 'They'll be back soon.' She did not sound convincing. 'How can Sandman do this? Wicked liar.' On their way back down the street Dele saw her mother's brown left slipper and Wale's blue toothbrush in the mud. She picked them up.

'Koseri look why don't you go in, fetch Dele's things and we'll meet you at home,' said Asafa, taking off her green scarf to reveal a receding hairline of fat cornrows. 'I'll let Mrs Oyenuga know that you won't be coming in to school today,' she said. Asafa set a plastic bowl of steaming vegetable soup in front of Dele and wrapped Koseri's bowl in a towel. Dele closed her eyes, put her hands together.

Please God keep mum and dad safe.

'This will get cold,' said Asafa, feeling Koseri's bowl.

'I'll go and get her,' said Dele. Just then Mama Taju burst through the door, her eyes as large as chicken eggs. Rivulets of sweat burrowed through her face powder.

'This woman why do you always have to shout?' said Asafa, cupping hands over her ears.

Mama Taju slapped her thighs, the Siroko woman's distress signal. 'Curse me if you like but you cannot go back…to…your house,' she said, pointing at Dele. 'Sharijujumen, the original juju people are coming. Anywhere they smell smoke they add more fire. Even Rokopats fear them.'

'Oh my God in heaven. Where is Koseri?' said Asafa. 'Wait here,' she said and dashed, barefooted, out of the kitchen just as Jonas, Mama Taju's barrel-chested husband, burst in wearing his trademark striped black and white T-shirt and trainers.

'Sharijujumen are looking for foreigners. They are blaming them for Mulou's death. Put this on, quick, inside there,' he said in a trembling voice. He handed Dele a dark blue bicycle helmet and a change of clothes, a white long-sleeved shirt and a charcoal skirt.

'What about Koseri?' said Dele.

'They'll look after themselves,' said Jonas, his face freckled with sweat. 'Quick, no time for debate,' he said and slipped out of the room. In a daze, Dele had to tie a knot in the waist of the skirt to make it fit.

Jonas was waiting. He lifted her on to the backseat and weaved his gruff-sounding bike through the late morning traffic. Dele clung on to the passenger's bar, her head in a whirl. The outsized helmet seeming to spin through the air. Fear, despair, anxiety buzzed through her mind. They arrived outside a blue and white striped two-storey building. It had blue United Nations curtains hanging half way down its windows. Jonas lifted Dele off the bike, went inside and Dele squeezed the wet out of her helmet. She hung it on a handlebar to dry.

Jonas soon came back with a worried look on his face. 'The madam of the house is not in, let's eat,' he said, pointing over the street at a general store. 'Remember, straight down on to the ground when the woman comes back. It will show her that you are not proud,' he said taking a big chunk out of a meat pie. 'Eat now, you don't know when your next meal will be born.'

At four o'clock a woman in a violet bandana arrived in a dark green jeep. With her came a girl in a pink dress. Dele threw herself on the rocky ground in front of them, her feet hanging over the edge of the gutter. The woman waved the little girl back behind her as if Dele carried some deadly bug. 'Did I not tell you that we were full?' she said to Jonas in a rasping tone of reproach. A corner of her mouth curled up and her eyes narrowed. She pulled Dele up by the collar and led her inside the house to plonk her on a three-legged chair at a dining table; but not before she whipped away a bowl of fruit. Dele brushed the dust off her hands and knees and tried not to fall off the wobbly chair. The girl in pink walked in soon after. Dele thought the girl was seven, maybe eight, years old, but she had a cruel face and a turned down mouth. Her eyes reminded Dele of the pointed end of a biro. The girl took her left thumb out of her mouth. 'Why are you sitting on our chair when you have pineapple skin,' she said, with a leer. She pointed at Dele's knees. Dele gulped. Her rash started to itch. A heaviness came over her: her arms felt like soaked timber and her hair like seaweed. She clenched her jaw and tried not to cry or scratch, rubbing her legs with the ball of her hand so that they did not bleed. The girl scoffed and, with her nose in the air, put her thumb back in her mouth and left.

Dele heard angry voices through the wall. She heard the word money come up several times. 'Last time I did not hear from you for...well, till after that child died,' said the woman.

'But Ajoks, Teri helped get you this job.'

Ajoks. She has a nickname like normal humans.

'She doesn't feed me,' said the woman as she walked into the dining room, followed by Jonas.

Jonas rapped his thigh with his bunch of keys. 'Let's go, this woman is a...a...is not a woman, thanks for your help. It is greatly appreciated.' The wiry bandana woman fanned her face, with the air of a woman who couldn't care less.

Even if she takes me she will only make me miserable.

Dele didn't like to see Jonas beg. 'I know somewhere else,' she said, thinking of Ambasi, the pastor at whose tables she played tennis.

'I told you, these small girls know more than you think,' said Ajoks.

Jonas smacked his keys against his thigh again. 'More *walaha* in our area. We can't go back,' he said, his voice striking several sorrowful notes. They got on to the bike. Back on the main road women and children jostled for space on long queues for fuel. They brought rusting jerry cans, bright plastic bowls, buckets; Dele saw that one woman had brought a teapot. Jonas flicked sweat off his face and glanced down at his fuel gauge. 'We may have to walk part of the way home, if we are to get you somewhere safe. And it will soon get dark. That woman wasted our time.' Dele wondered why Mama Taju and Jonas could not put her up for the night, but Jonas seemed to have read her mind. He shook the sweat off his forehead. 'They are watching. Spies can tell; and you are obvious...'

'I could go to the pastor, my friend, near Morocco Street,' said Dele, taking one sticky hand off the bar to wipe it on her skirt.

'Back, past Barracks junction? No way.' Jonas shook his head and put one foot down to steady the bike. The traffic inched forward. Jonas lifted his foot and pushed off again, from crawl to walking pace. Sensing Jonas about to change up, Dele leapt off the pillion and darted between a lorry and a white van.

'Hey, hey, come back,' said Jonas, grabbing Dele by the collar, but she tore free, vaulted over a yellow jalopy and did not stop running until she got to Ambasi's street.

Hungry and breathless, she arrived at Algeria Street in dusty orange twilight, but the sight of the leaning lamp post in front of Ambasi's wrought iron gate gave her a second wind; and hope. She staggered down the slight incline to cup her ear to the door and knock, but heard only a hollow echo from the wooden letter box. Needle, a tall thin man with bulbous eyes, hurried past. Needle played at Ambasi's tennis tables.

'Hey Needle...seen the pastor?' said Dele. Needle quickened his step, waved but did not stop. *Perhaps pastor's gone to the railway carriage service.* In the distance the last sliver of sunshine sunk behind a mountain of refuse and as the dark rushed in, as though starved of light for days, the first candle flames appeared in the windows. Dele sat down on the pile of bricks outside Ambasi's house to wait but everyone seemed to stop to stare so, pulling her shirt tight against the cold, she crossed the street to poke her head through the door of a beer parlour.

Inside, two men sharing a dwarf bottle of beer sat under a bunting of African national flags. A reggae tune chugged out of the radio.

'You blind?' snapped a woman in a yellow scarf. She steadied the foot-high stack of drinking glasses in her hand with a turn of the wrist and swerved round Dele.

'Sorry ma,' said Dele. 'I'm looking for my pastor, Ambasi. I play table tennis with his...' She turned to point through the raffia curtains.

'He's not here. Why your shirt is torn?' said the barwoman, waltzing off before Dele could reply.

'Sharijujumen took pastor,' said the older man.

'The man sometimes talks sense,' said the younger drinker.

'If he has sense why did he not tell them what they want to hear?' said the barwoman, prodding light out of a fluorescent bulb on the ceiling with a bamboo pole. Then she turned to Dele. 'What are you still doing here? Vamoose.'

FIVE

Dele crashed into a bench and sat down to rub the kidney-shaped bump on her shin. *Where's Mum? Where's Dad?* A street light blinked and died. The moon dived behind a cloud and the ensuing darkness came with a fear Dele had never known before; worse than when she was match point down at table tennis, or when she waited outside OY's office to be whacked for a prank, or when Mum went volcanic, or even when the soldiers came to their house in Zadunaria. Tonight, fear oozed from her skin dripped from her wet, seaweed-thick, hair. And it smelled of sour milk and rotten banana, beaded on her fingertips and made them shake and her lips trilled like insects' wings. *Please God help…bring back Mum and Dad* she prayed. A mist seemed to wrap round her to pump cold, yellow air down her throat. Scooped out spent, cold, hungry, she wanted to lay her head down there, close her eyes for ever and float away. But Mr Odutta, the school chaplain had said during assembly that that would be a sin.

Out from behind the massive cloud came the moon with its sorry shine. Street children scurried past Dele's bench. She had heard of them, the *scafos*, short for scavengers, who searched refuse mountains for scraps to sell, or eat. A little girl, perhaps five or six years old came past, dragging a car grille along the ground, the clanging sounded like a chainsaw grinding at metal inside Dele's head. A few yards behind the girl came a boy, wobbling under the car door he carried on his head. He stopped, stared at Dele for a few moments before he spoke.

'What you doing here?' he said in a voice that sounded like bursting blister packs. Fear booted Dele's heart against her chest. But she pushed off the bench on woolly legs to stand toe to toe with the boy and put on the best scowl she could muster, practised for weeks in her bedroom mirror.

'Waiting for my papa,' said Dele, pointing over her shoulder.

'You want to do?' said the boy. He looked down at his crotch.

'He is drinking, if he come out he will kill you,' said Dele, trying hard to suppress the urge to brush the boy's odour, a smell like that of a blocked drain, away. While they exchanged silent fire in the dark another girl came past dragging a computer on a sheet or blanket. The blanket gave way and the computer toppled over.

'Fucking hell,' said the girl. Her sharp screech made Dele jump. The boy chuckled, a look of triumph in his eyes, steadied his cargo with a deft turn of his neck and walked away.

Must find somewhere for the night. Dele sidled over to warm herself near the cooling embers of a cooking fire. A few minutes later a girl emerged from a shack to douse the flames with a bucket of water and shovel up the charcoal. 'For tomorrow,' she said.

Hungry, Dele swayed down the street to look for a shed, a kiosk, bus-stop, anywhere for shelter. She found none. Despair clawed her throat. She turned round and dragged her leaden legs back up the street. The hum from the main road grew louder as she drew level with the beer parlour once again. Then she saw, in the glow from a kerosene lamp, a man sitting on the pile of bricks outside Ambasi's house. When the man stirred his bowl and raised his fork to his mouth an aroma of fried plantains of such intolerable promise it almost felled her, swept over Dele; and if eyes could chew she would have had her fill from fifty paces. With her belly screaming attack but her head whispering caution, Dele bustled towards her target, bending over as if to retrieve or search for a coin, or stopping to wipe an imaginary raindrop off the back of her hand, whenever the man appeared to look her way. She had got to within a few strides of her target when the man shovelled more food into his mouth, put his bowl down beside him and lifted a flask to his mouth. He closed his eyes and turned away, towards the main road. Dele dropped all pretence. As she ran up the man's greedy glugs and chomps got louder, sucking her on. He still had his face turned when Dele pounced, swept the bowl off the bricks, stuffing the salty plantains into her mouth as she ran away. *Tule, tule,'* shouted the man. Fuelled by mortal fear, Dele threw the bowl over her shoulder hoping to slow her pursuer, but soon felt the man's spicy breath on her neck. She ducked, doubled back on herself, but twisted an ankle on a hard mud rut and fell.

'You are die, you hear me? Dead,' said the man, dragging her to her feet.

When Dele saw his Rokopat uniform she wished she could fly.

'Sorry sir...I thought it was pastor...Ambasi...uncle Ambasi,' she said, gasping for air and gasping in fear.

The soldier kicked her. Winded, Dele tried to roll away.

'Please don't. He calls me little sparrow...we have a game, hop...step and run for your chop-chop. Please, how can I do such a thing if I knew it was you? Pastor will pay you back,' she said, squeaking with pain between breaths.

'You think I fool,' said the soldier. He shook his fist in Dele's face and stamped on Dele's left foot again. 'Let me see you run now,' he said. What you civilians need is iron discipline. Sit up.' He barked into a walkie-talkie and forced Dele to sit cross-legged on the ground beside the foul-smelling ditch. She wretched, wracked with pain. Across the road the barwoman rattled down her shutters and shook her head; the fearful pity in her eyes obvious even in the dark. A van arrived. Two men jumped out and chained Dele's hands to her ankles behind her back. 'Take her away,' said the soldier. A man with a flat-bridged nose hauled Dele over the van's tail-gate.

That's a hard knobbly mattress. She heard a man shout. 'Ouch, ah, ah, my leg, my arm, oh,' said the man.

'Sorry, they threw me on top of you-'

'Shut up in there, now, now,' said a soldier, flashing his torch around the hold. He swung in over the tailgate. 'Ah chicken,' he said. He marched to the front of the hold, broke a few fowl off, as you would with a bunch of bananas, and threw the chickens out of the lorry. Clapping the dirt off his hands, he stomped over to padlock Dele's wrists to a floor joist, grunted, as though with satisfaction at his night's work, and leapt back out over the tailgate. Soon, Dele heard the rattling and clanging of the covers against the side of the lorry but the tarpaulin did not reach all the way down, and as her eyes adjusted to the dark, she picked out a huddled form in the opposite corner.

'Sorry, did I hurt you?' she said.

The man groaned. 'Rokopat men drove a jeep over my arm, to stop me writing, punishment for anyone who speaks English or looks like he will not swallow their pile of bullshit,' he said. 'Ah,' he groaned again and doubled up in obvious pain. A dark fluid ran down his face, seeping into his pale shorts and a soiled bandage hung round his otherwise bare chest.

'Why?' said Dele. A stupid question, but she had to ask.

The chains on his ankles and wrists clanged against the floor. 'I wrote article for fun. Saying that this our land of quarrelling telegraph lines, garbage tips as high as giraffe and farting gutters is like a form of tourist attraction for more developed countries. Because it is what they were like hundreds of years ago, difference is…now we have better ammunition to kill each other than they had then. Rokopats came to my workshop and charged me with misrepresentation of government efforts. That I am not transparent? How, I asked. I said I am too poor to have anything to hide. They said I could not be poor because I write in English and so must be one of those who are cheating illiterate market women.'

'Where do you work and do you-'

'I'm a tailor, but I am training as a journalist. I promised my mama a new dress for a wedding. If I don't turn up she'll know something is wrong.' Saro closed his eyes and sighed. 'What about you?' he said.

Dele told Saro about *her* day. 'I feel as if I've been beaten all over with barbed wire and I don't know where Mum and Dad are,' said Dele.

'This place, na wah oh,' wheezed Saro, coughing with the effort.

Dele recalled how her dad used to dance with her to that Kubaku hit song, *Na wah oh*, about life in South Roko. She knew the lyrics but didn't know what they meant. *My beautiful people, meek and mild, when we run and jump the wind cannot resist us…we smile, we smile, in rain or shine while he and his and anyone who knows him rob us so blind they are richer than Croesus.*

'They burned Kubaku's house down,' said Saro, groaning as the lorry lurched sideways. 'Roko. I call it a rock joined by giant zeroes…I am so…tired.'

***

Dele gritted her teeth against the pain in her back and neck and tried to keep out the stench of human and fowl excrement by pressing her nose into the gap between the side and back of the lorry for fresh air. After hours, during which she thought she had lost the use of her hands and feet and the back of her neck felt as if it had been turned on a hot spit, the lorry pulled out of another wrist-wrenching descent and rocked to a halt. Through a gap in the roof she could just make out the claret streaks of dawn in the sky. A few feet away Saro lay still, oblivious it seemed to the loud jocose banter, or the clang of pots and pans outside. The tarpaulin covers rolled back and a soldier vaulted in over the tail-gate.

'You deaf in there?' He poked Saro with a finger.

'He's asleep,' said Dele.

'Who asked you?' the man said, his black beret cocked to the right in the Rokopat fashion. Saro's frown had relaxed into what looked like a permanent and restful sigh. 'He is dead,' he said for the benefit of his colleagues. 'What do we do with his handcuffs?' he said.

'You signed for them?' said the man on the ground.

'Yes, if we don't return them…we could say they lost…when he ran away–'

'You are more stupid than a saucepan. Have you ever heard of government prisoner escape, in the history of Sankara central prison? Where did you train? Sandhurst or West Point or Guantanamo? There are different category of death in custody…accidental suicide, deliberate suicide, fall out of bed, swallow of singlet or toilet roll or fishbone by mistake, drink too much water from swimming pool or head-butt the officer's gun or bullets, but to escape?'

Dele heard a stamp to attention and another, superior, voice. 'Where is this person?'

'Here,' said the soldier from inside the van.

'Hah, they travel first class now? This is why this country is going down the pants,' said the superior, banging on the tail-gate.

'He lasted longer than my guestimation,' said the soldier, throwing the remaining fowls out of the lorry, and, flapping his arms like wings, he leapt after the cackling birds. As the feathers floated to the floor Dele looked through a chink between tailgate and the side of the lorry and saw the driver wipe his shaven head and salute. 'What of the girl?' he said.

That's me.

'What type question is that? Is gear engaged inside that half toolbox you call a head?' said the superior. Dele could not see him. The man laughed, hacked up phlegm. 'You know what they call me?'

What's he going to do?

'"ESBT, eliminate surplus before terminus", sir,' said the driver.

'OK. Do it one time…no mess.'

The driver climbed over the tailgate with a gun between his teeth. 'Please, I said I am sorry, it was only because I was hungry,' she said. The man shook his head. *Will it hurt?* A gun went off. Hot spikes clapped into Dele's ears. Then a firecracker went off in her arm sockets and the lorry spun into the dark.

SIX

Dele opened her eyes and flicked the blood-streaked mosquito net off her nose. *Dad must have mended that crack in the ceiling.* She sniffed the air and peeped over the side of her bed, but could not find a gutter or smell any soap suds. When she tried to lift herself on to her elbow a sharp pain in her left shoulder knocked her back. The door opened. A girl jumped off the bunk bed opposite. A bell rang. It sounded far away, like a tinkle borne on the wind on a school day out on a farm. *Where am I?*

A ceiling bulb flicked on. The mosquito net lifted off her face.

'You didn't hear? It's five thirty, time for prayers,' said one of the girls.

'Ah,' Dele said. When she moved another bomb went off in her arm joints. She squeezed her eyes shut with the pain, felt a wetness between her legs and put her hand down to check. The pungent aroma made her blush with shame. *Not again* she thought. *What will Mum say?* Then she remembered with that sinking feeling in the pit of her belly that there was no Mum here, only Yourlot: that terrible woman who called her Lazarus because of the rash on her legs.

Yourlot, thin, tall, had cold, pill-box eyes under heavy, seagull-winged brows that met over a gully. She had a fleshy nose with a small left nostril, as if it did not approve of the rest of the face, or its owner. Her long fingers had bulges on their ends, like drumsticks, or clubs. Yourlot stood in the middle of the room in the evenings, shook a blue can of mosquito insecticide close to her ear to see how much she had left, squirted one short puff above her head and left. You could count the droplets before they disappeared into the air.

The four other girls in the six-bedded dormitory stirred and groped under pillows for the little red prayer books. Dele did the same and rustled through to page 45. But the words seemed to start and end in the point of a dagger and told her nothing about her mum or dad. She put the book back under the pillow, closed her eyes and prayed to God once again to bring them back.

'Did you not hear the bell for end of prayers? Lazarus, it's bath time,' said one of the other girls. Dele opened her eyes to see Beni, the girl who slept opposite, hurry out of the door with a drib of striped toothpaste on the splayed bristles of a baby's toothbrush.

'I'm coming,' said Dele. She waited for the room to empty, peeled off her bedsheet and turned her mattress over, but the wet had soaked right through and previous emissions had dug an even deeper hole on this side. So she turned the mattress back over, tucked some straw from her pillow into the dent and went off for her shower. As she walked back to get ready for inspection under a doleful star, Saro's limp body dropped from the sky, bounced an inch off the ground, flopped down and was gone, borne on the wings of a guinea-fowl. *Please not another bad dream* thought Dele as she ran back to the dormitory.

Yourlot, the ward supervisor arrived at six-thirty. She pointed at the girl standing by the bed nearest the door. 'Let me guess. Who has messed the bed? You?'

'No miss,' said the girl, pointing at Dele with a mocking grin.

'You can go,' said Yourlot. 'And you in the middle,' she said pointing at Dele. 'You stand like you have messed. Guilty or not?'

'Not…exactly. I don't know how it happened. Soldiers chased me. I hid in the toilet and then it came. I'm sorry,' Dele said. A titter came from a girl standing by the door.

'We are doing the best for you until commandant and UN and government finish their talk. But you are a hard case, spoiling everything with your piss, so half ration this morning. Clear? Hurry up it's nearly seven and it is your week to sweep this room.' The thought of giving up part of her breakfast gave Dele stomach ache.

***

Built on the site of an abandoned mine, the camp had about half a dozen blocks of tin-roofed adobe huts arranged around a clearing the size of two football pitches. Soldiers patrolled a high barbed-wired perimeter fence. The commandant lived in a concrete bungalow in his own compound just inside the camp gates.

It was Tuesday morning, which meant the camp's favourite breakfast, a slice of bread an inch thick and a mug of soporific hot cocoa. Fifty or sixty children, in white tops and khaki shorts, squeezed into the old telephone exchange that served as the dining hall. It had only two oval windows set close to the high ceiling. Dele kicked a clump of red and blue cables from under her feet and took her place on the aisle bench on table 8, three tables from the exit.

A bell rang and Dele saw Yourlot appear through a side-door at the top of the hall. The room soon filled with the noise of chomping, chattering, clashing cutlery, satisfied murmuring and benches dragged along the wooden floor to make room for Yourlot. Dressed in a yellow top and dark skirt, Yourlot glided down the aisle with a jug of milk in her hand. With each eagerly held out aluminium mug she anointed with a drop or two of milk she clicked the silver counter in her hand. 'That's your lot,' she said and went to the next cup. Tingling with nerves, Dele rubbed a cigarette burn on her bench. *Should I not take my punishment and try not to wet the bed next time?* But her Dad had said *if you don't stand up for yourself you will die fed up and hungry.* A sour-faced girl on Table 5 looked as if she was about to cry because Yourlot had left her out. Indifferent, Yourlot glided on to table 6, two tables away from Dele's.

The boy with wispy orange hair and a red raw tongue grunted as he struggled to lift the pumpkin-sized aluminium teapot. 'You don't want tea Laza? Yourlot is nearly here,' he said. Dele corked her mug with her chin and shook her head. 'I thought you liked tea,' said Yinta, a girl with puckered lips.

'You heard me,' said Dele.

'Shush, I don't want Yourlot's *walaha*,' said Yinta. She turned her mug up ready for Yourlot. All, except Dele, got up to offer their mugs.

'Lazarus, no tea?' said Yourlot.

Dele shook her head.

'What do you do when I speak to you?' said Yourlot.

Dele got up. The other children sat down.

'This is not good enough for you. You are better than these others, with your craw craw skin?' said Yourlot.

Something inside Dele snapped. 'Why don't you use a bottle dropper, instead of a jug?' said Dele.

Yinta pulled Dele's elbow. 'Miss, please don't vex, it is hungry that is making Laza talk like this.'

'No,' said Dele, jerking her arm out of Yinta's grip. 'I saw cartons of dried fish and milk arrive from the depot yesterday. Even this jug is still half full,' Dele said. 'Where is all the bread and meat? Where is the mosquito killer? You come every night fizz, fizz, one second, that's enough for a whole room?' Yinta raised a keloid-crossed hand to her mouth, her eyes wide with shock.

The room had gone quiet but Dele could not stop. She spread her arms like a goalkeeper. 'Only two more tables and jug is still almost full of milk. What was going to happen to the rest? To wash the floor, paint the ceiling, sell, feed the cows?' she said.

Yourlot shoved the silver counter into Dele's chest. 'Show me respect you frog skin girl. You don't know who you are talking to. Mark this day. You dare answer me back? You will never become anything good in this life. Girls like you who crossed me before it is in the gutter they end up,' said Yourlot. A murmur went round the hall: a curse.

'I wish you the very best of the same,' said Dele.

'How dare you curse me back?' said Yourlot the whites of her eyes threatening to burst from her head. She slapped Dele on the face, hard.

'We are here under UN flag, not for you,' said Dele. She head-butted Yourlot in the stomach. The jug smashed to the floor. Yourlot pushed and punched Dele. Dele fell over the bench and cut her hand on a shard of glass. As she sprang to her feet again a dark shadow filled the doorway.

'What is all this commotion?' said the commandant. A thickset man with a goatee and an incongruously high-pitched voice, he was wearing his usual brilliant white shirt tucked over his paunch and into a sharply creased blue pair of trousers.

'It is this bed wetter here,' said Yourlot. 'All the children will hungry because…look what she has done.' As if by magic, a tear rolled down a cheek. 'I am doing my best for them…'

Commandant Lokilu ran his tongue under his lower lip while he nodded like a reptile. 'Come with me,' he said, turning on his heel. Dele staggered after him, her head spinning, stomach churning, and her bleeding finger in her mouth.

Outside, two soldiers in blue helmets smoked cigarettes under a no-smoking sign. Dele and the commandant walked up a footpath and across a field where egrets stabbed about for breakfast.

'I told you to do what we say, obey, because there is no other way to a nice life or day,' said the commandant, as he turned into hut 20. He sat behind his metal desk and unwrapped a sweet.

'I know sir. I'm sorry, sir,' said Dele.

'Don't do that again. Take this from me as a senior person. If you push lucky too far it will turn bad and bite you…where it will pain you most. You hear that?' said the commandant. He called his orderly. 'Take her to the Federated Block. She needs discipline,' he said.

***

A fluffy three-lobed cloud unravelled high in the sky. *Day 4 on detention duty. I'm starving. How many days to go?*

'Finished?' said the orderly. Dele nodded and tried to blow another day's smell of chicken ordure from her nostrils. The orderly padlocked the commandant's coops, wiped her hands on her apron and marched Dele through the iron gate to the Federated Block. 'Sit here outside your room. I'm going to the kitchen to get your ration,' she said.

Federated block stood outside the camp, had ten rooms, six or seven occupied by other detainees, and was surrounded by a barbed-wire fence ten feet high. Through the fence Dele could see the commandant's yard, with its goats and chicken coops and turkeys, where the orderly put her to work every day. Dele sat on the lower of the two steps outside her room. She stretched her stiff wrists and fingers and waited for supper. Dele hadn't bothered to ask what she was having for supper: stale bread and warm water again. Then, from the other end of the corridor she heard a door slam, a grunt and an anguished groan.

'Who is that?' said Dele.

'It's Aanu.'

'Ah, the boy with the shirt between his thighs. What are you doing here?'

'What do you think?' said Aanu.

'I mean why are you in detention?' said Dele, scratching her ear.

'For pissing too much in my shirt,' said Aanu.

'How many years in this place?'

'In the toilet?' said Aanu.

'In camp,' said Dele.

'Four, since I was seven,' said Aanu.

'The orderly asked me to wait…nearly time for my evening meal,' said Dele.

'Help me,' said Aanu.

Dele crept over to peep through a crack in the door. Two skinny legs dangled under the cubicle curtain. 'Can I come in?' she said.

Aanu grunted. 'Hurry up now. My usual helper…is not…in detention. Oh, oh my blum is going to quench.'

'It's all the orange rind I hear you eat,' said Dele. She checked to see if anyone was coming. Aanu pulled the curtain open. His shirt hung round his neck and sweat rained down his face. 'I will not eat green banana skin again,' he said with another grunt, the pain brimming his eyes with tears.

'I'm not promising but I have a plan. Saw it on TV in Zadunaria,' said Dele. She remembered seeing a pair of disposable garden gloves lying on the fence not far from the commandant's chicken coops. She dashed outside.

'It may not work,' she said as she donned the green gloves.

'I have choice? One hour, not even one small bean comes out,' said Aanu.

Dele rubbed soap on to the gloves and fished around like the vet she had seen on TV. 'Push, now, wait, I'm ready now. I can feel its head. Bend forward so I can feel better. It's hard like rock. Got it. Wait. Try now. Push. Good boy.'

'Ah, ah, yes, yes, I think you've…I can manage now. I'll never forget you,' said Aanu.

'Neither will I,' said Dele, wrinkling her nose in disgust as she peeled off the gloves. The heavy aroma made her swoon. 'But why do you eat junk?'

'They told me a full blum will save me from those men, the boy lovers,' he said.

'If I see you eat that cardboard again I'll chop your mouth off.'

'Someone's coming.' Aanu patted his thigh. Dele stepped on it and heaved herself over the wall into the next cubicle. She heard the clang of a steel bucket and a woman, a cleaner perhaps, humming a tune.

'Go away,' said Aanu, I'm having my pickin.'

'Where is that girl? I left her ration outside her room,' said the woman. She made a sucking noise with her mouth. 'Aanu, this smell is like chemical weapon. Is this what God put you on this earth for?' she said.

'To punish me. That is why he gave me the shit of elephant but the worm of a back passage,' said Aanu.

***

A week passed. Dele and Aanu took their places in line with three other detainees for the weekly inspection of camp worksheets. Aanu still wore a khaki shirt tied, like a nappy, over his pair of shorts. The duty sergeant shuffled a chair into the shade under the umbrella tree. He wiped his face, sat down, opened the detainees' register.

'You, yes,' he said, brushing a dry leaf off the table.

Dele handed him her worksheet. The sergeant stared at his signature and looked puzzled. 'How can this be? I don't remember you planting any tomato. And my book here says only ten baskets amongst all of you. Which row? Where?' he said.

'Did you forget? Aanu and I gave you a full basket of tomatoes last Tuesday,' said Dele. 'It says so here.' She pointed at the sergeant's forged signature on her worksheet. 'Here, from three to six fifteen.'

The sergeant slapped an insect off his hand and cursed. 'Something is not right, not right at all. And it is not my head that is not correct. If you work those hours Tuesday last, I must remember, especially you, with the long nose,' he said, pointing at Dele.

'It's the truth, maybe you did not see me because I worked in the ditch, digging, digging, sir and the sun burn my face and back. That is why we worked in shadow behind the shed,' said Dele, peeling burns skin off her nose. The sergeant made a face, took his cap off, scratched his head and inspected the signature again.

Dele stepped backwards. 'I almost feel sorry for him, commandant is not going to be happy,' she said to Aanu.

'It's not your fault that he has memory of brainwashed goldfish,' said Aanu.

The sergeant looked up and beckoned to Aanu. He looked both perplexed and angry. 'Come here, you boy, let me see yours,' he said.

Aanu handed over *his* worksheet. The sergeant flicked through the pages raising each to the sky like a teller would a suspected forged banknote. Aanu grinned. 'Ah, ah sergeant, are you happy with us now?' he said.

'Sarge, don't listen to him. He didn't work as hard as me,' said Dele. Dele performed an impression of the commandant, squeaky voice and all.

'Stop, Dele, my drum skin stomach will burst if I laugh. You want to kill me?' said Aanu, holding his sides.

The sergeant frowned and waved his finger at Dele. 'I am watching you. Any funny *mago mago* from you and even God cannot beg me. Go. As for you Aanu, when you will grow up, wearing shirt around your yansh like small pickin?' he said. 'Next.'

'How did you do that?' said Aanu as they set off for supper.

'Learned to copy graffiti at Ambasi's academy.'

'Who is Ambasi?' said Aanu.

Dele looked down at her feet and skipped over a trail of ants. *Where are Mum and Dad?*

***

'Praise Allah. You are back,' said Cel, the ward supervisor. She ran over to give Dele a hug. Dele wondered what had brought this on. She had never seen Cel smile at that time of the morning. A bell rang. The other children ran out of the schoolroom, their tiny shadows darting across the dusty playground in the bright midday sun. The boy with the orange hair and with tiny black teeth that looked as if they would crumble on contact with anything harder than a mushy tomato now had bushy black hair. He had a fresh smile on his face: and the tip of his tongue no longer looked as if it had been through the mills.

'Hey Lazarus, you want to play later?' he said.

Another boy, nicknamed the dozy tortoise by Yourlot, skipped up bouncing an orange ball.

Cel, the supervisor kissed her rosary. 'Yesterday they eat corned beef and bread and coconut milk. One girl drink so much her belly swell and could not lie down.'

'Where is Yourlot?' said Dele.

The supervisor shook her head. 'Sacked. Yourlot was selling camp food in the Kanjara market. Wait here, I have a present for you,' she said. She returned with an old easel and a set of pencils and paintbrushes. 'I found these in a cupboard in Yourlot's office. Omoti the orderly says you like to draw,' she said.

Dele danced a little jig. She set up her easel on the veranda out of the glare and stroked the paper, relishing its smoothness.

'I didn't know that Lazarus could draw like this, oh,' said Tuns, admiring the portrait Dele drew of him. Tuns was said to be twelve but already had a thick moustache.

'Can I go to detention too? Maybe I will learn to draw like this?' said Tuns. 'Draw this one,' he said. He beckoned to his mates to make space, took a stick and scribbled in the sand, the loops ending up in what looked like hieroglyphics. Dele skipped off the veranda on to the playground, had a quick glance at Tuns's writing, and after a practice squiggle in mid-air, copied it first on to the sand then on to a piece of paper with every whorl and curlicue. 'This one then,' said another boy, scribbling numbers and letters on to the piece of paper he grabbed from Tuns. Dele did it again.

When the children tired of that game, Dele drew a cow guzzling from a feeding bottle while a dozen calves fought for the straw emerging from its rear. The camp commandant waddled up.

'What is this?' he said, pointing at Dele's drawing.

'Milkgate,' said Dele.

The commandant laughed.

Dad used to make people laugh too.

'What's wrong Tuns, your eyes are bulging,' said Dele.

'Look,' he said pointing over Dele's shoulder. Aanu gasped. Dele turned round. *Mum.* And as the word splashed into her chest and head, Dele dropped her stick and pencils and leapt into her mother's arms.

'Is she your mama?' said Aanu.

'She is whiter even than Lazarus,' said one of the other boys.

'Where's Dad?' said Dele. Aanu lingered then trotted off. Dele could feel her mum trembling as they walked hand in hand. They sat down on a bench. Jane's once delicate dimples had deepened into troughs. She had new bow-shaped creases by her mouth; and when she spoke the soft parts of her cheek wrinkled like tin foil.

'I've not seen your dad since...since they took us,' Jane said.

At that Dele felt a heavy thump in her chest. They got up and walked hand in hand towards a square-shouldered woman in green fatigues. The woman pointed to a dark cloud.

'It's coming this way,' she said.

'Sorry Batari, I won't be long,' said Jane, raising a hand in apology. 'Got to go, darling. I'm so, so, sorry,' said Jane, brushing back a grey ringlet. Her voice sounded rough, like she had a cold, not husky and smooth like it did when they lived in North Roko. 'Good news. We'll be moving in here soon…week or two?' she said, turning to Batari.

Batari nodded. 'Seems they have come to some deal,' she said

Jane wiped her nose. She hugged Dele and ducked into the van. The van trundled off with Dele waving at it long after its rattle faded out of earshot.

***

Jane and a dozen other women moved into the camp ten days later. With Yourlot gone all that remained was to find Dad, get a visa and everything would be alright said Dele to her mum. Jane gave her a hug but did not reply.

Every evening, Jane and Dele sat on their favourite bench under an African Tulip tree to have a chat before supper.

A sweet and smoky aroma floated from the kitchen on the warm evening breeze. 'It's omelette or pancake tonight, a change after four nights of boiled yams,' said Jane.

'One of the eggs we'll have for supper could have hatched into one of these,' Dele said, pointing at the red cockerel prancing across the path. It puffed its breast out and crowed.

'It's the way nature meant it,' Jane said.

'Do the hens like it? Do they wake up and sing a song, happy that Dele's mum has come for their chicks?' said Dele. She smoothed her khaki skirt.

'Hens don't think like us,' said Jane. Dele leaned in to her mum, taking in her clean salty smell.

'Is it natural to take people away and lock them up?' said Dele. A mangy dog crept into the commandant's yard to Dele's right. An orderly chased it away.

'Maybe they think people who are not like them are not human, or they don't know what they're doing is wrong, or they're cross and taking revenge for some wrong they've suffered…lots of reasons…' said Jane. The dog barked over its shoulder as it scampered away.

'Aanu said the men work in a camp, sorting mountains of waste. If dad works hard will they still beat him?' said Dele.

Jane stroked Dele's hair. 'Wale will find a way, he's a tough man, and you take after him. I'm proud of what you did, standing up to that Yourlot woman.' A wispy cloud drifted overhead.

'Maybe Dad will make them laugh,' said Dele.

Jane smiled. 'If they'll let him. You remember how on Friday nights he use to do these silly routines, swing you round and between his legs. He said he invented break dancing in his student days in London.'

'And he said he used to DJ at parties…'

'Until he left his CDs on his car roof one rainy night and drove off, he had to improvise. He said that's how karaoke started,' said Jane, her laughter sending warm ripples down Dele's back.

'Dad said he invented everything.'

Jane sighed. 'You've grown up so fast…we didn't mean this to happen, like this…'

They fell quiet. Jane played with a leathery green leaf she picked off the ground. They exchanged nods with a woman as she walked past.

'Remember how he used to carry you to bed when you fell asleep downstairs?' said Jane.

'I was awake, but pretended to be asleep because I wanted him to carry me,' said Dele.

Jane tittered. 'I used to do that too….when I was small, sadly my parents, they had me late…gone now.' She stopped and looked into Dele's eyes. 'When you were born Wale took you in his arms and said "I'm your road sweep, your Sherpa, your baggage-handler, your carpenter." That's probably because he never knew his dad.'

'What's…baggage?' said Dele.

'He meant things that screwed people up, wrinkle their minds into the back of an old woman's elbow…stop them getting on. Sandman's wrecked the plans. We wanted to keep you safe…that's all your dad wanted…for you to be safe.' Jane broke off and looked away. Dele put her head on Jane's shoulder. She could feel her mother grinding her jaw.

'I'll get him one day,' said Dele.

'No, no, darling,' said Jane. She leaned forward and drew a line in the sand with her toe. 'You cross that line heaven knows where it will end,' she said. 'For now we live in the moment, get out of here and go and look for dad.'

'Mum, it's not easy to live in the same moment that Dad is sad somewhere else.'

Jane picked up a twig and snapped it in two. She smiled, a faraway look in her eyes. 'I know darling. But who would have predicted any of this? You just can't tell.' She dropped the twigs and rubbed the sand off her hands. 'Your dad and me? He in London, me a Zadunaria girl. But a friend of mine was getting married in London. Wale was there. He'd split up from his girlfriend. How did he put it?' Jane rubbed her sandy hair as if to summon the memory. 'Yes, his reluctance to extend himself enough to meet her needs to find herself. He'd lost his pharmacist job. And was staring at the bottom of the sack...at what he called his last grains of liquidity wondering what to do with the rest of it before the financial advisers punched a greater hole in the bottom of his bag. That's how he talked then. He could talk the venom out of a starving Cobra. When I told him about the problems I was having at work, I used to teach, he said why worry about a glass ceiling when your nose is pressed flat under a knobbled boot? I thought he was drunk. No, he said he was intoxicated with my heady elixir, me. I didn't believe him of course when he said he would come to Zadunaria. But there he was. We set up Veritreatable pharmacy, doing ok. When you came along we couldn't ask for more.' She drew another line in the sand with her toe.

'Dad said he wasn't allowed sweets when he was small and that's how he became a pharmacist...I thought that's rubbish...'

'It's true. He used to pretend to be ill so that he could gorge on the cough syrup his mum left in the room. He loved the medicine so much he decided to learn how they worked. Veritreatable was his dream, until…'

'Sandman.'

'It was Babubacka first.' She brushed a speck or twig out of Dele's hair. Dele nestled further into her mum.

'North Roko under King Dela – life was simple. You did what you wanted. When I finished my degree in Toronto…I came back to teach.' She interrupted herself to brush her nose with a knuckle. 'We went to all the festivals, temple openings, closing, Christmas, Muslim end of fast celebrations, we all joined in the fun bits. But in the South? Useless President Kofail ran the place like it belonged to his family. Then in 1999, a coup. Your dad's right. Cue the usual dancing, music in the street. Then they found Tantalum.'

'That's a rare metal, isn't it mum?' said Dele.

Jane nodded. Their faces rubbed together. 'In a seam lying mostly under the north. Where you find a rare metal in Africa, the Chinese are not too far behind. But King Dela in the north sent them packing with words of one syllable. He'd seen what happened on the African mainland. As Wale said…anything you dig out of the ground in Africa is grounds for killing people. But the Chinese stopped over to see Babubacka. Soon they became friends…one thing led to another, he invaded the north to take over the mines. We lost almost everything. Without Tantalum none of this would have happened.'

A horn sounded and a white van stopped outside the kitchen across from Dele's bench. A goat bleated and ambled out of the way, its udders wagging stiffly like a van's exhaust pipes.

'You'll be a teenager…gosh, a woman soon,' Jane said, with a glance at Dele's chest.

Dele blushed, the buds on her chest burned. 'I don't want to be a woman. I want Dad.'

She looked up. A van pulled up outside the kitchen and a tall, thin woman got out. 'What's she doing back here?' said Dele.

SEVEN

Dele staggered into the pantry with an armful of firewood. She had one more trip to make to the woods in the sapping heat before Jane got back from a late lunch with the world famous singer, Eniadudu. Her arms ached. She leaned her banging head against the cool, terracotta butt in the corner and closed her sore eyes. They did not like the dust. When she opened her eyes again the smudge on her white shirt reminded her that she had some laundry to do. The water butt stood just outside the door. She had reached the door with a bucket when she thought she heard a shout. Moments later she heard another shout: this time louder. Then came two sharp screams and what she recognised as the hollow blast of a flugelhorn. When Dele looked out of the open window her heart slammed into her mouth.

Their faces wreathed in black cloth, or hidden behind balaclavas, scores of riders wielding machetes careered around the yard, brown paper wrapping flapping from silver bicycle frames. Dele saw a rider drag a woman and child by the hair, and run them both through with his sword. Blood hosed out of the woman. Another man sliced through a breast with his machete and with another stroke sliced the suckling infant's head from its trunk. Blood pumped from the child's head. Dizzy and shaking with fright, Dele pulled the window shut, slammed the door and crawled behind a barrel. *Where is Mum?*

A siren wailed. Dele crept up to peep through a crack in the wall. It looked like some circus of nightmares had come to camp. Men ran out of the school room carrying books, tables, chairs, desks, her easel and parts of the blackboard to toss onto a fire. Dele heard a thump and scuffle outside. She leapt behind the barrel just before a man, naked from the waist upwards, his torso glistening with oil and sweat, dragged a whimpering woman into the hut. Yanking the woman to the concrete floor, he ripped off her clothes and straddled her, facing away from Dele. A loud banger went off in Dele's head. She grabbed her metal laundry bucket and swung its bottom edge hard into the man's right pate. She heard a crunch and the man collapsed forward.

'Yeowah, my jumata, burn for ever in hell, filthy banana leaf smoking dog,' said the woman, pushing the man off and pulling her tattered skirt around her midriff. She had wide, angry eyes, a flattish almost Northern nose and skin the colour of a strong cup of coffee. Dele did not think she woman was much older than eighteen. 'He's not moving,' said Dele.

The woman nodded and spat at the motionless man. 'Quick,' she said, grabbing hold of the man's feet.

'Where is Commander?' said Dele.

'They ran away,' said the woman with a show of resignation.

Dele helped roll the man up against a wall, made a sign of the cross on her forehead and squeezed up next to the woman. Through the crack in the wall Dele saw a man armed with a cutlass chasing a fair-skinned woman in a brown top.

'That's my...oh thank God...it's not her,' Dele said as the woman tripped over a dog. 'It's Eniadudu.' Eniadudu scrambled to her feet but ran into a handlebar. Blood ran from a gash in her leg. She crumpled, spread-eagled to the ground. A fight broke out between two Sharijujumen over Eniadudu. One man screamed and ran off with a bicycle spoke poking from his eye and a knife in his side. The winner, a man with a head shaped like a box speaker, leapt on to a crate. As he did so a jeep in the blue colours of the commandant's regiment crashed through the camp gates and knocked a pot-bellied goat into the path of another lorry. The goat collapsed with its head looking the wrong way. Dele's head spun. She thought she was going to faint.

'You are shaking,' said the young woman, taking Dele by the arm.

'That's Mum, beside that woman in the red scarf. Look through the legs of that man with the big head running towards us. Open the door,' said Dele as she saw Jane run towards the pantry duck under a bamboo pole then swerved past Dele's door and turned right. After her ran a man in white and green headgear, his face striped with green and white paint, neck jerking forward with each stride, like a bird's. Dele grabbed the bucket. She charged out of the hut, pumping her left arm as hard as she could, the blood-stained bucket swinging in the other hand and her baggy khaki shorts flapping around her thin thighs. Jane tottered, shortened her strides to hurdle a toddler but the man giving chase simply kicked the child out of the way. The child cried out and flopped over like a ragdoll. *What a wicked man.* Jane turned left between the cowsheds. *No, not that way Mum.* A goat scurried across the man's path. As the man slowed down Dele seized her chance, ran up and swung her bucket at his head. The man stepped ducked and Dele's momentum spun her off her feet. *Sandman. Is he a Sharijujuman?* Dele leapt to her feet and swung her bucket again, but Sandman kicked her legs from under her. Dele fell face forward. The searing pain in her left ankle forcing her to drop the bucket. When she lifted her head she saw, ten paces away, Jane on her haunches under the lattice shadows of the perimeter fence.

'Mum run, he's coming,' said Dele. But Jane, her chest heaving and face bright red, seemed too weak to run or fight. Sandman dragged her past Dele. Dele stretched an arm out, to fend off a boot aimed at her head. She ducked, but not in time.

***

Dele smelled smoke and burning flesh. In the distance the sun glowed bright, low over the treetops and the day looked and felt tired, nearing its end. Just over the fence the glistening boughs of a tall Iroko tree trembled under the weight of a white-backed vulture. Dele turned her head to the left. A few feet away lay two topless women, face down, side by side, one held a little girl by the ankle, the girl's guts splayed from a gash in her side. A naked child clung, bleating, to quiet breasts, one from each woman. *Where is Mum?* She heard the crackle of fire and turned her head again the other way. At the base of a neighbouring pyre lay Eniadudu, her right leg bent backwards. An inch of white bone poked through the fried skin on her shin. Dele heard a click. She flinched. Then came the glug and gurgle of fluid pouring out of a barrel. A fire took hold with a harrumph and purple-red flames tore up the pyre. Dele jumped away from the smarting heat, lost her grip and slipped downhill.

'What is this, a spirit child?' said a man. Flecks of soot flew off the cardboard burning in his hand. Dele limped to her feet. Her left ankle ached. She heard footsteps and turned to see Sandman loping up.

'Bandi, you go finish your work,' he said.

'Where's my mum?'

Dragged along by the ear, Dele limped along as fast as she could to keep up with Sandman.

'You sure you want to know?' he said, as they went past a man playing his flugelhorn on the bench under the Tulip tree. *Mum's tree.*

Sandman stopped outside the fifth of a row of garage doors. 'Go on then.' He banged a hasp back into place with the base of his hand and pulled the grey door open and over a clump of grass. Inside the garage a woman lay prone in the back of a truck.

'Darling, oh no...get away.' The woman turned her head. Blood bubbled up between her split lips. Dele stepped out of the light and round the side of the truck.

Oh my God, It's Mum. Jane had had her scalp shaved. Caked in blood, what she had left of her hair stuck out from over her ears. Her feet and slippers had been beaten into one red pulp. Where she once had a hand she had two crusted stumps, attached now to an arm that didn't look right, lying as it was under her body. A bolt of anger scorched through Dele's head. She leapt back and clamped her teeth down in the web between Sandman's thumb and forefinger. Sandman hit out, but Dele burrowed close and, like a terrier, would not let go.

'You will suffer, proper for this,' said Sandman, jerking his hand away. He showed her his bleeding hand and shoved Dele back against the truck. Dele's spat out a sliver of skin and flesh and as she stumbled caught sight of a rifle hanging on the back of the garage door. Feinting one way, Dele ran the other, jumped to flick the gun off its hook and pointed it at Sandman.

'You don't know what you are doing,' said Sandman. He stepped back. He was right but Dele didn't care anymore. She pulled the trigger. It felt stiff and for a second it did not give. It clicked. Sandman ducked. But instead of a loud bang Dele heard a sound like an egg dropping on the floor. Sandman leapt from his crouch. Desperate, Dele pulled the trigger again. This time a deafening bang, followed almost at once by an echoing clang, filled the room. She saw a flash and smoke and it felt like three class bullies had kicked her in the chest all at once. Dele fell back against a wall. She clambered up, hopping on her right foot, her left ankle aching as if crammed full of hot nails.

'Ah look what you have done now,' Sandman said, pointing to a black hole the size of a computer mouse in the back of Jane's head. Tears of anger and despair fried Dele's eyes. She grabbed at the gun and at Sandman. She missed and her right hand slipped over the blood-splattered wheel arch of the van and through the door. Sandman slammed the door shut. Dele screamed out loud but her mum did not move.

'Shut up your mouth,' said Sandman. He took Dele by the neck and back up the alley, past the smouldering pyres. 'Take her to that *yeye* commandant's rooms,' he said, pushing her to a man with a wispy moustache. 'This one is tougher than the bottom of your big mama's foot. She just shoot her own mama.'

'You don't say,' said the man.

'Watch her pam pam,' said Sandman.

I didn't mean to went the scream in Dele's head. Her smashed fingers looked like sausages frying from inside out and they felt as if about to burst. The minder dragged her round the back of the house and into a smell of smoke and pepper and salty meat. 'Sit,' she said, dragging a chair back to a wooden table. Dele sat down and blew on her fingers, lifted them to her chest, put them under an arm-pit, or in her shirt pocket, but nothing eased the agony. The minder tapped her on the shoulder and jabbed it with a needle.

***

Dele opened her eyes and looked through the window bars on to a grey, prelachrymose sky. Behind the perimeter fence the taller trees traded angry blows with the wind. A cleaner walked in with a broom and chipped pan.

'Is it morning yet? Where did I put my white swimming trunks?' said Dele. 'Mum will be cross if I don't find them.'

'I know you, your head tyre is not get air inside?' said the woman pointing to her temple. 'Don't you know that no sea water here for two hundred miles? Maybe you drink and sleep too much these three days past. Wear this.'

Dele got off the smelly sofa and put on the proffered white gown. The sound of water thundering into a bucket from a standpipe, drove spikes into her ears and she leaned her pounding brow against the window bars. *How did that happen?* she thought, when she felt the throb from her crocked fingers.

The woman left and a man walked in. 'Who sent you? Dad?' said Dele.

'Shut up,' said the bow-legged man. He unlocked Dele's leg chains and led her out across a courtyard to sit in a room with ten other tearful girls or women. A buck-toothed cleaner shuffled in to place a bowl of water on a wooden stool under the electric bulb to catch moths, termites, aphids, as they fell, roasted by the heat she hoped. But the bulb glowed barely bright enough to shame a sunflower and the woman kissed her teeth in frustration and whipped her bowl away. *Where is Mum?*

The national anthem warbled out of the TV set. Babubacka appeared on the screen. 'Some of you have been writing to abroad. Amnesty International. Human rights? You think anyone gives a...tossing; UN, EU, Arab states, USA? They appeal for restraint. We are restrained, but we must have order in this land.' A zombie pinched one Babubacka nostril. His leader inhaled the brown powder and blew out on to the proffered white handkerchief.

Where is Mum?

Babubacka didn't care. He peered at his pancake-sized watch. 'If you so-called elite feel sick I will offer you some advice or help, a finger down your throat?' He pretended to put a finger in his mouth. He licked his lips. 'Ah, you see, doesn't full participation feel that much better,' he said, with a wink at his zombie. A cock crowed outside the room. It sounded like a wail.

'Participation, my foot, full penetration more like. Who want fuck?' said a soldier. He bared his teeth and slapped his thighs, got up and dragged Dele up by the elbow.

'Come, inspector want to see you,' he said. A new cold fear gripped Dele.

EIGHT

An orderly shoved Dele over a threshold. The door crashed shut. The deafening bang seemed to slam Dele against the wall. She groped up the rough wall to flick a switch. A blue bulb came on. She saw that it hung from the ceiling by a short noose. A ceiling fan droned and creaked round under the bulb, its dust-stippled blades flicking grotesque shadows around the room and over the bare-mattressed bed pushed up against the far wall. Dele started to pant like a dog and her heart beat one way then the other against her chest.

Then she heard the panicky bustle of orderlies and the whirr from an engine. Gusts of wind and the sound of more shouting swept under the door. 'He's here, inspector, quick, quick, no time.' Sweat rained from Dele's armpits and her legs swayed like rushes on the riverside. She put an arm out for support but the door fell ajar and she found her fingers in the fleshy dip of Sandman's mid-riff.

'See what you caused,' said Sandman in his red fez and white gown. He had a cigarette dangling from his mouth. 'You can't answer? What your papa said pained me. If he does not know Roko history he should check before he opens his big mouth. It is your mama's people, Ligthausen, who took our land. You think it is by chance you landed on my street? No, that is the power of my great great Aunty Sumo's spirit. She died near a vet's clinic, eating dog's food, left by your mama's people as an insult after they took her land.' Sandman spat out a flake of tobacco and wiped his mouth.

'Mum had nothing to do with that and my dad's from England,' said Dele creeping backwards.

Sandman leaned the door shut. 'Maybe Ligthausen did not know that any bad you do will come back to catch you on this earth. The book of action and reaction must balance here before the final audit in the beyond of heaven. If you yourself escape…your children will pay.' Sandman reached inside his robe, took out a box of matches and lit another cigarette. 'As for your papa. Only luck is between us,' he said. Smoke, tinged blue by the light, spewed from his needle-hole nostrils. 'Because he is from England he is making big man here. I had scholarship myself to study there. Tings did not work out.'

'Where did you take my dad? Where is he?' said Dele.

Sandman drew a finger across his throat and shrugged one shoulder. 'Who knows, in the beyond of beyond,' he said, pointing to the ceiling, 'or the here and there?' he said with a dismissive clack. Dele's insides shrunk into a cold ball.

'Sashi, where are you? Mossa mossa, what do I pay you for?' said Sandman, turning to the door. Sashi, an old man in bearing but fresh of face, clattered through the door with a food trolley, set a tray on a table and lit a mosquito coil. A jeep snarled past. Insects buzzed in the bush. Dele glanced through the barred window. An indifferent blue-black night wore on.

Sandman sat on the bed, peeled a banana and spat off the tip. 'Sweet, sweet, fried on the fires of my enemies' remains.' The words slipped off his tongue as if he savoured or had rehearsed, them. He raised the lid off a blue bowl, devoured a mound of pounded yam with his bare fingers, swigged from a keg of palm-wine and farted. 'A sign of good living,' he said. He looked up at Dele. 'Do you know that song, sweet banana?'

Dele looked away. She did not reply.

'I didn't think so. When it comes to the most expensive real estate in the world you cannot tell men where not to dig. Ask those billionaires, paying money for ever for five minutes in a hotel room. Me...I can't afford to have that problem. I say if you can fuck, shit, piss when you want in your own time, you are already rich, the rest is fringe benefits,' said Sandman. He laughed and thrust his index finger through a ring made with his other fist. 'I plant in virgin real estate. You know they call me Sandman. Well, tell them that Sandman prefers to dig fresh pits, but he could not resist an open goal, pity that with your trigger happiness that hole is now closed; a well is dead and buried.'

Dele pressed against the wall to get as far away as she could from Sandman. She closed her eyes. *What's he saying?*

Before Dele could answer her own question Sandman pulled her away from the wall and shoved a flat pack into her hands. 'Open,' he said, with menace in his voice. Dele found herself fumbling with the wrappings. Her hands shook. Sandman gave an impatient suck of his teeth, snatched back the packet, tore it open and handed Dele pristine white bedsheets. 'Make the bed…don't waste my time, did your mama not teach you how to make bed,' he said. 'See this blue tablet? I got it from your papa's shop. You don't understand? All I need is to lick it, to make it last. That's what your dad said to that customer – papa, you don't have to stand on your head anymore to get it up. He had a sense of humour…your dad. You don't get it? If he was here he would say the way I tell his jokes is a joke.'

Dele spread the glistening white sheet over the mattress. The creases, one half convex, met in a cross in the middle of the bed. 'Good, now tuck in at the corners, not too tight.' He spoke in a creepy library whisper, but the labial smacks on his cigarette sounded to Dele like claps of thunder. 'Take this,' he said handing Dele a pillowcase. Tendrils of cigarette smoke wreathed Dele's face. Their spiky aroma and Sandman's flinty red eyes made her shiver. Sandman seemed to enjoy watching her tremble. He finished his cigarette, dropped it on the floor and clawed Dele to him. Dele arched her stiff back and pulled away but his arms dug in. *Can I crack my head on the mirror and stab him with broken glass?* She closed her eyes. He stopped his clawing and his breaths slowed down. Dele opened her eyes. For a moment she thought he would set her free. But he pushed her down on the bed and what hopes she had left dropped to the floor, like baubles off a hoary Xmas tree.

She squeezed her eyes shut and cringed when he licked the tears on her neck. Like a ram before its Abrahamic sacrifice, she turned her head and neck this way and that, but she choked, her lungs burning with pent up gases and her mind turned grey, then flashing red as Sandman forced what felt like a rubber toilet brush between her thrashing legs.

***

Sandman had gone. The fan droned on and on as though in lament at what it had seen. Dele sat on the floor with her back against the bed and stared into red space. Aching, burning, sticky, she smelt of dust, cigarettes, stale beer, blood and sweat and something else, like a salty boiled egg whisked with sour milk. She moved up to sit under the fan's breeze to wash away the smell. But the aroma of shame and fear and despair and defeat would not leave her. It clung to her hair, neck, all over her and seemed to waft up from under her skin and from her breath. Then the implication of Sandman's words about dry wells and holes and her trigger happiness hit her like a sandbag in the back of the head. *Mum.* Dele doubled up, her head dropped and tears banged down her cheeks like hot bricks. She closed her eyes, felt a furry scamper over her feet and screeched, only to open her eyes to the sight of a long-tailed rodent as it dived under the door.

A familiar voice came up to the door. 'Hey, bush rat too many here,' said a woman.

Dele shrank back against the far wall.

'Open up now, or real trouble.'

Dele shuffled over. She did not remember locking the door. She had never slept behind a locked door in her life. She turned the key in the lock and opened the door and, to her horror a tall woman in a nurse's uniform, blue frock and a wide red belt, waltzed in, swaying like a smug rapper.

'See how God works? To Him be the glory,' said Yourlot.

Shards of despair stabbed Dele in the heart.

Yourlot yanked the soiled sheet off the bed and tossed it at Dele.

'Flower, take this, wash your shame. And don't try any *mago mago* or you will not eat this morning. I'm in my office. You have one hour till seven thirty.' She poured a thimbleful of white washing powder into Dele's palm. 'Go,' she said, pointing through the door.

Dele took in the thick green algae on the bathroom wall, the shower head tied to its support by rope caked in slimy limestone. Her sorry reflection wobbled at the bottom of the green plastic bucket.

Not enough to drown myself in. She poured the washing powder into the scaly water and stirred it in with the stained end of the sheet. The flakes floated but did not foam. *How is this going to work? Oh Mum.* Her right hand throbbed. Trying not to think about the stinging bits between her legs, she felt doomed, defeated and empty but carried on beating and rubbing the stains against the sides of the bucket until cramp in her left hand forced a stop. But when she lifted the sheet to the light the stubborn red skid marks and spots stared back at her, defiant. Groaning in despair, she flaked soap off the floor and went back to work. But she slipped on the slimy floor and the sodden sheet tipped out of the pail. Her broken fingers jammed against the sides of the pail as she tried to save the sheet. She gasped out in pain. The pail rolled over and the bulk of the rest of the sheet slid on to the floor. Dele smacked her head and growled in frustration. A shadow fell across the door. She looked up and, to her horror, it was Yourlot again.

'Too slow. Food is finished,' Yourlot said. She turned her head to shout at someone in the end cubicle. 'I saw you arrive washerwoman. No pay today, you late,' said Yourlot, humming a tune to herself as she left.

Back again over the bucket, the red stains had been joined by green streaks from slime.

She heard a kind voice. 'Don't cry,' it said. Dele did not believe it until she heard it again. She looked up. Her eyes met the soft gaze of a woman in a grey tabard.

'I'm the washerwoman,' said the woman.

She had a wry neck, but her jet black skin, not the usual chocolate West African shade, reminded Dele of her friend, Koseri.

'I'm cleaner and washerwoman from village. Mariagra. They call me Mary.' Mary handed Dele a clean towel and scooped the sheet off the floor. 'Wait,' she said, returning minutes later with a squidgy sponge and a bucketful of steaming water. Dele closed her eyes and let Mary sponge her down. The water stung her legs and eyes but she would have stood there for ever to wash the memory of the night before, her 13th birthday night, October the 1st, away.

'That…that wicked woman will soon return,' said Mary, rubbing Dele's hair dry. Dele tried a grateful smile, buried her head in Mary's rocking warmth.

"I will get you a clean sheet. Past is past, like old and dirty cloth. Leave it where it is. Only go there if it will help make you strong. The rest, leave to God.' Mary pointed to the sky.

'Will he come back?' Dele said.

'That I can't say.'

***

It was the morning of October 10th. Sandman had come and come and he had just gone when Yourlot waltzed in to toss a bowl of watery baked beans across the floor. Dele waited for Yourlot's footsteps to fade away then pushed up on to her twiggy legs to empty the bowl out of the window. After, she went back to bed to wait for Mary to smuggle in an egg and a slice of bread.

A sultry afternoon arrived, but without Mary. Hungry and wilting in the heat, Dele tottered across to the window to stand on a chair. To cool down she pressed her face against the steel bars. She saw that the man in the white turban was back in his usual spot, popping his purple pimples and smoking his afternoon cigarette under a sapling to her left. A buggy loaded with pots, pans, tins of palm oil and rice trundled past and made Dele's empty belly grumble. She wondered what had happened to Maria. Then a wood pigeon started to coo. Dele felt a tremor go through the window bars. At that moment the bird stopped singing and the man in the white turban tossed his cigarette to the ground, leapt to his feet, hopped first away from, then past, her window. Then came a thud, like the sound of a dropped suitcase. Dele craned her neck. She heard doors slam shut, the sound of splintering wood, of breaking glass, followed by bangs, loud prayers, screams, more bangs, thuds, pleading, more bangs and two loud explosions. Dele curled up in the corner and closed her eyes. *I hope they shoot me quick.*

Her door opened. Dele put her hands over her ears. Nothing happened. She opened one eye and saw Mary. Next to Mary stood a female sergeant armed with a black revolver.

'You are safe now,' said the soldier, holstering her gun.

Where have I heard that before? thought Dele.

Maria bowed. 'Good luck my child,' she said. She had tears in her eyes. She hugged Dele, ruffled her air and turned to shuffle out of the room.

'Come,' said the soldier.

Dele stumbled, squinting, out into the smoke and dust outside. She coughed, saw a man lying dead next to a broken fingerpost and went over for a closer look. Bluebottle flies swarmed round his mouth, nostrils and bombed into the deep crater under his right breast.

'You know him?' said the soldier.

Dele shook her head. 'It's not the one I'm looking for. The one I want is called Sandman or chief or inspector. He wears a red hat.'

'That way, we have arrested some of them…Commandant's bungalow,' said the soldier, pointing down the path.

Good. Dele stumbled after the soldier.

A pile of furniture burned outside the Commandant's office. A woman ran up and threw on a tray of dead locusts. A few feet away four men lay face down in their underpants, one puffing sand into his neighbour's faces with miserable sobs for mercy.

'Nagati scum,' said Dele's soldier. 'They beat and killed farmers. Market women cannot trade. That's how we knew they were here,' she said.

'Where is he? You said you arrested him?' said Dele, waving away a gust of smoke.

'Go inside,' said the soldier.

The green door to the Commandant's bungalow had a splinter down the middle. A popular Kombo tune wafted through the windows. 'Enter,' said the soldier, refastening the bullet belt round her waist. 'Secure?' she said.

'Yes sir,' said a recruit. He saluted.

'I look like man to you?' said Dele's sergeant. The saluting soldier stuttered in reply.

Crunching broken glass underfoot Dele turned left at the end of a dark corridor, stepped over a dead dog and into the office. Mining, training and other certificates hung at varying angles from a pockmarked wall. On the desk stood a bleached white human skull filled with cigarette butts. Another skull stood on a pile of bank notes. Under a window in the corner of the room lay a broken sandal. *Sandman's.*

'Where is he? This is his,' Dele said.

The soldier did not reply.

'Escaped, how? You said…' She had no words to express her rage. She sat down on the desk and put her head in her hands. As the smoke cleared outside a familiar glitter caught the corner of her eye: her mum's ring lying inside Sandman's sandal.

'It's my mama's ring,' she said. The image of her mum lying in the back of the truck flashed into her head. Straightening up, she paused for a moment, rolling the smooth ring in her hand. The hot tears wanted to come out. She gritted her teeth and locked them in.

The soldier put an arm round her. Loud laughter rang in from the yard at some punchline.

'Do you know where they took the boys?' Aanu, Tuns. Galoro?' Dele said, shoving the ring over the knuckle of a broken finger. It fit.

'Come, this is no place for a child,' said the soldier.

'I'm not a child,' said Dele as a burning desire for revenge roared into her chest.

NINE

'Come on ward Townsend. It's six. Mossa, quick, Oluwole ward girls are up already.' A draught swept up the ward, the bulb flickered on and Sister Holly Ning appeared in the doorway wearing her awry white cap. *Morning at last.* Dele had lain awake in bed while the rest of the rehab dorm seemed to snore. Feeling as stiff as Sister's starched blue pinafore she pulled the coverlet back over her head and ignored the three girls rushing off to the bathroom.

The ward went quiet. The orderly rolled the squeaky weighing scales up to Dele's bed.

'Your turn, Verity.'

A corkscrew turned in Dele's belly. She groaned out loud and turned prone. The orderly's long fingers pushed through the net. 'Eh, God, only bone remain of you. Nearly twenty pound you lost in the last two weeks,' she said a note of concern in her voice. 'You want die?'

Yes, unless I find Dad. Dele forced her stick insect legs out of bed. The cold concrete floor chafed the soles of her feet. 'I'm ready,' she said.

'Dele, give me a smile. If you do well, the sooner we talk of discharge,' said Sister Ning, patting Dele on the shoulder. Dele wondered where she would go when she didn't know where to find her dad. She tried to smile but another wave of bellyache forced her to gasp.

'What's wrong?' said Sister, her dark eyebrows meeting in a frown of concern. Dele shook her head, wondering whether Sandman left scavengers inside her to scrape out his excess seed. She rubbed her belly and puffed her cheeks. At last the cramp fell away. She felt a treacly trickle between her legs. *Surely I'm not weeing again.*

'Shut the door,' said Sister, wheeling Dele back to the corner of the ward. 'Go, bring pain killers and my bag-'. The orderly dashed off before Sister finished. Dele started to tremble.

'Is this because of him?' she said, when she saw the blood.

'No, no. He is not the cause…'

The orderly stumbled in puffing hard. 'Put them on the cupboard over there,' said Sister.

'How's your belly?' she said turning to Dele.

'I wish my mum was here. I saw her on the beach with Dad last night. They looked so… beautiful, happy. Why can't I be happy?' she said.

'They're watching over you,' said Sister, brushing Dele's hair.

'There's another pain always there inside my chest.'

'It's because you miss them. But time is a great healer,' said Sister Ning.

'But what if he doesn't come?' said Dele.

***

Alisa, the happy clappy assistant therapist with her lilac lipstick, told Dele that the rehab block had once been a girl's secondary school dormitory. Built round an oblong, part-lawned quadrangle, the rehab block had six wards or rooms, each ward for patients in the same stage of rehabilitation. Two gravel walking paths bisected the quadrangle and in its centre, surrounded by a triangle formed by three benches, stood a flagpole and two stocky trees with yellow and green leaves.

Dele put on a light blue blouse over a darker skirt and, after the communal breakfast and prayers went to sit on the bench facing Sister Ning's office.

Alisa set up an easel. 'Try to paint good things,' she said. 'It will help you to recalculate. Now, your head is still like a ledger that is full of the wrong figures.' Alisa looked pleased with herself, perhaps because of the new red highlights in her hair. She wore a different style every week. 'You are in phase two now. Don't let another four weeks meet you still on this ward.'

How many phases? If I draw what she wants do I get out of here to look for Dad? Dele looked up, shielding her eyes from the sun's glare. 'I'm trying,' she said, but her head teemed with images of skulls without occiputs and ants wielding swords.

'Take this, wipe your nose. Why don't you go outside while I look for drawing paper?' said Alisa.

Dele ambled out on to the dusty dirt-track, the afternoon sun warm on her back. On her left, rows of yellow-crowned maize plants stood scores deep, glistening and proud. Beyond them gracile Iroko trees murmured and swayed to a languid rhythm, whooping with a shimmering frenzy, like possessed evangelists, when the wind got up. A ball of tumbleweed the size of a paw-paw rolled up, hopped off the track in the wind and exploded feet away. As Dele turned away from the cloud of dust, a piercing chirp from over her left shoulder took her ear. She looked up and saw, caught by a slanting ray of sunlight near the top of a tree, a pair of African Grey parrots feeding their chicks. And when the scarlet-tailed one dropped a squirming titbit into an eager beak, Dele's insides ran to warm cream. She stood transfixed, as happy memories, of life in Zadunaria – Innocent her pet parrot, dad's strong back, cake-baking nights, the charity run for Rwanda (she came second to last, but that was a virus), mum's honey and lemon in hot milk and the blanket on the sofa when Mum thought she was "coming down with something" – washed over her like raindrops made up of the softest cashmere wool.

Then a cloud passed in front of the sun and Dele lost the nest in the shadows. She turned for the wards. How, she wondered, if, as her teacher OY had said, life is made up of time spent in line, or on queues, from queues you join for the bus, to queues you aim to join for love and wealth, how it was that she had come to join the queue of daughters who would one day shoot their own mums dead; the queue of daughters who would lose their dads; the queue of little girls who would be taken by force by men who did not care whether they lived or not; the queue of those who would have no friends, or one to fight for them; the queue of those who would not belong to anyone; the queue of those who would have nothing to wait for, unless Sandman and Yourlot were right and God had ushered her on to those queues for something she had done wrong. But what she wondered. For mocking Little Mama, for throwing stones at the dogs when their backs stuck together, for riding horseback on sheep, pulling wings off the butterflies, for sometimes praying for Mum to disappear when she went all volcanic, or for praying for a different nose or skin from the one God gave her, or for putting off the trainee teacher during Maths lesson, or for forging school reports for a fee? Or was it for something Mum or Dad had done, or *their* Dads and Mums had done? If so, had she got what she deserved and was there more to come? If only in phase two rehab here in camp, in what phase was she with God?

Alisa stood waiting outside the block, with a paintbrush in her hand. 'Where were you?' she said, showing Dele to the work bench. 'I put a stone on your work to stop it blowing away. Your radio...I tuned it to your Mali station,' she said.

The radio sizzled, like an omelette in a frying pan. 'Thanks, correct station,' Dele said. It wasn't.

'Your feet are unusual, such small toes,' said Alisa.

Dad's cocktail sausage toes. Dele put the paintbrush down because it hurt too much to go on.

'Tim the TV man is coming after siesta,' said Alisa handing Dele a tissue.

'Who is Tim?' said Dele.

'You've forgotten?'

***

The typewriter in Sister's office had fallen silent and most of the other girls had gone to the afternoon session on domestic science. Dele sat outside her ward singing anything that came into her head, doggerel, birdsong or la-la-la-la-las with her hands clapped over her ears to keep out the image of the crimson-ringed jackbooted giant black ants on bicycles with Jane's head mounted on handlebars. The ants and bikes went away. Dele glared at a girl standing there. The girl ran off.

A car door slammed and a radio crackled. Sister Ning appeared with a man who should be white except that he had a face the same colour as his bright orange T-shirt.

'Tim brought you this,' said Sister Ning. She handed Dele a yellow and black TV/radio.

Dele got up to shake Tim's hand. 'Thank you, but-'
The crack of a stick under a cameraman's foot made her jump. Tim waved his crew back. 'Skittish aren't we?' he said. Dele did not reply.

'Mr Mullins, we thought you'd be interested in our Dele. For rehabilitation,' said sister, patting Dele on the head. Dele looked up at Sister. *This is your idea.*

Tim sat next to Dele. Dele pulled her skirt tight and moved away. Her left ear itched. She didn't scratch it. *Has he come to take what he wants by force, like Sandman?*

'How old are you?' Tim said, moving the bushy microphone under Dele's chin. 'Thirteen,' she said, leaning back.

A camera clicked. Dele jumped again. Tim waved his crew further back.

'Never mind. You look young for your age, and where I come from that's a compliment.

You would want your daughter to look like this, hair like rat-tails, nose like clothes peg, legs like the land on the moon?

'And these drawings, oh my. What have we got here?' said Tim. 'A headless horse jumping over a baby,' he said, answering his own question. Tim picked up another drawing. 'This one looks like giants snorting stuff through one nostril and spraying bullets through the other. Am I right? And what does this mean?' he said, turning another painting to the camera.

'Anything you want,' said Dele. *Dad didn't like these rubber neckers.* 'Attests to versatility. This one is a rifle farm, isn't it? They all make the same angle with the soil and the soil is made of children?' Tim turned to the camera. 'A raw talent; an anticipation, prefiguring perhaps, reinterpretation, celebration possibly of the tradition of the artist in the fugue of the aftermath of catastrophe in the developing world. It seems to me, it speaks to me...it seems to work, a brutally honest depiction,' said Tim. One of the crew, a man with a stern face and a greying goatee brought a short-sleeved arm down like a sword.

'Tim, I haven't the foggiest what you're talking about…you should have been a central banker,' he said.

Startled once again, Dele jerked backwards. She fell off the bench. Tim waved Jerry back.

'Art appreciation is an art in itself,' he said. He turned to Dele. 'Now, how about this one. A slipper?' he said.

'My mother's,' Dele said. The words burst out. She threw an imploring glance at Sister, like a boxer at the end of her tether would at her apparently indifferent corner.

Tim picked another painting. *I've been looking for that.* 'Is that Cupid's arrow or William Tell's bolt?' he said rotating the painting first one way then the other. 'Ah I see now. It's a child with thorns in her heart,' said Tim, turning to the camera. 'And what do you want to be when you grow up?' he said.

'A TV presenter,' said Dele.

'Ooh and why is that?' said Tim, his face lighting up.

'I will be the one to ask the stupid questions.'

***

A few days after Tim's visit Dele drew a picture of Alisa. The muse paraded it round the school, after which Dele noticed a certain coolness between Alisa and Sister, until she painted Sister a portrait of her own.

The morning post had just arrived. A door swung open and Sister Ning emerged from her office waving a white envelope. Dele affected a contemplative pose and crouched over her easel.

'Good news. Tim paid for your sketching, he liked the child with the thorn in her heart. More than two hundred Roko, that is plenty,' said Sister Ning.

'I didn't want to sell it.' Dele dashed her paintbrush to the ground. She heard a crash behind her. A ball had bounced out of Oluwole ward and knocked over her radio.

'Watch it windmill, it took me all morning to find this station,' said Dele. A lanky girl loped up to retrieve the ball.

'Yellow, shut your big mouth. You think because that TV man want fuck you, you can talk to me anyhow?'

Dele leapt at the lanky one.

'Hey girls,' said Sister. She jumped between them, grabbing the lanky one by the waist. 'Achu Boya don't be jealous,' she said.

'Jealous, does she want to swap places with me then?' said Dele.

'Perhaps. She sees you have a gift for drawing. And remember, there's always somebody worse off,' said Sister Ning.

'There must always be someone who is the worst off in the world even if only for a second…unless it's a tie for bottom,' said Dele.

'You like too much to prove logic,' said Sister.

Dele shrugged. She turned the knurled dial this way and that, looking for her Mali station but only got a screech and fuzz. So she switched over to TV. After some spluttering and blinking the screen cleared and a deep, mellifluous voice, with the most delicately formed vowels, emerged from lips that hardly seemed to move.

'It is a court, they are wearing gowns and wigs,' said Sister.

Beside the prosecuting counsel sat an intent fair-skinned young woman. A subtitle said that the sixth-former had won an international essay competition. A little man in a wig that came halfway down his neck called for Babubacka's regime to be indicted. 'Lest we forget, lest we forget we sing but too often we look away,' he said. 'Sermons at cenotaphs will not suffice,' he said.

Justice at last.

The man with the radio voice shook his head, a pained expression on his face. He chewed his lips, got to his feet again, looked round the courtroom, cleared his throat, and brushed his nose and the sides of his mouth with long, slender fingers.

'I looked in the mirror this morning…for bones sticking through my nose or blood dripping from my fangs. None, I'm afraid yet again. News of my lycanthropy has been doggedly and grossly exaggerated. I swear before you all and on any book you have in this house that there was no massacre or serious crime in South Roko camps. Not on our watch. As soon as we heard of trouble we called you in. We may be poor, but we are not bad. Like any people we have our moments. Like naughty teenagers. Give us space and let us grow up to trade our way out of this mess…our own messy bedroom…so to speak.'

The prosecuting counsel leapt to his feet. 'My learned lords, this typical classic, time-honoured, obfuscating tactic from the representative for South Roko we will not accept.'

The senior judge sat back and folded his arms. He pointed with his head at the screen again, a sceptical look on his face.

'How do you explain women and children cut down by gunfire and machetes? We are told that many had their hands up in the air or held over their ears as they ran, or fell.'

'Ah,' said the representative. 'Mannequins,' he said, drawing a female form in the air with sinuous waves of his long arms. 'We have been framed by our competitors. The waste you send to our land to process, how do you think it gets done?' He paused, ran his forefinger along his upper lip. 'If you think your industrial recycling will be done by prayer and a little persuasion, top marks for self-deception. But let me answer your question head-on. Classical case of North-South cultural divide. We played Wagner. Perhaps we should have started with the tippy tappy efforts of the early teenage Mozart or Mendelssohn. But in a nation in a hurry we were trying to do in months what it took generations to build in Austria. Many thought it sounded like a machine gun or like a powerful god had descended upon them. Ask them. A few died from fright and from the impact of freak hailstones…casualties of climate change, of northern hemisphere industry not too many leagues away from here. Anyway, our commander in chief has sacked the musical director and we are looking for the conductor.'

He turned to the left, adjusted his tie and bowed. 'It's over to you Interpol,' he said before turning back to the camera.

'So castrated young boys, genitalia traded like offal at the roadside; disembowelled pregnant women, all in the imagination of the peace keeping forces?' said lead counsel, banging the table.

'I agree it is not for this century. But do you know the situation on the ground? Years of enmity between tribes or nations will not end with one aid package. Did English not behead even a king? And surely you recall the vengeance his friends reaped? Did European armies not feed on corpses from graveyards, bodies from the gallows, snatch babies from their cribs and devour them? Are we not to make our own mistakes? And be allowed to correct them?'

'We are to stand by and allow these atrocities to continue? Your government has no case to answer? Your honour, you don't have to be very original to get away with blue murder,' said lead counsel. He dabbed his wide forehead with the tips of his fingers.

The representative for Roko went on. 'We, like you are fighting terror, defending the road to civilized values. But I knew this would happen; whatever we little countries do, we can't win. We tried classical music and from the unforeseen consequences you accuse us of genocide.' The man turned to the bench, to the six presiding men. 'But please. You cannot have it all ways. If we are not advanced we must be backward. If we are backward we will do what backward peoples do. Put yourself in the shallow, narrow mind of a villager. I would say put yourself in his shoes but he has none. Ok, now imagine, supporters of a foreign god kill his heirs. Will he take kindly to monuments erected in praise of that god on every street, to waking up and going to sleep in their shadow? And when his harvest fails who does he blame? What does he do? He grabs his machete – it is his nuclear weapon. Just as you were going to wipe us all out because your cousins put a wall up against Coca Cola so does he when he is hungry and angry. But of course he must be genetically barbaric. But you in this court are not. Please do not allow this court to inflate a cultural misadventure, a malfunction of historical satnav, into crimes against humanity. I humbly submit, in the name of justice, the Rokopat people, and its government, acquit.'

Dele picked the radio up and smashed it against a tree.

'Dele Verity, have you missed your afternoon tablets?' said Sister Ning. 'I am going to have to move you back a stage to Aggrey ward.'

TEN

Ten days later Sister Ning came to conduct the weekly senior inspection. 'What happened here, ah?' she said, pointing to a patch of soot on the floor.

Kamilo, the Hulk of Aggrey ward has been smoking weed. 'No breakfast for any of you. If I don't get an answer, I will send you to Crowther ward,' said Sister and she sounded as if she meant it.

From what Dele had heard Esdiefi, the Crowther ward supervisor, made Yourlot sound like Mary Seacole. 'It was her,' said Dele, pointing at Kamilo. Kamilo replied with a hate-filled stare.

'Miss Verity go shower. I'll deal with the rest of you, ah, later,' said Sister.

Kamilo will drown me in there.

'I'll wait here,' said Sister Ning in a reassuring tone.

Puzzled, Dele hurried off to the bathroom, but she did not let the water run over her head so that she could watch out for Kamilo.

'Let's go, my breakfast will be getting cold,' said Sister, handing Dele a clean white blouse. Dele hopped along after Sister, the over-sized pair of slippers she borrowed off little Nwokoye slapping at her heels.

Sister's main office, a musty room in the shadow of a large Acacia tree, had its walls covered in passport photographs. 'Children who have passed through us,' said Sister. She took a mobile phone out of a drawer. 'Verity smile. Do you want to be the worst in my gallery? Try,' she said, pointing the phone at Dele. Dele heard a click. Sister turned the phone round. 'Good,' she said. 'Maybe when you are famous we will show them this photo...sit there...breakfast. That's for you,' said Sister, pointing to a mug and a plate of pancakes set out on a table in the corner. Golden brown, they smelt and tasted of sugar, warm oil and salt with a hint of lime. The morsels melted in Dele's mouth. She had eaten all but one piece when Sister's phone rang.

'We're coming,' Sister said. She beckoned to Dele with a stiff wave of her hand. 'Come.' Dele popped the last piece of pancake into her mouth.

Cachectic clouds hovered high in the sky while a fat white cloud hogged the dazzling sun. Sister led Dele down a gentle slope to the narrow crazy-paved drive in front of the staff block. A man in a white cassock got out of a rusting four door saloon. He seemed to glide towards Dele. Like a clockwork soldier's, his arms swung by his side. Dele turned and ran back uphill, a picture of the orderly pushing her into that bedroom playing in her head.

'Traytop Mountain. It's me?' *Traytop Mountain. Ambasi. Ambasi.* Her head seemed to ring to the beat of the sound of his name. She stopped to make sure she had heard right, then ran back down the slope.

'How…how did you find me?' she said.

'Antikath here saw your painting on a charity website.' Antikath got out of the car and stepped forward. 'Your painting, child with a thorn in heart,' she said. About Mum's height, Antikath had midnight dark blue skin, laughing eyes the colour of organic dates and natural curly black hair. She wore a light blue frock and flat brown shoes.

'Tell Traytop what happened,' said Ambasi.

'TV man bought it from your matron or Sister and he gave to relocation charity. I saw your name in a brochure and a photo. I said to pastor…is this not the girl, the milk seller who played tennis at your tables?'

'I know that nose anywhere I said,' said Ambasi.

So my nose is good for something. Antikath sneezed.

'Your hand,' said Ambasi.

'Not here,' said Sister. 'Pastor wait in my office. Dele…go and pack. Don't forget your paintbrushes.'

Under a glittering silver-backed cloud and a blue sky, and waved off by Sister and three of the girls, who had heard of the departure of their mimic and painter, Dele got into the car with Ambasi and Antikath.

'Oh, leather seats, air-conditioning,' Dele said, rolling her head into the cold breeze. Ambasi patted the seat between them. 'Rust conceals the wrong impression,' he said.

'I couldn't find you...after they took Mum and Dad...' said Dele. She clunked her seat belt in.

'Yatingo, the drinks parlour owner told me,' said Ambasi.

'Where did they take you? Did you see Dad?' said Dele.

Ambasi shook his head and wiped his wet left eye. 'Sorry to hear about your mum. Me? They took me to their Security Office. Give us list of players at your tables they asked.' Ambasi paused as the driver manoeuvred the car into a tight space. 'How would I know people who just come off the street to play I replied. The one who slapped me was only a boy. I knew him. I knew his mother too. She sells soap in the market. They applied... the man I heard...was he not born of woman like them too...?'

Antikath sneezed. 'Those people will not enter heaven,' she said, turning round from the front seat. The coach in front of them lurched like a drunkard, revved up and spewed black smoke from its roof.

Dele tried to close her mind to what might have happened to her dad.

'We have to believe what they say that one day will be the Lord's day,' said Antikath.

'That's what my teacher used to say. When's the Lord going to stop them?' said Dele.

'His judgement cannot be rushed,' said Ambasi.

'My teacher said that too. But why didn't he wait for the Lord instead of caning me when he caught me doing his duck walk in front of class?'

'Because life is too long,' said Ambasi.

***

Dele opened her eyes. What a relief to wake up in a room of her own even if it had Ambasi's cartons and boxes stacked along its walls and the window gave on to next door's wall two feet away. What a blessing to wake up without the threat of Yourlot or Sandman at the door. Compared to the crackle of gunfire or the sputter of burning flesh, how sonorous the rattle of that old standing fan, the piercing crow of the cock of the roost, the parping from the handheld horns of the newsboys, the lilting chorus of the fish and bean seller and even the pathetic bleats of that three-legged goat. And what a miracle to wake up warm and dry between clean sheets, not wet with urine or petrol in the shadow of a funeral pyre, or shivering under the trickling shower, with your eyes smarting from the suds from the washing powder and with the ward bully on the prowl.

A muffled trill from under her pillow cut through her trance. Dele reached for her phone. Its screen read six o'clock. She sat up in the wan dawn light and ran her palms up and down her legs. In ten days her rash had gone. Then she remembered that Ambasi would leave at seven.

One Monday morning four weeks ago, a week after Ambasi took her in, Dele woke up to find that he had left without her. Getting through that empty day felt like climbing a mountain in leaden boots. Her mind had filled with images from the camp, of her Mum lying dead in the back of a truck, of the wilfully wicked Yourlot, of the rampaging Sharijujumen, of those funeral pyres; and of her ordeal with Sandman in that room.

Now she now insisted on going out with Ambasi in the mornings, on home visits or to the herb market or to the police station. She played table tennis at his "academy" in the afternoons and, when she was free in the evenings, or after Ambasi had gone to church, she would draw and paint or sneak into the dilapidated Jeba cinema to watch Spaghetti Westerns beside the projectionist. With Antikath she read the Bible. She preferred the Old Testament for its vivid stories of blood and gore and instant gratification. She tried an English translation of the Koran too, but it did not seem to have been written for Roko people and it reminded her of desert dwellers; and they reminded her of Sandman.

Antikath asked her one day if she was happy.

To Dele happiness used to mean tingling from her crown to the tips of her stubby toes, with a warm, blood-red flame glowing in her heart. She didn't think she would ever feel that fire again. Now, when she saw little Robi run into his homecoming mother's arms or when Antikath brought home a lush paintbrush, she felt only the flicker of a tiny candle flame in her gut, nowhere else.

'I'm glad to be here,' Dele had said. Perhaps sensing Dele's unease, Antikath had started back into herself and got up to make a pancake, a dish which more than any other reminded Dele of Mum.

The dog with the chewed up ear barked outside, reminding Dele that she had to hurry. She shook down the bed sheets, had a shower, and pulled on the three-quarter length brown trousers and the beige shirt Antikath laid outside the door the night before.

'Good morning pastor, where to today?' she said, settling into the back seat. The cool blast from the air conditioner soothed her already sticky face. The pips announced seven o'clock.

'Police station,' said Ambasi. The smile in his voice told Dele that she was just in time. 'I hope that stew's not too spicy,' he said.

Dele shook her head. *Why do Siroko people love pepper so much? Does it make them happy or forget to be sad?*

***

Midmorning Sankara rush hour traffic sat grumbling outside the police station door and the ubiquitous portrait of the Commander-in-Chief hung from the wall.

'Chief police commissioner mama is not well,' said the duty officer, brushing dandruff off the front of his starched brown shirt.

It was his uncle last time.

'For the past week, twice yesterday and now today we've been asked to report for clearance to look for Arimos, the missing persons,' said Ambasi, banging the desk. The officer snorted a finger of snuff and wiped his nose with the back of his hand. Dele wanted to shake the snuff out of him and replace it with some manners.

'Each time we come here it is a different story,' said Ambasi, cracking his knuckles. 'Two more unredeemable hours wasted.' Dele heard a murmur from the queue behind them.

'You are not the only ones with issues of this kind,' said the officer. 'Look at all these people.' He waved his hand at the queue which curled round the room like a scorpion's tale which meant that the last woman in line stood next to Dele. The officer leaned back in his chair and cupped his hand over his mouth like a doubles tennis player talking tactics with his partner. 'Hey, my man come here,' he said, over his shoulder.

Moments later an officer emerged from a dark room behind the desk, and went to throw a cigarette stub into the street.

'What is problem?' he said.

'I tell them there is no file for any Verity here,' said the desk officer.

The new man took his thick-rimmed spectacles off and rolled his eyes. 'You are a pastor.' He pointed at Dele. 'And you this girl, it looks like they born you overseas. So which of my comrade's simple English do you not understand?' From the look on Ambasi's face Dele thought the pastor would have jumped over the desk to strangle the man if he could.

From the back room they heard a cry, a shout a thud, then a noise like a spoon applied to a boiled egg. The room went quiet for a moment. The woman standing next to Dele wrung her hands and whispered a prayer perhaps. Laughter came from the back room.

'What is that?' said Ambasi. The tips of his ox-blood sandals gleamed under his red soutane.

'Oga, please do not raise your voice. This is my domain. Can I come to your church and tell you how to preach?' said the new man, smacking dust off his cap.

'No use crying over spilt ink. Let's go,' said Ambasi, with a wipe of his rheumy left eye.

'Before that...tell me pastor, is it your car outside, blue with rusty bonnet?' said the new man.

'Yes...yes, why?' said Ambasi.

'What's that got to do with my dad and me going back to school?' said Dele.

'Who is talking to you? Why you dress like office girl if you are schoolgirl?' said the desk officer. He took his cap off to scratch his head. 'Pastor, your windscreen has scratch. How do you see at night? Your trafficator is not up to Sankara standard. We will impound your motor for serious checking...if you are not careful,' said the new officer. He put his cap back on and lit another cigarette.

'How do you mean? There is nothing wrong with that car. I came here on a humanitarian-,' said Ambasi.

'Pastor, please don't waste everybody's time,' said the woman behind Dele.

Dele knew what this was about. It happened the week before. The first officer dropped his voice. 'I will not lie to you pastor. You could have avoid this mess if you had done the right thing,' he said.

'Mess? I can think of more appropriate descriptions for what is going on here,' said Ambasi.

The new man scanned Ambasi and Dele through greedy eyes. 'Pastor thinks this is London,' he said.

'Or Zurich,' said the duty officer, scribbling into a tatty ledger.

'Or Lagos,' said the new officer. They laughed.

Dele fumed.

'We are grown up men,' said the officer with the cigarette. 'Do you want to play by Geneva Convention or by local Sankara rules, it's up to you...and down to me,' he said with a belly laugh. The desk sergeant raised first one wretched ledger then another. A woman behind Dele made a sucking sound. 'Do what they say, ah, ah, we have homes to go to,' she said. Dele wanted to tell her to shut up.

The new man tapped Dele on the shoulder. Dele cringed. His touch felt sharp and heavy, like an axe. 'Tell pastor to sign here, to wash your sins away.'

'With Sankara police detergent,' said the woman in the queue.

Dele sensed resignation in Ambasi's grunt.

'Why are you dribbling us about? I come on behalf of this one's papa. Surely you have or want little ones yourself,' he said as he signed the papers.

The officer led them out into the boiling day and round the back of the police station to stand in a dip under a boarded up window. He dragged on his cigarette and stretched out a palm. Ambasi grunted, fished around in his cassock and crossed the man's palm with a wad of Roko notes. The officer tapped his takings against his thigh and threw his cigarette stub into a drain.

Daylight robbery.

'Pastor. When you talk as if you are the only one with mouth and tongue in your head you are spoiling our *sekewa*. To show no bad blood between us and for the sake of this small girl. I will tell you truth. Don't waste your time. Instruction to report for clearance is only for the benefit of UN inspectors. But Babubacka told UN that we are checking the camp girls for radicalisation first. Once UN hears this they are happy. They take away their inspectors to another country for election or another bad story and this government can do what it likes.'

'Radicalisation. That versatile blanket thrown over the bare threads of woolly thinking,' said Ambasi, rubbing his bad eye.

'Pastor. This is not the place for big grammar. On order of Oniseme, new minister of interior affairs and resettlements; no school will take camp girls until he says so…that is for at least one year, while he checks their particulars. As for Arimos, forget it, it is national security and even to mention them can turn you into a word of mouth - something you hear about but cannot see. Get me?' He poked his spectacles back on to his shiny nose.

Oniseme. That's Sandman's real name.

***

'I have a plan,' said Ambasi as they got into the car. He opened a bottle of cold water and gave it to Dele. 'Driver careful, if you want to die kindly drop us off first,' he said as the car lurched between a pushcart and a silver oil tanker. He glanced at his watch. 'I will see what I can do about Arimos. But care is needed. You heard the man.' He took the empty bottle off Dele, passed her a packet of tissues. 'Here take this. Sandman does not want the camp girls to go to school but he did not say school should not come to them. I'll get my people to teach you.'

'Who?' said Dele.

'You'll find out. First there is personal science. Mama Higuani is very good at bringing girls up to the right level in matters of women…not my field. Then Biker Bichi and a few others will teach Maths, English. Pick that chin of yours from the underworld. You can still come with men to the market to get herbs and play tennis again. Heard of *afinna?*'

'No,' she said.

'Ah, afinna broom disables or disorientates intruders and robbers until the rightful owner returns.'

Dele found herself laughing.

'Seriously, what I teach you will save you thousands of Roko in the future,' said Ambasi.

'Fair enough. But how can you be a pastor and a juju man?' said Dele, with another chortle.

A biscuit crumb tumbled down Ambasi's cassock. 'Call it dual accreditation. You can't be too careful,' he said. 'Turn left there,' he said to the driver as they joined the traffic on the roundabout behind a pushcart. He cracked his knuckles, bowed his head as if in sorrow. 'It's a shame, real shame what is happening here in South Roko. Answer me Traytop. Which part of Roko has more mosques and churches and temples?' he said. A motorcycle tooted as it went past.

'South Roko,' said Dele.

Ambasi nodded. 'Verily Verity, until Babubacka invaded the north, Niroko people were some of the happiest, healthiest people on this planet. They enjoyed religious feasts but were not religious. Spiritual, soulful, soul-searching even, but not all this foreign worship.'

'That's what Mum said,' said Dele.

Ambasi cracked a knuckle and brushed his left eye with a finger. He went on. 'But the South, a place thick with holy shrines, churches, mosques, temples and shocking towns without electricity. A million of us. In any league table we come bottom or second to last. What do we do? We live or kill *for* the moment our day will come,' he said. 'Worship foreigners from Mesopotamia or elsewhere and fight over which one is better.'

'I don't understand–'

'Imagine in a hundred years, Messi and Maradona's supporters killing each other in Argentina? Does that not strike you as incredible…if you let me stretch the point a little bit,' said Ambasi.

'Teacher said prophets are for all people…no matter where they come from,' said Dele.

Ambasi shook his head. 'Your teacher tells you to believe in prophet without passport. That's a symptom of Close syndrome…Continental or colossal loss of self-confidence and esteem. Traytop, I see your face. Ambasi is deluded, or he is high. Maybe. So what am I saying?' He waved a beggar away from the car and cracked his knuckles. 'Verily Verity, this is what happens when you leave your story to those born with a golden nib in their hands. I am going to write an African religious book. I may not live to see it finished but I will start…'

A little girl with wiry brown hair pleaded with the driver in front to let her clean his windscreen. She had a baby strapped to her back. The driver shouted and shook his fist at her. The girl gave up, waited for Ambasi's car to draw level and reached up to the windscreen with her tatty sponge.

'Too nuisance, these pickins, they mess the car, pastor,' said Ambasi's driver.

'Haha driver, what would you do if she was your own?' said Dele. 'Can you spare me a coin?' she said to Ambasi. She opened the window and gave the girl the coins. The little girl tucked her booty out of sight and gave Dele a gap-toothed smile.

'I'll pay you back...for everything. I'll get a job, help at your tables. To find my dad I'll do anything,' said Dele.

Ambasi raised his hand to stop her. 'Never say never and never say always, because you never know,' he said.

They set off again, with Dele wondering whether those long faces in the winding queues at the bus-stops also mourned missing Mums and Dads. After a humped-back bridge they turned off and bumped down Ambasi's Egypt Street. It looked like Nigeria Street but with more sand in the potholes, deeper ditches and fewer shacks. They stopped outside the gates of Ambasi's three-storey white block of flats. A wizened man tending an open fire roadside, got up to greet them and open the car door. Ambasi pressed a note into the man's hand, grabbed his Bible, crossed the ditch and leapt up the stairs to the first floor flat. Dele shuffled after him, the heat clinging to her head like a busby. Ambasi opened the door. The lime-green balcony curtains billowed apart and Antikath emerged from the dark corridor on the right. 'Hey you want to give me heart attack?' she said, starting back in shock. She pulled the white headphones out of her ears and with a broom in one hand, bustled into the kitchen where sat a small table set for two.

'What has the secretary general of Ambasi maintenance organisation come up with today?' said Ambasi.

'Don't disturb me. This is my office, I'll bring your food over there,' said Antikath, pointing with her chin to the brown leather suite in the sitting area.

'I'll watch CNN, Traytop Mountain...sit,' said Ambasi. While Ambasi flicked through the TV channels Dele washed her hands and picked a peanut out of the bowl. Above, a white ceiling fan turned in fruitless gyrations on the end of a short metal stem. The dark coffee table rested on a red rug laid over a terrazzo floor. Hanging on the outer wall and above the small flat screen TV, a three-quarter-sized foil of Ambasi in white robes, with cowries and colourful beads round his neck and a traditional whisk in his hand, cast a beguiling spell. She walked over to the opposite wall to look at the full-sized portrait of Ambasi, this time in a red soutane, large crucifix round his neck, black Bible in one hand, the other hand raised to the sky. He had his shaven head lowered in reflection or repentance, and his good right eye, bigger than it looked in real life, seemed to follow Dele round the room, like backache, or shame.

After lunch she called Needle, her mate at the table tennis Academy. He owed her one. His uncle worked at the Army Officers' Mess and Dele wanted to get close enough to Sandman to plan revenge.

ELEVEN

Dele got off the bus, showed her pass at the gates and slipped in through a side entrance for her third consecutive Friday shift at the Officers' Mess. She had to be home before Ambasi got back at eleven.

'You late,' said the barman, his wispy moustache and his baby pink lower lip rather undermining the force of his rebuke. He pointed at the clock on the far wall. It said five minutes past seven.

'That clock is fast,' Dele said, forcing her broken fingers into the yellow kitchen gloves.

The barman scowled. 'Start here,' he said and dumped a stack of tumblers into the steaming sink water. A wave of wild laughter drowned out what he said next.

Dele scanned the smoky hall. She saw the red tip of a fez poke up on a table at the far end of the hall. *He's here.* Beer flowed on that table with Sandman, the only man in mufti, the sponsor of a rowdy group of men who sat at four tables arranged, cabaret style, under a wall-mounted flat-screen TV.

'Leave the casualties,' said one of the men to the sweat-drenched waiters who had darted up to clear the empty beer bottles.

'That is so we can see all the empties and what a good time the minister is having,' said the barman. 'Get back to work.'

More shouts of 'Babubacka Power' rang round the room. Dele looked up and saw that Sandman had got on to his feet.

'We and you are the future,' said Sandman, waving his arms under his sprawling white lace *agagada*. Nods of approval leapt round his tables. One of the men got up to salute. The rest of his table followed and they sang the National Anthem.

At last the singing stopped, the waiters resumed their rounds and Dele went back to her steaming sinkful of dirty dishes. As she finished the batch she saw one of Sandman's men beckon to the main entrance. Moments later a group of women in their late teens and early twenties skipped into the hall, all undressed up, their smiles as wide as the grille on a luxury car. They fanned out across the room into the men's waiting arms and spread legs. One of them sat on Sandman's lap, another leaned her head on his shoulder, one of her breasts hanging out a mile. Dele's throat burned with anger. Then she felt the barman's presence behind her and bent back over the sink.

Another murmur swept round the hall. Dele turned off the hot water tap and looked up again. To scowls from the first group of girls, a younger, coltish, group had gathered by a side entrance, their bare arms held straight and stiff by their sides as though in plaster. Dele wondered where these girls came from. Probably from a camp she decided. The thought of it seemed to hold a struck tuning fork against her teeth. Seconds later she felt a tap on the shoulder and spun round.

'You don't have to box me, if you want help…ask,' she said to the waiter.

The waiter cast a look at the barman as though to ask where he'd got this one from.

'Aggro nose, get ready for his remnants,' said the barman.

Dele felt a thud in her chest. 'You are not an oil painting, either sir,' she said.

'Ok, don't vex,' he said.

'What am I to do with his leftovers, take them home?' said Dele.

The barman smacked the cash tray closed. 'Interior minister thinks that enemies can make bad charm against him from his leftovers. So he makes us bag and burn.' The waiter handed Dele a thick polyester bag.

'Take it. Have you not heard horses barking, afterbirths of stillborns running round town in the middle of a dark night?' the barman said, with a twinkle in his eye. Dele flashed a polite smile in return.

A man in a green uniform accompanied Dele to the open-air incinerator just outside the kitchen doors. Fighting back the memories they evoked, Dele scraped Sandman's leftovers off the plates, bagged and threw them into the fire. *Should be Sandman in there* she thought as the plastic bag warped and burst into green-tinged flames.

When she got back inside Dele saw that the younger group of girls seemed to have been shared out between the tables. One girl in a sleeveless white blouse sat between two men, doodling with her finger in her palm. Dele sensed that one of the men had his hand on the girl's knee. Sandman raised his arm. Dele turned to her boss. 'Can I take floor orders today for minister, sir?' she said.

'What is it with you and this floor show? You think I want small girl to serve these senior service people? Wash plate and glass is what I want. If you don't like just go. Every time you come it's the same thing ah, ah.' He swept a pile of clean plates back into the dirty water by accident. 'See what you made me do,' he said.

'Sorry sir,' said Dele. In her disappointment she forgot to put her kitchen gloves back on and scalded herself under the hot water tap. She refastened her apron. It had a photograph of Sandman on the back and one of Babubacka on the front, of course. That she had her enemy wrapped round her waist, in a fashion, while he sat a few feet away, yet out of reach, made her feel like a stowaway rumbled inches from the safe port.

'Anyway it's ten pm. How much I owe you? I'll settle you now or next week?' said the barman, scratching the back of his ear with a pencil.

'Ok, whichever is good for you,' said Dele. She lifted a handful of cutlery out of the sink and saw Sandman get up and rub his belly. He puffed out his cheeks and he seemed to belch. The man sitting next to him jerked backwards and looked as if he had swallowed a python whole.

'Who is that man…in the blue suit?' Dele said.

The barman kicked an empty crate under the sink and turned to look. 'Oh, oh, the one that look like bird shit on his head? Banusi…of external affairs. He talks more English than an Englishman, plenty French pass a Frenchman, he gets more degrees than man with Malaria Fever. But he does not like that interior minister not one quantum iota.'

I think he's the man at The Hague. Then why is he sitting next to Sandman?' said Dele.

'Maybe they don't trust each other…file that under useless info, my aggro face sister,' said the barman, with a wink.

Banusi doesn't like Sandman. That may be worth knowing. I'll tell Ambasi. 'But the girls, should Banusi not tell the foreign newspapers…'

The barman's eyes bulged and turned a glassy red. 'Look, too much talk, talk from you, ah, ah. We don't mess with customer business. Ours is to serve drink and food. Are you a CIA? If you can't just wash plates…in fact, as a matter of fact take your money and tell Needle you are sacked. Do not pass here again.'

***

'Can't we watch the film version instead?' said Dele, still sore after losing her job at the Officer's Mess a week earlier. She still had not come up with a plan against Sandman and to add to her woes, the rash on her legs had come back.

'Read these first three chapters,' said Mrs Ajango the English teacher. Mrs Ajango liked her purple saris. She opened the door. 'Movie versions are like vegetable with the nutrients boiled out,' she said as she left.

Tired of frowning at her pout, her darkening areola, and of looking for the best view of her nose in her mirror, which meant trying to make it look smaller, Dele put on her favourite pair of jeans to hide her itchy leg rash and set off to surprise Ambasi at the airport.

She ignored the touts and strode up to Arrivals, a grimy hodgepodge of glass and concrete crowned by a turgid windsock yammering at the indifferent green and white flag of the Federal Republic of Nigeria. At the door a soldier with bullet belts hanging diagonally from each shoulder glared at her.

'Hey, where you going?' he said, blocking the way with a rifle.

To Mars where else? 'To wait for flight,' she said, affecting a placatory mix of respect and fear.

Inside, loose panels hung from the ceiling of a hall recently renovated for only Babubacka knows how many millions of Dollars or Yuan. Tense and frustrated passengers of all shades and races queued behind counters of peeling Formica.

'Why so hot in here?' said Dele.

'Aircon is not get spare parts,' said a porter, rolling his eyes at the stupid question.

A rotund man in a three-piece suit of flowing green and white robes barged past Dele and through to a check-in desk. 'Look, only one finger to lift it, it's even too light to be called hand luggage,' the man said, with a crimson electricity generator swinging from his thumb. The check-in officer shook her head and broke off to help another customer. A belly belonging to a man of apparently equal distinction shoved the first rotund man aside. The shoved man went purple in the face. He put down the generator and pushed the culprit in the chest. The two men sized each other up. A female officer garbled into a black walkie-talkie. Moments later a stiletto heel jabbed into Dele's foot as passengers tumbled out of the way of a large black dog.

'Get back, get back,' said a soldier hanging on to the dog's lead. The rotund men must have taken too long to obey because a soldier punched them and pinned them to the floor. A pressman fell over backwards, crashing in to his colleague's camera and felling the metal ladder on which a man trying to open a window was perched. The window man cried out and landed on a metal chair. Dele winced for him. A flash camera went off. The hall fell quiet. Everyone turned to the Departure gate to watch a man in brilliant white robes and a gold-trimmed white cap, walk in through his own contra flow lane. He stopped, fanned his face with a languid wave of his whisk, and looked around the hall with the air of the fabulous snobbish optimist - one born to wake up each morning to look forward to looking down his nose. Dele stood on her toes for a better view. Behind the VIP a stooped, balding, grey-haired man with a wading gait emerged, his right hand held by a nurse. If Dele had not been caught by the young man standing behind her she would have crashed to the floor.

'Let me through, let me pass, I want to pass, yaga, yaga, ejioni, excuse, excuse, that's my dad,' said Dele, shouting out in pidgin English and Kombo and Nagati and elbowing her way towards the minister. 'Dad, Dad,' she said. The man stopped. He swung his head and body round in slow, cog-wheeled, stages. What Dele saw for a moment seemed to suck the brains out of her head. The man's nose and eyes looked as if they had been clawed at by a tiger, and his eyeballs replaced by pieces of slate. He had no teeth, no gum to speak of and he had a dark cave in place of his left cheek.

'Young girl. You call me papa, papa, but I father nobody,' he said, sounding like a toad on its death pad.

'Are you an Arimo, did you meet my dad? Wale Verity. Tall, short fingers, stubby toes…he coughs like this…' Her voice tailed off. The man paused, but before he could reply a nurse led him through a barrier, up a step and into the dark of a white van. A steward grabbed Dele by the shoulder, spinning her round. Dele cringed and pulled her arm away. 'I just wanted to ask him about the camp,' she said.

'What concern you with Bisuyi?' said a steward in an orange jacket. She smoothed down her jacket and puffed her chest, perhaps because a crowd had gathered.

Dele pointed at a girl in a white dress at the front of the crowd. 'I was a small girl like this when they take my papa and my mama. My mum is dead. I think this is my papa…he resemble him. Can I look again?' she said. The crowd pressed in.

'Back, stand back,' said the steward, striking out with a rolled up magazine.

'Don't listen to her. She's a *conny* girl, come beg for money,' said a baggage handler.

'Is it any of your business?' said Dele.

'Fuck off butter face,' said the woman. She belched, swayed towards Dele. She smelled of beer. Another steward arrived.

'Is there a problem?' he said.

'It's pig nose here snorting beer fumes in my face,' said Dele.

The offended baggage handler swung a fist. Dele ducked and the blow almost felled the steward. A police man pushed through, his baton poised in mid-air. He stepped on a carton, fizzing orange liquid on to a woman's blue jeans.

'Hey mind yourself,' said the woman.

'Officer, I've come to meet pastor. It is truth I talk, then I saw the man. I swear, he looked like my dad,' said Dele.

'Shush. Don't say that here if you love yourself. Causing commotion at airport is a potential terrorist offence. I have to arrest you,' said the policeman, grabbing Dele by the shoulder.

***

Dele closed her eyes. To get her nose away from an armpit smell of vinegar and rotting eggs she squeezed her other cheek between the bars of the detention cell and tried to imagine what life must be like for the man she had seen at the airport. Did Sandman do that to Dad too? Did Dad go hungry and cold? Could he see her here, trying so hard to be good, but not doing so good? She tried not to think about it. The woman standing next to Dele started to sob.

'Please I have pickin for house. She nearly will wake and cry.'

'You should have thought of that before you bring your business to airport. What have you got for me?' said the warder. Dele sensed the warder approach the cell so she kept her eyes closed.

'I have not had a first customer yet when police arrest me,' said the woman.

Dele felt sorry for this woman who had to roam the streets to feed her child.

'What of you, white girl. Are you a go-go girl too?' said the warder. Dele opened her eyes. Through the window up behind the warder's head shone the faint grey light of dawn.

'I came to meet pastor,' she said.

The warder chuckled.

'Next you will tell me that you are Obama pickin,' he said. He dragged a chair and had just swung his feet under the desk when Dele heard footsteps come through a door on the left. A few moments later Ambasi marched in wearing a light brown cassock and armed with his black Bible. Behind him came a man in a dark suit, a brown shirt and a green, red and white striped tie.

'Open up,' said the man in the suit. He had streaky sweat marks on his shirt and blinked nonstop as though typing the words out with his eyelids.

The warder fumbled through a bunch of keys and rattled the cell open. 'I'm the airport manager,' said the man. Dele and Ambasi followed the airport manager to a first floor office. On his desk two ashtrays full of bottle tops and cigarette stubs sat on a pile of aviation magazines.

'Sit,' he said, gesturing to a low table.

'I'll stand,' said Dele, sticky and stiff from her night in prison. She closed her eyes, but opened them again because her head spun.

'Smoke?' said the manager. Ambasi sat down and shook his head. 'I must get this one back home for fumigation.' The manager lit up, inhaled and sat back in his leather armchair. Grey tendrils of his cigarette smoke warped in the blast of air-conditioned air. 'You calmed down now?' he said, after another hissing suck on his cigarette. Dele nodded and stared out of the window. Her knees itched. A brooding dark grey cloud shaped like a bear hung over the runway.

'I saw a man…looked like Dad,' said Dele.

The manager slapped a fly off his lapel and tapped the corner of his mouth. He had a severe haircut and two deep wrinkles across his forehead. The black letters on his white lapel badge identified him as Mr Momoh. 'I am in this very position myself, my sister, I have to say. My cousins, two of them, disappear, vram, like that. I am monitoring the message and flights but no news so far, three years now,' said the manager. 'Prison rendition is ordered by Babubacka to cow the masses. Bisuyi and Babubacka were…tight once, maybe from school.' The manager clasped his nicotine-stained hands together to make his point. 'Then Babubacka joined army. Bisuyi is judge. He refused to jail Deoma in that notorious case. From time to time, government parades prisoners as an example. Today it was Banusi, foreign minister you saw with the prisoner. The new interior minister, Oniseme, is even more, er, let us say…harsh.'

'I knew Oniseme or Sandman as a cheap hustler. How did he become a minister?' said Ambasi.

Mr Momoh shook his head. He stubbed out his cigarette and closed his eyes for a few seconds. 'I think he did Banusi a favour over some land. He shot the headman at Alaga or somewhere like that. Soon they sold to Banusi. Banusi introduced him to Babubacka, then I think Sandman is now even closer to Babubacka than Banusi and Banusi is not happy at all.'

That's what the barman said. File under useless info.

'Thank you manager, we'll be in touch,' said Ambasi, tapping the side of his nose. He fished a brown envelope out of his robes and gave it to Mr Momoh. 'Traytop Mountain,' let's go home, we've got a lot to do.'

TWELVE

Dele banged into the living room door. Her pile of books crashed to the floor.

'What was that?' said Ambasi from his room.

'It's Dele. Since last week at the airport she's been walking about with her eyes closed,' said Antikath.

'Shush, don't tell him,' Dele said.

'He will vex. Those books are new and from abroad,' said Antikath.

Ambasi sauntered into the living room in his evening "homeboy gear", a loosely fitting white top and a pair of white linen trousers. 'It's growth spurts, she's almost your height now,' said Ambasi with a grin. 'Her elbows don't believe what the eyes are telling them anymore. It's like when they ask a minibus driver suddenly to drive lorry.' He pointed at the ceiling. 'We'll be up on the roof for supper. And Traytop mountain, about time we had our debrief,' he said, to loud sizzling from Antikath's frying pan.

Ambasi liked to eat supper up on the flat roof at night where he could smoke his spliffs out of sight of prying eyes. After supper of yams with grilled haddock he shook off his slippers and put his feet on a stool. 'Verily Verity, you were terrific the other day at the tables and Biker Bichi speaks highly of your studies and it was good of you to come to meet me at the airport. But next time you want to get arrested leave me out of it,' he said. He fished a box of matches from his top pocket while Antikath took the tray back down the stairs. 'Sit here, Antikath can manage,' he said.

Dele sat down opposite Ambasi and buried her face in her hands. 'It's my fault. I wish I wasn't born. Mum would have got away on Dad's visa and none of this would have happened.'

The tip of Ambasi's spliff glowed bright red in the dark. He smacked his lips round his cigarette and sucked until its tip crackled and glowed. 'Traytop,' he said, between puffs. 'Self-blame and pity bury many alive, many years before their time. Is that what your mum and dad would want?' He patted Dele on the shoulder. 'We all do or say things when the devil tenants our souls. But get that stupid notion out of that tray carrying skull,' he said. His spliff popped. 'I will tell you a story, I don't tell everyone this but I hope it will help.' He sucked his cigarette again. 'When I was your age I could have killed the people who called me shoe leather face. But does it bother me now? No. They said my skin was tough and shiny. Papa Madumi, my father, had about twenty of us. Death took six before me. Diphtheria etc.' Through the purple haze of spliff smoke Ambasi pointed to his shrunken left socket, the left eye looked wrinkled, like a senescent tomato. 'A hole in the side of my face nearly killed me, but Baba Ibeta, the man never saw the inside of any college, but he patched me...see how this part of my face is smooth. That's why they called me shoe face,' said Ambasi.

The street lights went out. A generator kicked off. Ambasi ignored the interruption and told Dele how when he was a boy his odd appearance gave him the aura of a survivor, good for his father's juju business, but not for reeling in the girls. He was about twenty years old when a friend told him about Tutu. Tutu had flawless black skin, oval face and thick hair, its line reaching down to the corner of her eyebrows. She was the first in her village to gain an overseas diploma. 'At first I thought my friend was pulling my leg, but Tutu did seem to have eyes for me. They say village women shuddered to think of us together. Me and that man. God forbid they said. How Tutu agreed to marry me I don't know. They say my father cast a juju spell on her.' Ambasi flicked the edge of his bad eye with a finger.

'Think of the hatred you have for Sandman for what he did to your dad and mum, turn it into love and multiply it by a million. That is how much I loved that woman. Maybe you are too young to know what I am saying.'

'What happened?' said Dele.

'As soon as Adire, our daughter, cut her first tooth, she was away.' Ambasi shook his head and looked into the distance.

'Should I go and fill the teapot? Antikath's gone home,' said Dele.

'Not to worry,' said Ambasi. 'Maybe it was not her fault. Perhaps the scales dropped from her eyes or the spell wore off. She left me for Bambo Crowther, the clerk from the west side.'

'Their family owned a chain of menswear shops. Are they still in Roko?' said Dele.

Ambasi shook his head. 'The next I heard…was that Tutu and Bambo had taken my little girl to England.' He struck a match but a gust of wind blew it out and the door to the landing slammed shut. Ambasi cupped the match in his hand, tried again.

'Dele, as I was saying.' Sweet grey smoke wreathed Dele again. 'If you think Sandman is bad, Tutu is not more than a shred of a whisker behind. She let my Adire die. We are now in 2007 so…' His voice tailed off. 'Let's see…she would have been twenty-five this month passed. I had it all planned. What I was going to wear at her wedding. Who I would invite. Whether they came from church or mosque or juju man's lair, I didn't care as long as they could share my pride. I was going to hire the best African Grey parrot to train up and serenade them on their way to the honeymoon.' Ambasi scratched a knee. He went quiet.

Poor Ambasi. Dele began to tidy up the mugs.

Ambasi started again. 'One day my friend Maja called me. Had I seen this bad, bad case in London?' said Ambasi.

Dele put the mug back down on the stool.

'There was my Adire, Lord rest her, in the newspaper with lumps on her head, her eyes so swollen they could not open,' said Ambasi. He put down his cigarette and closed his eyes.

Dele put her hand on Ambasi's elbow. 'Are you ok? Should I call Antikath?' she said, patting her trousers for the phone.

Ambasi sighed. 'Sorry, what is wrong with me nowadays? I shouldn't be telling a young girl all this…it's my problem not yours.'

'I'm not a little girl,' said Dele.

Ambasi's head jerked up. He fixed Dele in a gaze to size her up, or so Dele thought, before he went on.

'A London newspaper got me a visa. Tutu and Bambo in court, or you could say on stage. Composed, orchestrated and conducted by John Muldane, their barrister, Perry Mason and Simon Rattle of Islington rolled into one. Tutu played the crying victim and Bambo, the perplexed. Organs and violins wailing. Was it any wonder neither was convicted? They said maybe it was rare genetic defect...made her bruise like that. Pemphigus, pemphigoid different types, they used to bamboozle us. But the horror of detail. The horrible wrongs. Why didn't they return her to her dad, if they did not want my lovely cherub?' The chair grated on the concrete floor as Ambasi got up. He walked to the end of the roof.

'Pastor,' said Dele. Ambasi put an arm up to show that he was alright, pulled his white top back over his winged right scapula, turned round and sat back down.

'I could have killed those killers, but what could I do? Back in Roko my tears ran faster than the waters of the Congo.'

'Is that why you became a pastor?' said Dele. She sat down and put her hands between her knocking knees to keep them warm.

He cracked his knuckles. 'Not exactly. After what happened to my baby I was all over the place...backpedalling from the past. Believe me Traytop, I understand it when you walk around with your eyes closed, but you are young and I don't want you to make the same mistakes. When you walk backwards, backpedal forwards I mean, you may not see your best chances coming, until you have gone past them and they are far away...gone.'

He tipped his mug into his mouth, closed his eyes while he swallowed.

'I ended up in the church. It suited my temperament, studying the Bible, explaining it to others. Then there was this terrible earthquake, or was it a flood. Trustees took out a huge double-page advert, blaming sinners for incurring the wrath of God. Almost like it served the victims right. I spoke up against, saying they should be sensitive...but they wouldn't listen.'

'I thought earthquakes were caused by shifts in the tectonic plates,' said Dele.

Ambasi smiled. 'Ah, Miss Biker Bichi has succeeded in burying some knowledge in the Traytop Mountain.'

Dele slapped a mosquito away. 'I'm going to get Sandman...for what he did to Mum and Dad,' she said.

'Verily Verity, of a more admirable heart-felt proposition I'm sure you have not thought,' said Ambasi. 'But is Sandman going to meet you in central Sankara so you can run him through with your trusty sword? I say leave the man to destroy himself. He is burning with discontent. Who was it who got himself deported? Whose mother gambled away their land? His. What little I have now, I owe to that woman's profligacy. Now he wants to get rich by stealing from other people. Mark my word. His greed will be the end of him.'

'But...Dad,' said Dele.

Ambasi lit another spliff and took a few puffs. 'Verily Verity, let me show you my working. Life is like a game of billiards, but with our minds as the balls. It was Sandman's turn at the table. Now he appears untouchable. But your turn will come and until then do not abuse or misuse your cue, or it will end up of no use to anyone.'

Dele stamped her feet. 'First you ask me not to backpedal, then-'

'I am not saying forget. Who can ask that of one so young, or anyone? I say find another passion so consuming it will fry vengeance for breakfast. But if you let it hatch you never know who it will bite,' he said.

'Did I tell you about Galoro...in the camps?' said Dele.

'No, but as you know I left you to tell me or Biker Bichi when you are ready...'

'Galoro was shot by his daddy so he would not be taken when their farm was attacked. But his Dad missed. The dad killed himself and the rest of the family. The rebels took Galoro with them. Now

Galoro can't sleep without a gun by his side. When I grow up I want to help other poor children like Galoro to get better.'

'Perhaps one day there will be no need for such,' said Ambasi.

Amen. She looked up into the inky dark sky. An aeroplane roared overhead, the sight of the red light on its port wing rendered a flicking blur by her tears. *Dear aeroplane can you see Dad?*

Ambasi tapped the arm on his chair with long fingers. 'What do you have in mind?'

'Paediatric Psychology. I Googled it.'

Ambasi tapped his lips with his forefingers. 'Sadly, you'll never be out of work, but if you feel it right in here,' he said, placing his fist over his heart. 'What I do now, helping others, helps me.'

'So this ache or thorn or bucket full of what Antikath calls hot pepper soup swinging inside my chest is for ever?' said Dele.

Ambasi cracked the knuckles on one hand. 'We learn to live with it.' He went quiet.

'Pastor, I know what you're thinking. She's all talk. She can't do it, she's angry and stupid and will mess it up,' said Dele. *And Yourlot said I'll end up in the gutter.*

'What do you do if your rival farmer has a bigger hoe than you?' said Ambasi cracking the other knuckles.

'Dig harder…deeper…faster, but will she not do the same and stretch ahead again?'

'Do not shun an orange for fear of its rind or bittersweet seed. Let me show you my working.' Ambasi raised one finger. 'First this rival may underestimate you, just as that man did at the tables the other day.' He raised another finger. 'Second she may not be able to do any better anyway.' He raised a third. 'Third…but that's not the point, if you get the best out of a tiny hoe someone is bound to lend or offer you a combined harvester.'

'Show me the farm,' said Dele.

'You see, we all need a human mirror,' said Ambasi, patting Dele on the head.

'Who's yours?' said Dele.

THIRTEEN

One evening, a few days later, Dele had got halfway through peeling the potatoes in the kitchen, when Norma, Mama Robi, burst in to the flat.

'Where is pastor?' she said. Tears as large as orange pips bounced down her face and spotted her orange top.

Startled, Dele dropped a potato. The knife nicked her finger. *Shit.* 'Tonight is extra study and prayer night, he's not back till…after ten,' she said, sucking her bleeding fingertip.

Mama Robi smacked the sides of her head. 'Yeah, my pickin Robi two times this afternoon she is no breathing,' she said and waved her arms around in despair.

'My little friend Robi?' said Dele.

Mama Robi looked to the sky. 'Please God I am in desperate. I beg you leave this one. This is my third child you want to take. When she reached six years I thought he is safe. God. What have I done to vex you?' said Mama Robi. She wiped her face on the sleeve of her blouse.

Norma, Mama Robi, was the kindest woman in the universe. Dele put her hands round the weeping woman. Last week it was Landeke, the week before Olilonta, before that the twins. She wondered if Siroko children were like tadpoles and only a few survived.

'You are a good pickin, if it's God's will,' said Mama Robi, patting Dele on the head. She turned to leave.

'I'll come with you,' said Dele, cut up by Mama Robi's tear-riven face.

'Pastor will not like it. It's not a good thing for your eye to see and her papa is not here,' said Mama Robi.

'I can't leave you like this,' said Dele.

'If it's ok with you, it's ok with me,' said Mama Robi, taking Dele by the hand. It felt good holding a kind grown up's hand, even if the woman was crying.

Dele followed Mama Robi into a shed. Robi lay on a bare mat. In the dim candlelight her eyes and cheeks looked dark, dry, hollowed out and the slate grey skin of her chest, hammocked between beaded ribs, dipped in and out with each breath. An insistent rapid prodding under her left breast marked the apex of her heart; but Robi did not look like a child with many beats left. Mama Robi broke the candle stub off the wax drippings on the stool and held the light close to her daughter's face. 'If it's God's will,' she said again.

'Wait here,' said Dele. She dashed out in the dark and back to Ambasi's on her long legs.

Back at home Dele emptied her table tennis winnings, a hundred and ten Roko and some loose Bobo change, out of her green money belt and ran into Ambasi's room to look for anything with his signature on. After five minutes of frantic rummaging she found none. *What do I tell Mama Robi?* Then she remembered that Antikath had found Ambasi's note to the Notary Public in his trouser pocket and put it in a drawer in the living room for safe keeping. Dele yanked the drawer but it stayed fast. *Locked, Antikath locks everything.* Dele slapped her face, trying to remember where Antikath kept the key. She looked under the table mats, under the table-cloth, flicked through the newspaper – futile she knew – went back to glare round Ambasi's room and prowled round the living room. And there it was hanging from a nail above a window blind. *Is it the right one?* In her haste she pulled the drawer too far out and it clattered to the floor, scattering pens, papers, keys, erasers and paper clips. An empty bottle of ink smashed on to the floor. She found the note at last, tidied up, practised the signature on a scrap of paper and wrote a letter asking the doctors to take care of Robi in the name of the Lord. Signed Pastor Ambasirika.

Back in the shed, Mama Robi had her daughter in her arms. Robi's floppy head lolling back and forth as her mother paced the floor.

'Enough there for taxi, registration and diagnosis at Mile 4 hospital,' said Dele, stuffing the money belt into the weeping woman's hand. 'Say pastor sent you. It does not matter whether the doctor on duty knows you. Just say pastor sent you and give them this note.'

Dele went to look for Mama Robi the next day. She picked her way over the detritus, the heavy aroma from the crumbling bin lined with straw and newspapers reminding her of the nightsoilmen's industrial action. Pinching her nose against the smell she banged on Mama Robi's corrugated tin door. She waited, knocked again, heard nothing but the three-legged goat bleating its sad song. In the end she fled, saddled by sadness, convinced that little Robi, Norma's baby, was no more.

***

One braising afternoon a few days later, as she wondered how Ambasi could possibly walk so fast when her mouth seemed to be lined with parchment and her legs dipped in boiling treacle, she felt a pat on her thigh. It was Robi, on her mother's back.

'Meningitis. We've just come back from the clinic follow-up,' said Mama Robi, flicking sweat from her forehead. 'That day we just make it. Small more time, she would have gone, *pam pam*. Thank God that you were home that night. First two days it was touching go.' Dele blushed, proud that her winnings had helped save Robi's life.

Ambasi wiped his face with a white handkerchief. His left eye twitched.

'We, also have been on a medical errand, buying fresh produce from Eba the herbalist. I see now why the hospital called me,' he said. 'They showed me an invoice with my name on. It was you…Traytop.'

Dele opened her mouth, but could not speak. Shame and heat prickled the back of her neck.

Mama Robi tweaked Dele's cheeks. 'But if it was not for Dele only God knows what would have happened,' she said with cheers in her eyes.

'The bone I have to pick is with this…not so veritable Verity here,' Ambasi said, turning to Dele

'I forgot…to tell you,' said Dele, her head bowed.

'Good afternoon pastor,' said their next door neighbour, the seamstress, as Ambasi strode past her gate. Ambasi did not reply. Dele followed him out of the dazzling brightness and into the flat. She stood by the door, tachycardic, with her hands behind her back. Ambasi sat down. A heavy silence drifted between them. Dele inched along the wall to scratch her itchy legs. A dog whined outside.

'I used my winnings…from table tennis. I'll pay it all back,' said Dele.

'By the way when were you going to tell me about the Officers' Mess?' said Ambasi.

Dele's belly seemed to fall through the floor. Ambasi got up. He patted Dele on the chin. 'You went to look for Sandman. When it comes to the Arimos we have to be careful. And stop going on about money. I owe you more than you will ever know.'

***

'You passed and here is your radicalisation clearance certificate.' Antikath, in a yellow and blue frock, swept down from the kitchen, weeping and sneezing for joy.

'Two months backdated,' said Ambasi. 'You're fourteen. The school will take you in the remedial section, only two and a half years behind. But I trust you to catch up.'

PART TWO

ONE

Riding high on the "Tantalum boom," on the crests of waves made by his new friends, Babubacka announced a Five Year development plan. He awarded the contracts to his family and friends. Five years passed. Babubacka arrested anyone who dared point out that not a single contract had been honoured, only the contractors' inflated invoices: for doing nothing. Then he announced another plan and all talk of the Arimos, the disappeared, he banished: to talk of them gave treasonable notions oxygen. In some inchoate way the decree gave Dele some hope that her Dad might still be alive and she lived with the longing for her Dad and for revenge, day and night.

She had won a place to study Medicine and Georgina, the daughter of a cabinet minister, had the dissecting scalpel. Lying there without a care in the world in a trough of Formalin, the cadaver, a man with a bullet in his left eye and with his breast bone missing.

'Hey, this man's nipples, larger than some students' breasts,' said Georgina, smirking at Siuru across the dissecting room. Dele saw the hurt in Siuru's eyes.

'Miss spotless G spot, if your fucking life is so great why so much of your head in other people's windows?' Dele said.

'What's eating nose Kilimanjaro? Something not complete in here,' said Georgina, pointing to her temple, 'or down there, no action is equals to frustration,' she added in a market woman accent. Someone giggled.

'Your dissection time's up,' said Dele, pointing to the wall clock. Georgina, in a blue silk blouse under her plastic apron, pulled a pale string from inside the dead man's groin. 'Femoral nerve or a branch of?' she said.

'I'm talking to you,' said Dele.

Georgina raised her head in a slow arc, gave Dele another slow, condescending, stare and fished out another piece of tissue.

With that, weeks and waves of inchoate simmering at Georgina's patronising comments, at her impossibly shapely long legs and at her smug Mum and Dad in their ministerial car outside the hostel on Sundays, and of various other resentments, Georgina's display of the new shoes that lapdog of a lecturer bought her, her ever so self-satisfied look at her marks in last week's test, welled up and smashed into a blinding explosion in Dele's head.

'Had enough of this,' she said. She snatched the scalpel out of Georgina's hand, jabbed it into the man's leg then into his heart, slicing and cutting and slashing until, with little but pulp in the dead man's chest, the blade jammed into a rib, dropped out of her hand and into the trough behind the man's shoulder. 'There I've finished, whose turn next?' she said.

A male classmate sank, glassy-eyed, to the floor, tipping the body and wriggling maggots and preservative out of the trough. A smell like that of a public toilet spread round the room.

'Ponto. Ponto, come, this mad girl wants to kill me,' said Georgina. Ponto came running.

'Infection risk,' said Ponto, caressing Georgina's hand.

'Ponto, before you say anything, you are just her insurance choice,' said Dele. 'Everyone knows she is fucking a married lecturer.'

'How can you let her insult me like this?' said Georgina, holding her wrist under a running tap. Ponto left the room. The sight of his sorry face tweaked Dele with remorse.

'Hey you.'

Dele turned to find the Indian supervisor staring at her through a connecting door. 'If you are doing one more performance like that I am calling Professor Degenhardt…he expel two like you already this term,' said the Indian supervisor.

'I know your type. No decorum,' said Georgina, jabbing the air at Dele. Dele did not reply. She turned and walked away, sensing everyone's puzzlement through the door.

***

Ambasi called from France that evening. He'd been to the Museum of Mankind. 'Did you have a happy birthday Traytop? Twenty, no longer a teenager with tantrums?' he said.

Dele closed the Physiology textbook and rocked back in her chair. 'Could be worse,' she said.

'What's wrong?' said Ambasi.

'Lost my head again. I can't seem to help it.' She put her chin in one hand and phone in the other. Moments of silence followed. 'Say something. I've let you down again, haven't I?'

'I'll show you my working. Would you have reacted so to anyone else?' said Ambasi.

'Yes...no. I don't know,' she said.

'We've all been to that green and unpleasant land...where time stands as still as a hill.'

A twig seemed to snap inside her chest. 'Me? Jealous of that one? Pastor, for once the wind has blown off your thinking cap,' said Dele.

'Why not join a club?' said Ambasi.

'I have, after the session with the anger management counsellor. Table-tennis club turned me down because of my broken fingers. I hadn't played for years anyway.'

'You're tall enough for netball and it appeals to a certain atavistic tribalism,' said Ambasi.

Dele got out of her chair to get a better reception. 'Can't stand all that cheating they call mind games.'

'Horticultural society? Perhaps not, for you their labour will take too long to bear fruit...'

'...and Mrs Enameli of the Writer's group said I had barely the imagination of a pair of testicles?' said Dele. They laughed. 'And...hold on, I need to shut the balcony door. Mosquitoes,' said Dele. She pulled a shirt in off the balcony rails and shut the door. 'Still there?'

'Traytop, we're being acutely obtuse. Apart from head-butting tins of milk, what's the one thing you like and do well?'

Pick fights? Dele did not answer. She tossed the clean shirt on to the top shelf of her wardrobe.

'Paint, Traytop, you need to create.'

I could have been expelled thought Dele later that night in bed. And what did Georgina mean by *I know your type?* My race, my temper, my late nights out in town at seedy Jeba cinema watching old Spaghetti Westerns, my fondness for the odd binge of palm wine and soda, for hip hop and drum and bass and rap? Or, Dele wondered, with a clang of dread in her chest, had Georgina already seen through her façade of pretended aloofness and practised indifferences, to the closet in which she kept her envious anger and, under them all, the shame of her days in the camp: the legacy of that evil man, Sandman?

TWO

'Where've you been?' said Mr Dada the consultant as the registrar walked into the clinic room, his full-length white coat smudged with rust, blood stains and fingerprints.

'Cardiac Physiology lecture, sir,' said Dele.

'I wasn't talking to you,' said Mr Dada in a nasal drawl. The clinic was running late and Dele did not think it a right time to ask about the patient's swollen abdomen. Mr Dada would only grunt a reply over his left shoulder anyway.

'I was in main theatre,' said the registrar.

'Haba, haba, I asked you to take your time…not waste mine,' said Mr Dada, rolling his head like a boxer before a bout. A wave of the arm dismissed the waiting patient – a stooped man with an Ayatollah beard. Mr Dada got up from behind the clinic desk. He had a square face, small, atavistic, eyes, the type seen on suspects on the police posters. His baldness exaggerated a forehead that swept almost straight back from his brow and a knobbly vein stood out on each side of his giraffid neck.

Dele wondered whether the man was just arrogant or bad.

'I was waiting for my prescription, doctor,' said the elderly man, tattered cap in hand.

'Don't start reading any fat novels…life is short,' said Mr Dada, with a chuckle.

'Wing 4 doors wouldn't open. They were washing the walls so I had to go round the outside,' said the registrar.

'Look my dear man…at this rate you have as much chance of making it in this profession as the sun has of catching a cold. What time is it? Four?' Dada stabbed a glance at his watch gain. 'Ok, yeah. I'm off. You know how not to find me, keh,' he said, with a Nagati kick to his consonants. 'Follow me,' Dada said, turning to Dele.

The lift doors opened and two men in green theatre trousers got on. 'Going up or down,' said the shorter man, eyeing Dele up. Dele looked away. 'You'll have to go up in the world first then,' said Dada.

'You are looking fresh my brother,' said the other man.

Dada rolled his head. 'Barbados,' he said, chuckling.

'This new post, Academic Supervisor must pay well. Don't forget us, oh. Keleks told me you ordered new cabriolet,' said the shorter man.

'It's for Obinda, anniversary,' said Dada. 'Five point four litres. Man must enjoy.' He licked his lips.

Dele wondered how a surgeon who 'operates in theatre like a camel trying to juggle fine sand' could be so well off. Perhaps the rumours that he was related to Sandman were true.

She followed Dada out of the main hospital block into the warm afternoon sunshine and down the deserted corridor of a prefabricated building. Charts and projections and other data Dele did not understand covered Dada's office wall. He switched on the desktop computer and juggled with a ball of paper while the machine whirred into action.

'My essay on comparative cardiac anatomy?' Dele said, shuffling her feet on the floor to get his attention. Her legs itched, even in linen trousers.

Dada opened the drawer beside his left knee and produced Dele's essay. 'Ah, my friend, I've read this...piece of...fill in the rest,' he said, waving Dele's rolled up essay on commercial awareness in his hand. 'Anno Domino this time I'm afraid.'

'I don't understand,' said Dele shutting the door behind her.
"Anno Domino. You get A...D.' Dada laughed, baring unnaturally white and even teeth. Dele saw that her third essay had more red marks on it than did the previous attempts put together.

'Where have I gone wrong this time, sir?' said Dele.

'I cannot bear to be reminded of this insult to my optical apparatus. In actual fact I read this travesty with one eye closed and a hand cupped over my other eye, as insurance, keh. You may not have seen that announcement. They used to make it after some TV programmes when I was in the UK.' He paused, swivelled away and back again, looking pleased with himself. 'If you've been affected by any of the issues raised in this programme call this line. Where's the help line for me, keh, for other tutors, supervisors who have to read this mess, my friend.'

'But I followed…advice.'

Dada clapped his hands, the sleeves of his grey suit rippling smoothly round his wrists.

'At last my friend, the stirrings of a coherent argument,' he said. A neck vein snapped back and forth as he rolled his head.

'How long do I have to the next submission?' said Dele.

'It's due already. And each second spent here making *yeye* trouble wastes you time to rectify,' he said. He turned to the window and dismissed Dele with a wave over his shoulder. 'I've said it many times. Give students an inch they'll put light years on you.'

Dele backed out on to the corridor. A mouse scurried between her feet, down the corridor and under a nearby hut. Dele leaned over the wall to compose herself, checked that she had the correct essay in the green folder and pushed the door back open.

'Excuse me, I'm so very sorry to disturb you again. Could you do me a favour? I've read your comments and have come to my own conclusions.' Dele fished Panny's folder out of the folder. 'If I'm not mistaken you gave this essay here an A. Mine…what did you call it, you gave "A D." But mine is an exact copy of this. I copied it word for word. Same essay, same marker but different result. As a matter of fact, very different. Shall we ask the University Senate to work it out?'

Dada's face turned from dark brown to ash-grey. 'Give that to me,' he said.

'You can have it sir. I made copies,' she said.

THREE

Dele did not want to attend that week's multidisciplinary meeting on reflections about complaints and medical errors, but the alternative session on ethics had been cancelled. The meeting room smelled of dust and stale teabags. Mr Kabi sat at the head of the long Iroko table, flanked by a pair of dark brown floor-to-ceiling curtains hanging over a bay window. His white badge identified him as a service manager. To his right sat Mr Dada, representing the consultants. Dele did not catch the names of the two other women sitting next to the legal trainee, Christine Magasa.

Dele opened her little notebook wondering whether she would ever be good enough to produce one of those green, leather-bound Theses stacked in the bookcase beside her.

'Mrs Lagbaja will soon be here. She and her family worked for the Kolos in the civil service in colonial times,' said Mr Kabi, flicking through his file.

'Kolos are descendants of the former European colonial powers. Whenever they use a local hospital they bombard the hapless, junior, Siroko doctors, with sheafs of typewritten questions, to which they think they already know the answers,' said Ms Magasa.

We know that thought Dele.

'Like you,' said Dele's classmate digging her in the ribs.

Dele returned the compliment in kind.

'Thank you,' said Mr Kabi, looking even more drawn of face by the second. 'Her complaint is so wide-ranging, citing doctors who claimed that they had never even met her, that it is threatening to bring some HealthSmart departments, even catering, services to a halt,' he said.

'What are they doing here?' said Dada pointing at Dele and her three classmates.

'They're observers,' said Mr Kabi, picking loose skin off a thumb. 'Coffee or a coke?'

Mrs Lagbaja appeared at ten minutes past two. About five and a half feet tall, perhaps three inches taller in her prime, she had large, watchful, eyes, a long, grey-tinged brown, protean face with a forehead as grooved as a heavy duty tyre. Her light brown top hung like a tent from hunched shoulders and she had fastened her pleated dark brown skirt with a thick, six-inch long safety pin. In her left hand she carried a beige leather bag and in the other a white handkerchief. She muttered something about the receptionist, swept the room with her black eyes, then, with the straps on her slippers flapping along behind her, she shuffled over to the seat reserved for her, next to Mr Kabi. Someone offered her a cup of coffee. Mrs Lagbaja slammed her bag down on the table and refused the cup with a vigorous shake of the head.

A man stumbled in. He mumbled an apology. Dele recognised him as Azeez Sharli, a journalist who took up writing about the health sector after he lost his mother at HOSS, the Hospital of South Roko, before it was renamed HealthSmart by Sandman's conglomerate, Britsandchindarusa. Azeez bowed to the room and sat next to Mrs Lagbaja who took out a size A5 notepad and flipped through the pages.

'Please, we are listening,' said Mr Kabi.

Mrs Lagbaja had a clear loud voice. 'First point. You made my dizziness worse and those tablets you gave me I read somewhere shorten average life span and look like the same tablets that nearly killed Darwin…my pet parrot. It made my hair fall out,' she said.

'I thought that started forty years ago,' said Ms Magasa from across the table. Senior Sister Surina nodded. Her cap fell off.

'It's worse now,' said Mrs Lagbaja, dabbing the corner of her mouth with a knuckle. 'Food… abysmal. Had to get the kitchen staff in to tell them that the meat was too tough.' A jowl flapped against her neck. 'How they can take a perfectly decent piece of beef and turn it into patent leather beats me.' She bared a stretch of whittled canines and paused for breath, wiping the spittle from her lips. Dele thought that Mrs Lagbaja's prominent forehead, crooked neck and back and her huge black slippers made her look like a human question mark. Senior sister Surina started to say something but Mr Kabi stopped her with a shake of his head.

'Go on, Mrs Lagbaja. We're listening,' he said.

Mrs Lagbaja's tone and countenance gave the most benign intercourse a querulous edge. She glowered at Sister Surina. 'What's more, the radio in the patients' common room was too loud and the music dreadful. You may not want to hear this but in my discharge summary you don't say you sent me home too early.' Turning to Mr Kabi she said, 'disgraceful the way that awful man chucked me out, not even bothering to ask whether I had any food in the house. And I had to find my own way home by taxi. He charged me thrice over.' She swept the lank cigarette-stained hair back off her face. 'I have to tell you Sister. Some of your staff are not fit to look after bathroom scale, let alone patients.' She squinted at Dada's badge. 'Are you real or just borrowing the badge? Never seen one of your lot before. Consultant are you? Well, whatever your name is, I hope you don't let them treat *your other* patients like this. Look at my legs.' She pushed her chair back and pulled her skirt up so that everyone could see. Dark purple veins coursed over her calves. Dele thought the bleb on the inside of Mrs Lagbaja's right ankle was about to burst. Dada rolled his neck. Sister Surina looked impassive.

'You took your own discharge. You always do…against advice. Your legs? Varicosities distend with gravity…and age,' said Sister Surina.

'See what I mean by her deeply, deeply offensive commode level bedside manner?' said Mrs Lagbaja.

Am I Kolo? thought Dele.

Azeez dropped his notebook. 'Shit.' Mrs Lagbaja jerked her head round and gave Azeez a cold stare. Azeez ducked under the table for his book and buried his sweaty nose in it again.

'On the ward I could not understand what that registrar was saying. How he qualified as a doctor with diction like that I cannot fathom. Most of them do not have the courtesy to tell me who they were. I was just left to surmise that that was the case. In Austria where I worked, PA to the Meister, they would be deeply, deeply, deeply affronted by being addressed like that,' said Mrs Lagbaja. She pushed her tarnished gold ring back down her wedding finger.

A waiter brought in a fresh tray of tea and biscuits. Mrs Lagbaja stopped to inspect the fare and passed the tray to Azeez. 'Don't scoff them all,' she said. 'I'll take some home to Confucius.' Azeez broke off half a biscuit and popped the pieces into his mouth.

Mr Kabi raised his hand. 'Mrs Lagbaja how can we…redress?'

'A formal apology, refund, and a detailed reassessment of my case by seniors, preferably,' she said.

A one way ticket to the moon would be more like it.

'We value you as a customer, sorry…client. Mr Dada and I will put our heads together and book a date for you to come in to hospital. Say, for a week.' Mr Kabi turned to an assistant. 'Tell bookings.'

'Confucius doesn't like it when I'm away.'

'Siroko people and their dodo parrots,' said the girl sitting next to Dele. Dele looked at her watch. It was three fifty. She had a ward round at four.

Mrs Lagbaja turned to Dele and the other students as they trooped out. 'And I'm not going to have anything to do with that lot,' she said.

I'd rather lick spittle too. But Dada grinned.

***

'Stand or sit over there for patient allocation for your projects,' said Dada's secretary. She waited as the ante-room filled with students, clucked, tore a sheet from the jaws of her smudged laser printer, and pushed through the throng to the corridor to pin instructions on the notice board.

'You're just as bad as your boss, why couldn't you just say he wanted to meet us in the other room?' Dele said before she trooped down the corridor with the other students.

'Keep that bouche of yours shut, don't you ever learn?' said a classmate, nudging Dele in the back.

'It's my mouth I can chew what I want,' said Dele.

In a pink suit, white shirt, striped blue and red tie and blue brogues, Dada was waiting in front of a large wall to wall blackboard. *I hope this will not take long; I've got to call the airport manager to see if he's heard anything* thought Dele as she took her seat. Dada seemed to be in his element, doing his neck exercises and hopping about in front of the blackboard, rubbing out the outline of his lecture before the students had time to copy it down.

'Each of you will be allocated a patient, yeah. Write your report or case study...submit in ten weeks. Failure to do so or to obtain a pass mark, you repeat the whole year. If you fail again, that's it. End of career, yeah. That's what the minister said. And he who pays the piper, calls the tune, that much I know my friends.'

Murmurs and gasps of dismay, woe, and excitement went up as the students opened their envelopes.

'Something's not right here, I have no patient,' said Dele, waving her blank sheet of paper.

'More drama from the profane parrot,' said Georgina.

'Shut your effing gob.' Dele waved her empty envelope at Talabu 'the soprano'.

'Now...if the rest of you don't have any questions,' said Dada.

'How many words in the essay?' shouted someone from the back of the room.

'Enough,' said Dada, an evil glint in his eye. The class emptied.

'You like your surprise?' said Dada, after the rest of the class had left. 'We didn't have enough volunteers, so I had to pick your patient and you are not the only one. But I know she'll make a great case report.'

'Who is it?' she said, with a sense of unease.

'Mrs Lagbaja.'

'But you heard what she said about students...'

'You'll just have to persuade her, keh?' said Mr Dada after he scratched his shiny pate, feigning bewilderment. Then he dialled a number, pushed the red speakerphone button and Professor Degenhardt's voice came over the line.

'Is she there?' he said.

'Yes, sir,' said Dada, standing to attention.

'Miss Verity. I hear you are trying to subvert the academic process.'

'Not at all, professor. My allocated patient is not likely to cooperate.'

'A tenuous hypothesis I doubt you have put to the test. Dada, your opinion?'

'Miss Verity has a track record of this sort of...hysteria,' said Dada.

***

On her way back from the library late that evening Dele had only just found her way back on to the hospital corridor after a wrong turning when a nurse hurried past and disappeared down a dark stairwell. In the dim orange light of a lonely light bulb Dele could just make out the sign for the laundry and mortuary at the end of the corridor. As she moved over to let an electric buggy past her phone rang - Ambasi.

'I called to tell you about Dada,' she said.

'Show me your working,' said Ambasi.

'I told you about the way he marked my essay. Then he gives me this witch. The last student she had failed the project beyond redemption.'

'But don't you know that Dada is as crooked as a handset cord? He may not even have read any of the project essays-'

'Are you saying he just scattered marks and red ink on a whim?' said Dele.

'Traytop, you can't climb a mountain without rubbing a stone the wrong way. This Kolo woman may be just…the kick, the spice you need.' said Ambasi.

The buggy drew ahead. Dele saw a girl facing backwards on the back seat. The girl's lips shone with glossy makeup and her red skirt rode up almost to her crotch. From her flat chest and thin arms, poking from a low-cut white blouse, to Dele the girl looked no older than twelve years.

'You wouldn't be saying that if you'd met this Mrs Lagbaja,' said Dele. 'Sorry, the reception is not great.'

The little girl's white high-heels dragged inches from the floor. She raised her head. Her sad gaze met Dele's just before the buggy clattered over a crack, rounded a bend and turned off the passageway.

'I'll call you back,' said Dele to Ambasi.

Keeping a safe distance in the dark, Dele followed the faint glare from the buggy's reflector down a dewy path, flexing her toes to stop her clogs sinking into the mud. The buggy stopped outside what looked like a wooden block marked "Medical Records." The door opened, casting the driver's thick-set form in misty light. Dele crouched behind a hedge.

The girl stumbled off the buggy and tottered through the door. The door closed. It went dark. *What would a girl be doing in Medical Records at this hour?* Dele waited behind the hedge until the buggy hummed past and out of sight. Then she crept towards the door and knocked. The door felt as cold as steel and hurt her knuckles. A woman came to the door.

'We've closed. Come tomorrow,' said the woman. She had what Dele's dad, Wale, used to call "attitude." The woman made a grab to pull the door shut again but Dele shoved a satchel in the way.

'I saw the light and the girl and thought you were doing overtime,' said Dele. Over the woman's shoulder she saw a girl shuffle up the corridor and turn left into a cubicle. *What sort of Medical*

Records department has no storage cabinets? I'm a medical student, and I'll give you my identity and the name...'

'That was my child. Stupid girl went to party. I will teach her. Sent her uncle, Babansha, to get her. Go now or I'll call security and your Dean,' said the woman.

She's lying.

The next day it took Dele an hour to find the building hidden behind scaffolding. It looked empty and the sign for "Medical Records" lay broken under a boundary hedge. She could not risk another run-in with the Dean, so, reluctantly, she shoved the encounter with the girl to the back of her mind.

FOUR

South Roko's annual Arts Festival, held under floodlights on a large open space next to the National Stadium, attracted youth from all over the island and thousands from the African mainland, Nigeria, Togo, Benin, Mali. The drummer brought his solo to a shimmering crescendo on the high hat and rounded up with a sudden stop on the bass drum. 'Thank you, ladies and…gentlemen, give it up for the Beat Ovens and for the mind-bending artwork by Dele, the slap and dashing medic,' said Tafawa, the impresario, to flashes from the multi-coloured stage lights.

With the artists' materials Ambasi got her, Dele had become the go-to student for set designs. She threw her banner into the cheering crowd, peeled off her black gloves and put the large paper clips, braces she designed for her floppy fingers, away in the pocket of her jeans.

'See you tomorrow, parrot,' said Ukwu the band leader. They called Dele parrot because she crammed for tests, but the nickname reminded her of her long nose. 'I'm off to see if I can find the Malians,' she said.

Dust motes swirled and darted in the floodlit night as though frenzied by the clashing polyrhythms. The ground underfoot, even the air seemed to throb, shimmer and heave in time to the music booming from huge box speakers stacked storey-high. Dele pushed through the crowd, ducking round hawkers selling anything from a few nuts or slivers of tangerines to electricity generators. Every few minutes she stopped to snatch a few notes from a weeping guitar, or to mime to the punchy blasts of a brass section or the call and response of a West African choir. She had just swerved to avoid a man carrying a live goat on his head when three loud cheers went up on the other side of a gaudy arcade. Dele decided to find out what the fuss was about.

She squeezed between a bandstand and a snake-charmer's stall to find the culprit, a young woman with what looked like light brown skin. She had a nose of tropical, perhaps African, provenance, but long, wavy European hair and she pranced about on a door mounted on bricks. Behind her fluttered a white banner with the name, *Hanili*, written on it in bold black italics. Her audience, a hundred or so young men and women, stood, eyes glued to the stage, mesmerised.

Dele stood near the back of the crowd, noting with a little purr of content that Hanili's skin looked a little lighter than hers. Hanili was wearing a bright orange crinkle cotton kaftan with angel sleeves and multi-coloured braid trim. Like Dele, she wore her dark hair long, shoulder length, but with her fringe swung low over her left, rather than right, brow. *Is that the girl I saw on TV? At The Hague?*

'What have they made dear Roko?' said Hanili. She turned the microphone round for a reply, like a pop star.

'A tax heaven,' the crowd chanted in return.

'A tax heaven for the globals,' she said, punching the air with the microphone. 'To she who has more will be given and from she who has little even that will be taken away; until she opens her eyes to claim what is hers?' She paused with a cheeky glint in her eye. Dele craned her neck round a knapsack for a better view.

Hanili went on. 'Someone comes to your garden, to harvest your vegetables, cooks them with your water, your power, your stove, takes it all home to her family, leaves the scraps, just enough to keep you alive...and a new bucket and sponge for washing up for which you should be grateful because her husband will sell you insurance and spare parts for the bucket until you kick it. His premiums compulsory, your token tax bill, voluntary.'

She laughed, pushed a strand of hair behind her ear. *Her hair's so free and easy, mine's like starched twine. Look at her slender fingers.*

'Bills inflate...'

'And hopes deflate,' sang the crowd.

'To the minister of less this and that, can we have some water to drink seeing as you own half of Thames Valley...sir?' said Hanili, with a bow. The banner billowed back. Hanili wiped her freckled nose and puffed her cheeks out. She raised a clenched fist to the floodlit sky. 'Enjoy…be safe my sisters…and brothers,' she said. When Hanili pulled off the Alice band and tossed her hair back Dele could have sworn that she saw tears in her angel's eyes. A gust got up. Hanili put the Alice band back on, patted it down. The crowd dispersed, but Dele would have given anything to swap places with the three young women in red T-shirts and black jeans helping Hanili fold the banner into the back of a battered white Volkswagen Beetle. The car had the words "Pleb bus" scrolled on one door, "Pleb Mobile" on the other. *That's the girl at The Hague, what's she doing here stirring up trouble. Has she got a death wish?*

Dele called Tafawa to ask about Hanili.

'My slap and dashing doctor. Are you still here…yes if you are at Hanili's stage, row Z, I'm not far from you on row V. Yes…I can hear…oh I see you now.' He puffed into sight a few moments later.

'You know Hanili?' said Dele, ducking under a hawker's tray.

'Haba, how I will not know Hanili? Works for Voluntary Foundation. Top girl. They say in UK she entered wrong exam hall by mistake, wrote two essay at the same time with pen in each hand and got First Class for each.' Tafawa fiddled with the medallion hanging round his neck. It had his initials, TB on it.

'I think I saw her on TV at the Hague–'

'That must be when she was schoolgirl. She won a prize to the trials. Then she became a journalist. But when they ask her to write one thing, she write another thing, but before they shot her she shot them, resigned to come and cause trouble here,' said Tafawa.

'I've not heard of this Foundation,' said Dele.

'Billionaire Olaf started it. His profile is so low even snake cannot find him, but he wants to help our grassroots. Hanili is high up in his South Roko branch.'

'Family?' said Dele, hoping that Tafawa would not notice the strangled note in her voice.

'That's no concern of mine, not my type,' said Tafawa.

'And she's mine?' said Dele.

'Hey, no need to jump on my neck. Look, see trouble,' said Tafawa.

Dele heard a man call out through a megaphone. 'All you women turn away at once. Now,' the man said, cracking a whip. Tafawa disappeared behind a magician's stall. The crowd parted. Two masqueraders skipped up, yelping in headdresses made up of a multi-coloured crown of interlacing pythons, turbans and cutlasses, worn over a white veil and a facial mask. The white mask had the eyes and mouth sculpted in black. Perched on top of the crown stood an African Grey parrot which held in its beak an object that looked like a scorpion with two human heads.

The women covered the little girls' faces with their hands, pulled them in and backed away. Dele tried to hide too but one of the masked men screamed and pointed her out. Bamboo poles held at the ready and chattering like Colobo monkeys, the other masked men charged up. They came to a skidding halt in an arc in front of Dele. The men in the crowd closed in as a masquerader sloped towards his quarry, so close did he come that Dele could see the whites of his eyes. He snorted, sniffed the air, raised his baton and whipped it down like a conductor. The chanting stopped. 'Leave this one to me,' he said, raising his baton again. 'Kill, kill, apapa,' said his mates, stamping their feet. Dele knew who they were, the GeleRoko. Made up of young men, the group performed on special occasions, to mark a coronation or an important anniversary for example, but other larrikins joined the group to cause trouble, beating a young man senseless on Mengistu Lane in 2011 because he winked at one of their girlfriends. Dele braced herself, her heart tapping its own poles against her chest.

Her nerves screamed but the man brought his weapon down on to Dele's shoulder in a gentle arc. 'You are the artful forger, remember?' said the masquerade. He had a deep voice, but it sounded familiar.

Dele shook her head.

'I'm Aanu,' said the man.

'Oh my God, nappy shirt Aanu, my constipated…patient?' said Dele.

'Shush, shush. We Gelerokos do not cavort with ordinary *sifitis* in public. Yes it's me from the camp. Remember Robi? With meningitis? I'm Robi's cousin. My aunty Norma told me. I have seen your artwork…and with the Beat Ovens.' He gave Dele a few more playful blows on the shoulders, tossed her a card. 'Call me,' he said.

FIVE

Groans went up and the students streamed out of the Students' Union Hall into the warm moonlit humidity of a February night in Sankara.

'The end of term party has not even reached go and no light again. How can you run a band and not have a generator, in this day and age?' said Musi 'broadband' Kalango. Musi had ears as large as saucers.

'We shouldn't need a generator in 2014,' said Dele. She cupped an ear with her good hand. 'Is that singing I hear?' she said.

'That white woman who talks at festival last month is at a meeting of the Ashi Sankara local women's co-operative. It's not far from here,' said broadband Kalango.

'She's not white. Am I white?' said Dele, baring a forearm.

'I don't care what you say here in Sankara. Where I come from she is white and so are you,' said broadband.

'To you Filipis even charcoal is white, no, even blackboard with chalk writing on it is white,' said Dele.

'Parrot, I haven't got time for your big mouth. If you want to see this woman go round the back of that church, past that broken soak away. It will take you fifteen minutes,' said Kalango. Dele made it in ten. She found Hanili in full flow in front of a small group of women and children.

'How can they close your clinic when it is making your mother, your sister, your son and your daughter better? Don't listen to them. We know their tricks. Our Foundation will fight them, show them pepper, or, as we say in London, bring it on.' Hanili flashed a smile. 'Everyone say yeah, yeah, this is your land, you go nowhere, until they give us water,' she said, her hair radiant even under two weak light bulbs dangling from a cable twice coiled over a craggy tree branch. She raised a clenched right fist and waved the cordless microphone in her left hand.

'We are here to stay,' chanted the women over the rumble of an electricity generator. A little girl in a red bandana using a rolled up newspaper as a microphone skipped to the front to mimic Hanili.

'My name is Hanili, be mine, stitch in time saves nine…lives, but not as many as a borehole instead of landmine,' said the little girl, rocking and jerking her head from side to side like a hip-hop artist. After her song, she presented Hanili with a large bunch of green bananas.

'Thanks, Tessa's after my job,' Hanili said, her freckles bunching up in a smile. The women rolled around laughing and clapping. Hanili flicked her thumb with the tips of her fingers and patted the girl on the head. As she straightened up a scrawny woman in a pale top nudged her on the shoulder and gestured at Dele. Hanili looked at Dele. Gazes blent. Hanili smiled. Dele's heart flopped. The moment went.

What's happening to me?

Hanili tapped the cordless microphone, clapping with her free right hand against her left wrist. 'You must all be tired. Remember what we say. Safety first. A problem shared may be a problem halved but it may be the start of an epidemic.' As Hanili turned to help with a folding metal table a woman stepped out of the dark. Even from where she stood Dele could see that the woman had a face several shades lighter than her neck and she seemed to tower over Hanili. The woman gave Hanili a pointed tap on the shoulder.

'What you are teaching our people? You think I don't know what you are saying? Go back to where you came from to teach them your dirty mind. We God-fearing people do not need your chemicals and rubbers here,' she said, prodding Hanili in the chest.

Dele jumped over a bench, shoved a chair to one side and confronted the angry woman. 'Yellow fever, what's your problem. Is it with your ears that these women hear?'

'Who are you calling that?' said the tall woman.

'You bleach and you talk of natural? Look at you…you look like bush leopard with chicken pox. Is it any wonder that flies dance round your mouth, when your brown moustache looks like heap of shit.' The woman pushed out at Dele. Dele leant away and made her miss. Hanili tried to jump in front of Dele but a man dressed in dark trousers and a skin-hugging T-shirt appeared from behind the hut. 'What is it Bose?'

'Felix, these stupid girls are calling me names.' She grabbed Dele's shirt. 'Ah, this one in particular. I don't know her problem…it is the foreign talker I have *jibi* with. This one has no home training. Look at her sharp head and nose.'

'Please no need for all this,' said Hanili, nudging between Dele and Bose.

Felix ducked under a bough and drew himself up. He glowered at Dele, his jaws clenched and fists at the ready. Dele got a crick in her neck looking up at him.

This is not good. 'Bose, let go of me so that I can defend myself,' said Dele.

Bose pushed Dele into Felix. Dele burrowed in close to smother Felix in a clinch.

'Help us, help,' said Hanili.

Out of the corner of her eye and to her relief Dele saw a man bound up and leap over the benches to her side. 'Leave her, you want to kill the girl?' he said. Dele stopped fighting. Her left eyebrow stung and air scythed down into her burning lungs.

'Felix, ah, ah, it is woman you are now sparring with…what happened to Digsy in the gym?' said the passer-by. 'What could she have said to make you swell like dead goat so?' he said.

'She disrespect Bose and myself,' said Felix.

'In what way?' said the man, turning to Bose.

Bose stopped Dele with a wag of a finger. 'Don't dare you repeat what you said,' she said. 'Felix leave her. She not worth it.'

Dele snapped her arm back from Felix. She smoothed down her blouse and jeans. 'Ogun, the god of iron must be on your side. Thank the kind man for saving you my…I would have shown you Sankara hot pepper,' said Dele, her heart juggling beats and dropping a few.

Bose and Felix left. The Samaritan waved a playful warning finger at Hanili and Dele, smiled and also melted into the night.

'Gee, thanks, I'm, em, Hanili, by the way.' Hanili puffed her cheeks out. She was wearing a plain cream kaftan and a red pair of sandals.

'I'm Dele. Verity,' said Dele. *What sharp, kind eyes. Her nose, with a little nob on the end, perfect.*

'You're the medical student Tafawa calls the slap and dashing medic, something like that.' Dele drew herself up to about the same height as Hanili. Hanili flashed a smile and tossed her head and hair back. She smelled of warm breakfast cereal and had five freckles on the bridge of her nose.

Dele's words seemed to be pounded into some sort of disorder by her heart before they came out. 'Need some help?' she said after another aching pause. Before Hanili could reply Dele hopped round the back of the tree and tried to lift the black electricity generator off its brick stand. *I shouldn't have done that* she thought as cramp gripped her hands. Hanili appeared, looking puzzled.

'I know, this is a mess,' said Dele, untangling a knot in the power cable.

'I meant…your hand, can you manage?' said Hanili.

Dele tucked her right hand out of sight, but Hanili coaxed it out with a gentle tug on the elbow. 'Oh gee, let me see.' Hanili's shoulders dropped and the colour drained from her face. 'What happened?' she said.

'It's nothing,' said Dele, blushing.

'Sorry, em, didn't mean it.' She pointed at her nose. 'Pokes its tip everywhere,' she said. 'Oh, my splitting headache, that frigging generator.' She disconnected the electric bulb and with a practised flick of the wrist, like a Federer overhead back hand volley, tossed the power cable back over the bough.

'Overdone the coffee, where's the…you know…'

'Gee oh gee, that's the first thing I ask for when I arrange a meet,' Hanili said. 'Where's the loo, failing that, the girl's big tree trunk?' Hanili pointed at the hut. 'Round the back; you can't miss it, but mind the wind doesn't blow it all back in your face,' she said, with an impish grin.

I want to hug her.

Dele returned to find Hanili standing over the generator. 'Might have to leave it over there in the guard's shed. My usual helpers cried off,' said Hanili, pointing past a hut.

Dele shook her head. 'We can manage,' she said flexing her biceps like a victorious Olympic weightlifter. They dragged and wheeled the generator up to the front of the VW Beetle, braced the machine against their thighs and heaved it over and into the boot. 'There, we've done it,' said Dele, trying to clap the life back into her hands.

'Do let me drop you off.'

Half an hour later they swapped smiles and taps of the wrist on the approach road outside the hospital gate. Dele got out of the car and pressed the door closed with a hip. 'Nice to meet you,' she said. Her right hand shot out in a nervous flick. *What lovely skin she has. I'm sure it doesn't itch like mine.*

'You too, take care,' said Hanili.

'Your number...just in case,' said Dele.

'Of course, I'll tell you mine, call it now.'

Dele leaned back inside the car, into the dizzying aroma of what smelt like warm cornflakes and pancake. She called Hanili's number. 'Great, I'll put your name on. Contact. There, done,' said Hanili her voice even, clear, with a timbre hinting of promise; like a TV voiceover for a miraculous new drug.

The car rolled back. Hanili pushed the gear lever and Dele stepped away. The words Dele wanted revved up too, then stalled, perhaps for fear that they may be ever so politely diverted should they come out of their hangar.

'You wouldn't mind one...one of these days, a drink that is, as my guest...as you are new to this place?' said Dele, the thought, since she first set eyes on Hanili, of her daily commute between desperate longing, resignation and despair thrust the words out of her throat. But, to her anguish, a car roared past as she spoke and she could not tell whether Hanili heard what she said. Dele cringed and got ready to flee but she saw Hanili flick a thumb with a finger and nod. Hanili made a sucking noise. 'I'd love to,' she said.

Dele leapt out of bed at five the next morning and sliced through the awkward chapter on acid-base and fluid balance in kidney failure with unprecedented ease. When her phone rang during breakfast she shook so much she closed the call by accident and dropped the phone on the floor.

'How's your revision going?' said Hanili.

'Didn't do any,' Dele said, searching for the right response.

'And your wrists?' she said.

'You saw, rubbed them away last night,' she said. *What am I saying?*

A pause followed during which Dele stewed in adrenaline juices. 'Are you there?' she said.

'Thanks for your help,' said Hanili.

They fell silent again, Dele wondering whether she had heard right last night. *Say something you fool.* 'Your car...how long have you had–'

'I'll pop round to pick you up for that drink, em, but on one condition,' said Hanili.

'What's that?' said Dele, holding her breath.

'That you empty your bladder first...can't afford accidents in the Plebmobile,' said Hanili with a smile in her voice.

'I'll be ready,' Dele said. The teaching session with one of the friendlier registrars would have to go.

'Oh, gee, you haven't asked when yet,' Hanili said.

Dele boiled, cursing herself for her awkwardness. 'I thought...six-thirty,' she said.

'Twisted my arm. Seven is safer, after the ministers' procession,' said Hanili.

Seven. A lifetime. Dele went back to her room. As the words on the page would not keep still, she closed the books and set up her easel. Lunchtime came. She went to the cafeteria but could not eat. Adidu, the steatopygic lover of yams, cleared it for her in three mouthfuls. At six o'clock Dele had another shower, sat in front of the mirror and because she found a tiny hole in the right sleeve of her blue blouse, where she'd stuck a safety pin during a ward round, decided that she would have to stand to Hanili's right all evening. Georgina, next door, must have sensed the unusual activity and she came in wearing her most patronising face.

'I hope it's worth all this,' she said, waving at the make-up on Dele's table. 'Parrot keep the noise down. Some of us have better things to do,' she said.

'Get some fucking earplugs,' said Dele.

More nervous than a rookie schoolteacher, Dele hurried out so that she could catch Hanili at the hospital gates, before Georgina or any of the other nosey ones saw them.

At a few minutes to seven Dele felt a tap on her back. Hanili. She had on a light orange blouse over a dark brown baggy pair of linen trousers and black court shoes. A pair of dark basic stud earrings shone from under her bob. She did not wear an Alice band. *If this girl were a movie she would win best picture and all the major categories* thought Dele.

'Did I take you by surprise? Gee, goody. I parked over there, came in through the other gate,' she said.

Oh my lovely defib, you make my heart beat.

***

At the junction of Angola and Nile Roads, a red van driven by a young, long-haired Chinese man crashed through a rusting dustbin and cut Hanili up at the traffic lights. Hanili slammed on the brakes and Dele's head jerked to within an inch of the windscreen. 'Are you ok?' said Hanili. Dele rubbed her head, nodded and glared out of the windscreen. The Chinese man put up a two-fingered salute and tossed a can of beer out of the window into the roadside ditch. Hanili muttered under her breath and a few minutes later turned left into an underground carpark.

'We're there. It's called "King Belly."'

'Owned by retired Rokopat Army officer as usual?' said Dele.

'Not sure,' said Hanili.

In the foyer oriental music tinkled and warbled from ceiling speakers. A man in epauletted red livery showed Dele and Hanili to an airy hexagonal hall packed with diners. In the middle of the hall a four-tiered service section looking like a wedding cake rose from floor to ceiling, with the food lifted on trays through the central aisle from a basement kitchen. A tepid aroma of fish, soy sauce and pepper greeted them at the second, marine food, level.

'That brown lake is prawn and shark soup, whale, the red stuff over there they say is from crocodile,' said Hanili, pointing at a pink bowl. 'Is that all you're having, salmon pancake with rice?'

Dele nodded. 'Never seen so much food in one place, buffalo testicle, fried, broiled, barbecued pig, boar, rabbit, goat, tongue of chameleon, shark's eggs. It's freaking me out.'

'Always wanted to see Africa,' said Hanili, as they took their seats at a dark brown Iroko table overlooking a gaudy fountain display.

'Don't give me that earth mother Africa's so natural bullshit. Africans are dying to get out,' said Dele.

Hanili rummaged through her handbag. 'It was the Hague inquiry into the camp massacres that got me going. UN...pathetic. Babies bludgeoned to death, but, oh no they fell out of their rollercoaster in a playground on a school day out. Banusi got away with bluster.'

'Is that why you left your newspaper?' said Dele.

Hanili shook her head. 'More prosaic I'm afraid. Every day the same thing in the papers to distract us. How many more cans of beer you can afford after the budget. In the land of Shakespeare ten year olds cannot read. But what do we write about? Royal hairline. I wrote this piece…if it's all to do with economic benefit then the ideal immigrant is a black slave you wouldn't have to pay,' Hanili said.

'You didn't?' said Dele.

'Up struck the orchestras of the age of entitlement, on period instruments…that's social media to you and me. Death and other threats from racists and trolls, the usual stuff. My boss apologised to the proprietor. I refused and left for Olaf's Foundation.'

'The world's not all about schools and hospitals though and at least they don't shoot you or lock you up…for what you write.' Dele told Hanili about Saro.

'We've been there too…but you're right that was a long time ago,' said Hanili, teasing the skin off her breast of fried duck. Chinese, Europeans, in casual dress and a couple of locals in suits and green cravats, Rokopat colours, filtered in.

'Hanili's a strange name,' said Dele.

'Mum's from Africa but burned her bridges. End of story. Dad wanted a boy, to play cricket for Yorkshire, but out popped…me. Dad always liked the name Emily, but a favourite aunt of his wanted Hannah, after an actress or a movie.' She flicked a thumb with a finger. 'So Dad and Mum combined the names to get Hanili.' She tossed a pill into her mouth and chased it down with a glass of water. 'Anti-everything pill,' she said. 'Couriered from Oslo, too many counterfeits here in Roko. Anyway enough about me.'

Is she on the pill? 'I was born in North Roko and here I am,' said Dele.

Hanili leaned over the table. When she rested her hand on Dele's for a second and gave it a squeeze Dele's stomach jangled like a pea in a referee's whistle.

'Whose is the ring?' said Hanili.

'My mum's, my dad's…I call the airport manager to find out what happened to him. But there's an embargo on any mention of the Arimos. We raised a petition. No answer. I just want to know what happened…not even a photo. All I have left is in here,' she said pointing to her heart. 'Otherwise, rootless, Mum's gone, our old house razed to the ground by Sandman and his land grabbers,' said Dele.

'Sorry, didn't mean to prod my proboscis in again,' said Hanili.

Don't frighten her away with your issues, stupid. 'You must meet Ambasi. Pastor, juju man, he's been helping me and he's writing a book. Will he ever finish his research on history and anthropology of Siroko…? Did you know that a Niroko's nose is on average two millimetres shorter than a Siroko's?'

Hanili shook her head. 'I *do* know that Nirokos are called basket mouth though, because if you have a big bum, ugly wife, spoiled brats, or bad teeth they soon let you know,' she said.

'So that's why Prince Philip didn't come to North Roko with the Queen,' said Dele.

Hanili laughed and tossed a blue capsule down her neck.

The swan and the ugly duckling. Ambasi might like that as a book title. 'They seem to be doing back of envelope calculations,' Dele said, pointing at the next table with a nudge of her elbow. The Chinese man at the top of the table picked a cherry off a fruit cake and popped it into his mouth. He made a face. The black men laughed.

'Roko's next high speed rails fiasco. That's Warana sitting on the right side of the Chinese man. They say everyone in Sankara has a book in them, one for the shelf, the other for under the counter. I've got my eye on Warana,' said Hanili. She flicked her thumb with the tip of a finger. 'Africa needs truly heavy movers and shakers,' she said.

'African pile drivers,' said Dele.

'They're right pain in the arses,' said Hanili.

'Like gigantic haemorrhoids,' said Dele.

'Heemo rods…that's bloody scaffolding, right,' Hanili said in a South London accent. They burst into laughter.

'Miss Verity I've got artistic pretensions myself you know.' Hanili took a piece of paper out of her bag and started to read. 'That farm boy, the terrorist crooning in prison, knew just what he was doing, stuffing a weapon into the cow while it was mooing, so when

Babubacka comes past the kitchen farting and chewing, the irked cow replies by groaning and pooing, exploding old lizard face into the broth the cuckoo was cooking,' she said in a singsong voice. Dele burst into laughter.

'Can I do anything for you?' said the waiter.

'Gore-Tex corsets, my side is splitting, my friend here is full of sh-'

Hanili raised a hand. 'Oh, you can't say that here. You meant to say I'm full of the figs and mints of my emerging notions,' she said in a high-flown English accent. They started to laugh again, heaving and panting, until they wheezed and shuddered to a halt with tears rolling down their cheeks.

'These accents you do kill me,' said Dele, wiping her eyes.

'Gee oh gee, I must meet this friend of yours…Ambasi. He's helping you look for your dad?' A police siren went off.

'The owner is coming,' said the waiter, sweeping crumbs of their table with a broad blade before hurrying off to line up at the entrance.

Sandman walked in seconds later, surrounded by a dozen armed police officers and a trinity of heavyweight bodyguards, their reptilian heads swivelling on necks as thick as planks.

SIX

Dele put a cream blouse on over a black pair of jeans. She would have much preferred a quiet meal but Hanili had insisted that they all met at Babubacka National Stadium as a thirteenth birthday treat for Keli, Hanili's friend, who wanted to see her idol Ami, the newly crowned world junior javelin champion, in the flesh. Bookended by Keli and Ambasi, with Hanili, resplendent in a Keli-designed deep blue kaftan, to Ambasi's immediate left, the group of four sat at a horseshoe-shaped table in one of the dining rooms overlooking the track. *I hope Ambasi likes her.* A blast of cold air from the vent above reminded her that she should have put on a long-sleeved blouse. Ambasi, with several glances at the ceiling, also looked as if he could have done with a cap.

Applause sizzled round the stadium. Keli's eyes lit up. Then, with thousands of white balloons fizzing into the floodlit sky, Ami bounded in to the first few bars of the Roko national anthem. Ami turned to the VIP dais and clapped his hands in the air. The giant stadium screen showed Sandman sitting next to Monday Babubacka under the national flag which featured the national mascot, an African Grey parrot, sitting on an egg: the ovum of prosperity. Sandman nodded, like a fictional Roman emperor at the Coliseum.

The heads to Dele's right turned left and the heads to her left turned right. Ami started his run, his back arched, javelin in his fist, a grey and red band on the wrist. He loped up side-on, his steps quickening until at the end of his run, he planted his left foot just behind the line, whipped his arm and trunk forward and let fly. Light teetered on the javelin's wobbling tip. The white flag went up and the crowd sighed its relief and delight as the javelin arced through the sky. Four shadows and all eyes met at its landing point. Ami raised a clenched fist to the night and bowed. Keli jumped off her seat to clap, her hands a blur, like the wings of a humming bird.

'Brill, thanks aunties,' she said. Her toothy smile lifted her ears up and out, just as Hanili had described them. For a bitter second, Dele recalled where she was on *her* 13th birthday.

'What about me?' said Ambasi, in a splendid silky white soutane.

'Thank you…pastor,' said the gleeful Keli. Ambasi said something but Dele didn't hear him for the applause. She flashed a surreptitious look at Hanili and with a nod of the head asked Ambasi if everything was alright. She got two slow nods in reply.

'I'm expecting a call, but you can take a few photos…birthday girl,' said Hanili, passing her phone to Keli.

Sandman and Babubacka appeared on the stadium screens outside and on a giant TV monitor in the dining room. A scratchy rub, like a thorn tapping the strings in her heart, started in Dele's chest when Babubacka, in his trademark white robes, got up to speak. 'Today I announcement the confirmation of Chief Oniseme, former Interior Minister after doing a good job, a man who can block and unblock anything from nose to airport runway…to confirm him as Haka of Roko,' said Babubacka. He lifted Sandman's right hand. Sandman beamed like a double Olympic gold medallist.

The scratchy tapping in Dele's heart got faster. Hanili leaned her head on Dele's shoulder and gave her a long hug. Dele saw Ambasi flinch.

'Does the man's mouth really smell?' said Keli.

'Shush, you'll get us all killed,' said Hanili, looking round to see if anyone had heard.

'The man behind him. Who is he?' said Dele.

'Chinese ambassador,' said Keli.

'Clever girl,' said Dele.

'He looks as if he owns the place. So he should. After what happened to the child at Gole?' said Ambasi, shaking his head. 'They get Tantalum, we get cheap slippers and ChinAfrican babes in orphanages and dustbins,' he said. A waiter arrived with a commemorative T-shirt. 'No thanks,' said Ambasi. 'Probably cheap Chinese import.'

'It's why we are here to help...with water projects,' said Hanili, leaning back to let the waiter in.

Ambasi will like that.

'You'll be chewing our food for us next,' said Ambasi, muttering into his drink. He dipped the tip of a serviette into the corner of his teary left eye.

Hanili lowered her fish fork. 'But the WHO...'

'Life is not played out on paper; unless you are a bottle of ink...or a pundit,' said Ambasi. 'But don't get me wrong. I'm sure you're doing an excellent job.' He looked to see if Keli was listening. Dele looked too. But Keli was away with her fairies and idols on the field and track. 'You could say this place was shit before the Chinese came, but it was Siroko shit and we knew where to bury it. But this dried powdered colonial shit gets in your hair, between your feet, deposits millions of eggs that hatch inside your head and take centuries to wash out. 'The fruit salad. Where's the fruit salad?' he said to the waiter.

Hanili patted her chest as though a spicy morsel had gone down the wrong way. 'Pastor does it not matter who is robbing you as long as he's one of your own. I asked the ministers the other day...where is the money set aside for waste disposal and rural water supply? In reply a projectile bilious bluster from repeatedly rewarmed bits of his botched reforms,' she said, chopping the table with her hand.

'Blood is thicker than water,' said Dele, squirming in her seat.

'In South Roko money is thicker than blood yet only light travels faster,' said Hanili.

Ambasi looked out on to the track and frowned. 'All this fuss tonight for tossing a stick. When a Kombo man won the medal at 800m a few years ago...greeted with bombproof wall of indifference.'

Hanili flicked her thumb with her elegant forefinger. 'Yes, but a dirt poor island punching above its weight in the world of athletics is worth celebrating,' she said. Dele stole a glance at Keli, but the little girl, agog at Ami's trackside "warm down", seemed oblivious to the discussion.

'Poor countries can compete in these one – dimensional sports, throwing, running jumping, because…the laws of nature are blind to race…,' said Ambasi.

'The laws of nature are blind to race, but the laws of humans are not, is that because it is in our nature?' said Dele.

Hanili shook her head. 'Law should be blind.'

'In theory,' said Dele.

Hanili hiccupped, flicked her thumb with her fingers. 'What do you think, pastor?' she said.

'Evil is our second skin, how do we shed it?' said Ambasi. The table fell quiet.

On the track the white flag for a legal jump went up for Busi, the veteran female athlete.

'Can I go for Ami's autograph?' said Keli.

'Take my phone, call Dele if you need anything,' said Hanili.

Ambasi pointed to the bottle of white wine. 'Tell me when,' said Dele as she poured him a drink. Sandman appeared on the big screen in the dining hall. Dele sat down and popped a piece of yam into her mouth. It tasted sweet with a bitter and salty aftertaste.

'I just want to run him through with a sword laced with Polonium,' said Dele.

'What good will that do, in theory or practice? It's your dad we want to-' said Hanili.

'I have a Ghanaian classmate. His widowed mother rang him from home because some man refused to pay the rent. Mama had sued the tenant and won. Still he wouldn't pay. Tenant is thriving, mama is wasting away. What did my friend do? Sue again? No way, Jose. He got his mates to drag the tenant into the square, had his pants off, pulled his you know what hairs out one at a time…yes, in central Accra. Do you think that man will default again?' said Dele.

'Good attempt, Traytop, but this friend's mother went to court first. Therefore, no matter how crude, what he did was law enforcement. You were talking about revenge,' said Ambasi.

'I agree with pastor,' said Hanili

'Law enforcement in Roko? Where the law is bent and the bench is bent, and even the air we breathe we take in with large sniffs of smoke and salt?' said Dele.

'So you all surround Sandman. Each of you with a sword. You shout go, you plunge, but one of you could get hurt, and if another sword kills him before yours will you feel avenged?' said Hanili.

'Ask not what revenge will do for you but what you will do for revenge,' said Dele. 'When you slap a mosquito you are not thinking what the slap is doing for you, but what it does to the mosquito. It will not bite you or anyone else again. Why? Because it's effing dead.' The back of her neck itched.

'Slapping a mosquito is a one on one. Human revenge is more complex,' said Hanili.

A thought occurred to Dele. 'What if I managed to trap Sandman with his own bent rule of law?' she said.

'The man's untouchable,' said Ambasi.

A retort stuck in Dele's throat. She rolled the dregs of wine in her glass. Hanili squeezed Dele's wrist. 'I'm off to powder my nose. Keli…coming?' she said. Keli trotted after Hanili and they disappeared down a corridor.

'Your friend is very gifted,' said Ambasi.

Dele nodded. 'I know…it's so unfair.'

'Can you afford this… ?' He waved a small circle in the air as he sought the right words. '…this liaison could be…awkward. Don't you think her a little…should I say…reckless? In the present climate…we are not ready for her brand of life,' said Ambasi.

Hanili's phone rattled across the table.

'Let me,' said Dele, but Ambasi shook his head and wouldn't hand the phone over. 'I'm not stupid…ah, got it,' he said with a grunt, raising the phone to his ear. 'Who is it?' he said. 'Ah, Hanili. She has gone to use the facilities.' He sounded as if he was talking to a tax officer. 'Of course…your number will show on her log. I'll make sure she returns the call,' he said. He stared at the phone as he put it down on the table, nudging it away behind an empty plate, as if he had just seen his wraith.

'Who was it?' said Dele.

'Insurance scammer I think,' he said. Dele noticed a slight catch in his voice. 'You're sure it wasn't-'

Keli skipped back to the table to show off her idol's autograph, his name, "Ami", in a neat hand. 'Can I take your photo as well?' she said. Ambasi posed. 'With aunty Hanili as well?' said Keli.

Hanili shuffled in closer to Ambasi and put her arms around his shoulders. Their smiles looked forced, like that of an estranged couple posing for the sake of the children. Dele wished Keli would hurry up with the photograph. Her clenched bum was beginning to hurt.

'Ready?' said Keli and clicked the button. 'Urgh, wait, it didn't flash.' A man in pursuit of a young woman in a flowing cobalt blue frock bumped into Ambasi's elbow, making him spill drink into Hanili's lap. 'I'm so sorry,' said Ambasi.

'The tyranny of emperor testosterone,' said Hanili, brushing herself down.

The flash went off. Dele stood her clenched buttocks down.

Ambasi got out of his chair and waved a tired hand. 'Hanili, you had a phone call, but got to go. Lovely evening. Nice meeting you. You've given me new ideas for a sermon or two. And Keli.'

Keli snapped up in her chair, chirruped. 'Yes pastor.'

'Ever need any help, anything, you know where to come,' said Ambasi. 'And Traytop…we did not quite finish our discussion.' He gave another tired wave. A wistful look clouded his face.

SEVEN

Dele knocked. Antikath opened the door and her eyes glittered with joy. She was wearing a brown top over a green, ankle-length skirt. 'Welcome my pet, welcome, where did you meet pastor?' she said. She gave Dele a long, warm hug.

'I was on my way back from a seminar. Thought I'd drop in to see pastor at table tennis because he looked a bit tired last week,' said Dele. A smell of pepper, fish, prawns and a low hubbub from the kitchen filled the living room.

'Traytop, I'll shower. Should we eat on the roof, like the old days?' said Ambasi, closing the door and Dele squeezed past a sofa out on to the balcony. 'Nice, this velvety texture and shade of blue,' she said, of the new balcony curtains. Her eyes scanned the room; the same tired light fittings on the wall and the 'grandfather' kerosene cooker on a table under a sooty ceiling in the alcove; and Ambasi's portraits on the walls.

'Pastor wouldn't let me touch your room. It's just the way you left it. Go and see. Your netball team photo is still on the wall and that green book of yours is now under a spider's web as big as a farmer's basket,' said Antikath.

The softy. Dele dragged the door closed. 'Smells as if it's going to rain...we'll have to eat here,' she said and, like a gymnast on the pummel horse, she leapt over the back of a sofa to land on a cushion. She did not want to be grilled by Ambasi alone on the flat rooftop before he gave her a cheque. 'Anyway, I haven't seen Antikath for ages,' said Dele.

'That's the aid worker's doing,' said Ambasi as he disappeared down the corridor.

You mean Hanili.

Ambasi returned fifteen minutes later in a light brown shirt and a baggy dark pair of trousers.

'Who is having what?' said Antikath. She hovered over the dining table, juggling two plates, plonked them down with a flourish and a pout. Dele got off the sofa and took her place opposite Ambasi, with her back to the main door.

'Is this the bush meat dish I like?' said Dele, her long legs banging under the table.

Antikath nodded. Her shadow slid off the table as she sat down. 'Dele, bad university food is making your eye hide inside your head. Today pastor, see how my stew makes Dele eyes dance about.'

'That's because they're trying to escape the fire burning in her mouth. Her tongue is hanging out as well,' said Ambasi with a chuckle.

And my nose is dripping. 'I thought he was going to hit you out there,' said Dele, wiping her nose with a tissue paper.

Ambasi ducked an imaginary blow. 'Just like the old days, Traytop. Ali-Foreman fight. Rope a dope then sucker punch.'

'Pastor is it not time to retire from these…tricks?' said Antikath, gesturing with a wing of fried chicken.

'Traytop was knocking up with Jaygrala when that fool got out of a taxi. You could tell they were Niroko,' said Ambasi.

'The basket mouths and their usual effrontery of the first degree. I hope you taught them a lesson,' said Antikath.

'Niroko pride is a particularly capricious companion. Traytop pulled it off by the edge of her pimpled bat. I thought we were gone,' said Ambasi.

'It was your business school pep talk - it is a bat not a cutlass – that gave me a boost,' said Dele.

They laughed.

'Oh, smells super,' said Dele as Antikath opened a steaming bowl of giant prawns.

'Anything could have happened. What if your bogus policemen, Hairy and Baldy, had not jumped over the wall to arrest them?' said Antikath.

'But they did, with impeccable timing, like cartoon heroes. And as one of the men ran off grateful not to be detained for disturbing the peace, he tripped over the base of that electric pylon and cut his arm on a broken bottle. I affected agency with a glare… it's good for business…see what pastor did to that man…he didn't even have to touch him they will say,' said Ambasi with a grin. 'Traytop, drink up,' he said. Antikath swivelled to lift a bowl of fruit out of the fridge.

'To the three musketeers.' A can of beer and two glasses clinked in a toast.

And to Mum and Dad. 'Absent friends,' said Dele, raising her glass again but Ambasi lowered his can before the clink and tapped his lips with steepled hands. For a beat or two an awkward silence followed.

Antikath turned to Dele. 'Do you want more water?' she said and leaned over to open the fridge.

Dele shook her head. 'Gee, as Hanili would say…almost forgot. The other night I saw this young girl. The nurse said it was her daughter and she'd sneaked out to a party. Didn't sound right to me. Am I putting too many twos together?'

'You don't have to be a barber to cut hair. You saw what you saw,' said Ambasi. 'But keep your nose clean. Your trigger happy Dean is waiting to pounce,' he said as the clock struck the hour.

'Stay the night. I can make your bed before I go to late service,' said Antikath.

Ambasi put his can of beer down on the table, waited for Antikath to leave for the kitchen. 'Something's been troubling me,' he said, fanning the leaves of his cheque book.

'It's Hanili isn't it?' Dele said.

'The association could end your career,' said Ambasi, with a half blink of his bad eye.

'I don't deserve to be happy?' she said.

'Verily Verity. The blind pursuit of happiness drowns many in the well of discontent.'

Dele threw her napkin down and leapt off her seat. 'But-'

Ambasi closed the cheque book. 'Yours is no ordinary friendship and it could ruin you. This is not London. So why should I support it?' he said, slamming the cheque book down. His good right eye narrowed to a slit. They heard a knock at the door and Hanili walked in.

'Hi, pastor, Antikath I presume.' Hanili shook Antikath's hand. 'Dele, where've you been? Your driving lesson,' she said.

***

On the hospital perimeter road an ambulance tore past, blinding Dele in its headlights and making her stall "The Pleb bus." She tapped her head against the steering wheel in frustration. 'I'll never do this,' she said.

'Calm down, it's dark, no one can see you,' said Hanili.

'Except you,' said Dele. The wipers flicked on, squeaking against the misty windscreen like jesting clowns. 'What have I done wrong now?' said Dele.

Hanili leaned over to flick the stalk switch down. 'You haven't said a word since we left Ambasi's, except bark.'

'Just tired, it's not a crime.'

'Biting my head off is. Are you hungry?' said Hanili.

'If you want a take away, why don't you just say so?' said Dele. *What am I going to do for food?* She turned the key in the ignition and revved up. The car lunged out of a pothole, headed straight for a parked car. Hanili tugged the steering right. They missed and Dele drove into a car park beside the nurses' block.

'The clutch has got a fever, the engine is burning up and the exhaust smells foul but what the hell it's only Verity wrestling her future at the wheel,' said Dele. *Yourlot said I wouldn't amount to anything.*

A white truck rumbled in and splashed into a puddle. Dele grappled with the window winder, but too late. 'Brilliant,' she said, flicking mud off her forehead. *How am I going to fund the rest of the term?*

'Not exactly…it's mud,' said Hanili. 'Sorry,' she said when she saw Dele's face.

'When did that…that boy learn how to drive…oh, can't see, where's the wiper switch again?' said Dele. She pressed a button and the hazard lights came on, then the wipers. 'Sorry, should we try next week. I'm…knackered…is that how you say it?'

'Cream crackered in cockney rhyming slang,' said Hanili. Dele managed a smile.

She reversed into a space next to an abandoned ambulance. The news came on. Babubacka had been nominated as presidential candidate to both main political parties.

'The men in khaki rule forever…khakicracy,' said Dele, with venom.

'A unique Roko form of *kakicracy*,' said Hanili.

'Power without steering,' said Dele, slapping the radio quiet.

Hanili averted her gaze and wrung her hands in her lap.

'What's wrong?' said Dele.

'Er, my mum, er, rang the other day. I've got to go away. I mean away away…England. Dad needs an op and Mum's not coping.'

'You'll be back soon though,' said Dele, trying to ignore the anxious whirring in her head.

'Depends,' said Hanili.

The ugly duckling's fucking luck strikes again.

EIGHT

Dele saw Hanili off at the airport. She cried most of the way home, her head turned into the window shine on the bus and her face hidden behind a fist. She spent days listening to Ennio Morricone's score to Once Upon a Time in the West in her room or just staring blindly out of her balcony.

'Parrot, your mate has flown; is that why you look for a spare bird in the bush from your balcony?' said Georgina one evening.

'It's my marathon bird watch, for charity. I'd explain what that was but I can't spare the breath,' said Dele. She went back inside, the sound of the breeze chuckling through the bushes near where she played "spot the psychopath" with Hanili dragging brambles through her chest. *Hanili's gone. Was Yourlot right? Am I worthless?* Two weeks passed without word from Hanili. Dele was broke. Hunger raked her stomach, but she would not beg Ambasi. What right did he have to tell her whom to fall for? She couldn't even explain it herself. One evening, after a stale slice of bread washed down with a litre of water, she drank gallons of water to give her trips to the toilet to look forward to, Dele was standing on her balcony when she saw a white car drive past. It looked like Hanili's Pleb Bus. *What if that was Hanili and she came back to find me like this? What will Dad think of me?* thought Dele, with a shiver of shame and self-reproach. She peeled off her sticky nightshirt, had a cold shower, got dressed, sat down at her desk and started to draw.

First she sketched Hanili as she remembered her at the Festival, Alice band and all, one arm in the air the other holding a microphone, but gave up that effort because her friend looked too remote. She tore the drawing up and started another of Hanili sitting next to her on a wooden bench in the back of the open-air Jeba cinema: its roof had blown off that night. Dele smiled to herself. They had seen *Once upon a time in the West* together for the first time that night.

'I wonder how Harmonica felt afterwards,' Hanili had said, her eyes wide, bright, and lips forming a wistful smile.

'Never thought of that, just feels good seeing Frank get what's coming,' said Dele.

'Vicarious vengeance at the movies is a free lunch, like a stolen glance at a stranger's watch or newspaper. As Ambasi would say, real life equation is not so simple, sinner and the sinned against both pay a price…the equation can never balance, no matter what,' said Hanili.

'It's only a movie, Hanili,' said Dele.

They had gone on about the film over dinner, then got back on to the subject of her dad and Sandman. 'All I want is to find out what's happened to Dad, so I can say finito, is that too much to ask?' said Dele.

Real life crashed in with the slam of an outside door. Dele heard footsteps, laughter, and pious clinical banter as her mates returned from the day's teaching rounds. Dele locked her door, sharpened her pencil and returned to her drawing. She gave the corner of Hanili's eye a steeper slant. Then she sat rocking from side to side in her bed and listened to the hiss and gurgling crackle of the paper under her palm as she rubbed the drawing over her heart. How, she wondered, had she come to move up this queue for same-sex attraction? Had she started off on the line to so-called normality and been torn off it in the camp by Sandman, and was it the fear of a repeat or the wish to bury his memory that drove her to Hanili; or had she always stood on this narrower, shorter, queue and known it, even as a little girl fumbling with Koseri on Nigeria Street? Dele closed her eyes, lost in her thoughts. *Why do I keep asking myself questions to which I can never know the answer?* she asked herself. Then she smiled to herself as though she found the new thought itself comforting. *Asking myself why I ask myself such questions…is this what it means to be a fucking fucked up human being?*

***

Franko in the 4th year called. He missed her scolding he said and wanted her to lunch with him in the cafeteria. They met outside the sliding doors to the canteen, Dele grimacing as her long-term unemployed stomach juices rumbled, sprucing themselves up, it seemed, in anticipation of rare and august visitors. Beyond the check-out counter rang laughter from lucky throats and bellies. Franko placed a packet of biscuits on his tray.

'I thought you liked these oatmeal ones?' he said, shoving his tray along the rails.

Dele shook her head. 'Not anymore.' She shoved her empty tray on, wondering how to tell Franko that she could not afford lunch.

Franko swept her with a puzzled glance. Then as he made way for a drinks trolley he must have guessed the truth. 'Why don't you let me pay? To thank you for the boot up my Gluteus Maximus,' said Franko.

'Your Distinction in Pharmacology was all your own hard work. All I did was give you a pep talk. But we can get past checkout,' said Dele, nodding round the corner.

The queue moved on. For the plan to work Dele had to keep her place just behind Franko. She ladled a heap of boiled rice on to her plate. 'Don't go too fast, Franko. You go past check-out first, as if you forgot to give him your ticket. When checkout turns to ask you for the ticket, you say sorry you forgot and turn back to give it to him and while he's looking your way I'll slap…put my hand on the pile of old tickets on his table and walk past as if I've paid…bluff my way, yes?' said Dele.

'So you don't want my money?' He sounded hurt. His Dad owned oil concessions in Gabon and he had overheard Dele denouncing the meteoric rise of the oligarchs.

'You think I'm a charity case?' said Dele.

'I'm not saying that but…remember, pride comes before a ketoacidosis,' said Franko. He tapped Dele on the shoulder with an air of suppressed exasperation. 'I'm ready, as long as it's not…him at the till,' he said.

Ketoacidosis? Can he smell my starvation breath? Dele inched towards the checkout, her stomach stabbed by hunger. Beyond the checkout counter sat the lucky ones with their plates of steaming rice and beans, boiled yams and sweet potatoes. She rounded the bend, looked up and saw Jabu. Her stomach sagged. *Gendarme* Jabu, senior cook, had telescopic vision, arms as long as a famous brand of toilet paper and more foresight than the IMF. A few days earlier Jabu had stared Dele down, until, with an impatient queue building up behind her, she had had to abandon her tray and flee.

The queue pressed forward. Jabu leaned back in his high chair, fixed his knowing eyes on Dele and hung his long fingers out for the tickets.

'It's Jabu,' said Franko and Dele almost together.

'Old news,' said Dele. She dropped out of the queue and watched her rudderless tray, stewed rice and all, glide down the rails. Grinning, Jabu put Dele's tray aside, knifed the leg of chicken and thrust it into his mouth, each roll of his jaw pounding a fork harder into Dele's guts. Dele wobbled off to the conveyor belt in the canteen to save a discarded banana before it disappeared down the hatch.

'And are you on a diet?' said Sara, a research nurse, as Dele sat down at the table.

'Can't get the anti-oxidants anywhere else these days,' Dele said, sprinkling a tablespoon of salt over the rotting banana to douse its smell and taste. Sara gathered two great box files and made to leave. Dele raised a hand to stop her.

Sara paused. 'Everyone, secretary says you are looking for me. Stalker are you?' she said.

'Has Medical Records moved?' said Dele, folding the empty banana skin on to Sara's tray.

Sara nodded. 'To an annexe, Dada is renovating the old Medical Records…they say with a grant from UNICEF.'

Does Dada know about the little party girl? Dele nodded to Franko as they walked past his table.

'Parrot, I've kept some for you,' he said, holding up a red packet of nuts.

'Thanks, you're my hero,' said Dele.

'You don't need a diet, parrot, you must be a size 10,' said Sara.

Believe me this skinny catwalk figure is not by choice.

Outside, milky rays of sunshine peeped through a clump of doughy clouds. Dele and Sara stepped off the pavement to allow a wheelchair user past.

'You know Dada?' said Dele, trying to keep up with Sara. With legs so weak, the pavement felt like sticky rubber.

'The big mouth surgeon? Can't stand the man,' said Sara. 'One time a shaky surgeon with one *jarara* motor, the next minute he and Obinda are like Jay-Z and Beyonce.' It started to drizzle. Sara quickened her pace. Dele struggled to keep up.

'The man cannot connect a hammer, a head and a headache. So how can he be Academic leader? And did you know that he is in-law of that chicken face minister?' said Sara.

Sandman.

'Files are getting wet,' said Sara, pressing on up the slope in the drizzle. 'From day one, all Dada wants from HealthSmart are data on length of stay, expected and actual days of discharge. I can tell horse manure from dog shit. Excuse my gutter speak,' said Sara. She pointed at the carpark. 'Is that not where your friend gave you driving lessons? I've not seen her lately,' she said.

'I need to see Diana in HR, for a job,' said Dele.

Sara let Dele into a ground floor office. 'Diana no longer works here,' she said, closing the door on the pitter patter of rain. 'She had bargy bargy with Dada's wife, Obinda, over recruitment. Obinda filled the posts with her mates and in-laws. Diana got fed up. We go back to elementary one. She has a big mouth. A bit like yours if I can say so-'

'Use it or lose it, I say,' said Dele.

Sara smiled. 'Diana tells her that whatever funny business she is involved in with her husband will come out one day. Obinda reports her to Head of Service for insubordination. HOS is in minister's back pocket, the same minister who wangled UNICEF grant for Dada in the first place. Now Diana has no job, her husband is not well,' said Sara, shaking her head as she put a file away.

Dele tried to make sense of Sara's story - the girl in the party dress, Dada and the length of stay data, his conversion of Medical Records to a rehabilitation ward, UNICEF grant and the minister - but hunger befuddled her. She looked at her watch. *Shit, I'm going to be late for revision.*

***

The exams arrived too soon. Dele had still not found a job. Feeling awkward and overdressed in a dark mid-calf length skirt and a black pair of court shoes, Dele shoved her last minute revision back into a green folder and set off for the exam. It had stopped raining and the air smelled of wet sand and grass. Gleaming in the wet, the main block looked even more like a cake baked by bickering chefs. The limestone ground floor, with its four-column portico, multipane double hung windows and green shutters, leaned a little to the right, just below the left-leaning red-brick first floor where the exam was held.

Dele's pale blue blouse had two new smudges down one side. *Brilliant.*

To get into the exam mood, Dele played "spot the diagnoses" as she hurried up the ramp. An old man in an oversized coat lifted his torn boot high into the air and slapped its sole down on the ground with a thud. *Foot drop.* A backfiring exhaust: *dysentery, amoebic, or was it cholera, no amoebic, choleric diarrhoea ran like a tap.* The pretty woman posing with a steaming cup of cocoa on the large yellow billboard opposite the porter's lodge had a goitre. *Perhaps I've still got it.* At the reception desk she found Emile, son of the missing Tantalum millionaire, trembling, sweat dripping from the end of his nose. He was repeating the exam and if his nerve failed again he was out. *Good luck Emile.*

For the exam Ward B4 had been divided into 12 cubicles or stations. Professor Krimu, a round-faced Siroko man with short brown hair, set some green size A4 papers down on a chair near the entrance. His companion, Professor Agosi, nodded at the patient in Cubicle 2 at the far end. 'You are late young woman, and you have missed the first station. I'm sure the Urology patients won't hold it against you, unless they have been holding it in,' he said. His knobbly Adam's Apple bobbed up.

'It's five to four, sir,' said Dele.

'Check, you were due at 3.45.' Dele fished the schedule out of her pocket. With her vision blurred by hunger, she had read her name against the wrong column. 'Sorry, my mistake, sir,' she said.

Professor Agosi showed Dele to the cubicle. 'Catch your breath young lady and please examine your patient's legs,' he said.

'Legs sir?' said Dele, her mouth as dry as a Saharan windsock.

'Yes, lower extremities, the bit between the floor and the pelvis.' The examiners exchanged glances.

'Legs, legs,' said Dele. The patient pulled his trousers down. Dele crouched as she approached, to give the impression of competence. *What do I do? Should I draw the curtains?* Was this station a test of empathy and consideration for the patient or of pure clinical acumen? She guessed the former. Professor Krimu jerked his head back, holding on to his pince-nez as Dele drew the flowered curtains past with a flourish. The curtain got stuck, resisted further frantic tugs and left a gap through which the whole world could see the patient's hydrocele, a swelling of his scrotum, hanging down to his knees. Dele smelled urine.

'My name is Dele Verity, may I have the privilege of examining your lower extremities, sir.' *That "sir" sounds sweet.*

'I'm a woman,' said the patient.

Dele grunted. *I may be hungry and under rehearsed but I know bollocks when I see them.*

'You have one minute,' said Professor Agosi.

Dele smiled and nodded in the vague direction of the examiner's voice. Inspect first. But what for? She looked without seeing anything of note: asymmetry no, rash no, oedema no, missing digits no, but she had forgotten the rest. The exam buzzer went off. *Already?*

'Time's up,' said Professor Krimu, scratching his palm with a sheet of paper.

The next patient, a plump, middle-aged woman of Asian descent stood behind a desk in Cubicle 8, halfway up the room. She had droopy eyelids and downy hair on her cheeks. Professor handed Dele a card instructing her to ask the patient about abdominal pain.

Dele sat down. 'Good afternoon ma'am,' she said. *I am sure you are a woman.* 'May I ask you some questions about your pain?'

'It's not a pain, it's an ache,' said the patient.

Of course it is a pain. It says so on this card. The inside of Dele's head sloshed like a waterbed. She looked at Professor Krimu for support but the professor gave his check-board a quizzical look, then Dele, then the patient. The patient folded her bright red velvet skirt under her and sat down.

'You don't mind if I sit down too?' said Dele.

From Professor Agosi came a rustle of paper and a rasping sigh. The patient pointed with her eyes at something to Dele's left. Sensing that the patient was trying to help her, but not knowing how, Dele reached out for the patella hammer to buy time. But she missed. The hammer fell off the desk, landed on its rubber end, bounced off the floor and the leg of a chair before rolling under a bed. Dele crept under the bed. An examiner's chuckle echoed from the other end of the hall. The buzzer went off. The end. Professors Krimu and Agosi lined up, bowed low, nodding their mocking visages like model railway signals. Dele bumped into a tea lady's trolley, sprinkling granulated sugar over the sandwiches. 'Oh. No sugar,' said the tea lady. 'No it's shit,' said Dele. She knew she had failed. *Was Yourlot right? Am I going to the gutter?*

'Take this,' said Emilio outside the hall. 'I saw you in the canteen,' he said, handing Dele a few Roko notes. 'Fifty. Not much.'

'You're sure about this? You have a better chance of being paid back by wood chippings,' said Dele.

'It's of more use to you.'

'How did yours go?' said Dele, thrusting the notes into a skirt pocket.

Emile walked away. Dele counted the notes again. She needed four hundred Roko more before the end of the week or she could say bye-bye to medical school. Sandman would have won and got away with everything. So would Yourlot. She called Sara again. 'I'm in the land of desperandinhos, give me anything,' said Dele.

'Heard of Abha?' said Sara.

'The Abattoir?'

NINE

Abha Community Hospital, known as the "Abattoir", sat in a sandy valley two hundred miles from Sankara. Everything in the claustrophobic staff room, the walls, the aprons hanging on the wall, the table-legs, gleamed with sweat, or steam.

Special Matron Danankara got out of a low armless chair. Oh...that.' She followed Dele's glance to the steel kettle that stood on a stool next to what looked more like a plastic bread bin than a medical device. 'That is the incubator. We boil kettle to keep it humid and for tea,' she said. 'But I hope you brought your own drink Miss Verity. Because you are medical student don't expect us to treat you like Tantalum shines from your backside,' said Matron, adjusting her belt.

'Thank you ma'am,' said Dele.

Matron cleared her throat for her Friday weekend shift pep talk. 'You may have read WHO report about South Roko,' she said, directing her words at Dele. 'I quote "two out of ten women who leave home in hope to put to bed do not return from that confinement." A side-long glance from Matron shot two nurses off their loll against the wall. 'But our figures are much better here. Why?'

Creative discounting.

'We are the A team,' said a nurse.

'We prioritise,' said Matron, looking askance at the nurse.

A squat, portly middle-aged woman with a small head crowned by a spindly tuft, Matron Danankara had a red belt that just about reached round her brown uniform. She turned to Dele again. 'Leave the singletons to the midwifery students, you deal with the multiparas. If you are caught between the two spill the wine but don't break the keg. Men can always pour in new wine. You get me?'

'Yes ma'am,' said Dele. *If the child dies the woman can always get pregnant again.*

157

'You get paid on Monday morning. In Roko currency, not the internal market Hakas made up by the minister. But we deduct for mistakes. Shake my hand if you agree with our terms and conditions, yes, no?' said Matron.

Dele shook the Matron's hand. 'I agree, but could I end up owing you money?' she said almost staggering back from another lungful of Matron's perfume, which smelled like a mix of rotting orange and PVA glue.

The Special Matron's piercing glance brooked no further questions. She stepped over to the whistling kettle. 'Go on, it's six sharp. Start on Labour ward,' she said, shaking coffee into what looked like a vase, but was her a mug.

Dele's phone warbled. She peeped at the message from Franko and quaked with shock. Emile, dead. Overdose. *Poor Emile. They found his missing Dad dead in the gutter.* Dele tucked the phone back into her green hospital togs.

'Go, now' said Matron. She ushered them all out and shut the door no doubt to resume her evening beverage. A nurse led Dele through a dank, gloomy corridor in which patients sat leaning against the peeling walls, looking too weak to crush a grape, their faces as dry and as long as garden benches.

'They are pissing shit or shitting piss because the sun set twice on their labour and their undercarriage cannot take it,' said the nurse.

'Could be you,' said Dele.

'God forbid,' said the nurse.

Labour ward Two, lit by a palpitating light bulb, had ten beds arranged in two rows of five. The patients looked like pregnant seahorses. They lay three to a bed, diagonally across bare, plastic-covered mattresses, their globular bellies facing the door. 'You are not fully dilated. I'll be back, I am showing this doctor to the annexe,' said the nurse. The patients replied with desultory nods.

In the small dim side-room, Dele found two ashen women, groaning and rolling around on their beds. *One bed each. It must be serious.* Dele checked her handbook, donned a glove over her left hand and had a fumble inside. 'You are ready to push,' she said. The baby arrived twenty minutes later. Dele welled up as she gave the little bundle to the exhausted mother. Then as she sat down to wait for the afterbirth she heard scuttling in the eaves over the sound of the whimpering child. Dele turned round. Moments later a rat the size of a puppy, dropped through a hole in the ceiling.

'Shoo,' said Dele. The rat stopped a bed's length away. Dele threw an empty packet of cigarettes at it, but the rat did not retreat. It seemed to duck, watch the missile sail over its head and come back up grinning, like a superior pugilist in the ring. Dismay, disgust and fear crawled up the hair on the back of Dele's neck as the rat crept closer, whiskers twitching, glinting eyes fixed on the glistening placenta cruising out between the mother's trembling thighs. Dele thought of throwing the rat the emerging afterbirth, so ravenous did the rodent look that she thought it might jump on the baby or snap her own toes off instead.

'Come, we have some third degree tear upstairs,' said a nurse at the door. Dele flicked the cold sweat off her brow and put the pair of forceps she was about to launch back in the bowl. 'But I haven't finished this delivery and look at the rat.'

'You want to get paid or what?' said the nurse.

'Who cares, the need of this hungry rat is greater than mine,' said Dele, chucking her gloves into a bowl.

'I don't see any rat, it is a shadow of the toy in the cot maybe. I think you are seeing things,' said the nurse.

'I'm sure...'

Dele hurried after her, still wondering whether she had indeed been dreaming. The nurse showed her to a trolley in an alleyway – minor ops.

'Ten Roko per patient and I will inspect before I sign you off for your money,' said the nurse. Water dripped down the wall and pooled under a commode.

Dele got to work, dragging and pushing frayed sutures and rusting needles as blunt as a fist through the ragged perineal tears. 'Water, water. I need water. Nothing here to drink but drips from the ceiling…and blood,' she said to no one in particular. A clock somewhere down the corridor chimed for six o'clock and Dele heard the patients stir from their beds for Sunday prayers. *One hundred and fifty Roko, but how much do I owe for breakages?*

A nurse walked in. 'Neonatal ward. The cannula tissued,' she said. *Tissued.* The word sounded like a thunder clap. 'I spent hours getting it in. *For only five Roko.* What happened?' said Dele.

'It tissued.' The nurse clucked and turned away.

One hour later, with the anxious mother beginning to fret, Dele was still trying to find a tiny vein in a baby no bigger than a man's fist. She tried first with her left hand then with her right but the little one, flitting in and out of conscious, its eyes sunken deep in orbits set in a head the shape of Africa, bounced around its cot, rigid and convulsing with Tetanus from the dirt sucked up by its cord cut by the juju man with a broken bottle or with a blade dipped in hot manure. *I've got to do this or she's on the short queue to misery.* Dele trembled almost as much as the child.

'Ah, got it,' she said. She looked at her watch. An hour had passed in what she thought was no longer than twenty minutes. *Time rolls faster under pressure.*

'You could have thrown the saline into the peritoneum,' said the nurse, a note of exasperation in her voice.

'Don't you ever say thanks?' said Dele, ripping her glove off. Just then a woman limped in with her hands between her legs. 'Thank you doctor,' she said, swinging her wobbly legs on to the couch. 'Two days I have wait.'

Dele felt a crunch, like a cracked eggshell, in her head. 'Finished,' she said, slamming her glove into the waste bin.

'God bless you,' said the woman, pleading with her eyes.

'How many children do you have?' said Dele. 'Fourteen, but only six remain,' said the woman. She smiled with pride, baring the one tooth and a bit left in the front of her mouth. *This is Sandman's doing. His internal market with his useless Haka currency and the WHO family planning unit's hard currency in his pocket.* The nurse brought Dele a pair of gloves.

'New, it's my lucky day,' said Dele, tearing the packet open.

'Thank you doctor, God bless,' said the woman fifteen minutes later.

Hoping the repair would withstand the first test, which would come when her patient got down to use the toilet, Dele risked a sly glance at the table clock. *Twenty more hours in this place. Jesus wept.* She looked at her time-sheet. *Two hundred and four Roko. Gross.* Dele lumbered back upstairs, her knees grating as if lined with sand.

Back on the ward one of the pregnant seahorses had been moved to the side-room. She soon delivered a baby girl. Six pounds. Dele sighed. *No perineal tears, so I get twenty Roko?* She checked the tariff in her pocket, straightened up and almost lost her footing because the frightened eyes she saw staring at her from the other trolley belonged, she was sure, to the so-called errant schoolgirl she had met that night outside the Medical Records department in the hospital.

'What are you doing here?' *Rephrase that, stupid.* Where's your mama?' said Dele.

The girl shook her head and blinked. She shuddered and pulled her knees up tighter against her chest, her plain white gown trailing over the edge of the trolley like a wedding dress. 'Mama no dey,' she said.

'I saw you at the hospital…in the night, you went to a party?'

The girl's big eyes searched Dele's face. A tear burst on to her plump cheek.

Dele tried a reassuring smile. 'Who brought you here?' said Dele. A baby's cry drowned out the girl's reply.

'She's only a pickin herself,' said the new mother, shaking her head.

'Obviously not everyone agrees,' said Dele. 'Have you had operation inside…you know?' she said to the girl.

'Two times,' she said.

The new mother gasped.

'This time or before?' said Dele. The girl did not reply. 'What sort of operation?'

'Same last time…four months,' she said, her smooth face filmed with sweat. 'They buy us new dress and send us out to birthday party to make us happy but…' Her voice cracked. She closed her eyes and rested her forehead on the wall as if succour came from bare bricks. Her fuzzy shadow flickered around her in the lantern light.

A man brushed past Dele. 'Are you ready?' he said to the girl.

'Who are you?' said Dele.

'Duty doctor, rehabilitation,' said the man. He had a long face, a chin studded with moles and small, flinty eyes.

'Patch her up, repackage her, and recycle. Is that it?' said Dele.

The girl slipped off the trolley and on to her feet. 'My mama and papa and my sister don die, I had nowhere,' she said. She shuffled to the bathroom. The sight of the oval wet patch on the back of the girl's gown swung steel balls of anger round inside Dele's head.

***

She submitted her time-sheet at six o'clock on Monday morning, the end of the shift. Matron paid her one hundred and fifty Roko net: ninety eight Roko deducted for breakages, time spent on the tissued drip, for opening a set of brand new instruments and using them only once; and other incidentals. Dele put the cheque away. Better than a slap in the face by a rodent's tail, but still three hundred Roko away from what she needed to keep her in college.

TEN

The lecturer stopped for a sip of water. 'Did he say muscular or corpuscles?' Dele said with a long yawn. Two consecutive weekend shifts at the Abattoir seemed to have crammed her head with screeching rodents. Sitting high up at the back of the lecture hall, she lifted her chin out of her hands, rubbed her eyes and tried to wrap her mind round the topic, but the picture of the little girl in Abha hospital kept breaking in.

'I didn't hear him either,' said her classmate. He peeped at Dele's scanty notes and gave her a smug grin.

The lecture ended. 'Parrot are you not coming for practical?' said the ever conscientious Elati. 'Parrot is not serious,' scoffed another classmate. Dele did not reply. She had an idea and scribbled *officer's mess, the little girls, UN, Dada, Sandman, rehabilitation, connected?* into her notebook, then packed her bag and headed for the main hospital block. *Why didn't I think of Baba Funi before?* Nothing, prosaic or profound, escaped *his* bespoke security cameras.

An ambulance arrived outside the hospital, siren blaring, a tongue of dazzling sunlight reflected on its roof. When the hospital doors swung open for the patient Dele caught sight of Baba Funi, the Deputy Head Porter at Main Reception.

'Hey Baba Funi, how are you?' she said, trying to sound jolly. They shook hands over the counter.

'We cope,' he said. Well over six feet tall, bald but for a narrow strip of jet black hair over each ear, deep-set eyes and a ragged tribal mark extending from his left ear to the point of his chin. 'What brings you over here during lecture time? I owing you?' he said. His globular belly wobbling with his chuckles. "Sankara, city of brilliant excellence" played in the back room.

'Baba Funi. I need your help. You are like papa and mama for me. I see bad things but God sees everything,' said Dele adopting Ambasi's pious tone. 'And in my time we did not have good care like these young girls have now.'

A veil dropped over Baba Funi's face. 'Yes…I know that,' he said, fingering the hospital logo on his shirt. 'Things have moved on, the country is more secure,' he said. A driver leaned across him for a bunch of keys.

'Do your men help with moving rehab patients? One of my patients ran away and her mama said one of your people brought her back.' said Dele.

Baba Funi shook his great head. 'My men are not for that. Yes, we used to help with the Americans. When that Siroko man Jofol Raisis went to Princeton University in America and he graduate in sums come louder degree in Maths, many black American women, came here for South Roko sperm. Sandman opened a bank or clinic here in Sankara. The only extra work my men have done is to take Sandman's clients from the airport.'

"Sums come louder? Oh, you mean Summa Cum Laude. Latin, Baba Funi. So you don't have anything to do with the rehab of camp girls?' said Dele

'When we were called HOSS, Hospital of South Sankara, we did all the portering and security work. But minister brought in his conglomerate, changed our name and Dada got money from abroad, UN.

'The surgeon?' said Dele, trying to hide her surprise.

Baba Funi nodded. 'He invited another subcontractor with their own doctors and nurses. But it doesn't concern me anymore, they should call us Healths *Market*. It's all about business.' He shrugged his huge frame. 'Expect my bill for this,' he said with a chuckle and disappeared into the back room. *Dada has to be involved with the girls and so must Sandman.* Dele dragged herself back to her room, said a prayer for her missing Dad and, dead beat, she fell asleep with a textbook on her chest.

***

The bright light in her room and the grating sound of the turning fan blades when the power returned must have roused her. Thinking that her eyes were up to their old gimmicks, she snapped them shut and braced herself for the return of those crimson-tinged jackbooted soldier ants that so often invaded her sleep.

'Do you always sleep with your ear on your fist and a book in my place?' said a familiar voice, mimicking the growl of the philandering General's camouflaged jalopy. Dele opened one eye, then the other. She leapt out of her trance and sat up. Hanili had had her hair cropped close and in a burgundy top and pale pair of trousers looked more stunning than a Taser gun. Dele pulled Hanili down and hugged and rocked her like a long lost pet.

Georgina knocked on the door. 'Power's back, you still need this or not?' she said. Dele opened the door and Georgina walked in waving a green medical journal. Dele grinned and shook her head. *I'm sizzling hot enough as I am.* Georgina cursed, stormed off and slammed her door shut.

'Nothing better than giving envy a polish,' said Dele. She locked the door and put on her favourite compilation CD.

'Dad didn't make it,' said Hanili. Her head dropped. 'I'm ok, really, expected,' said Hanili, dabbing a tear with her finger. Dele stroked her friend's hair, still not quite believing that she was back.

'With all the running around I lost my bag, phone and passport. Mum played up. She rang the passport office to tell them that I was going to a place worse than Syria. You'd think I was fifteen. She said working with and standing up to a corrupt regime was not a good idea. Roko was riddled with viruses…that Dad's going and my losing my passport was God's way of getting me out of the place. When was I going to get married? Had I been radicalised?' said Hanili. She rested her head on Dele's shoulder, to Dele's delight.

'You poor thing,' said Dele. The CD player wheezed and after the Marvin Gaye, the soundtrack to *Once Upon a Time in the West* filled the room, borne on notes of the plushest eiderdown.

'Your eyes, like a pair of dark, delicate tulip buds, and your nose…'

'What about my nose,' said Dele?

A smile played along her Hanili's lips and creased the corners of her shiny eyes. 'It's straight, to the point, like you, it's what makes you…it stands for…Verity.'

'No one has ever said that about me before.' *It's either big mouth or pineapple legs or parrot nose.*

Hanili's eyes sparkled with tears. 'Love you all the same,' she said. She flipped off her black shoes. 'New nail polish,' she said, in reply to Dele's unspoken question. 'Stocked up at the local chemists. They call this the African dawn,' she said.

Dele cooed inside, like the crowd in a hall when the cute child star appears. 'I love you too,' she said.

They merged into one.

'Wonderful,' said Hanili after, untangling her limbs, a smile on her tumescent lips.

Dele replied with a long wet kiss. 'First thing I've done that feels right first time in my life,' she said. They fell silent. Dele listened to her sprinting heartbeat slow to a trot. A door banged shut outside, at the other end of the corridor. 'Will you have to go away again?' she said, her words clipped by fears.

'From you, never,' said Hanili. 'Hey, who's that?' She swung her long legs out of bed, wrapped them in a loincloth and got out of bed.

'It's Emile. Classmate. Wind blew it over…I started again. Took his dad's…what happened to his dad…badly,' said Dele not knowing how else to say it.

'Hey, it's not very good,' said Dele.

'Don't get your gorilla knickers in a twist,' said Hanili, moving along the wall to the next picture.

'You're one to talk,' said Dele. She sat up and flipped Hanili's red lace underwear up with a toe.

Hanili hopped into her knickers and turned back to the painting. 'Wow African Grey parrot feeding its young, with a barb through its heart. They're endangered you know.' She stroked Dele's hair. Her voice cracked. 'Dele you don't mind me saying…your lines are softer, but hey, I'm no critic.'

'That's a copy. Sister sold the original, anyway I don't mind what you say as long as you stay,' said Dele, squeezing Hanili's hand.

'Did you know that Sandman's son, Arami is to marry Pupa?' said Hanili.

'General Giradona's daughter? She's only seventeen…and Sandman's son is barely out of nappies,' said Dele.

'If you ask me boys should wrap their balls in a helmet and their heads in a nappy, until they're thirty,' said Hanili with a chuckle.

'They should be kept in deep freeze when they're born and have to apply for them, like a driving licence, or passport,' said Dele.

'And when they turn up you'd say they got mixed up or squashed in the Friday night crush and they'd have to wait a month for the next batch of processed applications,' said Hanili, new tears of laughter in her eyes.

'That's awful,' said Dele. They laughed out loud. *These would have been the best hours I ever lived. If only Dad and Mum were here.*

***

'What did the Dean say?' said Hanili, starting the car engine. She had been back for ten days.

'I told him I had only a few hundred Roko. He called the college Bursar to accept it as a deposit. I could stay on till after the resits. If I fail I'm out anyway.'

Hanili pulled down the sun visor. 'I thought the Dean was supposed to help the country produce doctors, not strangle them in their cots. On a more serious note I'll be free next week to take you to practice exam technique at Elugba clinic. And I've thought up another mnemonic,' said Hanili.

'I've got so many mnemonics I can't remember them all. What's this one for?' said Dele. She fastened her seatbelt.

Hanili reversed out of the space. 'It's for the intermediaries of the pathways in Diabetes you were moaning about. Dad had Diabetes,' said Hanili with a sad catch in her voice.

Dele rubbed her friend on the neck. They stopped.

'I'm alright now,' said Hanili after a minute. She drove off. 'Phew, lend me your handle. I need to wind this window down, it's like an oven on my side,' she said.

'By the way did you hear back from Mr Momoh?' said Dele.

'He'd gone to lunch and then some meeting,' she said as she slowed down at a junction and then turned into the entrance to the Majestic Hotel.

'Where are we going?' I've got a project to write up,' said Dele.

'It's a surprise.'

***

Hanili parked the car and led Dele to the hotel tennis courts. A bellboy produced a thermometer from his top pocket and opened a fridge. He emerged not with cold drinks but with a tin of tennis balls.

'Who are they for?' said Dele.

'Mr Chou,' said the boy. 'Mr Chou will be here soon, before six, and likes his balls at just the right temperature for the grass court,' he said with a shake of the thermometer.

'When he fucks too?' said Hanili. 'Gee, did she hear me?' she said as an elegant woman in a white top hat walked past.

A helicopter landed beside a tennis court in a pall of dust. Hanili made to walk up its steps. 'It's my treat. Mr Olaf was feeling chirpy. So cheeky me asked him if he didn't mind lending us this for an hour or two.'

April 23rd. Dad's birthday. Dele fought back the threat of tears. 'How did you find out?'

'I have ways,' said Hanili. They hugged. 'Come on.'

Dele hesitated. 'I can't do it. Take me home. It looks like a grasshopper with a bad haircut on a bad day.'

'Oh come on,' said Hanili. She pulled Dele on board.

'How do you get this rich?' Dele said, sinking into the blue leather seats.

'Olaf made his dosh from vaccines,' said Hanili. 'He says a rich man is one who can afford to spend his time only with those he has time for…but doesn't.'

'That sounds like the gospel according to Ambasi,' said Dele, then wished she hadn't brought him up.

'How is he by the way?' said Hanili.

'We're on trial separation for a few weeks until after my resit,' said Dele with a pang of guilt. The helicopter took off, leaving Dele's belly earthbound. She clutched her seatbelt.

'I'll get Olaf to see what he can do about the Arimos. I'll say the issue is affecting morale and the water projects, something like that,' said Hanili, popping a pill into her mouth.

The helicopter banked to the left, setting off more chimes of alarm in Dele's chest.

'You're looking a bit worse for wear?'

'It's my rollover stomach,' Dele said. She cast a nervous glance at the cockpit.

Hanili leaned forward to pat Dele on the wrist.

'Why don't you stick to digging boreholes, instead of mouthing off at rallies? It's not clever,' said Dele.

Hanili nodded, looked into the distance as if deep in thought. Then she shoved a glossy pamphlet under her seat. 'Ordinary Siroko are a people that time expends faster than any on this planet. You say stick to boreholes. But who owns the land?' Her freckles darkened. 'In theory the people, in practice anyone with clout. They take what they want.' She cut across her throat with a finger. 'Sankara central, the hotel was built like that, but we managed to get the family compensation. So…worth it in the end.'

A bright orange sun bathed the cabin in eerie light. Dele looked out of the window. Yachts the size of small islands glistened and bobbed in the turquoise waters of Roko Bay.

Hanili's freckles folded into a crease in her brow. 'The generals ask us not to teach or preach against…their culture,' said Hanili, making two bunny ears in the air with her fingers. 'But where in

Roko culture does it say you must have a Swiss bank account? Look at this.' Hanili pointed out of the other window. Dele leaned over to look. 'That one's Sandman's, the other one's Banusi's, side by side,' said Hanili.

'Was Banusi not the man I saw at the Officer's mess?'

Hanili nodded. 'Probably. He can't stand Sandman, but can't afford to thumb his nose at Britsandchindarusa either…the largest landowners in the southern hemisphere.'

'That's except for that Australian actresses' family,' said Dele, with a slight frisson of pleasure at the titbit.

'Turbulence,' said Hanili, as Dele's belly flopped once more into her bladder.

'Talking of the Roko Mafia. That flash surgeon, Dada's making money from little girls. I'm sure,' said Dele. Hanili took notes while Dele told her what she saw in Abha and at HealthSmart.

'Life for some must be like living in a stranger's latrine. How old was this girl?' she said.

'Twelve? Thirteen?' said Dele.

Hanili's frown turned blacker. 'You are sure?'

'I put my head in her little mouth to count her milk teeth. Of course I'm sure,' said Dele.

'Dele, only asking. Oh gee.'

'Also…something dodgy about the length of stay data. Sara the research nurse told me. Sandman appointed Dada Director of Research, Development and Rehabilitation which puts him in charge of UN grants…'

'That was over distinguished Professors Jega, Yinkaso, Dike,' said Hanili.

'If I can expose Dada, maybe I can use that to get at Sandman…somehow,' said Dele.

Hanili's sceptical look turned a screw in Dele's chest.

'If you don't want to help me why don't you just come out and say so,' said Dele. 'Perhaps I should jump out of the window and leave you to condescend with the pilot.'

'I arranged this trip to tell you stuff…personal stuff…about my trip to England …but seeing as you've got that boiler under the collar again…I'll pass…'

'No, tell me,' said Dele.

Hanili frowned and looked out of the window, while Dele searched for the simple words to lob back into play.

'Have you heard of the woman who flashed her headlights to thank the car *behind* for letting her in?' she said.

Hanili did not reply.

'The joke about the biscuit tin form of birth control?' said Dele.

Dele saw a flicker of interest in her friend's face.

'How does that work?' said Hanili.

'I'm not telling you…until you cheer up.'

Hanili bared her teeth, like an angry carnivore. They fell silent again. Dele listened to the whirring helicopter blades. Moments passed. Her head started to spin.

'Gee, are you ok?' said Hanili.

Dele nodded. The queasiness passed and she reached over to cup Hanili's hands in hers. Hanili squeezed her hand and smiled.

'That's better. I was thinking the other day,' said Hanili. 'I've had everything, education, free healthcare and even here I've got pills for this and that. Locals have nothing. What makes me so special? I've decided. If I fall ill don't cart me off to England. I'll take my chance here just like you would have to,' she said.

Dele threw her hands up in the air. 'That makes no sense. You could catch bad Malaria. You've got no immunity. And what if it's nothing to do with boreholes or parasites or Rokopats or landowners? What if you had some fucking autoimmune disease, some crazy blastoma, glioma, cardiomyopathy? You want to throw your life away? I know you're grieving for your dad but…'

Hanili raised her hand to cut Dele off. 'Gee oh gee, don't go on. I've thought long and hard about this and made up my mind. It's my absolute clear line in the sand or, as the Jehovah's Witness said to the surgeon, it's *my* blood in the line, or nothing.'

ELEVEN

Results day arrived four weeks later. Dele spent a nervous day doodling, drinking coffee and quaking in her room. At four o'clock she shuffled downstairs to hover around the notice board opposite the Porter's cubicle to watch one of the Academic Registrars pin a green sheet of paper to the noticeboard. Students milled around like randy goats. Dele's heart rattled as she pushed her way through the melee. For a minute her eyes missed out a middle section of numbers then landed on number *6856*. *Where's 6828?*

'Parrot, you passed. Those ones are the Pharmacology results for year 4,' said "broadband Kalango." Dele checked the number she had written on her palm against the numbers on the next column of green sheets and leapt into the air.

'Passed, passed,' she said, hugging Kalango. 'What of Emile?'

'He passed,' said Kalango. She sounded disappointed.

'You don't have re-sits. What are you doing here anyway?' said Dele.

'I like to be the first with news,' said Kalango.

'Why don't you make it up…as usual,' said Dele.

Dele called Hanili. No reply. She went back upstairs to her room on the second floor, stuffed Hanili's birthday present, a hardback, "Winners and losers in the latest scramble for Africa," back in a bag and called Keli's mother.

'Is everything all right? It's not like Hanili or Keli not to call if they were going to be late,' said Keli's mother.

'I'm sure it's nothing,' said Dele and rang off.

A white car pulled up behind a lorry. Dele's heart leapt but it splashed back down in disappointment because it was not the Pleb Bus or mobile. She called Hanili again, for the third time in fifteen minutes, but the calls went to voicemail. Her hands started to shake. *Something's not right.*

At half past six she trudged off towards the main hospital block. While she waited for a red lorry with a long list of consonants on its side to crawl past she dialled Hanili's number once more. *Fucking voicemail.*

'I can't find my friend,' said Dele to Baba Funi. Baba Funi guffawed and leaned over the counter.

'Teach me this juju, doc, maybe I can use it to make my wife disappearendo too...come, ah, ah, only a joke, why you are looking as if I packed your mouth with sharp sand?' he said, tapping Dele under the chin. He lifted a thick ledger off a shelf behind him, laid it open on the counter, licked his forefinger and flicked through the pages.

'Hey Padi. Where is the big blue book?' he said. Padi did not reply. Baba Funi shouted louder. 'Padi you come here to dance or to work? Don't make me vex.' Padi trotted in with a sheaf of papers. 'Padi, my friend here is looking for Hanili,' said Baba Funi.

Padi was wearing a large red T-shirt outside a black pair of jeans. 'How do I know that you are not a kidnapper?' he said.

Dele slapped the counter. 'Baba Funi, do me a favour; get this man out of my face,' she said.

'Padi, this is not the time to practice lawyering. Sorry my friend, he's been like this since he started evening classes,' said Baba Funi.

'Keli is thirteen, with long braided hair pulled back and tied in a pigtail. She may have been in a school uniform, white blouse under a pink petticoat.'

'That's the girl I saw. Crying like Mary of Magdalene after our Lord died,' said Padi. 'She is not in this book though.' He shuffled in to the back room singing along to Bob Marley's *Exodus*.

'Can we check the security camera then?' said Dele.

Baba Funi reached up to fiddle with some buttons on a wall-mounted screen.

'Who is that?' said Dele.

'That is the southern gate bus stop...' said Baba Funi, rubbing his nose. An ambulance arrived at the main gates, siren wailing.

'There she is, walking towards the camera,' said Padi. 'Ah.' Padi pointed back past Dele and up the main hospital corridor. 'Behind the woman in the blue dress.'

Dele ran up to hug Keli. 'Keli, you're safe, thank God.' Keli's puffy face showed that she had been crying.

'You know her?' said the nurse.

Keli nodded.

'Hanili is on our ward…C6, third floor,' said the nurse. Her doleful face said enough.

'Call your mum.' Dele handed a phone to Keli.

'It's me, mama,' said Keli. 'When I got home Hanili was not well. She was shaking, sweating, scratching her head and her nose was bleeding. Neighbours were standing outside her flat because she had the music on too loud.' Keli nodded to something her mother said and wiped her nose. 'Mrs Fedi brought Hanili to hospital,' she said. 'On my way home I got on the wrong bus so I got off and came back to the hospital.'

Dele waited for Keli to stop crying and left her with Baba Funi.

***

As she turned into the ward, an array of red numbers flashed from the dark monitoring screens hanging above the beds. Then she saw Hanili in the bed, shrivelled, eyes closed with palms turned to the ceiling, her hair and ears flaked with blood. 'How much urine?' said Dele, pointing at the dark brown fluid trickling into a plastic bag.

'About twenty mls,' said the nurse.

'That's all, in two hours?' said Dele, flicking through the charts. The nurse nodded. Dele prodded the tubes hanging over the bed rail as if to milk more urine into the bags. *Acute Kidney Injury*. She squeezed Hanili's hand again but got no response. *At least she's breathing*. She blinked back the tears. The sight of poor Hanili lying there helpless reminded her of Eniadudu's body smouldering on the camp pyres. She dragged a chair and sat down while the nurses flitted about, changing tubes, tutting and clucking at the numbers.

'Her pressure is a little on the downside,' said one nurse.

Dele was not fooled by the euphemisms. *Could it be Malaria* she thought? Had Hanili bought a faulty batch of prophylactic tablets or simply forgotten to take them? But she was always ever so careful. *What for fuck's sake was wrong with her. Please God, don't let her die.*

It was three minutes past midnight when Hanili opened her eyes. 'I'm here,' said Dele.

'Where's Keli,' said Hanili. The pupils in her eyes bounced like roulette balls when she turned her head.

Nystagmus, cerebellar, what next?

'Oh, gee, she's in trouble isn't she? They put a red-headed lizard on our doorstep,' said Hanili. When she tried to get up the tube in her arm fell out, dribbling a syrupy pink fluid on to the floor. A nurse came along, tweaked a syringe and Hanili soon fell asleep.

'She needs blood, but you have to give first to keep the bank topped up,' said the nurse.

Dele ran to the blood bank to give the collateral pint. They needed "liquidity." Even on the ward that early in the morning, she thought the first bag of blood looked a trifle transparent. Perhaps HealthSmart did indeed dilute the blood with brine and kept some for the black market. She wouldn't put it past Sandman. And one day, make no mistake, she would make him pay.

***

Dele walked in to the staff room. The microwave oven whirred to a halt.

'What have we here?' said Dr Waladi, a dapper man with a pocked yellow-brown face, thick black hair and an accent straight out of a 1950s film noir. Dele thought he was South American. Sister Mirada said he was French.

'Medic. A friend of our new admission, the conundrum in bed three,' said Sister, an elegant woman with her cap perched on a neat Afro. 'Coffee?' she said, turning to switch on the kettle beside her.

The doctor nodded. 'She's not new, five days. Two sugars, thank you.' Dr Waladi ran a hand through his oily hair and rummaged through a red tin of biscuits. 'Ah,' he said when he found the chocolate biscuit he wanted.

Never eat on this ward again.

Sister Mirada handed Dr Waladi a steaming mug of coffee. 'Your friend had a cardiac arrest last night, six shocks,' she said. At that, the floor seemed to sweep Dele off her feet. She grabbed on to a table and sat down.

'Straightforward case. Malaria,' said Dr Waladi, picking his nose. 'Probably not taking her prophylaxis. These foreign aid workers think they know best.' Leaning back against the far wall he sipped from his mug and nodded his approval at Sister. Sister Mirada replied with a beaming smile.

'With the greatest respect sir, could I ask a favour? Has a *consultant* set eyes on my friend?' said Dele.

Sister refastened her cap with a pin and came over. 'It's not their fault. Haka, the health market currency, has been trading so low that consultants cannot afford to work here,' she said, kneading Dele's shoulder as she spoke.

So we end up with these "lowcosts", paid in useless Haka. 'Too busy ferreting for mining concessions,' said Dele.

'Or contracts with the Haka's many companies. He sets the exchange rate. Do you blame them?' said Sister, adjusting her cap.

'Can't you transfer her?' said Dele.

Dr Waladi put a finger to his lips. 'You are only a student, until you get your licence, leave us to make clinical decisions, yeah?' he said.

Dele shot to her feet, jabbing the air like a demented rapper. 'Every day a different doctor comes here late, to express dismay…each in their own cultural way. One day you're squeezing out inflation with a kidney machine, the next you are putting it back because she's dehydrated, or deflated. I've had more sense from a …boiling kettle.'

Sister turned to Dele. 'We've used all our transfers to North Roko this month, dear and it'll spoil their figures if they take any more high risk cases. Your friend's case is too risky. What if she has Swine Flu, Avian Flu, Ebola they ask. It could spread to other patients. Fred...sorry, Dr Waladi's doing his best.'

'God in heaven. So Hanili's stuck here because she's bad for business,' said Dele.

'Don't forget that she signed paper to the Foundation to say she did not want to be transferred. It is with Matron. But her mama is coming…if she gets a visa. Our minister was dissed at Heathrow so we are making it hard for British to come here in retaliation or is it revenge?' said Sister. A man with jaundice in the opposite corner coughed. It sounded like his last.

***

The next day Dele was on her way to see Hanili when Baba Funi, the Head Porter, hailed her. 'Any news?' said Dele.

'Yes...,' said Baba Funi.

'And?' said Dele.

'Bad,' said Baba Funi. 'Keli and her mama, stabbed in the railway line area, not far from their house.'

Shock thwacked Dele in the stomach. The old familiar smell of cordite and burning flesh in a yellow mist seemed to whirl round her head. 'No, tell me it's not true. Was it robbery?' Feeling faint, she held on to Baba Funi's arm for support.

Baba Funi shrugged his shoulders. 'Maybe she got lost again. Camera shows she did not go home the usual way.' He turned the wall-mounted CCTV screen round for Dele. 'Look, here is Keli running down the hospital ramp that day. This is you. You call her back and chase after her because she left her school bag at reception,' he said.

'I caught her at the pedestrian crossing at the foot of the ramp and she said she'd see me the next day. That was three days ago.'

'See, but she did not go the usual way, look, behind the man carrying the dead sheep on his back. She is getting on the bus,' said Baba Funi. 'But that's the Mosalasi not the Bauya bus.'

'Where was she going?' said Dele.

'Maybe she is selling janija. Not the first girl this has happened to for the sake of money palaver. That is why I tell everyone not to go to railway line. It is thief and night workers' market.' Baba Funi cracked open a sweet wrapper and put the rest under the counter. 'Bring fan, it's getting hot in here,' he said.

PART 3

ONE

For two days Hanili's condition swung between hopeless and terminal. On the third day she turned a corner back to critical.

The rainy season arrived, the whole season crammed it seemed into a few days. Dripping like a waterfall, Dele charged through the suffocating sheets of rain. Her momentum took her past the nurses' station. She missed a dustbin by a nose tip and her squelching sneakers brought her to a squeaking halt just before she hit the cleaner's bucket.

'Marie Teresa, late again. Fighting evil empires on the seabed?' said Dr Waladi, tapping his silver watch, his sidelong glance at Dele filled with disdain.

'Sorry, the storm seemed to have saved its best shots for me,' said Dele.

Dr Waladi made a dismissive sound. He stopped at Hanili's bed, the only one occupied in the four-bedded cubicle. 'As I was saying the more antibiotics we buy, the more Haka we have to convert to Roko from ward reserves,' he said. Three weeks. Give it another twelve hours. By eight tomorrow morning…if kidney is lagging the predicted index…bail out?' he said, polishing his moustache with his finger.

How much more of this man can I take?

Hanili had a new feeding tube in her stomach. 'Where's Keli?' she said, in a croaky whisper. 'She's in danger. She wouldn't tell me who threatened her family…but she got me…antidote. She hasn't been to see me, no calls…no nothing.'

'Maybe her phone's broken or she's lost your number…ah, I think her mum said she was going away, school trip to the Abata lake district,' Dele said. She squeezed Hanili's hand.

'Then she's out of the way, safe,' said Hanili. A tear rolled down her cheek.

Dele felt like crawling under a divot. Blood rushed to her face. And as she turned away to hide her shame she heard Sister call out.

'Listen everyone. You know that woman with the sharp mouth and teeth. Mrs Lagbaja. She took her own early discharge against advice but they say a tree fell on her in the storm. Get Dr Awe. We can't have you know who.'

Mrs Lagbaja, again.

Dr Awe appeared on the ward fifteen minutes later, in a shiny wet tuxedo. He leaned over the reception desk, teased off his bow-tie. 'Pure silk,' he said handing it to Sister. 'Why must this woman feed parrots during a hurricane?' he said. Shoulders hunched, he charged past Hanili's bed but just before it looked as if he was going to head-butt the wall he stopped, straightened out, in tremulous self-restraint.

Dele squeezed Hanili's hand. 'He looks really…put out, as you say.'

For a few minutes everyone went quiet while Dr Awe fumed. Then he turned round and walked back to Sister's desk to continue his rant. 'If a tree fell on the old woman it was probably in revenge for all the parrot mess on its boughs. My old Professors used to say the mark of a civilised society is how many lives it puts at risk to save the one, but on a filthy night like this even David would think this is going too far.'

'Hanili, he's looking back this way, oh no, he's looking at me,' said Dele.

'Verity, yes…you, if that badge is correct and you're not a terrorist in disguise,' said Dr Awe.

'Medical student,' said Dele.

'Well we're two short in theatre…so you'll have to do,' said Dr Awe.

'A night on the theatre tiles with a cardiologist. I might learn something. Humility perhaps?' said Dele to Hanili. She squeezed Hanili's hand. *Or honesty.*

***

Mrs Lagbaja arrived on the ward on a trolley, tiny beads of sweat running down her greying face. 'I'm cold, it aches, my chest,' she said. A wisp of steam clouded the nasal mask with each brief breath she took. Dele helped the porter wheel her to theatre.

'BP's critical and ECG's not much better. Is this not futile?' said Dr Awe. He arrived in the anaesthetic room already changed into the green theatre togs.

'It's your call, I'll tip the bed head down,' said Dr Bewasi, the anaesthetist, with a shrug of a shoulder.

'Who else is on surgery-wise?' said Dr Awe.

'Camel hands, Dada,' said Dr Bewasi. 'Should I call him?' she said giving the air bag another squeeze. One side of Mrs Lagbaja's chest rose higher than the other.

Dr Awe grunted. 'Him? You hate this woman that much?' he said. 'I'll deal with the heart but if any other part of her body raises more than a mild protest I'm out, on grounds of qualitative and quantitative futility, at least. Agree?'

They rushed Mrs Lagbaja into theatre where, the nurse on duty, Abuli "special prize", after the TV quiz *Bull's Eye*, had a crystal clear frosty air about her. In a flash Dr Awe confirmed by angiography that Mrs Lagbaja needed a stent.

'Hand over please,' he said with a practised air. He held out his hand. Nothing happened. He looked up at Abuli. Abuli returned his gaze with an aggressive frown. Mrs Lagbaja groaned. Anxiety etched deeper into the anaesthetist's face.

'Guidewire please,' said Dr Awe, deep notes of frustration in his voice.

Abuli had now scrubbed up. 'Why didn't you say? It's my job to unpack the guide wire,' Abuli said. She grabbed the plastic packing off Sid, the "runner" and with the showy care of the clumsy or incompetent, proceeded to open the pack, first forcing the clam plastic shell open at the wrong end, then snagging the tip of the wire on the end of the introducer.

Like a fired missile, Dr Awe went both ballistic and extra-terrestrial. His face turned plum purple and his eyes into red tomatoes. He spluttered, trembled and let rip. 'Your paws have made a spider's web of this wire. And what am I supposed to do with this, eh?' he said, flicking the sorry tip of the wire with his finger.

'And that was the last one,' said a nurse. Mrs Lagbaja moaned.

'I'm not taking any more of this,' said Abuli.

'Abuli, Abuli, wait,' said the radiographer, but Abuli pouted, sucked her teeth, snapped her gown and gloves off, and went to sit behind the reinforced glass panel in the viewing room.

Where have I seen her before? Dele saw Dr Awe's chest heave as he tried to contain his anger. But he seemed to calm down just as quickly as he had flared up.

'Verity, yes, you, student, wake up and scrub up, it's not this woman's fault that that woman is useless,' he said. Dele got scrubbed and tried to focus on the grainy screen. If this was war, all they had was a bent rapier, but it might as well have been a bunch of bananas for the success the doctor was having in opening the blocked artery. Mrs Lagbaja stopped breathing. Dele's tired mind drifted. *Is this what it is to die a natural death, but all death in the end is of natural causes. What is a supernatural death? Juju death? To die with a tree on your chest would be natural. To survive would be a fucking miracle. I'm going round on a board of snakes and ladders? Verity concentrate.*

Dr Awe's elbow bumped into Dele's ribs, by accident or to wake her up. He handed Dele the firm bottom end of the wire. 'Blasted thing,' he said. He swore again, at the wire and at the pool of blood spreading at his feet. The anaesthetist looked away, tapped a red knob on her console and gave the breathing bag a long squeeze. Dr Awe sighed, pulled the wire all the way out, kneaded it between his fingers, passed the scalpel handle over its tip. 'Fix it,' he said, placing Dele's finger on one end. He plunged the other end of the wire back in.

'Can you adjust my mask please?' Dele said, dancing on the spot to stay alert. She bent over so the nurse could reach. When Dele looked up again Dr Awe had got the wire across, and was about to deploy a stent.

'STs are coming down,' said the anaesthetist, sounding both relieved and impressed.

'And pressure's up,' Dr Awe tossed his gloves across the room and into the bin.

'Good shot,' said the "runner" assistant.

Dr Awe winked and shrugged a shoulder like an athlete who always knew that he would come from behind to win. 'Where's that…nurse?' he said, wiping his gleaming brow with the back of his hand.

Dele hurried off for something to eat; but the vending machine had run out of fruit and she did not trust the soggy sandwiches. She lay her throbbing head against the cool wall of the changing room and closed her eyes. Minutes later an argument in the next room perked her up.

'I have work in the London, St Thomas's, not ramshackle East End place like you. And I am not going to take insults from some Kombo village doctor.' It sounded like 'special prize' Abuli.

'A mild reprimand for an absolute balls up and you're bleating like a lost sheep,' said the man. 'I wouldn't trust you with my son's dead pet hamster and if it wasn't for Dada you wouldn't have a job.' Dele heard a booted foot stamp on the floor. *That's Dr Awe.*

'You treat everyone like they are dog shit…nobody likes you,' said the woman.

'Better to be envied or resented than despised…like you are…,' said Dr Awe.

A door slammed. The argument stopped. *That's it. Abuli is the woman I saw with the little girl in so-called Medical Records. She works for Dada. And as Mondays follow Sundays, Sandman must be involved.*

***

Dele went to see Mrs Lagbaja the next morning to make a start on her project.

'She's over there in her own single cubicle having breakfast. She will *not* share,' he said. 'Loco,' he added, stirring the air in front of his head. 'Dr Awe says to get a head scan, see if she has any brain left. I can tell him…she has plenty, just the wrong type.'

'What did the ambulance crew say?' said Dele.

'Ambulance? You are being funny or what, parrot? Taxi dumped her and offed it,' he said.

'How did she get a taxi if she was outside under a tree?'

The registrar shrugged his shoulders.

'Cantankerous *and* confused,' said Dele trailing after the ward Sister to Mrs Lagbaja's bay.

'Tougher than rhino hide. She nearly quench, but here she is a day later sitting up. It's thanks to Dr Awe,' said Sister Surina.

Hunched over a breakfast tray, with a tube draining pink fluid from her chest into a bottle on the floor, the subject of much attention pored over her breakfast like a lottery-winning miser would a bank statement.

'They call this soggy piece of foam toast? I'd have the chef and steward back up here if it would do any good,' she said.

'I thought you wanted white bread,' said Sister Surina.

'How can I tell white from brown when it's burnt to cinders?' said Mrs Lagbaja, picking up a slice of toast between two knobbly fingers.

'Please keep that arm out of the way if you don't want to bleed to death,' said Sister.

'Don't take that tone with me, young woman. My God, is that blood all mine? Were you going to tell me that you nearly killed me in there? After such a simple procedure I would have thought that you would have wheeled me back as soon as you finished, no, they made me wait for that porter,' said Mrs Lagbaja.

'Gandi only stayed late for you as a favour. It *is* a hospital…with other patients in it,' said Sister. She pulled her blue belt back up over her waist and made to leave.

Please don't stop, this is fun thought Dele.

'Keep her in till her renal function's stable,' said the registrar, from the other side of the bed.

Mrs Lagbaja's eyes swivelled left under their great hoods. 'You're not a consultant I take it and I'll not stay here for a second longer than I need to. Expecting a delivery of high protein parrot feed. If I'm not there they'll only sell it on the black market and charge me for the trouble.' She retched. Dele looked around for a *Papier Mache* kidney dish, but Mrs Lagbaja soon recovered.

'Saved her life, this is all we get from nail-gun mouth,' said Sister, yanking the blue plastic curtains to behind her as she left. The registrar and other nurse soon followed. Dele waited while Mrs Lagbaja cut the toast into little triangles. With one slice despatched she looked up, her jaw rolling like a cow's at the trough.

'You're a medical student aren't you? I thought I made it absolutely clear that I did not want to take part in your intrusive experiments,' she said.

'Fair enough, then please could you do me a great favour and sign a paper...to show the Dean?' said Dele.

'I made it clear in the first place,' said Mrs Lagbaja.

'But-'

Mrs Lagbaja appeared to size Dele up, her eyes and head moving up and down like a paintbrush on a wall. 'Sit down. Where are your parents from...originally?' she said.

Dele blushed, brushed her hair back and sat down. 'Father's from England. Mother, Niroko.'

'Unusual, she said. 'And your hand?' she said, after a long pause.

'Used it to claw my way into medical school. Please can we talk about my assignment?' said Dele.

'You nearly killed me and I should be grateful?'

Dele got up. 'May I ask, with respect, what you were doing outside in the storm Mrs Lagbaja?'

Mrs Lagbaja shook her head. Her wattle wobbled. 'Rubbish, I wasn't outside and it was a wardrobe not a tree. I got home from hospital early...that's what happened...it's coming back to me...he said he heard a crash as he came back past the house…he came to see…'

The lady's brain cells need grouting. Dele sat down on the windowsill and poured Mrs Lagbaja some more tea. 'The wind blew the wardrobe through your front door and it landed on you…like a Tardis?' she said.

'What's your name again? Verity' said Mrs Lagbaja, squinting at Dele's badge. 'I can't stand names with more than three syllables. Waste of breath. And don't think for a second that you're smart with remarks like that. Maybe they were burglars. But I'll have you know that that man Sandman and his greedy conglomerate want me off my land. He says it's for affordable housing. Affordable house my bleeding heart. One man's mansion is another man's eminently affordable. The only huts there will be for the houseboys and I'm sure they'll pay through their dear nostrils for it.'

That's what Hanili said.

'You look as if you've burst an eardrum,' said Mrs Lagbaja. She leaned back and tapped her free hand on her knee. 'Now tell me what happened to your hand?' she said.

'It's a long story and Sandman's in it.'

Mrs Lagbaja dabbed her chin and the corner of her eye with a napkin. 'That man is rotten from crown to sole.' The tufts of grey hair on her eyebrows rose and fell as she spoke. 'That land's been in my family for generations. My sister sold her half. Passed two years ago. John, my husband was a farmer; lost his livestock to some disease, but locals said it was because he offended some local deity. Nonsense. Anyway he went into his shell and when he died even garden moss would have tired of life with him. I told the undertakers to take the gramophone and his Glen Miller LPs and bury them with him. Been on my own since. Forty-six years. Does that help?'

It's a start. 'Any other relatives?' said Dele.

Mrs Lagbaja shook her head. 'Never wanted kids. Too selfish. Or is it selfish to have them? Foisting your genes and foibles on another human being, throwing them out into the world before they can walk or even talk in some cases, then blaming the teachers, the environment, the government, everyone else for the results of your deeply selfish experiment. Anyway, I decided that the world does not need another version of me. I'll give my cottage and land to that Olaf Foundation lot if they promise to look after Confucius and my other pet parrots.'

I'm sure Sandman and Britsandchindarusa will be delighted.

Mrs Lagbaja glared through the curtains apparently irked at the presence, in the adjoining cubicle, of a nurse to whom she had taken an instant dislike. The nurse, probably sensing the strong antipathy, left soon afterwards.

'As for your request, or favour as you call it, let me be. Let me be? Song title if I'm not mistaken. The Quarrymen? I do keep up with the latest trends in popular culture you know.'

TWO

Mrs Lagbaja's comments about land seizures and Abuli's behaviour filled Dele with a renewed urge to thwart Dada and Sandman. The next day, in afternoon heat a degree below steel-warping unbearable, she hopped into a crowded bus and headed for central Sankara.

Two white mobile air conditioner units moaned away in the corner of the internet café, trickling a rust-strewn pool of water over the scruffy tiles. To Dele's left stood six curtained booths, against a wall. Dele tucked ticket number 24 into the front pocket of her jeans and perched on the edge of a three-legged plastic chair to wait for her turn. Her neck prickled in the heat. The keyboards in the customer booths rattled the minutes ticked away. At last her number came up. Dele leapt out of her chair, but a boy in a tight school shirt beat her to the terminal. 'Number 24,' he said waving a receipt in her face.

Dele felt like tearing the boy's head off. 'That's my number,' she said.

'What is the problem?' said the manager, a muscular man in a skin-tight black T-shirt.

'This boy-'

'Your receipt, madam?' said the man. He put out his hand.

Dele fished the receipt out of her pocket but, soaked in sweat, the flimsy piece of paper came apart in her hands like a ball of fluff. The manager shook his head. He glanced at his watch.

'Sorry madam, but you need to start again. We will soon close.'

Counting to ten over and over to quell her anger, Dele squeezed back through the throng to queue once again for the ticket dispenser, behind a man studying the football pools forecast. Half an hour later, just as it got to her turn, the dispenser ran out of tickets. 'Hey, what do I do now?' she said.

'Wait for recycle ticket,' said the manager.

If I didn't know any better I'd think Sandman knows that I'm here. She heard a slap from booth 4. The schoolboy cried out, tumbled out of the booth and through the main door, helped along by the manager's kick up his backside. 'Forged his ticket,' said the cashier. 'Sorry madam. Go in,' said the cashier.

Dele's anger changed to frustration. She had forgotten her login details and lost the mnemonic. After another plea to the manager she made up new ones. Login: SandmanandDada. Password: Tohellwithyoutwo, and composed her email. *'I am aware of your interest in length of stay data and the girls at HealthSmart. Your in-law the minister will not be pleased by your showiness. You know he does not lick when he can bite. When you meet tell him that I say if the eye picks a fight with even the smallest grain of sand it must end in tears. From concerned who knows you both well.*' She read it over, and pressed *send*.

***

'She's stable these last four days,' said the sister on duty. The ward orderly rang the bell to announce the beginning of the evening visiting session. Dele kissed Hanili goodbye and, with her heart burdened with worry, she set off to buy a jotter at "Bari's." There she found the shop assistant, a mean-faced teenager in a bright red blouse, engrossed in gossip with Abuli "special prize", the theatre nurse.

'Haba, not this Roko, oh,' said the girl, clasping her hands over her mouth.

Abuli nodded. 'That's it. I talk true.'

Dele waited, scratching the back of her neck.

'That Dada man with long neck, but I saw him in blue sports car, let me see…stock taking day…yesterday morning?' said the assistant.

Abuli fanned her face with a magazine. 'I heard with my own two ears.' She picked up a packet of cigarettes. 'Original or fake?' she said, squinting to read the packet.

'Sorry, original is here,' said the shop girl, reaching under the counter. 'I meant to give you this one,' she said, handing over a packet a shade darker.

Dele coughed, heaved her satchel off her shoulder. 'Excuse me, can I-'

'Wait your turn, you can see that I'm busy serving another customer,' said the girl, rolling her eyes. Abuli pulled on a bra strap and shook her head at Dele. 'Do I know you? Why are you looking at me like that?' she said as she turned away.

'Hunh, medical student. They think they are special,' said the shop girl, making a sucking sizzling sound with her mouth. She clunked loose change on to the counter and cursed when a coin rolled on to the floor.

'Can I have this refill paper pad? Quick please,' said Dele.

The shop girl twirled the biro in her hand. 'Miss medical student, you are going to answer my friend or not?'

'Leave her, that's how they are,' said Abuli. She dabbed on her deep purple lipstick and set off.

Dele ignored the shop girl's handful of small change and shouldered through the evening crush on the main hospital corridor. She caught Abuli outside the blue swing doors of the Physiotherapy department.

'Excuse me.'

Abuli wheeled round. 'Do I take food from your mouth…can I not buy cigar in peace?'

'It was you I saw with the girl in front of the…medical records…in the middle of the night. Admit it. She's not your daughter.'

'You are drunk or high or what?' said Abuli. She lit a cigarette and puffed the smoke in Dele's face.

Dele blew the smoke back at Abuli. 'You call yourself a woman. You should be ashamed of what you do to young girls.'

'How is it your concern? I work extra in rehabilitation ward. When they come back from camp I am looking after them. That is all. As God is my witness.'

'I know what I saw. And Mr Dada must be involved. He recruited you.'

Abuli sucked her cigarette but her features softened as she exhaled and she looked afraid and sad. 'I have mama for house. She has stroke. Three sister, junior to me are still in school. Who will feed them?'

'I just want the truth, the girls are…only children.'

A security man wandered over and flicked a switch on a hand-held console. Only one of the three ceiling bulbs agreed to shed their light on the evening.

'Are you ok Abuli?' the man said.

Abuli nodded and sidled off to lean against a pillar. She looked away from the corridor and wiped her face with the back of her hands.

'After what happened to Mr Dada…I don't know…'Abuli shook her head and sat down with her feet on the grass. 'There has been a serious incident,' she said, in a sad voice. 'His secretary has gone to see what….' She shrugged, lowered her forehead even further. 'This life. You don't know what is coming over the bridge. It was only the other day I saw him,' she said crossing herself.

'What are you saying?' said Dele. *Perhaps it's not her fault.*

'Mr Dada is dead.'

Dele's innards did a bungee jump. 'Are you sure?' she said.

Abuli sobbed. After a pause for breath she went on. 'They find the houseboy in singlet shaking and walking zig-zag, like he drunk. He say doctor is lying by the fridge. He say he turn off the electric, but too late. So many times he told them to buy new fridge in that room. Had it not been by God's grace the fault may have killed that boy too.'

'Where is this houseboy?' said Dele.

'Fanti? Under arrest. Maybe he did it for money. What will I do if they sack me?'

Dele's head spun, full of questions. She had sent the email only four days earlier. *Was Mr Dada's death an accident? If not would the police find her email and link it back to her? Did Dada show the email to Sandman? Or am I thinking out of the box and going round in circles again?*

She put her arm round Abuli. 'But maybe now the truth will come out. Abuli I wish I could help you but I have athlete's foot and only one slipper and many miles to travel myself.'

THREE

'You again,' said the Dean from behind his tidy desk. The white filing cabinet in the corner with its middle drawer open looked like a ventriloquist's dummy.

'Professor, I've waited a week since Mr Dada...went...my classmates are making progress on *their* projects and my patient has disappeared,' said Dele.

An angular white man with skin peeling off the tip of his nose, Professor Degenhardt had wiry hairs fanning out of his ears. 'Surmounting obstacles is part of the test,' he said, tearing a green and red journal out of its packing and flicking through its pages.

'Professor how-'

He waved Dele away and tucked his red kipper tie into his trousers. 'Don't raise this matter again. Case dismissed,' he said.

Dele's phone buzzed. 'Mrs Lagbaja where have you been?' Dele backed out of the Dean's office.

'Sorry young woman, I've been away at an aviary conference. I just heard about the doctor and I need to talk to someone...,' said Mrs Lagbaja. 'I live in a red and white bricked cottage. It's behind a wall a hundred yards off the track leading to the beach. Even you can't miss it.'

'See you tomorrow,' said Dele.

***

Arriving at the bus station at eleven the next morning, with a ghostly moon high in the sky, Dele got on to a half-full bus, still pondering Mr Dada's death. *I'm probably making too much of it. Maybe he had a heart attack, or pulmonary embolus and fell in front of the fridge.* Then her thoughts went back to poor Keli. A foghorn went off, blasting her out of her trance. She looked around. After half an hour the bus was still only half full. *What's going on, we were only two short when I got on.* Then she remembered that sham passengers attracted fare by making the bus look ready to depart. *I've fallen for that one again* thought Dele with a rueful shrug of the shoulders as the bus set off at last, at half past eleven.

Two hours later Dele took a left fork off the unpaved Roko Beach Road on to a dust-track. The sea whispered in the distance, and, roadside, smooth-trunked palm trees sparred in the lazy breeze. Dele walked up a gentle rise, ducked under a mango tree and squeezed, side-on, through Mrs Lagbaja's weed-bound gate.

Mrs Lagbaja lived in a red and white double-fronted bungalow, its oak-brown window shutters spattered with birds' mess. In the walled front garden, dozens of bird cages hung from the lower branches of Breadfruit or Acacia trees or stood propped up in the rockery or wedged amongst red Blood Lillies. At Dele's approach a purple-breasted bird chirped and hopped about the lawn. One parrot replied in kind and the others soon joined in a jarring chorus. With a finger over her left ear to keep out the noise, Dele walked up the concrete path to bang on the door with a grey knocker shaped like a parrot.

The dark brown door creaked open and Mrs Lagbaja appeared in a sandy brown shirt over a black ankle-length skirt. Streaky grey and brown hair hung over her brow. 'Good afternoon young lady,' she said. She led Dele to a dining area. On the table lay a number of windowed envelopes, an aviary magazine and a thick blue dictionary. Six or seven cages, a few of them empty, glided on rails in a slow procession around the ceiling. One of the caged parrots had joined the feathered debate going on outside.

'Shut up Ukrani,' said Mrs Lagbaja. 'Miss Verity, can I offer you a drink?'

Dele declined. Mrs Lagbaja cleared the papers to one side and clicked a remote control. The parrot cages swayed to a halt. 'Sit down,' she said.

Dele heard a 'fuck, fuck', from a bird in a back room.

'Whatever's got into Confucius while I was away last time, he's so...disgusting, making those noises you see...you know what I mean, like they make in the blue movies...not that I have any course to view them, and swearing like a trooper. It's all been eff this eff that since I came back. Of course the poor thing doesn't know what he's saying. I left him on his own, not the first time. So can't explain why he's so rude and grumpy.' Mrs Lagbaja pursed her lips and dabbed them with a knuckle. 'I needed someone to talk to...'

'Did you ask me to come all this way as a substitute for your profane parrot?' said Dele.

'Come, follow me,' said Mrs Lagbaja.

The dim rhomboid-shaped back room had diamond-shaped black and white tiles on the floor. Deep mauve curtains hung from the ceiling, against the pale walls. A white coverlet featuring a parrot in an academic gown graced a king-sized bed. Confucius's cage, formed by welding two cages side by side, hung from the ceiling to the right of the door. It cast a blurred figure of eight shadow along the floor and adjacent wall.

'Fuck you, fuck you,' said Confucius, looking askance at Dele with its large yellow eye. Dele thought she saw flecks of red in the bird's eye, perhaps a sign of tiredness, or anger she wondered.

Mrs Lagbaja waved at the cage. 'You would have thought I got him off a porn star,' she said. 'Yet I raised him from hand. I dare say I still have the certificate.'

'He's twice the size of my old Innocent, look at that great head,' said Dele.

'Fuck,' said the parrot and smacked its black bill against the cage.

'Obnoxious, most unpleasant, I'm sure your Innocent did nothing like this,' said Mrs Lagbaja. 'It's nothing to do with me leaving him on his own. It's that new gardener, I'm sure.' She lifted Confucius out of the cage, stroked its grey wings, fluffed out its red tail and smoothed down its legs. Confucius let out a fart.

'Where on earth have you left your manners, Comfy?' said Mrs Lagbaja.

'Fuck me,' said the parrot, out louder than before.

'Mrs Baby Doc Duvalier's once had a swearing parrot. Even Dr Awe swears,' said Dele, trying to bring the discussion round to medical matters.

'She's angry, oh not with you Miss Verity, something's upset Comfy while I was away. Feathers have lost their sheen. Bright red they used to be,' she said. Mrs Lagbaja went quiet. She lifted the parrot's undertail coverts and while she rubbed them between her fingers Dele went to wait by the door. After a minute or so Mrs Lagbaja sighed and put Comfy back in the cage. She shuffled her feet into her brown slippers, hobbled past Dele and back to sit in the dining room.

A tap dripped outside, at the back of the house, the water drumming on to what sounded like an upturned plastic bowl.

'That man hasn't fixed it. Why did I go in there?' said Mrs Lagbaja.

'To show me Comfy?' said Dele.

'No…not that, it'll come back to me,' said Mrs Lagbaja with a worried frown.

'Mr Dada, the wardrobe?' said Dele.

'Had that fixed and sold it. No…something else, can't for the life of me remember…' said Mrs Lagbaja, scratching her head.

You'll pull out the rest of your thin fuzz thought Dele.

'I've got more grey cells on top of my head than inside it. Young woman, don't get old. No, it's not Dada, though dreadful what happened to that man, no great shakes as a surgeon but…,' she dipped a teaspoon into a jar of honey.

'An electrical fault I heard,' said Dele.

Mrs Lagbaja licked one side of her spoon and shook her head. 'Expunged, like a stain on a shirt. I used to work in the security sector you know, long before the island split. Sizing up communist threats…native insurgencies. We are not allowed to use that word anymore. Threats from indigenous activists, the radicalised, is the current term. First my flying wardrobe, then Mr Dada and the leaking fridge. And that awful man and his mates want my land.' She licked the other side of her spoon.

'Mrs Lagbaja, I must say you have the most imaginative imagination,' said Dele.

Mrs Lagbaja tutted. 'Say what you like. What you call coincidence is, in the condescending light of retrospective clairvoyance, often a blinkingly obvious disaster in the making.'

Dele did not know what to make of Mrs Lagbaja's story. The old woman had been through a major procedure and had nearly died. So she could have dreamt it all up. But what if she had indeed disturbed intruders? Were they simple burglars or men trying to frighten her off the land? And why had her parrot gone all fuck-mouthed? What was it the old woman wanted to show her in Confucius's room?

FOUR

Dele went to see Hanili the next day. She found her in a bright new side-room. It had flowery window blinds and Senior Matron Heather in it making a fuss.

'What is the matter Hanili, should I get Dr Deya?' said Matron. 'Do you not like the room?' She came over to feel Hanili's brow. 'You're burning like hellfire. Who upset you?' she said. Senior Matron Heather shot an angry glance at Dele and went to open the window.

'I've only just arrived,' said Dele.

Hanili started to cry again. 'Where is she, not back from the school-trip, er, two weeks?' she said.

Dele hugged her. 'I'm so sorry, Keli's…gone. Baba Funi told me.

Hanili groaned. Dele wiped her friend's runny nose. 'I just knew it. You must have known too…and for almost a fortnight,' said Hanili, shaking her head.

Dele nodded. 'You were on the critical list, I didn't know what to do.'

'But I could have told the police. Someone threatened Keli.' Hanili buried her head in Dele's chest and sobbed. Dele shuddered at the thought of rats and vultures picking at dead Keli and her mum on a railway line. She rocked Hanili to the elegiac piano music floating through the wall. Matron Heather sidled out.

The tune ended. 'I know it's not your fault,' said Hanili. She lifted her head. Tears shone on her steroid-bloated cheeks. 'We're a right pair,' she said, wiping her face with the back of her hand.

Dele got off the bed. Her head ached. Garrulous drums beat on the radio next door.

'It's the toothpaste jingle,' said Hanili with a sniffle. She blew her nose. 'Have you met Dr Deya?' she said.

'Not exactly,' said Dele.

'The nurses call him Dr Idea, Dr Waladi sent for him…after you chucked your toys out of the pram the other day,' said Hanili.

Dele blushed.

Hanili pointed to the pink cannula in her arm. 'His …beautiful handiwork. He'll kill me if it falls out…but he has this theory, em, about my illness…'

***

Dr Deya met Dele in his cramped office after that afternoon's ward round. Aged about forty, he had thick tightly curled black hair, and what looked like a broken nose. The tiny knot on his blue striped blue and white tie squeezed his beige shirt collar into a pair of dog ears.

'My wife,' he said to Dele, cupping his hand over the mobile phone. 'She's not used to the slow pace here.' He stopped while a young woman tested the table for sturdiness with a nudge from her hip before she put the food tray down. The spicy aroma of fried rice made Dele's stomach rumble. 'And one more plate, for my colleague here,' said Dr Deya.

Dr Deya ate like a man on a speed trial. He didn't seem to need to chew his food. 'I came back from Belgium, a few months ago,' he said, between heaped mouthfuls of steaming rice. 'I was born not far from here.' He put his toothpick in a saucer. 'Waladi asked me to take a look at your friend. You must have upset him. Unusual for him to ask for help…'

'And what did you think?' said Dele.

'Call me Iyan.' He jangled a tiny bell and licked his lips. The woman came in to clear the table. Her face dropped and she gave Dele and her empty plate a cold stare.

Don't blame me, it was your ideal doctor who ate all the rice.

'Simulated Immune Deficiency Syndrome, at least that's what they called it in Leuven. I have heard it called Dilaids- Disease like Aids,' said Dr Deya, rubbing his nose.

He's sound. Where have you been all this time? 'I've never heard of this...condition. Prognosis?' said Dele.

Dr Deya licked his lips again and smiled. 'One good thing. It's not contagious. There is no single test, but your friend is like the patients I saw as a trainee. Many from the Congo. You wouldn't imagine. La crème de la crème, yet they thought that some witchdoctor crushed magic weevil into their millet. Politicians, teachers, oui, doctors. I did not believe them, initially.' He put a palm out to the scowling woman for a squirt of soap.

'You do believe them now?' said Dele.

Dr Deya nodded while he washed his hands in a bowl.

'In a way. We saw a few cases so they sent me to Congo to investigate. I continued the research here.'

'Not a waste of time?'

Dr Deya wiped his hands with a napkin. 'First few months I said to myself this is like looking for mermaid in the desert. But it's been worth it...published several papers. It can be caused by a unique brew of local herbs...starts like a bad case of pneumonia, Malaria or Dengue or Yellow Fever, then lungs collapse and cavitate. Patient drowns in toxic waste. Some may be complicated by parasitic superinfection, there is an argument for saying it's all about infection and not juju, so it is always worth finding out more about the ingredients. In other words Sids is an alloy of microbiology and psychology and immunology, *c'est vrai.*'

'I can't believe this, poor Hanili...'

The doctor's left eye twitched. 'Your friend has many who do not take so kindly to her...ways. But few are likely to know how to make this, and to have the means of delivery. Very difficult to make proof.'

'Poisoned? Any antidote, immunoglobulins, plasma exchange, something like that. Can we still salvage her renal function?' she said.

Dr Deya shook his head, licked his lips. He tinkled the bell. A different woman came back in to clear up the rest of the plates. Dr Deya gave her a tip. The woman crept out and closed the door.

'I had a guardian…knows a lot about this sort of medicine. Pastor Ambasi,' said Dele.

'Him, hah. He refused to speak to me…claims that I am trying to steal secrets of Roko people for overseas companies. Me?'

'You explained…?' said Dele.

Dr Deya nodded. 'You say this man was your guardian? Perhaps you can convince him to help me. Fifty percent of cases suffer a fatal relapse. I can sniff it. Her CRP is climbing, more cells in her urine. We can't just keep dosing her up with steroids and climbing down again. Your friend and her kidneys are not out of the path of this storm. Perhaps if this pastor can help us, tell us what is in the concoction…may be her best chance to save her kidneys, her brain, her life.'

FIVE

Dele got off the bus. It had rained earlier that July day, as always, and wispy steam rose from the shimmering tarmac. She crossed the road to avoid a group of demob happy children and stopped at a convenience store to buy a pack of beer. As she turned left off Sankara Central Motor Road on to Egypt Street she thought she caught a glimpse of Ambasi standing on his balcony. She waved and tried to keep him in view, but a pushcart full of bric a brac crossed in front of her and forced her on to the muddy sidewalk. When she looked up again Ambasi had gone. *Am I dreaming again?* Trying not to agitate the six-pack of beer swinging in her hand she hurried down the street to knock on Ambasi's door. A silent minute passed. She knocked again, harder. A door clicked open behind her.

'Who are you?' The woman in the doorway had a tower of grey hair and a silver chain with a name tag "Sylvia" dangling round her neck. 'You want break the door?' she said.

'I've come to see…pastor,' said Dele. 'Sorry, my name is Dele and Ambasi is my guardian. I'm a student.' Dele pointed through the corner of the wall to where she imagined she saw Ambasi on the balcony. 'I saw him standing…around here, there,' she said.

'You are student? Is that why you bang his door. Typical, you want to cause a riot?'

I haven't the time for this. 'Can I get in or not?' said Dele.

'He not well, I make him cocoa and juice for fever yesterday,' said Sylvia, with a flinty stare.

'Antikath didn't say anything about that. I thought I saw him a few minutes ago.'

'Come,' said Sylvia. Dele followed her. Sylvia's flat smelled of stale tobacco and fresh coffee. Out on the balcony a plank bridged the scaffolding between the flats.

'No other way?' said Dele, with sweat gathering on her lip.

'Do you see one?' said Sylvia.

Dele handed the tins of beer to Sylvia, rolled her jeans up and climbed, gingerly, on to the plank as if it were a piece of string. It started to rain. Half a dozen nervous and slippery shuffles later Dele vaulted into Ambasi's wet balcony and looked through the steamed up window between cupped hands. Two bare feet dangled over an upturned chair. *No, no.* Dele smashed the window with a vase, put her hand through the broken pane to open the door, ran into the dining area, found a knife in the kitchen sink, and leapt on to the stool. A spark of static from Ambasi's white gown stung her as she grabbed him by the waist. She tried to take his weight but the noose pulled up tight. Ambasi's bulging eyes rolled open. 'It's me, Traytop,' said Dele, sweating like a horse. She lifted herself on to her toes to reach the rope with the knife in her left hand, but it was all she could do not to drop Ambasi and stop him rotating while she tried to keep her arm and hand going in an awkward and frantic sawing motion through the thick rope. After an aching eternity, the rope snapped. Ambasi's dead weight thumped into Dele's chest. She teetered on the edge of the stool for a moment, fell backwards, but pulled Ambasi over her to break his fall. Ambasi's elbow dug into her midriff. Dele crashed into the coffee table, gasped, winded. *Is he alive?* She rolled on to her knees. Her lungs burned but some life returned to her arms. *Airways, Breathing, Circulation, Disability, Exposure. It's all very well with a dead mannequin.* She put her cheek to Ambasi's face, listening for a breath, looking to make sure his tongue or the noose was not blocking his airway.

'Help, help me,' she said at the top of her voice while she tried to feel round the noose for a pulse on his whealed neck. And, to her horror, when she put her head to his chest she sensed neither beat nor breath.

She got to work. Sweat rolled off her face. The acid returned to gnaw at her neck and arms. Ambasi's neck and head jerked and rolled with each chest compression. Soon, in spite of what she had been taught, Dele found herself kneading and rocking from the waist instead of pushing straight up and down. Acrid sweat, tears pooled in her eyes and the images from the camp, the goat with the head the wrong way round, Eniadudu on the funeral pyre, Jane in the van, flashed into her head. Angry, afraid and despairing, she counted to the end of the third, or was it fourth, cycle of compressions. She checked his neck again. Again pulseless. She pressed on his chest. On the first upstroke the front door crashed open and two burly ambulance crew dressed in green togs strode in carrying a yellow and red defibrillator.

'How long have you been...going?' said the first man as he took over the compressions.

'Not sure,' said Dele, stretching her limbs and back.

The second man attached a monitor. Ambasi's heart tracings had gone from flat to little tremors, to rapid jagged, coarse deflections, back down to flat until, after the fourth shock and more thumping one of the men said, 'we have return of spontaneous circulation. Let's take him to hospital before something bad happen.'

Dele waded through ankle-deep flood waters to get into the back of the ambulance. 'I'm a medical student,' she said. They let her pump air into Ambasi's lungs with a laryngeal mask. The driver cursed and did a multi-point turn, keeping the van in the middle of the road to avoid hidden kerbs and gutters. With siren wailing, they lurched through the floods, the driver crouching to peer through the foggy windscreen and past the piece of cardboard plastered to it by lashing wind and rain. 'What's your name?' said one of the crewmen.

'Dele.'

'Well done, Dele.'

Dele rubbed her sore wrists. She gave the bag another squeeze. Ambasi's chest rose and fell. 'Are we going to HealthSmart?' she said.

'They don't take this sort of patient,' said the ambulance man. Dele tried to hide her disappointment. She had hoped to see Hanili.

'Aloisi centre has good people too,' said the shorter man, bracing himself against the door as the ambulance rocked over a mound of refuse.

***

Dele got up at five the next morning, put on her hardest wearing pair of jeans and waterproof jacket and set off for the Aloisi centre.

The flood waters on the road outside the hospital had reached waist high, the odour of ordure, rotting milk and eggs and animal flesh, strong enough, it seemed, to knock the earth off its path. The wash from a passing van almost knocked her over. She bumped into a black bin bag. It burst and the snout of a dead rat poked through a slit. Dele shrieked and, as if on cue, a fridge paddled by a man in a broad-rimmed black hat and a red scarf drifted up.

'How you dey?' said the man.

Dele pointed to the hospital, half a mile away.

'Enter, but pay me first,' said the man.

After half an hour on the makeshift raft Dele arrived at the main entrance.

'Your smell can kill well person not to speak of patient on edge of life,' said the hospital receptionist. With a showy waft of a palm over her nose she directed Dele to a staff shower and showed her where to get a fresh pair of green togs.

On Ward 12 Ambasi had his eyes closed in bed, the wheal on his neck as thick as a man's thumb. The blood pressure monitor read 76/50mmHg. A bag of intravenous saline fell off the drip stand. Dele picked it up, held it over her head and gave it a squeeze. *Every little will helps.* Ambasi sat up. 'Traytop,' he said, in a weak voice. Dele hugged him. He let out a soft cry.

'Sorry, I forgot about your cracked ribs.' *Resus officer was right. I push too hard.* 'Anyway, as you're a man, according to the Bible you can spare the odd rib,' said Dele. She patted the corner of the bed and sat down.

'Where are your proper clothes?' he said.

'Why did you do it?' said Dele.

Ambasi's eyes glazed over. As he turned to the window the bed sheet fell off his thin legs. 'Sin is our second skin how do we shed it...'

'Are you pastor? Dr Saura's patient?' said a passing nurse. Ambasi nodded. The nurse muttered to herself and set off for the next 4-bedded bay.

'I thought you were under Dr Dariani,' said Dele, pulling the sheets back over Ambasi.

Ambasi shrugged his shoulders. 'Easier to agree.' He stroked the wheal on his neck. 'Can you bring my book? It's the one that has been going round in my head all these years. Everyone has nuclear weapons, except us, everyone has a holy book, except us. So I told you I was going to start one from African point of view, but I will never finish. Haven't even made a proper start.' He seemed to brighten up. 'I was tracing our story from early human life in South and East Africa, from that 1st great great...great grandmother they call Lucy – I'll call her Ibere. Then I go on to Zimbabwe, Mali, Egypt, mix in myths and heroes, and end with Mandela. This is how all the imported holy books started. The bits they did not remember they made up. But they are good stories. I enjoyed them and I believe so did you: burning bushes that are not consumed, water turned into wine. Shame the authors are anonymous. They would win Nobel Prize for Literature every year.'

'But you'd still end up with followers of Mandela fighting those of Mansa Musa fighting those of Lumumba. It is our way is it not...as human beings?' said Dele.

Ambasi stroked his wheal again and coughed. 'If the gods are not colonial imports, perhaps we will be less likely to attribute their powers to the supernatural.'

'We can only hope,' said Dele.

Ambasi coughed. It looked painful. 'Go to the flat. I don't trust the lawyer. It's all there. Pay the hospital. Don't let them say pastor did not settle his...his...bills.'

A nurse arrived with four pink capsules and a cup of black coffee. Ambasi grimaced and chucked the pills down his throat. 'Fair trade coffee. So, is the other coffee they sell us not fair? Nurse, can I have a smoke?' He squeezed Dele's hand. 'When do I see you again?

Call me tomorrow. When are your exams? I hope you understand. Traytop, please forgive me. I was goaded by an urge that I truly thought that I had defeated. Desires, urges, make fools of us, twist us in and out of shapes. But if you rid us of urges, will that make us good, or free? Or will we become like flowers in the field, at the beck and call of the wind and the rain and the sea and at the mercy of the bee?' Ambasi sighed. He shook his head and patted Dele on the cheek. A nurse arrived with a bedpan. Ambasi swung his thin legs over the side of the bed and waved with his half-clenched fist. Dele sailed back over the floods on a raft made of flattened kerosene tins, wondering what Ambasi was trying to say.

***

Back at the flat Ambasi's bedroom smelt vaguely like the hospital, or was it the antiseptic smell of the wards that she could not get out of her head. She beat the dust out of the cushions and replaced them on the chairs then scrubbed the brown blood stains off the floor. At midnight she crept into Ambasi's bedroom, even knocking before she went in, out of some vague sense of respect. The room smelled of dust and camphor. She found Ambasi's cheque books in a drawer and put it in a bag ready to take to the hospital in the morning.

Sleep announced its imminent return with jaw-cracking yawns but Dele did not want to receive it in Ambasi's bedroom. Ambasi had blacked out the window in Dele's old bedroom and her bed lay under piles of dusty papers. On the other side of the room stood boxes full of vinyl records, papers, old bills, souvenirs. A signed photograph of some visiting dignitary, an Archdeacon perhaps, stood on one of the boxes. Beside it Dele found a bundle of papers, a draft of Ambasi's history book. But he did not seem to have got past the first chapter titled, "Dear Ibere", a fictional account of the life of the first family in East Africa. From the scribbled entries, crossed out and stapled on text from other sources, it seemed that as soon as he finished the section some new discovery or debate forced him into yet another revision. *Surely writer's block was not enough to lose him his bearings* thought Dele. He had no money problems and did not press his attentions on female parishioners. She wondered whether it had anything to do with the Rokopats. Had his potion let down one of the top brass for example?

Dele put Ambasi's aborted opus back in its box and found his furry Bible under a pillow. He had highlighted several Old Testament passages in yellow, but his choice seemed arbitrary because he had ignored the New Testament, his usual source of texts for his homilies. When she opened a wardrobe to search for fresh linen a box file labelled "pills and potions for patients, invoices" fell at her feet. Its first page had the date written at the top, followed by a list of antipyretics, balms, snails and reptiles, types of insects and tree bark. The bottom half of the page, consisted of a code written in numbers as well as noughts, crosses and short strokes. Dele didn't know what to make of them.

An old conversation, something Ambasi said on the day he dropped her off at college, stirred a stagnant pool in the back of Dele's mind, but for the life of her she could not recall what Ambasi had said. With her head weighing a ton and the letters on the page beginning to limbo dance, she could not keep her eyes open any longer. Her arms stretched out in a yawn and as she reclaimed them her phone rang.

'What I have to say is not for the radio or airwaves,' said Mrs Lagbaja.

SIX

Dele arrived at Mrs Lagbaja's in the dark.

'Come in, I'm sure that moped taxi fleeced you,' said Mrs Lagbaja in her crumpled brown blouse.

'Sorry I'm late, lectures and a friend wasn't very well,' said Dele. A whiff in the air reminded her of the camp commandant's chicken coops. She followed Mrs Lagbaja through the eerie moonlit hall into the dining room, feeling the glacial and gravelly crunch of what she thought was broken glass and crockery under her feet. Mrs Lagbaja struck a match and groped her way along to light a lantern.

What? The room looked like the aftermath of a battle. Mrs Lagbaja's ornate dining table lay covered in parrot mess, feed and empty cages. Bird parts and feathers lay strewn about the floor.

'Who did this?' said Dele, suppressing a swear word.

'My pets…Comfy…gone,' said Mrs Lagbaja and lowered herself into a dining chair, wincing with pain, effort, or sorrow.

'Are *you* alright?' Dele said.

Mrs Lagbaja shook her head. 'I was feeding the birds in the afternoon, heard loud banging at the door, shouts of police, police. How I fell for that one I'll never know, but maybe it's one of the tablets they gave me in the hospital. Wouldn't have made the slightest bit of difference anyway. They nearly knocked me over. One dressed like Arab, his head like the front of a canoe.'

'Sandman.'

'I know his type. He pushed me along. Hobble faster he said. In my own house. The other one had one of those wicked faces, like you see in movies, stony eyes, lumpy features, trumpet ears and lips. They pushed me into this very chair and asked me to shut up. I'm praying for Comfy to keep his beak shut, but it didn't matter a jot. They knew he was there. Tipped all the birds out of their cages, snapped Little Russia and Big Ukrani's head off. Cooked them on my own stove.'

Dele's face prickled. 'Why didn't you call the-'

Mrs Lagbaja raised her hands in mock surrender. 'The police? Army. Airforce? Who's the one with the wild imagination now?' she said.

'We can't let him get away with this,' said Dele.

Mrs Lagbaja flapped at the wisps of grey hair over her face, drew herself up. 'Won't let them,' she said, dabbing the corners of her mouth with a knuckle. Except for the ticking from the wall clock lying on the floor, the next minute passed in silence.

'I'll make you something hot,' said Dele. She picked her way through the debris into the kitchen to boil the kettle, dropping a teabag into a white mug inscribed with the blue and red logo of the South Roko Birds' Society, before swapping it for a plain yellow mug to spare Mrs Lagbaja's feelings.

'Thanks,' said Mrs Lagbaja. She took a sip, gave Dele a weak nod. 'They took Comfy. The wrestler one was going to kill me, the other one stopped him.'

I wonder why? 'Playing good cop, bad cop, or for some other reason, could be due to some superstition about older women,' said Dele.

'But I'm not going to die in some old people's home. All those people sitting around, waiting for a coffin in front of a wind-up radio.' She paused for another sip, clunked the cup down on a coaster and dabbed the corner of her mouth. 'Let that man go somewhere else to build his fancy condominiums.'

'He must be desperate…to come himself,' said Dele.

'Maybe he doesn't want to lose face…must have promised his cronies he'd make them a fortune and I'm still here, or maybe he's borrowed money and needs to make it back.' She folded her arms across her chest. 'I'm not going.'

Dele got up to pick a smashed parrot cage off the floor.

'Stack those ones in the corner. I'll sort them out. Gifts from friends. Many of them long gone,' said Mrs Lagbaja. She got to her feet, gravity yielding to her demands in crepitant instalments.

Dele swept the floor with a long broom she found in the kitchen. She washed her face in the toilet and put her jacket back on.

'You're not going are you? Do you know what time it is?' said Mrs Lagbaja. 'Pancake? I've got some eggs and milk. It'll do till I get some more supplies.' She shuffled into the kitchen. Dele followed but Mrs Lagbaja waved her back to the dining room.

'Here; two thick one's for you and a special salty one for me. Stuff Dr Awe. If I'm not going to die sweet, might as well die salty…oh my knife,' she said. Mrs Lagbaja returned with her knife. It had a worn bone handle and seemed to be a favourite. She sliced and honeyed each nugget, nodding down each mouthful with a sip of tea with patent relish. Dele gulped her pancakes down and tapped her feet under the table while she watched Mrs Lagbaja. Twenty minutes later, with Mrs Lagbaja still half way through her first pancake, Dele leapt to her feet. 'Getting late,' she said, heading for the exit.

Mrs Lagbaja raised a hand. 'I remember what I was going to tell you last time. Sit down.' She opened a walnut cabinet and produced a gold chain with a medallion inscribed with the letters TB. 'I found this in poor Comfy's room when I got back from hospital, must have been left by those robbers. Funny thing is… they didn't take anything.'

'Are you alright? Oh, my dear, you look as white as baking flour,' said Mrs Lagbaja.

'It's nothing.' Dele went through to the toilet. She leaned over the sink and let the cool water wash over her hair, face and neck. *That's Tafawa's. The impresario.*

She found Mrs Lagbaja clearing up in the kitchen. 'Can I keep it? It may have something to do with your Tardis wardrobe,' she said. She scraped the food remnants left by Sandman into a bin liner and put them in the fridge.

'What on earth are you doing?' said Mrs Lagbaja.

'What's left of Little Russia and Ukrani, I'm bagging up. Keep these safe. I have a plot of my own to hatch,' she said, tapping the side of her nose.

'You know who it is? What dubious company you keep.'

Dele tapped her nose again and let herself out. Under a starless sky the lawn twinkled amber and green as though teeming with tiny aliens. A frog begged a princess from the undergrowth, each croak more plaintive than the last. Dele wrapped her arms round her chest against the whistling cold wind and hurried back up the road. She had to find out what Tafawa was doing in Mrs Lagbaja's house. Was he working for Sandman?

SEVEN

'Is Tafawa here?' Dele said, flicking her earrings. In a pair of three-quarter length trousers, a pink top and a black denim jacket with large copper buttons, she thought she looked a right clubber.

'What are you to him?' said the bouncer. He looked like a constipated Sumo wrestler.

Dele tossed her hair back. 'His wife, what do you think,' she said. She showed him her ticket and brushed past into Tasadi nightclub without waiting for a reply.

Inside the club, polyrhythmic guitars chirruped over a thudding bass line and under the flashing strobe lights, the dancers seemed to jerk and snap like manic marionettes. Dele pushed through to the bar to buy a drink. She sat down behind a pillar in one of the darker alcoves. A man leaned over. Supple and lithe of frame with an unlined face he looked late twenties. He had a bright scarf around his neck, a green and black probably satin top tucked into a pair of jeans.

'How much…?' he said. Dele did not catch the rest. The man leered at her, jangled notes and coins near Dele's ear. He had a sharp smell of beer, sweat and nicotine.

'I'm not sure,' said Dele, raising her voice to be heard.

'Listen to this one. You think I no pay you, what you doing here in Tasadi? Is that how you ended up in this country? Your mama missed road?' he said with an angry look on his face.

'No need for that,' said Dele. This is my friend's club. I know the band "Jiju Brigade", well.' She looked him up and down with affected disdain. 'You are not my type. I want Tafawa.'

The man poked his pumped up pectorals through the open shirt. 'You know who I am? I'm Sikiru, band member. Guitar. I know where to find him,' said the man.

'I thought I recognised you,' said Dele, playing along. 'Was it at festival? I do some artwork.'

'Pah, band for students. Jiju Brigade…we are international. Next month, Togo. Benin…'

'Tafawa tells me you have a good time here. But I no see road myself…get my saying,' said Dele in her best downtown drawl. She eyed Sikiru over the brim of her glass of beer and winked. *This is what they call going with the flow.* 'Is he here?'

The next number started with a sampled James Brown riff. Marshall rolled on to the stage with a girl on his arm and a microphone cable wound, like a snake, round the other arm.

'That's Efun. The latest Marshall…recruit,' said Sikiru, taking a seat and wheeling round to face the stage. The girl had the cherubic looks of teacher's pet on the first day of term and did not look much older than fourteen.

'Come. I'll take you to Tafawa.'

Dele followed him, glaring and swaggering like a Lag, local area girl. They came to a set of pale double doors.

'Hey,' shouted a bouncer. In a baggy pair of lopsided blue dungarees, held on by the left strap thrown over the right shoulder, his boxing career had come to an abrupt halt when he snapped a head of his right biceps during a famous bout. 'Dararasinha, how you dey,' said Dele, prancing on the spot.

Dararasinha looked straight through her.

'Hey Daras, do I not see you right?' said Sikiru.

The man's blood-shot eyes filled with menace and the corner of his mouth twitched. Dele got ready to duck.

'It's only because it's you my Siki. Is she game?' he said, after a moment. He gave a half salute and dropped his arm. *What is game?*

'Who no know will know my man,' said Siki and saluted by shaking his fist above his head. Sikiru guided Dele to the far end of the floor, pushed through what looked like another fire door. Dele found herself in pitch darkness. *This is not good.* She heard a girl groan, heard lips smack and suck and saw a dozen glowing red spliffs flit about in the dark. Buttocks gyrated, wagged, floated, stiffened and fell. Sikiru reached out for Dele's left wrist, gripping it harder than she thought he should and placed it over the hard lump pushing at the front of his trousers. Dele flinched. Shrill warnings went off in her head. But Sikiru pulled her harder. 'This one followed me here,' he said.

'Bring,' said a man in a deep baritone voice. He sat up, putting on pause a girl's oral gyrations on his obelisk. 'Siki my man, you do well, fresh meat, hot flesh,' he said.

'Marshall ah, ah, how many you want do?' said Sikiru.

The image of that room and the aroma of Sandman's cigarettes in the camp flashed into Dele's head. *Must get out.* She rubbed Sikiru's swelling crotch and, sensing his guard drop, swung her right elbow as hard as she could into his right ribcage. She heard a crack. Sikiru cried out. 'Ah, what do this woman?' he said. With head swimming and ears ringing, Dele ran, trampled over a leg and a saxophone, tripped back out of the yard and through a door. She ended up in another dark but busy corridor. 'Kakakolu, shansha, baluba,' she said, adding other what she thought were credible night-club phrases as she shoved and bounded through until, stumbling down some steps, she found herself back on the oval dance floor. A short man gyrating to the music bumped into her, grinned and staggered off, bouncing into another girl, whose man shoved him away. He collided with a table. Bottles crashed on to the floor. A drinker at the depleted table leapt to his feet and dropped the clumsy dancer with a right hook. The erstwhile dancer got up, his rheumy eyes fixed on Dele.

'You caused this,' he said, winding up his fist. At that moment a strong hand grabbed Dele by the left wrist and spun her round. 'Ah, ah, what you do here at Tasadi spot?' It was Tafawa.

Tafawa had a large gold ring in his left ear and had a wide-striped red and beige shirt open from the waist. The tips of polka-dotted black and red brogues peeked from under a pair of white bell-bottomed trousers: on his chain the initials, TB.

'This is my dad's place,' said Tafawa, scratching his goatee.

'I come to chill, look what happens. Now I run into a renegade like you,' said Dele, shouting to make herself heard above a scratchy vinyl rendition of "Brown Sugar." The live band had gone on a short break. 'I thought this was a busy time for you medics,' said Tafawa.

'All work and no play…,' said Dele.

'What?' said Tafawa. 'Oh, no worry. I know medics who did not know nothing, everyday so-so club and girls, kai, many are top doctors abroad.' He dragged Dele off the dance floor to the bar. A young woman in a raffia red and yellow bikini skipped up to Tafawa to shout into his ear. Tafawa fondled her breasts. *Lucky her, at least a 34D.*

'Do me a favour. I need somewhere to stay for a day or two, my room-mate's fiancé is visiting and I want to give them space,' she said with a knowing smile and tap on Tafawa's forearm. Tafawa detached himself from the girl. The girl scowled, fished a couple of bank notes out of Tafawa's top pocket and flounced off. The band reassembled on stage in animal skin tops over red pairs of trousers embroidered with a black map of South Roko.

'Let's go to my base, too much noise and I don't want that girl… are you coming?' He scratched his chin.

They walked through a backstage door and up a narrow spiral staircase into a large room shaped like a coffin. A single ceiling bulb washed the room in dilute light. Tafawa peeled off his clothes and planted himself on a red chaise longue. With his hairy belly hanging over the broad waist of his Chelsea football club boxer shorts, Dele thought he looked ridiculous.

'Sit. That is my sister and her kids,' he said, following Dele's gaze. A handsome woman and three boys beamed down from the framed photograph on the wall. Dele sat down in a one-armed chair, grateful for the rest.

Tafawa snapped out of his chair. 'Jesus. It's nearly two and no fucking arrangement,' he said. He pulled on his goatee.

A cork popped in Dele's stomach. *What does he mean, fucking arrangement?*

'Fried chicken? Microwave chicken, boiled chicken, baked?' said Tafawa, counting off the choices on his fingers.

'An egg or two will do, with a soft drink,' said Dele with relief.

'Egg and what? Ah doctor, you don't know how to enjoy.' Tafawa fished a mobile phone out of his pocket and ordered a double serving of fried chicken. 'Sleep through there, it is free today.' He pointed down a dark corridor. 'For me for me I like to enjoy first. I sleep well, well, after fuck. Fuck works better than any pills…and you can't overdose. Do they teach you that in medical school?' His tone changed and he fixed Dele with red eyes. 'Are you like saying that this fiancé man is want the both of you, that is why you hide here?' he said.

'Don't be ridiculous,' said Dele.

'Man must ask,' said Tafawa.

Dele called Ambasi's ward at three o'clock. 'No change,' said Sister. The news dropped a barb into her heart.

***

The sun shining red through her eyelids woke her up at nine the next morning. She called Mrs Lagbaja, who sounded frantic.

'All day this giant's been watching the house. Won't even let them deliver the newspapers or the parrot feed. I'm at my wit's end. I gave some freelance men money to get rid of him but they took my dosh and disappeared.'

'Can't talk. I'm in the house of the medallion man. I've got to go. Someone's coming,' said Dele.

Tafawa's house-girl brought in the breakfast. 'It good?' said Tafawa, waddling in with his shiny belly button peeping over the top of a red loin cloth. He opened the dish and forked two large pieces of yam on to a plate, folded an omelette between them to make a sandwich and disappeared across the landing to his room. 'For stamina. By the way I disciplined Sikiru,' he said, over his shoulder. Dele waited an hour before she crept over the landing to eavesdrop at Tafawa's door. *Perhaps the "sleeping tablets" have worked* she thought and tiptoed back to her room.

She switched the TV on. Babubacka's usual lies oozed from his greasy mouth. *Another initiative to provide clean water. Billions of Yuan in bilateral kickbacks.* Dele turned up the volume, bolted the door top and bottom, rummaged through drawers and cupboards, under the mattress and cushions, but found nothing to explain what Tafawa was doing at Mrs Lagbaja's. She wondered whether she could not just come out and ask Tafawa about the pendant, but decided that that would be suicide if the impresario worked for Sandman.

Dele went on to the sunny balcony to clear her head. She watched the people go by until her arms started to tingle from resting on the hot balcony rails. Back inside, as her eyes got used to the light, the one spot she had not searched stared back at her. With her heart thumping with bated hope, she went over to check the door again before she got on to her knees to fish around the TV cabinet. Tangled amongst the plugs and wires and cobwebs underneath the cabinet, she found a DVD labelled "Pumped Friction II" in a white jacket.

She slotted the disc into the player. The crude credits rolled on to a jerky movie of a muscle-bound man in bed with a prepubescent girl, who fondled the buds on her chest while she bounced up and down, an otherworldly expression on her face. The man's pay check seemed to be based on the word count of expletives. Dele was about to switch the player off when the scene segued into another. *Shafts of fucked lightening.* The cage in the corner of the room, the pale wardrobe with the broken handle, the picture of the parrot on the wall, the black and white tiles, it had to be Mrs Lagbaja's house. And there was Confucius hopping about repeating what he heard from the bed below. *So that explains Comfy's vocabulary.*

Questions rolled up in her head. *What was Tafawa's job? Cameraman, producer, director, editor, actor? Did Mrs Lagbaja disturb them? Is that why the wardrobe toppled over her? How did they know she was not in in the first place? Would she rent out her room for cheap spanks?* She tidied the room in a frenzy and got up to brush the dust off her clothes. She had just slapped a cobweb off her trouser leg when she heard loud banging on the balcony window.

'Why you lock door? Eh, what the *dogoni* are you doing?' said Tafawa. He swung his trailing leg on to the balcony and hopped into the room.

Dele shoved the DVD into a bag and leapt for the exit. She kicked the bottom bolt open but the top bolt would not budge. Tafawa's hands closed round her neck. She felt the heat and aroma of his morning breath on the back of her head. Summoning all her strength she pushed backwards against the door. Tafawa wheezed and they both fell on to the floor.

Dele leapt for the door again, grabbed the bolt and tugged, but she might as well have been towing an oil tanker with a paper clip.

Tafawa grabbed her by the neck and threw her to the floor. 'I will kill you this girl,' he said.

'Why the old lady's house. Are you working for Sandman?' she said, as Tafawa yanked her up on to her feet and the room spun round her ears.

'You want die, doctor?' he said, but Dele saw a flicker of fear in his eyes.

'I have no quarrel with you. It's the mama I'm trying to help. How did you know that her place was free?' she said, panting for breath.

Tafawa paused as if he had not thought of that himself and in that split second Dele shoulder-charged him. He tripped over a stool, caught his head on the end of an armchair. He groaned, and tried to get up but fell flat on his belly, heaving for breath. A wheal ballooned over his right eye. Dele skipped away from his desperate grab at her foot and yanked again at the stubborn bolt. It came away from the jamb and hung off a crocked nail. With another desperate pull from Dele the door flew open and a dinner lady, probably eavesdropping, tripped and staggered along to land on Tafawa's knee.

'Stupid idiot, you've broken my leg,' said Tafawa, shoving the woman away.

Dele charged out, collided with a late riser on a landing, leapt down the flight of stairs, brushed herself down with a pretence of nonchalance, put on a drunken gait, and, once out of sight of a bemused couple in the hall, picked her knees up and ran.

***

A brisk and stiff-legged ten-minute walk later, she ducked into an alley and crept along the narrow backstreets until she found a space in the oblong shadow of a church. To loud drumming in her head she sat down on a step. Her thoughts went back to *Pumped Friction II*. *If Dada was making money from dirty movies Sandman must know.* Then she remembered that in her haste to escape she had left the tape behind in Tafawa's room. *Daft and useless, you.* She was still cursing herself when her phone rang.

'Two men came…here this afternoon,' Franko said with a breathless stammer.

'What did they want?' she said.

'Please tell me the truth Dele. Your friend is in hospital you don't know…what's wrong with her. I heard that her young helper dies. Then these…ugly looking…urgh, men came this afternoon. Are you into heavy stuff? I know you were short of money…'

'Of course not. Trust me. Franko, do me a favour. I can't come back to college at the moment but I need your help.'

'Keep me out of your trouble,' said Franko. He went quiet. Dele sensed that Franko was talking to his precious girlfriend. 'Ok. This and I'm done. I am moving out of college…until it is safe,' he said.

'I'll tell you where I am. And it's not the Majestic,' said Dele. Dele closed the call and wandered around till it was dark. She bought barbecued beef from a roadside hawker and washed it down with a bottle of water. After that she had only loose change left. She went to sit on the steps outside a petrol station but an oil tanker arrived and proceeded to smoke her out. At eleven, hungry and shivering in the cold night, Dele shouldered into the departure hall of Dili Chuchu bus company.

About twice the size of a schoolroom, the ground floor reception hall heaved with passengers. After half an hour of pushing and shoving, past the grumbles of vented frustration at some delay or perceived insult, past the boy and girl cursing each other and a woman clouting her son about the ears for being tardy or perhaps for being there or born at all, Dele hurdled a cage of hens to reach a cracked noticeboard. In chalk, the time-table said the bus would leave in about five hours, at five o'clock. *I can stay here all night then.* Affecting an aggressive mien, she found a space on the edge of a benign-looking couple's mat, next to a girl crying for her dress that had split but not at the seams. The couple's toddler strained at her leash. 'Let her come,' said Dele. The mother eyed Dele's torn blouse, but must have seen something reassuring as well. 'Take,' she said, letting the little girl roll into Dele's lap. The little girl smiled up at Dele with wide, ash-grey, eyes. Dele tapped the toddler's tiny shoulders with her fingers and rocked in time to a silly ditty she made up. The ditty put her in mind of Hanili and goose bumps tickled her neck.

'She's not good with strangers usually,' said the mother. Dele handed the sleeping girl back and called the hospital.

'Miss Hanili has been more up than down. She is asleep,' said Sister. Cheered up a fraction, Dele rested her chin on her chest and fell asleep.

An engine's growl yanked her out of sleep. She saw the passengers push and shove and bump, cursing their way out through the door as if in flight from a plague. The hall emptied in under five minutes. Dele crouched under a water spigot in the corner and had a wash. Her hair was still wet when Franko arrived in a shiny metallic grey sports car.

'I have liquidity problems but at this short notice, take this, about fifty-five plus some Bobos,' he said handing her the notes through the car window.

It'll have to do.

'And Lari said to give you this,' Franko said, handing Dele a white cotton blouse.

'You are a big sweetie,' said Dele. She leaned in through the car window to give him a hug. Franko drove off and Dele called Ambasi's ward. 'Not so good,' said Sister.

'Give him my love,' Dele said with a knot in her throat. After a spicy hot breakfast of rice and beans and fried peppers served in broad banana leaves, Dele turned her mind to the next stage. She needed Sandman's recent autograph.

EIGHT

At one o'clock armed with a notebook she had filled with bogus addresses and signatures to make it look like a delivery record book, Dele pulled her cap down over her face and crossed the busy road in air so heavy she could have done with a shovel for her lungs. 'There is no Gobi Street. Only new Gobi Street, since last month,' said the bedraggled blind man on crutches.

'What do they call the old Gobi Street?' said Dele.

'Arami Boulevard,' said the blind man.

After Sandman's son. At about two o'clock, with her new shirt soaked with sweat and beginning to grate in her armpits, Dele arrived outside a pink three-storey building. Sandman's signpost hung from a first floor balcony and a window. '*Versatile Associates: no mission impossible, no matter too small,* a tagged on phrase: *the unblocker of anything from nose to airport runway* had probably been scrawled on to the end after his promotion. Dele pulled her cap down over her face and tried to make herself small by holding her arms across her and hunching up. In the foyer she found an envelope addressed to Chief Asiri Oniseme, the Chairman of Versatile Associates, lying in a red plastic tray. She picked it up and tip-toed up the wooden stairs. With each step she took her heart seemed to beat its own path up her tightening throat. A door opened. Sandman's squawk echoed down the stairwell. *He's in.* Dele leapt down the steps, her momentum carrying her into the road. Hurdling a thick finger of molten tarmac, she swerved round a wheelbarrow and crossed the road to crouch behind a silver petrol tanker.

When, after fifteen minutes, Sandman did not re-emerge, Dele crossed the busy road again. Pausing at intervals to see if anyone was watching, she walked up the stairs sideways so that she could make a rapid escape if needed. At the top of the stairs she found a young woman sitting at a desk with her back to a wood-slatted window.

'I have a personal document for your managing director and chairman, where he?' said Dele.

'What do you mean?' said the receptionist shuffling papers to one side. She was wearing a blue lace blouse over a white bra. 'You can leave it with me,' she said. Her hand shot out.

'I mean where is he?' said Dele.

'With a client,' she said, pointing down the corridor to Dele's left.

'You don't understand me. I need for him to sign and for me to tell the head office that I was here. You know what they are like.'

'Come back tomorrow,' she said.

'They will kill me. You want me to die?' Dele said, leaning over the desk.

A shy smile softened the young woman's face. She looked down at her bangled wrist. 'How can, no, why would I want that? You have not done me harm.'

'So if I vex you, you *will* kill me?' said Dele.

'What you need?' said the receptionist, placing her elbow on some papers as the breeze from the wall fan above swept the table.

'Only your office paper, only thing I can think of to show my *poga* that I came. Your name?' said Dele.

'Mabel.'

'God bless you,' said Dele, like Ambasi.

Mabel looked uncertain. She looked around as if to look for help, then leaned backwards and opened a desk drawer. 'Take,' she said, holding out three sheets of Sandman's letter-headed paper. Keeping her broken fingers out of sight, Dele turned away to fold the papers into her notebook.

'Mabel, tell him that I'm waiting. My *poga* will not be happy.' Dele looked at her watch. It was a quarter to four. Some offices closed at four. A door opened round the corner.

A bug-eyed man in an ill-fitting grey suit appeared. 'What does this one want at this late hour?' he said. He made an impatient noise.

Dele bowed low. 'Barracks delivery service, sir,' she said in her most obsequious and gruff downtown Roko accent.

'Who are you?' said the man. He pointed at the logo on Dele's cap.

Dele couldn't remember what was on her cap. *Run, now*, shouted her shrill inner friend. 'Courier sir, are you the chairman sir? Please sign here, sir,' she said. Hiding her right hand under the newspaper she handed the man the brown envelope with the other. She heard another door open.

'I've never heard of such useless company,' said the bug-eyed man in a loud voice. He gave Dele back the envelope.

'Who is that?' Dele heard a door shut and Sandman coming round the corner. *I warned you intoned her little friend. This is not good.*

'Morning sickness,' said Dele, pointing to her belly. She clapped her hands across her mouth and raced for the door to the men's toilet, reaching it just before Sandman.

'Someone is inside,' said the receptionist. Out of the corner of her eye Dele saw Sandman coming. She bent over double and retched and, hiding her face behind her hand, wheeled round and raced the other way back to the receptionist's desk.

'Turn right,' said the receptionist.

'Which right?' said Dele, wondering whether she should just dash for the exit.

'By my left,' said the receptionist, pointing away from Sandman. Dele tumbled into the ladies' toilet, waited for her chest to stop heaving, simulated half a dozen deep-throated croaks and retches and splashed water on to her face. A few minutes later, with her face screwed up in feigned anguish, she opened the door and crept out with her hands and notebook over her belly. 'Do me favour. I need doctor for woman problem,' she said, sidling gingerly into a chair with her left hand over her face.

Sandman was standing by the desk. 'Don't die here,' he said. 'Mabel, get her out.'

'What about this signing, sir?' said Mabel.

'Me? Nonsense,' said Sandman and walked away. Dele watched him through a gap in her fingers and racked her brain for ways to salvage her plan.

'Mabel why don't you sign? Ah, oh, this my belly go kill me. Then I can tell my *poga* that you are co-operate and show that I reached this place. Your *poga* can answer for himself. Just in case the General office want to know...'

Mabel looked unsure. 'Can I sign my own part sir?' she said as Sandman disappeared round the corner. 'Can I not go to piss in peace?' said Sandman.

'God knows what will happen when I tell them back at headquarters,' Dele said.

'But I have no authority to sign when–'

Sandman returned too soon to have used the toilet. He gave Dele a puzzled glance, during which Dele almost passed out, grabbed the notebook off Mabel, grunted and signed a page.

Dele fled. Outside, the rush hour had started and ordinary Sankarans milled around on foot, fighting to get in the queues for the mopeds, the smoke-belching taxis, the lopsided buses. Some, with heavy goods queued for donkeys. Sticky with sweat, her mouth as dry as a groundnut shell, Dele went to sit on a roadside brick wall to gather her thoughts. She waited for a lull in the traffic noise and called Aanu.

NINE

Aanu arrived half an hour later on his black and gold "John Player" motorbike.

'Why black leather in this hot sun.? Is it what you GeleRokos wear?' said Dele.

'My one and only true medic…me I don't sweat,' said Aanu. He jerked the zip on his jacket up and down, made a sign of a cross, kissed his knuckle and raised it and his eyes to the sky. 'I'll drop you at Aunty Norma's. See you after urgent business,' he said.

Mama Robi, known in the church as Norma, lived in a single-fronted bungalow on Ethiopia Avenue. With her bright eyes, round cheeks, Mama Robi still looked just as sweet and kind as Dele remembered her. Sobbing, she held Dele in a lung-defying hug. After a long shower Dele had fish stew, sweet potatoes and fried eggs with Mama Robi at a low wooden table in the kitchen. As in many other houses in South Roko, the kitchen doubled as the living room. It had a double-hobbed cooker against the wall on the right as you walked in. The cooker was supplied by a green pipe from a caged gas cylinder outside. Round the table sat four chairs, one metal and four wooden, and on the table a portable black and white TV sat on a frilly plastic doily. One door led to the private quarters and another, to a store-room or pantry.

'They force us to move here to Ethiopia Avenue after all the daily trouble from Rokopats, Sharijujumen, area boys. You want more curry?' said Mama Robi, fanning the smoke from the stove away with her hand.

Dele shook her head.

'Here, we have tarred roads. Every week, maybe two, cleaner come to clear the street. We have park for children to play,' said Mama Robi.

'Not like my old Nigeria Street,' said Dele.

'That is because mama of the mistress of army officer lives not far. Any trouble maker they shoot *pam pam*.'

'What if the shot are innocent?' said Dele.

'It is worth it. Even Americans with all their satellites cannot avoid clatter and die image?' she said. She got up to fill a kettle from the orange water butt by the sink.

Clatter and die image? Ah, collateral damage, probably nearly the same thing.

'I hear your mama…died,' she said.

Dele nodded, fatigue almost cracking her resolve not to cry. 'I can't talk today…about it,' she said.

'Sandman caused this,' said Mama Robi. 'Only God save Aanu in camp. They think he is Nagati. All Kombo boys they finish with machete. Three months in the bush. The things that enter his eyes, fear to come out of his mouth. I don't blame too much for how he is…he just want enjoy life because you no know when they will end it for you. That is what he says.' She pulled a red handkerchief from her cleavage and blew her nose. 'And you?'

'Me?'

'Aanu saw you in camp. How it be?' said Mama Robi.

The image of a funeral pyre and Eniadudu's broken leg flashed into Dele's head. She adopted a world weary shrug. 'We thank God. UN peacekeepers saved us,' she said. She felt the blood rushing to her face so she started to clear up.

'What are you doing? Sit down let me wash the plates,' said Mama Robi. 'I will never forget what you did for Robi. God bless.' Mama Robi closed the window against the noise of a barking dog and switched a fan on. 'Is it true? Pastor helped you these last years?' she said.

'I don't know what would have happened without him. In fact I do. But isn't it funny that I should run into Aanu like that the festival? With his GeleRoko mates, or what do you call them,' said Dele, fanning her face with her hand.

'That's how God works. Was the pepper too hot?' She handed Dele a bottle of iced water.

Aanu came hurtling in to the room with a cardboard box stuck to his right foot by a piece of tape. 'Evening mama,' he said, kicking the carton off his foot. He tried an Ali shuffle, of which he seemed unjustifiably proud and made alternate cutting passes above his close-cropped hair with cupped hands.

'Why do you jump about like a jackass? I needed that box for returns, cans and plastic bottles,' said Mama Robi.

'My one *genuine* knock out doctor, know what I'm saying, wicked,' said Aanu in an American accident, emphasising the "genuine" by banging his fist into a palm and touching Dele's chin with it. 'Aunty Norma, you know where I found doctor? By the big oil drum near Greg's house.' Aanu stood a fingerbreadth or two taller than Dele, about 6 ft. tall, his thin face as smooth as the inside of a coconut shell. When he laughed his nostrils flared out into pink lozenges and his playful eyes shone with tears. He had a narrow waist and a jutting, behind, Dele thought like the back end of a horse. His long chin must have come from his father. Babubacka's thugs killed him.

Aanu dragged a carton from under the cooker stand. 'Ah, ah, I thought it was beer,' he said with a hint of disappointment. 'Only milk.'

'I planted another word in the ear of Pali's mama. She said-'

'Marriage is for those who can't get it for free; know what I'm saying.' He ducked under an imaginary blow, pulled his zip up and down his jacket. His aunt shot Dele a knowing glance.

The boy with the shirt round his balls is now the babe magnet.

Mama Robi tutted and shook her head. 'If your mama could hear you talking like a common hooligan...'

Aanu peeled his jacket off, found a can of beer in a cupboard and clicked the ring open. 'I *am* a hooligan, but not common. I am a prince. Sorry Dele, I heard about your friend Hanili. All the market women say it's juju, straight up,' he said taking a seat on the stool next to his aunt.

'Juju is your explanation for everything?' said Dele.

'How you think we escape police?' He bared his forearm to show Dele a tattoo of a parrot standing on an eagle. 'That's my *anjima*…makes me invisible. Police arrest thin air or wrong man.'

'If this hocus pocus really worked sell it to Americans as stealth bomber technology and retire rich.'

Aanu rolled his eyes. 'Ask pastor. He knows about these things.'

'I need your help,' said Dele.

Mama Robi tapped Aanu on a shoulder. 'As long as it's not bookwork,' she said and pulled the mosquito blinds closed.

'It's a patient, one Mrs Lagbaja that I met in the hospital-'

Aanu broke off mid-glug. Beer frothed down his chin. He banged the table and made it rock. 'That witch. She is like Kolo. Kai. Mama, you know her, that woman with tongue sharper than the blade they use to shave elephant. Even Lady "armour face" Fatima cried one whole shift because of that woman.'

Mama Robi nodded.

'Why should they drive her off her land? Sandman took her African Grey parrot and probably killed it,' said Dele.

'Why didn't you say that? If they kill sacred parrot, I will be first in the line to stone the bastards,' said Aanu, his eyes lighting up.

'Clean that mouth out with Dettol,' said Mama Robi, straightening the artificial flowers in the vase.

'Aunty, how can you say that? When they found Manio guilty of selling parrot stew you called all your friends to Nanita quarry to stone him.'

'That's different,' said Mama Robi. 'You can sleep in Robi's room,' she said, turning to Dele. 'Robi is in boarding school. I will bring her to see you one day. That meningitis killed one of her ears but we thank God.'

Mama Robi showed Dele to a dark semi-circular niche near the back of the house where, amongst the pots and pans cowering in the corner, she had made a bed out of old tea crates.

'Will you help me with Mrs Lagbaja?' said Dele while Mama Robi was out of earshot.

'Sweet,' said Aanu, with a duck under another invisible blow.

***

A car exhaust backfired. Minutes later Aanu walked in to his aunt's kitchen heaving a large carton. 'Where is Aunty Norma?' he said.

'Market…she woke me early for breakfast. Yam and pepper soup.'

'Sorry I did not come yesterday. Did you find Mama's yam good? My clutch is more slippery than mashed banana,' Aanu said. 'You finished at the court yesterday?' Dele nodded and washed the red oil off her plate under a dribbling tap.

Aanu looked at his watch. 'Ezeowah. Work and hypertension will kill that woman. Wait.' He bounded out of the room and returned with a trunk box. 'I brought you this to try…GeleRoko costumes, for when we go to your Kolo mama's house,' he said, heaving the lid open.

'I like this one, it's got a carving of a parrot sitting on top of a mongoose with a snake in its mouth. Reminds me of Innocent, my old pet parrot,' said Dele.

'Black mask, white eyeholes, ebony face, ivory eyes…sweet.'

Dele put the mask on and Aanu fiddled with the veil. He stood back. 'That's sic, man,' he said.

'One day I'll hang this up in my wardrobe like a wedding dress,' said Dele. She drew the curtains round her bed and tucked the documents under her Geledo gown.

Back in the front room she met a gangly teenager.

'This is my friend, "Snake legs"' said Aanu.

The teenager had bowed legs and a flute in his left hand. 'Pleased to meet you,' he said. Then he raised the flute to his mouth, stood on one leg and played the first bar of a Siroko folk tune.

'Tell him I'll slice his legs like bread if he doesn't put that thing away...know what I'm saying,' said Aanu. 'Let's go before it is too late in the afternoon.'

Aanu got in the front of the van with Snakes Legs. Dele sat in the back. After an hour and a half they turned off the main road to don their headgear and masks.

'The paint fumes, making my throat and eyes itch,' said Dele with a sneeze.

'Haba, I forgot the menthol,' said Aanu.

'How do I wipe my runny nose?' said Dele.

'The sun will dry it. Is this the place?' said Aanu. He stalled the van and cursed.

Dele peered through the eyeholes and patted the envelope strapped to her waist. 'Drive up a bit closer, so the van won't roll back,' she said.

Aanu crashed the van into gear and it lurched on to within ten feet of Mrs Lagbaja's gate. Before Dele could react a burly man in a brown leather waistcoat and a pair of jeans seemed to drop out of the sky. His bloated face seemed to fill the window.

'Where you are going? Off your masks, now,' he said, making an elephant trunk with his lips. He banged a fist on the roof of the van.

'Geledos cannot show face near seawater,' said Dele, quoting something she had overheard after lights out at school.

'Rubbish, me Burutu, I have *ajesaria* protection,' the man said, thumping his chest. Muscles the size of a child's arm rippled along his temple.

Dele cleared her throat. Sweat and snot ran down her lips. She leaned over the front seat and tapped the Aanu and Snake legs on the shoulders. 'Get ready,' she said.

'What?' said Snake legs.

Dele got out of the car, swayed and tapped her feet as if about to launch into a GeleRoko dance. As she drew level with the man, who was standing on the other side of the van, Dele let out a loud shriek as if it was part of the ritual, leapt into the air and galloped as fast as she could up the slope. Burutu gave chase.

'Hey, no go,' he said and grabbed Dele's right foot. Dele kicked out. Her ankle bracelet snapped off and she wriggled free, but, top-heavy from the headgear, she stumbled and fell as she tried to clamber over the gate.

'Comfy, Comfy,' she shouted at the top of her voice, heaving herself up by the branch of a mango tree. Through the slits in the mask she saw Aanu and Snake legs run up and dive for Burutu's legs. But Burutu soon swatted them away. Leaves and branches tore through Dele's fingers and her head swam from the warm fumes in the mask as Burutu reeled her in with his right leg. Soon she felt his forearm up against her neck. She coughed to clear her throat and shouted out again.

'Comfy, Comfy.'

A parrot squawked and seconds later Mrs Lagbaja appeared at the door. Burutu let go. Mrs Lagbaja scratched the side of her mouth, looked puzzled and turned to go back inside. 'Comfy, it's a Verity dance for Comfy,' said Dele. Mrs Lagbaja paused, tottered back round. 'Comfy and Verity,' said Dele.

'Is it you?' said Mrs Lagbaja, a glint of recognition in her eyes.

'We have a booking. For Comfy, remember,' said Dele.

'I not agree,' said the guard, his breath smelt of pepper and cigarette.

'Why all this commotion? Let them dance and go,' said Mrs Lagbaja.

'No,' said Burutu. 'I'll tell him—'

'You kill me then what? Is it not to make our papa's spirit to sleep well that we dance the parrot dance?' She turned to Dele. 'I give you five minutes and five Roko between you. You'll only waste it on weed anyway. And you too, guard, do you want a bottle of imported spirit?' said Mrs Lagbaja pointing a spindly finger at Burutu. Dele hurried towards Mrs Lagbaja.

'It's me, Dele,' she said.

'I know,' said Mrs Lagbaja and withdrew inside. Dele turned to Aanu and Snake Legs. 'I need toilet. Do the fire dance till I come back. Drum and play the flute. Give me a few minutes,' she said in a loud voice. As soon as they got through the door Dele shoved the envelope into Mrs Lagbaja's hands. 'Take these, sign. Keep a copy. I'll tell you what to do, it's to get Sandman. Have you still got the parrot leftovers?'

'I don't understand. No need to go to all this trouble on my account. And who are your friends?' said Mrs Lagbaja.

'No time to explain, just do it,' said Dele. Then she remembered Tafawa's medallion and dashed into Confucius's room, ripped off her headgear, grabbed a chair to stand on and pushed up the ceiling panel near the corner of the room. 'Torch, torch, have you got a torch?' she said.

'Oh, it's broken. Ah, under here somewhere,' said Mrs Lagbaja, wheezing for breath. She rummaged behind the bed and reached up to hand Dele a silver pen torch. Dele scanned the roof space, pulling at anything she could see in the dim light.

'You've brought all the dust down, young lady; and disconnected the bulb and wires. Oh, what's that?' she said.

'I'm going to find out,' said Dele. She held the pear-shaped camera in her palm and shoved it under her costume. Just then Burutu stormed in. He punched Dele on the shoulder and snatched the brown envelope out of Mrs Lagbaja's hand.

'Get out now,' he said. Dele grabbed the envelope back. 'Ah, it is ash inside – what is remaining of mama's parrot, it burst out.' She waved at the swirling dust. 'Mama take, it is yours.'

'Thank you my child,' said Mrs Lagbaja, turning to let Dele dust her down.

Burutu stared at the hole in the ceiling, then at Dele. 'What you do inside there?'

Dele gulped, for moments lost for words. 'Mama's alarm system, the man no finish work well,' she said, hoping for the best.

Burutu shook a menacing fist in her face. 'If you don't go now now I will smash your nose proper,' he said, shoving Dele to the front door where he lifted her by the waist and threw her into the back of the van.

***

Back at Mama Robi's that evening Aanu brought a laptop and they played the footage Dele got from Mrs Lagbaja's ceiling space.

'Dele, why your face look as if it wants to sleep with your feet?' He popped a piece of fried mackerel into his mouth and licked his fingers.

'I saw Pumped Friction at Tafawa's. Nothing here we can pin on Sandman, either,' said Dele, snapping the camera screen shut.

'Wait, I bring data sticks and you make copies for me,' said Aanu. 'Switch on.'

The screen changed to show a naked man lying prone and sweaty on the conjugal bed, nodding with each heave of his barrel chest. Aanu chuckled. 'Snakes Legs, see…the man no get stamina, one round he done finish,' he said.

'If you can do better, maybe you should audition,' said Dele.

'I'm a natural, knaamsaying,' said Aanu.

Dele affected an older sister's air of droll condescension.

TEN

It was Dele's sixth night at Mama Robi's, two days after the trip to Mrs Lagbaja's.

'How are your studies, hope generator not disturb too much?' said Mama Robi, getting up to clear the kitchen table after supper.

"I found time between two and four in the morning when the generators are a not so loud and I put cotton wool in my ears.'

Aanu laughed at Dele's clumsy pull on the oversized blouse of white lace his aunt lent her.

'How is your friend?' said Aanu.

'Kidney trouble,' said Dele.

Mama Robi struck a match and leaned over to light a candle. She screwed it into the liquid wax drippings on the saucer. *She hasn't asked after Ambasi so she must know.*

Dele called Mrs Lagbaja. 'Did you speak to the minister, Banusi?' said Dele.

'Who is that?' said Aanu. Mama Robi carried the laundry out of the room.

Dele waved him silent. 'Mrs Lagbaja,' she said in a stage whisper and went back to her call. 'Sorry ma'am. You were saying. Banusi?'

Dele heard Mrs Lagbaja clear her throat. 'I laid it on, said I thought it was a consortium thing but this man called Asiri, Sandman's real name, that he had killed my parrots and taken the African Grey and got me to sign for him instead. Was it alright I said. I thought he was signing for all of them I said. Told him I had copies with me if he wanted to see.'

'What did Banusi say?' said Dele. Aanu leaned closer.

'In the time it took me to cook a bowl of rice there he was outside my door with the original Britsandchindarusa papers, unsigned. I think he came by helicopter. I showed him your copies, on the Versatile Associates' letter-headed paper-'

'Then what?' said Dele.

'For a second Banusi looked like a man who had had a mouthful of Sandman's bladder contents, then he perked up, dredged up an oily smile and said of course he knew what his friend Asiri was trying to do…return a birthday favour on the sly. But when I showed him the bag of parrot remains I could see the devil crawling into his mind. That, my girl, his big eyes could not hide,' said Mrs Lagbaja with a cough.

'Now we wait,' said Dele.

***

For four days Dele fried in her own greases, hoping that Banusi would take the bait. Aanu called early on the fifth morning.

'Wake up wake up,' he said. 'Snakes legs says they found Sandman. They charged him with UNCA.'

'What is UNCA?' said Dele. Dele scraping an elbow on a crate as she jerked out of bed.

'Unpatriotic and unnatural cultural activity. His head of family, Chief Abbiaba Oniseme, the man's belly looks as if he ate a baby elephant. He says he has not seen his cousin the minister for…since the man was appointed. Sandman left his people hungry while he filled his faces. The family has disowned him: with immediate effect.' Aanu chuckled. 'Banusi will be on TV tonight or tomorrow to make official announcement.'

'You mean to gloat,' said Dele.

***

Banusi's special broadcast was to start at ten minutes to seven in the evening. Aanu and Dele watched a 12" battery-powered black and white TV in Mama Robi's kitchen. The first bar of the national anthem rattled from the television, the credits faded and Banusi appeared, sitting on a sofa, unctuous and eager, like a contestant on a talent show. The hostess, Aju Kiaka dressed in a beige top wore her dark hair pulled back off her powder-caked face.

'We know you are a very busy man and are grateful that you found the time to speak to us,' she said.

Banusi put his hands out in front of him as if to say he could do no other. 'I'm here on behalf of the Supreme Commander of the Armed Forces of Roko but also as a citizen of our young republic.'

'Who elected them?' said Dele, munching on a fried bean cake. Aanu shrugged and nodded Dele's attention back to the TV.

'What motivates you…gets you out of bed in the morning?' said Aju.

'Money,' said Aanu, playing with his jacket zip.

Screwing defenceless people.

'The love of my country,' said Banusi. He dropped his voice and bowed.

'The matters we are about to discuss are…painful. Water?'

Banusi picked up the glass of water, inspected it and put it down again. 'Indeed, but I had to act,' he said.

'Please take your time,' she said.

Aanu cracked open a beer can. 'The man is a worm, turning this way and that,' he said.

'It is true that Oniseme and I work closely. My colleague was in charge of…delicate negotiations.' Banusi straightened his pristine white collar and dark tie, uncrossed his legs and leaned forward. 'Then I received a tip-off about activities of way below salubrious provenance, land being sold or resold, to third or fourth parties. Of course I did not believe it. I confronted my bosom colleague. Next I hear are unkind and unfounded counteraccusations…the matter is in the extremely capable hands of our esteemed and venerated indigenous Guilds and courts. I have a copy of the documents here…somewhere,' He tapped his breast pocket.

'So this is not a private disagreement between ministers?'

Banusi stiffened, and appeared to be about to mouth a retort, but his features softened again in a beat. He smiled at the camera like one would at a potential lover. 'No, it is an attempt to hijack our plans to build affordable houses. I was a poor orphan. Others should not have to go through what I did. But money is not my motivation. Yes, a big bank balance is nice, but it is like a new toy, at first you want it to yourself but the novelty soon wears off and you want others to come and enjoy it with you. At least that is what I think. Ask Bill Gates, not that I'm comparing myself to...' Banusi threw his head back and laughed.

'What do you do to relax?' said Aju.

Banusi sat straight up. 'Relax? When our people have no water or electricity or money? They leave in droves and are being fished out of dangerous waters to power economies with cheap labour. We must pay them, pay the rate to retain top talent. With the reforms I had in mind, top hospital cleaners will one day earn as much as English Premier League footballers...otherwise we will die of dangerous bugs.'

'This Banusi man can weave spider's web into wings for a hippo,' said Aanu, making the sign of the cross over his jacket zip.

'For the sake of the devil's advocate I hope that his boss was not watching,' said Dele.

'Snakes Legs just texted me. Sandman's trial is next week,' said Aanu. 'At Goke Rocks.'

'At last,' said Dele.

ELEVEN

The chrome trimmings on the motorbike gleamed in the sun as the rider turned on to Goke Rock Approach. In the distance, a broad coalition of wispy clouds pulled apart and drowned in the deep blue sky.

'This is our Olympics. We Siroko are world champion in criminal justice - stoning or hanging is best,' said the rider to his passenger, Dele. The thick hairs bulging from under his helmet shone with sweat.

Dele puffed air over her boiling face and peeped round the man's broad back. Just ahead of them, Kendrick Lemar's "Fuck your Ethnicity" boomed out of the back of an old jalopy, the car bouncing, as if mounted on pogo sticks. They inched through the crowd in swirling dust. A cacophony from blaring trumpets and ringing bells sounding to Dele louder than they could ever have on earth before, *and that probably includes Jericho* she thought. Then, as they went past a woman who appeared to be seeing a vision or having an epileptic fit or simply vigorously berating her fate, a man in a replica Man U football shirt muscled through the milling crowd. He ushered Dele to a gate where a man clad in leopard skin handed her a ticket and a red sash. 'As you are witness, wear this,' he said, waving her through.

'This is our world famous Goke Rocks…and Caves. Our culture which nobody can take away,' said the usher. He pointed to a three-story high outcrop of jumbled black rocks under which workers arranged chairs in curved rows about ten deep.

'Oh,' said Dele, almost collapsing with shock when she saw the scaffold. Its shadow lilted over the front row seats. 'Is this your first time?' said the usher. Dele nodded. The usher beamed, like a host at a long-awaited guest, sat Dele on the end of the second row of chairs opposite the packed galleries. 'Only elders sit in front,' he said. 'They will soon come out.'

Dele threw the identity sash over her right shoulder, thanking her stars for cotton blouse and baggy trousers in this heat. She would have melted in jeans. At the gates on her left stood men armed with snub-nosed machine guns; to her right sat the black Goke Rocks, stern and forbidding, like a judge on the first day of a difficult and orphaned trial. Behind her tree branches groaned under the weight of eager onlookers.

At half past four, to blasts on a horn, Dele counted nineteen men, in white robes and white caps, as they emerged from a cave in single file. Each man carried a horse whisk. The most senior elder brought up the rear in a purple wheelchair pushed by a one-armed man.

Seconds later, to deafening drumming and cheering, a hunchbacked woman with a large goitre danced into the clearing. 'That's the head of the Guild of women priests. The rhythm of the drums spells out Niputi's name. Red and black scarf she is wearing means blood and rock,' said the man sitting next to Dele. He looked odd in a monocle and bottle green suit. 'It is to wake up his ancestors, to let them know that their son may be joining them soon.' Dele caught a whiff of the man's woody perfume. She turned away and tried not to look at the scaffold. *Who is Niputi?*

The elderly woman with the goitre poured libations out of a bottle of Scottish whisky and the elders screwed their left heels into the dust. 'It means their verdict is-'

'Grounded in tradition,' said Dele. The man turned to Dele in obvious disbelief. He wreaked of condescension.

'Fair enough, but why is that one screwing in his right heel?' she said.

'There's always one. I'm Musa, anthropologist,' he said, offering a handshake. Dele did not quite catch which museum Musa worked for. *I wonder if he knows Ambasi. Get well Ambasi.* Ambasi had bilateral pneumonia.

'Dele Verity, witness,' she said. They shook hands. The elders turned to the scaffold as one, first touching their own, then their neighbours', chins with the end of their whisks.

'Bizarre,' said Dele.

The woman priest walked backwards, and the porters erected red-cushioned stools and black umbrellas for the elders in the front row. To the bleats of a flugelhorn, a man dressed in sheepskin dragged a goat to the scaffold and forced it on to its knees. After a brief struggle he knelt on the goat's neck and signalled to the elders. Tall, a little stooped, with a neat white beard, he had on a red toga and a white cap. He strode up to the scaffold to bring a shiny cutlass down on the goat's neck; severing its head in mid-bleat. Blood spurted in four red jets.

'He's done that before,' said Dele.

Musa chewed his nails, his eyes fixed on the young boy pouring a bottle of whisky over the blood-caked stool.

An usher handed the most elder a cordless microphone. 'Let the court begin,' said the most elder. The crowd cheered as two men dragged a convict from the caves.

'Who is that?' said Dele.

'Niputi, a vicious armed robber,' said Musa.

On a nod from the most elder a tall masked man placed the noose round Niputi's neck. The most elder touched the stool with his cutlass. A masked man gave a massive axe to a young woman. 'Do as you wish,' he said.

The crowd went quiet, hushed, expectant, like a football crowd just before a penalty kick.

'Why did he give her the axe?' said Dele.

'He killed her father and seized their land,' said Musa behind his cupped hand.

To another long blast on a flugelhorn the girl swept the axe down. A man in a white hood rode up on a white horse, circled the gallows, shouting "Aboka, Aboka," justice. He leapt on to the gantry and plunged his sword into Niputi. Niputi squeaked. His dusky innards snaked out, then plunged straight down, like an apron, to his shins. The crowd cheered. They threw stones, banana skins, yam peelings, coconuts rind, anything to hand, at the stricken Niputi as the warders carried his body back into a central cave.

Dele retched and looked away. *Could I kill Sandman like that?* Her breaths came short and fast.

'Case file closed,' said the most elder. He sat down while a posse cleaned up for the next case: Sandman's.

'They probably put that on for the benefit of novices and tourists,' said Musa. Dele saw, for the first time, foreign faces in the crowd.

The wind got up, scrooping through the microphone in the elder's hand. A young man ran up with an umbrella to shield the elder from the wind and dust.

'We now come to the main case of the day,' said the most elder when the wind died down. Dele craned her neck round a bright purple umbrella twiddled by the elder in front of her.

On the third of three long blasts on a trumpet, each one echoed by the excited gallery, Sandman appeared out of a dark cave. He had a broken nose and streams of sweat on his face. Squinting like a neonate, his ridged bald head bobbing, hands tied behind his back, and hustled along by a thick-set warder, he stumbled, pigeon-toed, towards the elders while trying to keep as upright as the overlong loincloth and his limp would let him. The warders sat him down under the scaffold.

'Take his cuffs off,' boomed the senior elder. 'Do you know what you have done?' he said. Sandman shook his head.

'You have kept us away from siesta,' said a man in the middle of the first row. The crowd laughed.

'Baba Waru, this is a special session,' said the elder. He turned to his other colleagues on the front row. 'Keep your minds open. Hope you had the kola nuts Mama Buhariti brought from the forest of Goodluck.' They all bowed. He turned to Sandman. 'What is a parrot to Siroko people?' An usher handed Sandman a microphone.

'To a Siroko a parrot is the symbol of everlasting life and the spirit of our ancestors; and of luck,' Sandman said. He sounded shrill.

'Rotila, you are a lawyer. Take over,' said the most elder. An usher rushed a microphone to Rotila. Rotila swaggered to the front of the clearing like a drunken football mascot, the rim of his red cap dark with sweat, his white robes riding a foot higher at the front. His bat ears detracted somewhat from his otherwise smug bearing.

'Roti, Roti', cried the crowd.

Rotila tapped the microphone and the crowd went quiet. He turned to Sandman. 'You have been in the practice of packing up your remnants after meals?' he said.

'To kill bad medicine,' said Sandman.

'Not to destroy evidence?'

Sandman looked down at the ground.

'You have been eating parrot, confess and don't waste our time, my dear minister *oh jareh*,' shouted Baba Waru. The most elder shook his whisk at Baba Waru. The offender shrunk back into his seat.

'My son,' Rotila said. A young man in a pair of jeans and a hooped black and yellow T-shirt skipped up to stand next to his father. They shared the same design in ears. 'Very…very brilliant,' Rotila said. 'Trained by Lagos-trained lawyer who was trained by London-trained lawyer. He turned to his son. 'Billi, the exhibit please.' Billi waved a billboard in front of Sandman and lifted it to show the crowd.

'That's Comfy,' said Dele.

'Do you know this parrot?' said Rotila to Sandman.

'No,' said Sandman.

'You are sure?'

'I have seen many but not this one.'

Rotila muttered under his breath. 'Show him the house,' he said. The young man produced another large board. It looked like a photograph of Mrs Lagbaja's bungalow.

'Do you know this place?' said Rotila junior.

Sandman nodded and made a sucking noise. 'We are in negotiation.' The crowd booed.

'Now we're talking,' said Baba Waru. 'The man is guilty. It remains only to sentence him.'

The crowd cheered. 'Rope him, necklace him,' they shouted, banging drums, whistling, blowing trumpets and sundry other wind instruments.

'Remove Baba Waru,' said the most senior. Baba Waru threw himself face first on the ground in front of the senior. The most senior waved the guards away. Baba Waru brushed himself down and shuffled back to his seat.

Rotila turned once more to Sandman. 'Don't hedge your lies, you must know the great Grey African parrot, Confucius. It belongs to our senior citizen present here.' He wheeled round to turn to where Mrs Lagbaja was sitting, in the shadows. 'I put it to you that you killed it.'

'No, I did not,' said Sandman.

Rotila puffed his cheeks out. 'Play the clam if you wish but I have just the thing to open you up.' He wheeled round to the guards. 'Mama, are you here?'

Eyes turned to Mrs Lagbaja as she got out of her chair.

'Gently,' said senior Rotila. Two young women shuffled Mrs Lagbaja forward.

A few in the crowd shouted "Kolo Kolo."

Mrs Lagbaja arrived at the front of the assembly. She pointed at Sandman. 'That's the man. He of the nose that his eyes cannot bear to be near. I'll recognise him anywhere, in my bed asleep, in my dying grave, in my flowing waters,' said Mrs Lagbaja.

The crowd hummed at "Big English."

'Mama tell us what happened,' said Rotila.

'Certainly,' she said, her hectoring voice booming from the microphone held in front of her by an usher. 'This man and his accomplice whom with regret I descry not in this assembly, ransacked my house and compound first to destroy my parrot cages but to compound their egregious transgression they returned to remove my precious Comfy. It's grade one avicide and I will not rest until-'

A hum went round the ground again at Mrs Lagbaja's outburst. Senior Rotila clubbed the air with his short arms to calm the crowd and turned to Sandman. 'Minister, you heard mama. What do you have to say? Do you want my son to translate?' he said. 'Mama you can return to your seat now.' Mrs Lagbaja did not move. 'Pilu, help mama, perhaps she didn't hear me.' Pilu the usher led Mrs Lagbaja away.

'I wanted at least an hour's session, not testimonial interruptus,' she said, snatching her elbow away, to loud laughter.

Junior Rotila waited for Mrs Lagbaja and the crowd to settle down. 'Continue minister,' he said.

'As a minister of health I have mandate to clear up the mess from the parrots in a potential tourist area,' said Sandman. 'Parrots should be free in the forest not in mama's house or cages,' he said.

Senior Rotila got up and turned to the elders. 'On this Roko island, can you believe this; when our people have no food to eat, minister is talking animal welfare?' he said. He wiped his face with his cap. His son pulled a face. 'This man came to the house, he cooks the parrot and we have the evidence. Case open and closed, in...thirty-five beautiful minutes. Not bad, eh my brothers?'

'Does the accused have anything to say?' said the most elder from his wheelchair.

'A Guild man myself. Never would I do a thing like that,' said Sandman, looking as if he regretted his reference to animal welfare.

'Are Siroko allowed to kill animals?' said most elder in his rich voice.

'Yes, to eat and feed our families,' said Sandman. He sucked in a deep breath.

Dad, I don't believe it they're going to let him off.

'Are you allowed to kill a person?' said most elder.

Sandman paused. Dele thought he looked like a man asked to leap into an abyss. 'As a last resort, if my life is in danger,' he said.

'So how many times would you say that your life had been in danger? And speak up,' said the most elder.

Sandman cleared his throat and drew himself up. 'My life is in constant danger. I am a minister, after all.' Baba Waru guffawed. The crowd booed. Dele felt better.

Rotila stepped forward but the most elder raised a hand. 'I have not landed.' A little boy ran up to fan the back of most elder's neck. 'Mr Minister, we inspected the remaining fowl. Slips off your tongue landed in the bag that Mama here kept to protect herself from the usual evaporation of evidence…in these matters,' said most elder with a glottal click. He turned to Mrs Lagbaja. 'My elder citizen Lagbaja, this was a special parrot?'

Mrs Lagbaja dabbed an eye and nodded. 'He's eaten it, it's written all over his face,' she said. An usher rushed her a microphone so that she could repeat what she said.

Sandman shook his head. 'Jealous people are behind this,' he said with a squawk, like a chicken about to be put down.

'Let the people be the judge of that. Call the next witness,' said the elder.

TWELVE

On the last of a series of three short blasts on flugelhorns from each corner of the arena a man in a loincloth shuffled out of the cave. Taller and wider than his warders, the pink dressing peeling off his right ear, the right arm in a sling and his left eye half-closed by a purulent eyelid, made him look like the poster boy for a charity for destitute veterans.

'That's Burutu. Sandman's man,' said Dele.

'Masseurs have got to him...pressed him for the truth,' said Musa.

A young man set up a microphone for Burutu. Beside him, Sandman wore the pained look of a man at the mercy of an ataxic dentist.

'What is your name?' said the elder.

'Burutu.'

'How are you to this minister?'

'I am his inside right man.' The crowd hissed in derision. Sandman shook his head.

'Mr Burutu. We want you to clear up a few matters.' Burutu nodded and made a sucking sound. The crowd booed.

'Tell us what happened to the doctor,' said the elder. A hush went round the arena.

Burutu scratched his brow. He stole a sheepish glance at Sandman.

'Don't fear,' said the elder.

'Quenched,' said Burutu.

'You will quench yourself, quench yourself,' roared the crowd.

Sandman leapt to his feet and tapped the microphone. 'Listen to me, not this nonentity of a dummy. What does he know of the big picture? Dada is my in-law. I promoted him to find a way to raise money for the hospital to treat more patients.' He took a deep breath. The amplified rasp soared round the gathering. 'When a patient is admitted she can rent her house to other patients' relatives, those who have to travel far. The sick person gets a little money and someone to look after their house, the people from afar have somewhere cheap to stay, the hospital gets a fee. Everyone win, win. Then I saw that Dada was living like king. I told him to stop whatever he is doing. He did not listen. Maybe he was dealing drugs. It pains me to say but that is the truth,' said Sandman.

Burutu shook his head.

'How can he say he didn't know that Dada ran a porno ring from the patients' houses?' said Dele.

'Which of them is telling the truth?' said Musa.

'Does anyone care?' said Dele, turning her attention back to the proceedings.

'Sit down minister. Mr Burutu tell these people what you told us,' said the elder with an expansive wave of an arm.

Burutu got to his feet. 'When girls come from camp they have no mama and no papa, minister admits them to hospital. I collect them from airport and hospital. They are not to go to school because he says they are mad and useless and should be in rehab…rehabilistation, stabilisation. I take them to parties, or Officer's Mess. Dada and his nurses dress them up. After, we take them back to hospital. One day, maybe about one month or so ago, Dada is rush to minister's office. He is fearing and almost wetting his trousers. So I listen outside the door. He says to minister that he received message on computer that they know what he is doing with girls. That minister should give him a millions of Roko and help him find and quench the person who sent the message.'

'A strange request. If this Dada man is so rich why did he ask for more?' said the most elder.

'Most senior, papa it is true I talk. The reason doctor is panic is he is making films inside the patients' houses. One of his camera people ask me if I want do. I said not for me to do small girls.'

'And what was the minister's reply?' said the most elder.

Sandman leapt to his feet. The most elder waved him down.

Burutu went on. 'Minister tell me to pafuka Dada.' A gasp went round the ground. Sandman shook his head.

'How did you achieve this… pafuka?' the elder said.

'Inject air and piss into the vein in his neck the night he working in hospital,' said Burutu.

Another gasp went up from ten thousand throats. Dele thought she heard a man cry out behind her, looked round to see that a man had fallen out of a tree.

My e-mail must have panicked him. But I didn't want this.

Sandman shot on to his feet but Burutu ignored him. 'We pafuka the chief at that Alago development. If it was not for her age and she is woman, this mama here, Lagbaja, we would have quench and pafuka her too. And it was we who put that poison in the tea of –'

'We don't need to know the names and causes of death of everyone in your funeral parlour,' said the most elder, bringing his whisk down on Burutu's testimony.

'Why didn't he let Burutu finish?' said Dele.

Sandman cleared his throat and started to speak. 'This is all lies. I rose from the dirt of the gutter,' he said. Ten thousand heads in half shadow turned his way like ears of corn in a breeze.

'Are you the only minister in the world to rise from the ranks on this island?' said the elder.

'He's not even the only one on his own street,' said Baba Waru.

Sandman replied. 'Please my elders, hear me out. Some of you may know that I won scholarship to study Engineering. In London this South African man is making *yanga*, in the take-away where I was working. He say he has just come back from throwing bananas at kaffirs making monkey noise for Mandela outside his embassy in Trafalgar square. He did not want me to serve him. As customer is always right and I am in another man's country I didn't say anything. Then he called Mandela a monkey terrorist, that their own kaffirs don't starve like those Sirokos in Roko or Rastas in Ethiopia. The fire of his insult in my belly was too much for me to bear. I jumped over the counter, gave him one Ali and a Jankoko, that is one fist each and a head-butt. The man's teeth jumped from his mouth and scattered into a takeaway box.'

Sandman turned to acknowledge a cheer. He went on 'Police came. They didn't ask any questions, just held me like halal goat, pressed their boot and knee into my neck, saying I was resisting arrest. I nearly died. Then dey deported me. Me,' said Sandman stabbing his chest with a finger. 'Not de man who started the trouble.' He pointed at the sky, perhaps in the general direction of the culprit in the northern hemisphere. 'The man who throws shit from bridge may not remember, but ask the woman who has to wash it from her head, she will never forget,' said Sandman, after a pause. Dele heard sympathetic murmuring, saw exchanged nods and glances of support and understanding.

The most elder stroked his beard, beckoned for a glass of water.

What's he thinking?

The elder's glass arrived just as Sandman punched himself out. He sat down. The heat from the metal chair burned through the thin linen of Dele's trousers but her knees knocked together as if she was in Antarctica.

I don't believe this. Hey, has he seen me?

The elder finished his drink. 'Minister, this talk of yours is full of what the Brazilians call rubbishinho. Is it not the truth that you are using camp girls? You had Dada killed? You have mansions, on land you seized. But we should feel sorry for you. You think we have forgotten what happened at Enugo? And the head of that woman that you cracked open just wide enough to let in just enough of your sense of common-sense. Will that woman forget? Anyway who sent you to England to fight Afrikaaners in England? Mandela?'

'Madiba, Madiba,' shouted the crowd.

Sandman jumped back on to his feet. 'I did not eat parrot. Burutu, did I eat the big parrot?' said Sandman.

Burutu did not look so sure and squirmed on his seat.

Sandman started again. 'You allow foreigners to bear false witness in our Siroko court. That white girl over there forged my signature. May be it was she who sent Dada that letter.' His angry stare make Dele blush.

'Wait,' said the most elder, shuffling towards Dele. 'Should we not be hearing from you too my young friend?' He fished some papers out of his gown, looked up. 'Ah, identify yourself for the sake of this court.'

'Dele, Dele Verity, most elder,' her words escaping from the grip of a tight throat.

'How do you know this minister?' said the most elder.

'On Nigeria Street and in the camp. I was invited, brought here by your order to bear witness, just like Mrs Lagbaja over there,' said Dele.

'Her mother was from a wicked Kolo family; Ligthausen,' said Sandman. On hearing the name the crowd hissed and booed. The elder swivelled back to Dele, like a predator eyeing up juicier prey. 'They didn't tell me this. Ligthausen? Bring her over here,' he said.

Dele walked to the front to stand with the elders to her right and Sandman to her left. She put her hands behind her back to show respect. Hundreds of eyes bore through her, some elders looking dubious, sceptical, neutral at best. None of them smiled. One elder four places in from the end stared through thick, rimless glasses, his eyes pinholes of ice. Leaning back in his chair, with his arms folded across his chest, he looked as if he had the mind to replace Sandman with Dele in the dock.

'Which Ligthausen are you,' said the most elder. He handed Dele the microphone.

'My mother's family is from near Zadunaria I think,' said Dele. The gallery booed.

'Basket mouth people,' someone shouted.

The elder waved the crowd silent. 'The Zadunaria Ligthausens,' he said. 'The Zadunaria Ligthausens,' he said once more, with added gravity. Dele looked round the arena, at all the bowed heads, heads lowered as if in prayer or in quiet contemplation of whatever Ligthausen meant to them.

'Is Asiri correct? You have born false witness to this case?' said the most elder.

Dele's stomach twisted and turned. *Asiri, on first name terms with the elders all of a sudden.*

'Yes,' said Sandman. 'She came to my office...'

Burutu joined in. 'And she came to the mama's house to take things from the room. I remember her well now. From roof place. It worry me. After, I think and think what is this girl doing in this house. Then I remember. It is camera not alarm in that roof place. Dada people put it there. I checked with mama after. This girl took a camera,' he said.

Out of the corner of her eye Dele saw Sandman's jaw drop open. She sensed his shock and heard him hiss at Burutu. 'Why didn't you tell me about this camera before?' he said, wiping spit from his mouth.

Burutu did not reply. He looked at the ground.

'The parrot was missing when I went to visit Mrs Lagbaja,' said Dele. *Did Sandman really not know what Dada was doing with the hidden cameras?*

'So you know the old woman,' said the elder. He smiled and frisked Dele with his whisk. Dele nodded. *Better.* She took in a deep breath, then went on. 'He ransacked her house and cooked her parrots, as you heard in this same court. Dele mumbled over the last words. Fur seemed to clog her throat.

'She is making fool of you. It is in her blood,' said Sandman, flapping an arm at Dele. He sounded hoarse.

A couple of elders nodded, scorn for Dele obvious in the odd pause and sidelong glances at her from behind their whisks. Dele's heart seemed to stumble from beat to beat. She drew herself up, sucked in another deep breath and let it out slowly as though to blow the floods of fears from her chest. She raised the microphone to her lips and turned to Sandman.

'This man did bad things in the camp. My mama's body…he cooked his food on fire from burning my mama,' she said, rushing the words out before they stalled.

'Fire is for cooking, what is wrong with that, your people did worse,' shouted one elder.

What does he mean by "my people" Dele thought.

'Yes, they did worse,' she heard some say in the crowd.

A passing cloud cast the seated section of elders and the crowd in front of Dele in shadow. In the sunshine, Dele felt even more exposed, like a genetically modified bald hedgehog amongst a raging prickle of giant porcupines.

'That is not why we are here,' said the sceptical elder. He crossed his legs under his robes, uncrossed them again, tapped his friend on the tip of the elbow and shook his head.

'My dear elders, this man did this…to me…my hand, put my dad away, killed my mum. My great grandparents are not here to answer these charges. If this man standing here condemned by your court had died in prison or run away, or even died a natural death, would you hang his son in his place? And if you did not find the son, would you hang his grandsons…even if they are innocent?'

A murmur went round the ground. It went quiet. 'If I was the parrot's grandson I would,' said the sceptical elder, his voice carrying to a microphone. Laughter rang round the arena.

'The issue the minister raised is a serious one, young lady. Did the evidence presented at the first hearing have a touch of what we know as *mago mago* - remote control signatures on stolen letter-headed paper?' said the most elder.

'Mago mago, mago mago,' shouted the crowd.

Dele gulped. 'It is true. I represented the signature of the minister on the property-'

Another roar went up from the crowd. 'Shame. Kolo girl. Go home,' they screamed. Dele looked into Sandman's eyes. Sandman stared back, his eyes shooting laser-guided missiles of hatred and contempt so accurate that their impact threatened to tear the door she had pulled shut against the horrid past from her hands. *No I'm not going back to that. Not to the nightmares of Mum on funeral pyres, of heads sawn off by gunshots, and of giant soldier ants.* Dele's right arm shook so much she had to cradle it in the other hand behind her back. She waited for the hubbub to die down.

'You want the truth? You have children many of you. Little girls?' Someone behind her booed and started to bang a drum. 'My dad did nothing to harm this man or his family. He decided to take his revenge on him. My mother is dead. He smashed my fingers in a car door. You want to know the truth? Ask yourselves if that happened to you, if someone destroyed your family, whether you will stop at forging a signature. Ask them most senior elder. Ask the little girls he took to the Officer's Mess. Ask the broken, soiled, instrumented little girl I saw at Abha Community Hospital. So I forged a signature. So what? For what? To bring him here for you to judge him. I had no choice. Let him deny what he did in the camps and at the Mess and swear on the bones of his ancestors.'

The crowd fell silent. A calmness came over Dele. She nodded at the elder to show that she had finished. *I've done my best. I love you Mum and Dad.*

The most elder silenced the crowd with a wave of his whisk. He walked round Dele and Sandman, in a figure of eight. With each circuit the elder completed a crown of thorns seemed to sprout from Dele's scalp. She tried to speak but the most elder silenced her with a finger to his lips. 'My bones are clicking with the ancestors,' he said, as if weighing her fate in his swaying head. 'My bones have spoken,' he said, at the end of his fourth circuit. The crowd hushed.

'Verity, go.'

Dele made her blind way back to her seat.

The elder turned to Sandman. 'You know that this missing parrot was like a person to this woman.' He waited while an aeroplane passed overhead. 'Therefore if you can kill human beings like Dada you can kill a parrot. QED.'

'I see where you were going my senior,' said Rotila. 'Respect, my senior, you have landed well.' The most elder raised his hand and the murmuring stopped. A child's wail echoed from within the cave. 'Tell that woman to shut the boy up,' he said. 'Minister. But you say that the parrot is still alive and it is in the forest?'

'I have told you I did not eat parrot,' Sandman said. Sighs of disbelief rose from hundreds of throats.

'It's always someone else's fault,' said Dele, her stomach churning. *What will they do?* The most elder sounded far away. He swivelled his head and chair round to address his colleagues.

'We will be fair?' said the elder. *What?* 'Tell Gareem and his men to provide an escort.' He turned to Sandman. 'If you can bring parrot back to this mama within a month you will be free. If mama dies before you bring it or you cannot find it, you will die. That is the law of the Goke Rock. Take him away.'

THIRTEEN

For the next week the story of two men who died fighting over the remains of a python that had fried in an electricity transformer, dominated the news.

'It's probably not a bad thing. Keeps your name out of their sharp focus,' said Mama Robi.

'Two weeks and Babubacka still hasn't ratified the sentence,' said Dele anxious that Sandman would get off. She heard a car engine rattle outside. Moments later Aanu walked into Mama Robi's kitchen with a colour TV under his arm.

'Been in North Sankara all day, on business,' he said.

Dele raised a hand. 'Say no more,' she said.

'Am I in time?' he said, tapping the side of his nose.

'For what?' said Dele.

'You didn't know? Babubacka is going to make announcement,' said Aanu.

Dele's hopes rose. *Special TV broadcast. Maybe he'll ratify the sentence.*

Mama Robi made room for the plates of fried fish beside the TV.

After the weather forecast, presented as usual by "scattered showers," an excitable man in a bright yellow suit, Babubacka came on TV, wearing a shiny-buttoned, double-breasted, dressing gown.

'Why is he wearing that…nonsense?' said Mama Robi. She sucked her tongue in disgust.

'Looks like a cross between a convict and a football agent. Last time it was that cloth that looked like gall bladder contents?' said Dele, shifting away from the heat of the kerosene stove.

Aanu cracked open a can of beer. 'His friends bought him that for his third official birthday of the year. He is in New York. Mama Robi face this way. If that woman next door sees your angry face she can report you,' said Aanu.

Dele turned her attention to the TV. Babubacka went on. 'Chemical weapons? That is abuse of language. It is the chemicals in the words of the international press that destroy truth,' he said in response to a question from Pete Angel, the world famous reporter.

'Go on, your Excellency.'

'State money has to be under good husbandry. Do you want to know what the economists in World Bank call us now?" Babubacka paused for breath and jabbed the air with a tobacco-stained forefinger. 'Emerging. One day the "R" in BRIC will be Roko not Russia. That is due to our efforts. You may have heard of "sponsor a poor child in Knightsbridge." Well, we, my cabinet, started it and it makes Roko people proud.' He coughed.

'He sounds chesty, but he hasn't said anything about Sandman's trial,' said Dele.

'God let him choke to death,' said Mama Robi, whispering into her cupped hands.

'Your Excellency, when they saw you shooting hyena in the forest with gun belt round your waist to many you looked…irresistible,' said Mr Angel.

'My friend, I've…had…my moments.' Babubacka sipped beer from his hotel tumbler, stopped and held his throat as if he had swallowed a hot marble.

'So, if I may put this, as it were…delicately. You have a reputation. Last time you came here there were rumours that you made certain requests about your…sleeping arrangements…

Babubacka's eyes narrowed. 'I thought this was serious interview? I am talking to UN soon…and my man is appointed to the Hague (pronounced Heck), you ask me about this? But I will answer your question. I meant I need beauty sleep, maybe that is why they said I asked for brunette, no I needed beauty sleep, not beauty to sleep with. Ah, you people…read too much into my simple words. Am I Shapespar?' He started to cough again. 'Water please, water, where is my aide-de-camp? I need a drink…water…' The screen went blank.

***

Aanu called Dele early the next morning. 'Have you heard? Babubacka don quench. Turn on your radio. Wait five minutes it's on repeat. There is God. Only last week that King of North Roko and Archimedes II, his Grey parrot that teaches children alphabet, died on that island. What's it called?'

'Fernando Po. The king died in exile there where Babubacka put him,' said Dele.

'Now look what's happened to Babubacka himself,' said Aanu.

Dele flicked on the transistor radio. 'The President, Head of Supreme and Revolutionary Council, Commander-in-Chief, Head of State, the Father of the Young Roko Nation, Number One Servant of God, the first and only Husband of the First Lady, Monday Babubacka, has died. The Supreme Military Council declares a week of mourning and a lying in state of emergency. And in anticipation of unruly, unpatriotic fifth columnists, the University of South Sankara, including the medical school, will be closed with immediate effect, until situation stabilises.'

Aanu called in at ten that morning with a rip in the sleeve of his leather jacket. 'Soldiers, tanks everywhere. If not for my conny way I might not have got here,' he said, feinting and bobbing like a practising stuntman. 'You may have to stay with mama…as long as you like,' said Aanu.

Dele shook her head. 'I promised to look after pastor's flat. Mrs Lagbaja will move in with me in a few days. But I don't buy that "Babubacka died after a brave illness he caught in the peace-keeping force" shit,' said Dele.

Aanu cracked the tops off the bottles of cola with his teeth. 'If you ask me that was not him on TV. Maybe he was already dead. He overdosed on Viagra and those waxed men from Brazil, but Snakes Legs says that it was the Russians who did it with radioactive sugar because they did not like the way he gave China the Tantalum. My tailor said that it was a Kombo guard who punctured the man's lung with bamboo stick. Taxi man said it is that Kama Sutra expert who killed him with her yansh when he would not give her password to Swiss bank account,' said Aanu.

Dele opened a packet of biscuits. 'Maybe he's hiding in Switzerland after plastic surgery. This new regime could close the unis for years you know,' said Dele. That's what happened in Somalia. Their first doctors to graduate in twenty years in a hall to take the oath. Bang. Bomb. All fucking wiped out. Allah is great.'

'This is Roko, not Africa, knaamsaying,' said Aanu waving a biscuit in the air like a sword.

'But it's got Africans in it,' said Dele.

Aanu stopped mid Ali shuffle. 'You know how to wag my tongue,' said Aanu just as his phone rang. 'You are serious? That's a palace coup man. Calamity on the mountain of nonsense,' he said. He grimaced and closed the call.

'What is it?' said Dele.

'Bloodless coup. Giradona is new Head. He has pardoned Sandman because the minister's son is going to marry his daughter.' Dele's stormed out to kick the life out of the crates of her makeshift bed.

FOURTEEN

Dele went to bed that night feeling like one who had run out of fuel during a joy ride and had to walk all the way home only to find that she's lost the key to her front door and her wallet and been sentenced to jail for attempted robbery; with no chance of appeal. A new rasping ache in her chest joined the chronic gnawing longing for her Dad. *What do we have to do for justice in this place?*

She went back to Ambasi's flat on a gloomy afternoon, two days after Sandman's pardon. But she could not sleep. So she got out of bed early in the morning, plucked Ambasi's old Bible from under her pillow, lit a candle and trawled through the book's finger-worn pages, and tried once again to decipher his code. Hours passed. Her head ached. *This is like trying to fork water.* When the power came back on she snuffed out her candle and wandered round the living room while the kettle boiled. Ambasi's eye followed her round. *Antikath was always talking about making a calendar from the portraits. Calendar. That's it. Silly Dele Verity. The code has something to do with dates. Pneumonia or no pneumonia, I need to talk to him.* Dele called the hospital. The nurse paused then passed Dele on to a senior colleague.

'We tried to reach you but switchboard phone here is like wheel without spoke. Pastor closed his eyes not more than an hour ago.'

***

They buried Ambasi two days later. At the funeral service, the priest extolled Ambasi's strong Christian faith. *If only they knew.* Surrounded by a large congregation, Dele felt all alone once again. *I'm re-orphaned, God. Please don't let Hanili die too.*

'We are now going to sing pastor's favourite hymn,' said the minister.

'*Those returning, those returning, make more faithful than before,*' they sang. The dam burst and Dele's tears tore like acid through the printed order of service she held in her bunched fists.

After the service she went home with Mama Robi.

'You must stay here a few days. Not good for you to go back to that place. But why would pastor do this kind of thing?' Mama Robi said in a whisper after everyone had left.

Dele sat down on the bench next to Mama Robi. 'He seemed fine when Antikath spoke to him. But I have to go back…Mrs Lagbaja needs company. She's lost her friends,' she said.

Mama Robi, Norma, shuddered and made a sign of the cross. 'A bad thing to take the life that God give you,' she said. 'You found note? Pastor is the type of person who would explain himself. There must be note somewhere.'

Dele counted the bubbles rising in her glass of fizzy water. An image of a man hanging from a noose swam up from the bottom of the glass.

***

'Got us out of the house this morning, didn't it? She's getting better under that clever doctor,' said Mrs Lagbaja, lowering herself into a chair. They had been to the hospital to see Hanili.

'Lost 2 and a half stones, a quarter of her kidney function and the little toe of her left foot, but she is walking and talking, so mustn't complain,' said Dele. She lit the kerosene stove and blew out the match. 'Would you like a banana with rice later?'

Mrs Lagbaja nodded. 'What happened at the Interior Ministry the other day?'

Dele frowned. 'Didn't get past the receptionist,' she said. She swallowed the lump in her throat. Sandman's free. And Hanili and Ambasi said we need justice. Is this justice?' said Dele. She snapped the kitchen window closed against the draught and tucked Ambasi's plastic curtains out of the way. *Must get those changed.* 'Kettle's boiled.'

'Thanks for letting me stay here with you. With that man out and about again anything can happen. I'm going to get my sweeteners. I get them from a special source in South Africa and I don't want anyone pinching them while I'm out. I don't mean you,' said Mrs Lagbaja, shuffling off to the bedroom.

She's one of a kind. Dele hung her head in sorrow for Ambasi. She heard Mrs Lagbaja's shuffle up so she leapt up to light a candle and make a make a mug of tea for her lodger.

'I don't know why I bother to read this stuff. Look. And this one too. All the papers are full of them in big writing so we can see. It's as if nothing happened in those camps. They're laughing…even the Vice Chancellor and the Archbishop of Sankara Cathedral have taken out full-page adverts to congratulate the lucky couple,' said Mrs Lagbaja, shuffling on to the edge of the sofa. She dabbed the corner of her mouth and picked up her mug of tea. 'The wedding's not for two weeks yet.' She gestured at the ring. 'That's your mum's isn't it?' she said, in a low voice.

'Only thing I have left of her apart from…what's in here,' said Dele. She tapped her chest with her fist. The lights came back on and the candle flames cowered in the ceiling fan's breeze.

'Oh, I've got to go.' Mrs Lagbaja dropped the mug on the table and in her hurry she tipped her chair over. Dele saw fluid trickle down the elderly woman's foot.

'Oh my goodness, it's come away. Don't get old,' said Mrs Lagbaja as she disappeared down the corridor. Dele got up to mop the floor. Mrs Lagbaja limped back shamefaced a few minutes later. 'I didn't mean you to clean up after me,' she said, with a sad gesture at the mop and bucket.

'Put your things out and I'll get them washed,' said Dele.

'I've had a life. And I'd give it up if it would have helped your mum and dad,' said Mrs Lagbaja as she sat down. 'I'm truly glad we met. I learned a lot from you and want to thank you for trying to help me keep my cottage. Game's probably up I'm afraid.'

Dele blushed. She blew out the candle. 'I've not given up yet,' said Dele.

Mrs Lagbaja shook her head. 'Pointless now, even your pastor friend realised that in the end,' she said.

'I don't know why he did it,' said Dele. *Poor Ambasi. Why? I must get back to that code.*

'And we can't stay here forever,' said Mrs Lagbaja. 'I'm going in for tests tomorrow. Staying overnight. The doctors want a bladder biopsy,' she said.

'I thought you hated hospitals,' said Dele. *Biopsy?* A string of knotty worries tugged at Dele's mind. 'Did they say what they're looking for?'

Mrs Lagbaja shook her head. Dele poured her another mug.

'And you didn't interrogate them?'

'I'll sue or complain if it goes well,' said Mrs Lagbaja.

'And if it doesn't?' said Dele.

'I won't be here will I?' said Mrs Lagbaja.

***

Dele waited for Mrs Lagbaja to go to bed then laid Ambasi's Bible beside the box file labelled "pills and potions for patients, invoices." The first page in the file had a date at the top and a list of Ambasi's potions, ingredients, antipyretics, balms made out of limestone, snail shells and tree bark in ordinary lettering. The rest of the document consisted of seemingly random numbers, noughts, crosses and short strokes. They looked like entries in an accounts ledger. *Where do dates fit in?*

It came back to her at five. She jumped out of bed. Ambasi based his code on the first 31 Books of the Bible. The date at the top of each entry in his secret diary or ledger corresponded to a Book in the Bible, 1st for Genesis and so on, and the text in yellow highlights served as the cipher. Dele went back to the first page, the one that had the list of ingredients and recipes for potions in ordinary writing at the top and the code at the bottom. Then she opened the Book in the Bible corresponding to the number at the top of the page in the box file; and from the corresponding highlighted text she knew given time, she could now crack the code. The numbers and crosses at the bottom of the page represented the position of a letter in the highlighted Biblical text. Where there was no corresponding letter Ambasi left a gap. *Yes.* She punched the air in triumph.

Dele crept out of the room to make a strong cup of coffee, put on her lucky red pair of old slacks and flipped through the rest of Ambasi's box file. She found his will. Ambasi had left everything to her. She wept; tears of everything, for everything, tore down her face.

And as she wept a scrap from a tabloid, a photograph and a short account about the death of Ambasi's daughter, Adire, cut through her sore eyes. The next few entries she found seemed to be about Hanili. Dele splashed cold water on her face to put a stop to the tricks of her eyes.

Ambasi had made an entry on the day Hanili appeared on TV, another a few days before she fell ill and another when she was admitted to hospital and another when Keli and her mother died. Dele froze in shock. Ambasi, why? But the answer was as obvious as a nuclear explosion. *An eye for an eye.* Hanili was Tutu's daughter and Ambasi wanted revenge for his Adire. The man who advised her not to cross the line in the sand had crossed it himself.

***

At three o'clock that afternoon, with her head still swimming from shock and insomnia, Dele saw Mrs Lagbaja off to the hospital, After a long walk to try to clear her head she returned to the flat at about five-thirty. As her lodger was not around to complain about the smell and smoke Dele decided on a fry up for a change, of eggs, bacon and plantains. She poured the palm oil into the pan and lit the kerosene stove. Her phone rang. Dele blew the match out, turned the wick down on the cooker so the oil would not get too hot and answered the call.

'It's Mr Dada here.'

'Is this a sick joke? Mr Dada is dead.'

'My name is Dada too.' The voice sounded familiar. 'You remember Mrs Lagbaja?' said the man.

'Who are you? She was helping me with my project.' Dele heard the man's heavy breathing and footsteps on the phone.

'You have taken my colleague's...research, from the old woman's flat,' said the man.

Dele heard a loud crack and thought the caller had fallen or dropped the phone. As she put her phone away she heard another crunch and the front door caved in, splintered by a brown battering ram. A menacing, shaven-headed man with a long beard strode in. A few paces behind him, and to more clanging alarms in Dele's head, came Sandman, in a feathered red fez. With the sofa in her way, she had no escape. She backed away but stopped when she felt the heat from the cooker on her rump.

'Get out of my way Alubosa,' said Sandman. He barged past his man and slapped Dele on the face. 'Sit there and shut up,' he said, pushing Dele back into a kitchen chair. Dele tried to get up but Alubosa's fat fist a knuckle's breadth from her face provided compelling reason to stay put.

'You have no right to go in there, that's pastor's room. We haven't got anything that belongs to you...' Dele was about to add *here* but something stopped her.

Sandman turned round, an even angrier glint in his eyes. 'It was you who came to the house and to my office. It was you who caused all that *walaha* with forgery. I'll deal with you proper this time.' Alubosa yanked Dele on to her feet. Another slap from Sandman stung and brought tears of anger to Dele's eyes.

'I cannot fucking believe that you would raid a dead pastor's bed before it is even cold,' she said, rubbing her face.

'Shut up. Ah, want to know how I am free?' said Sandman. 'Wedding amnesty.' Sandman leaned over to leer in Dele's face. His breath smelled of beer and tobacco. Dele leaned away from him. 'Kolo woman, all that special attitude you got from your mama cannot lift one fingernail to help you... and I've not finished yet,' he said. His eyelashes looked like claws straining to scratch Dele's lights out.

Alubosa pushed Dele in the chest. He stood over her while Sandman went down the corridor. Soon Dele heard boxes crashing to the floor, papers being torn up or trampled on, swearing and cursing and the odd hack of a cough from Sandman. *Is he looking for the code?*

Sandman emerged about ten minutes later covered in dust and sweat. He told Alubosa to get the crate from the room. 'You think you are clever?'

'What have I done-?'

'Shut up, next time keep your pestle out of my pounded yam. Alubosa, you deaf? Go get that crate. It's on the left, by the door,' said Sandman. He clapped the dust off his hands, slithered towards Dele.

'What happened to my Dad?' said Dele.

Dele's head jerked back from the force of a slap from Sandman 'Shut up. You think I come all this way to answer your stupid questions. Do your worst. You hear me. Do your worst.' He leered, right up in Dele's face.

A gust of wind billowed the plastic curtains inwards, fanning the smoke. Long blue flames licked the frying pan. The oil fizzed and crackled. It spat and stung Dele's arm. 'Ooh, hah,' Sandman said, slapping his neck and face.

Go, go, go, get out, screeched the voice in Dele's head. She kicked the stove into the plastic curtains, sending the pan crashing to the floor. In the same movement she ducked under Sandman's lunge just as Alubosa, who must have heard the commotion, lumbered in carrying a crate, which he threw to the floor to chase after Dele

'Hey, hey, I will kill you,' he said, his threat lending springs to Dele's leap over the sofa and on to the balcony and to her swing from the railings long enough to glance over her shoulder and shout 'watch out,' before she let go and dropped to the ground.

'Thieves, thieves in pastor's house,' she said, hobbling on a twisted left ankle. 'He is one of them,' she said. She pointed at Alubosa. He retreated into the gloomy stairwell.

Distracted, a little boy stopped midstroke, his bat, a bamboo stick, poised mid-air as the ball, a crushed milk tin, whizzed into his wicket. 'I'm not out. Fire made me miss,' he said, pointing his bamboo stick past the demon bowler. Dele turned to follow his gaze. *Shit.* She saw thick, blue-grey smoke spewing on to Ambasi's balcony through the open door and from a crack under a window.

Sandman ran out, spluttering and coughing. He pushed the young cricketers out of the way, jumped into a white car. Alubosa ran after the car as it careered up the street.

'Catch them,' said Sylvia, Ambasi's neighbour, from her balcony. 'Yeah, my fish, don burned,' she said.

'It's not fish, Sylvia. House is on fire. Help fire, fire,' said Dele. She took the twelve stairs up to Ambasi's in four bounds. Sylvia and her boyfriend ran across the landing ahead of her and into the flat. The kerosene cooker lay on its side, the base of its broken fuel reservoir lying against an upturned chair. Ragged curtains in the kitchen dripped molten wax on to the window and down the walls.

'Quick, before it spread to the sofas,' said Sylvia. Her boyfriend threw a blanket over a lick of burning oil.

No, should it be sand? Is this a chemical fire? Dele pulled the sofa away. *I don't fucking know what I'm doing.* Before she knew it the room filled with helpers, some carrying buckets of sand. One man brought an ancient fire extinguisher. It looked like the WWII bomb they found in Zadunaria.

After an eternal and frantic fifteen minutes of energetic waving, shouting, praying, blowing and throwing, the neighbours got the kitchen fire under control. They trooped out shaking their heads, thanking their maker and imploring Dele to do the same for her narrow escape. 'I will, I will,' she said.

'Was that the man they call Sandman, the Haka?' said Sylvia, righting a smouldering chair. Dele nodded. 'I would offer you something to drink but as you can see…'

'What did he want?' said Sylvia.

'Maybe he had business with pastor,' said Dele. She sat down on the soggy arm of Ambasi's favourite sofa. The room smelled damp and of smoke and made Dele's eyes and throat sore. *He's taken the camera. Why? Anyway Aanu's got copies.* She called Aanu.

Aanu sounded angry. 'He came to Aunty Norma's house…broke her cupboard, and took the things you gave me,' he said.

'Why…it was only musclemen and young girls on the camera. Why all this…*walaha*?' said Dele.

'Must be something else, that he does not want our eyes to meet outside'

'Can you watch out for Mrs Lagbaja and get the carpenter, Tilati, to do some repairs? I'm sorry for what Sandman did to Mama Robi's house.'

'Where are you going?' said Aanu.

'Can you keep a secret?' said Dele.

'Yes,' said Aanu.

'So can I,' said Dele.

FIFTEEN

Special Matron Danankara extricated herself from her office armchair and made two predictably futile attempts at fastening her red rubber belt.

'Your bag and things are in this cabinet, please sit,' she said. Grimacing, she swivelled to squeeze between her desk and the wall, lowered herself on to her podgy knee to open the drawer. 'Here it is,' she said, handing Dele a blue satchel.

Dele thrust her hand deep into the false compartment to unzip the pouch. 'It's for probate...my guardian, the pastor, you know lawyers, eh,' she said, puffing her cheeks in relief when she felt the three data sticks.

'Don't forget us here when you qualify,' said Matron Danankara as Dele's red taxi rumbled up. The driver sounded the horn.

Outside Matron's door, a bright blue sky stretched into infinity.

'Any more...patients from HealthSmart?' said Dele, assuming a casual tone. The driver revved the engine.

Matron Danankara shook her head. 'Not for some weeks. With new man in government everyone is minding their own back yard.'

***

Dele found Zadunaria for the most part as she remembered it: palm trees shimmering in the dizzying heat, shiny cars humming along tree-lined avenues between steel and glass-fronted malls, a huge red ball of a sun majestic in a cloudless cobalt sky, and the shadows crisp, short, as though caught in the act of diving out of the glare.

Opposite the entrance to Breadfruit Street used to stand the brilliant black and yellow signpost to Mango Street. *Babubacka must have been learning how to play scrabble, or to read* thought Dele, referring to the letters missing on the rotting street sign. In her old front garden, behind a head-high pyramid of crumbling concrete, a red Chinese bulldozer hung over the edge of a large crater. Dele peeped into the cabin. Stalked controls stood spread-eagled around the driver's seat. She remembered that her dad taught her to read on that spot and two giant tears rolled down her chin, dived and shrunk into the hot footplate.

Two hours later she checked into Ambassador Hotel, an old colonial chalet which, had it not the good fortune of lying within ten-minutes of the main railway station, would not have survived for half a century serving burnt breakfasts. After supper she called Hanili.

'Where are you?' said Hanili.

'Zadunaria. I'm looking through this porno stuff I got from–'

'Oh–'

'I thought I told you…Mrs Lagbaja's was right. She took early discharge from hospital…Tafawa and his film crew weren't expecting her…poor woman ends up the meat in the sandwich between the wardrobe and the floor.'

'Whatever,' said Hanili.

'You sound tired.' Dele could not bring herself to tell Hanili about Ambasi, not over the phone. She did not quite believe it herself and wanted another read of the diaries before she shot her mouth off.

After the call to Hanili Dele watched the last half an hour of "Pumped Friction IV" grind to an end. *One data stick to go, nothing unusual. Have I missed something? Hope it's not in code again.* She had a biscuit and went to bed. Roused by guilt and anxiety at four thirty-five she made a strong cup of coffee and pressed the last grey stick in to her laptop.

The red bar along the bottom of the screen had crept along to within ten minutes and five seconds of the end when the scene changed. Dele jerked back in shock when she saw that head and those eyes. *Sandman*. But the flash of victory and discovery lasted only a moment. It was no big deal. Timothy Delita, the Minister of Transport, caught *in flagrante* in the back of his security detail's van, had even been promoted and still received countless tweets asking how, at his time of life, he had managed to get into some of the alleged positions.

At seven, tired and frustrated at finding nothing important on Sandman, she went downstairs for breakfast. The stuffy dining room, about the size of an average schoolroom, had pink paisley curtains flanking a large portrait depicting an English breakfast. It had no windows.

'Newspaper madam? Special complimentary copy with your morning coffee,' said the bow-tied waiter. 'To you only one fifty Bobos,' he said. He led Dele to a table behind a walnut pulpit. Dele sat down to flick through her newspaper but the stories about the impending "wedding of the century," made her even angrier. She ordered a pancake.

On the table to her immediate left a man with short fingers grappled with his pink broadsheet. The woman in the photograph on the back of his folded paper looked familiar. Dele put her fork down to flip through her own newspaper. *Oh my God, it's the lady in the video with Sandman.*

***

She spent another five days lying low in Zadunaria, then cut her hair short, pulled a wide-brimmed hat and dark veil over her face, more out of habit than proven need, and crossed the channel back to Sankara.

'Don't open the window. It's dark and you'll let the mosquis in,' said Hanili inspecting a blood red wheal on her arm. 'What have you done with your hair? Still wrapped up with Sandman are we?' she said and swung first one leg then the other, off the bed and on to the floor.

Dele bristled. She still hadn't decided how to tell her friend about Ambasi's diaries but thought she would test her with Pumped Friction first. A man in blue overalls walked in to Hanili's room with a fan under his arm.

'Matron called you at four. Where have you been all afternoon?' said Hanili. She coughed, winced with her palm on her chest.

Dele stepped sideways to make room for the workman.

An orderly cleared Hanili's tray. 'Olaf sent me some new clothes, books and a new laptop,' she said. She sat up and coughed. 'Blue top for a change and they got me this room. Brighter view and walls. And my creatinine is stable.' She cleared her throat. 'I caught a glimpse of my face this morning. Shock, horror and awe shattered the mirror but I've lost some of the chipmunkiness...not that you've noticed,' she said. 'I told everyone I dropped the mirror. That's my story and it's sticking to me.'

'It's your mind I find sexy,' said Dele.

'That won't get you far with anyone else,' said Hanili.

Dele yawned. Her hands shook.

'Bored already?' said Hanili.

'I've found a way to get back at Sandman,' said Dele, twisting the top off a bottle of water. Hanili went quiet and scratched her thumbs with her little fingers while Dele told her about the footage.

'Gee, oh, gee, oh gee, still can't get my head round it. But he'll not be the first, or last,' Hanili said, scratching a bushy eyebrow. 'But be careful...Beat Ovens have cancelled all their other gigs because of this wedding and Ukwu's struggling to feed his family. So it is a big one for him. If you do this it could wreck him,' said Hanili.

Dele's toes curled up. 'I haven't decided yet. That's why I'm here...'

'All I'm saying is that evil and revenge are not equal and opposite-,' said Hanili.

'Evil without reaction is the definition of hell on earth. The man killed my mum, took my dad away, all those poor innocent landowners and farmers. Dada,' said Dele.

'Was Dada blackmail then?'

Dele sat on the bed next to Hanili. A warm Hanili hug made her feel better. 'Dada helped Sandman move girls around. I heard they used a few as baby factories for military wives or girlfriends. Anyway, after my email-'

'What email?'

Dele told Hanili about the email she sent to Dada.

'You put the frighteners on him,' said Hanili.

Dele blushed, not sure whether Hanili approved. 'From what Burutu said at the trial Sandman must have had enough of Dada, period, even if he didn't know about the secret movie business.'

'And you believe Burutu?' said Hanili.

Dele gulped. 'It's the sort of thing Sandman would do…expunge as Mrs Lagbaja would say.'

'But then how did Sandman find out about the tape. You didn't exactly wave it in his face,' said Hanili.

Dele shook her head. 'The look on Sandman's face, like a chicken that had mistaken a snake for a worm, when Burutu spilled the beans? I think the first Sandman heard about the film or camera was from Burutu at the trial.'

'They left the camera running…by accident or for real? Reel, r,e,e,l, get it?' said Hanili.

'You are so dangerously funny, so please signpost your jokes,' said Dele.

Hanili laughed and while she poured herself a glass of water Dele turned to look out of the window. Below her lay Sankara city, the so-called city of excellence, a sprawling web of candle flames flickering in the dark.

She turned round to see a tear peep out of Hanili's right eye. 'I wish Keli was here,' said Hanili.

'You're making yourself ill,' said Dele. *I'm not feeling too good either.*

Hanili wiped her face and eyes and threw the hand towel into a bin. Dele went to the window. A nurse brought a pot of tea. Dele poured while Hanili tottered off to the bathroom. *I can't not say anything about Ambasi.* The toilet flushed and Hanili returned, her face wet.

'Without Keli's antidote it could have been much worse,' Hanili said. 'Poor Keli, caught between chariots of fire and flood waters, risked her life in the end when she told the elder.' Hanili blew her nose. 'I'd like to meet this elder,' she said.

Ambasi? Impossible. Their eyes met. Hanili had that familiar cerebral and intense cast of face that Dele had been dreading. She felt a thump in her belly.

'Oh my God,' said Hanili. She put her hands on her head. 'Dele hear me out will you…maybe Keli is threatened. Keli does what he says, realises what she's done…goes to this elder for an antidote. He asks who it's for. She tells him, or her, and if it was someone who didn't exactly fancy the pants off me, she, or he, trundles into the bush with their tropical chemistry set and returns with even worse…toxins…whatever Dr Deya calls them…'

Dele's heart rattled. 'I spy a big hole in your knitting, Hanili. What if this…elder didn't know who it was for?' she said. She went back to the window. 'Ah, those boys are up late. Is it half term?' she said.

'Dele, look at me. No more secrets remember?' said Hanili. She patted the bed. 'Come over here. You know something. First you say Keli was on a school trip. Now you're giving it the old inscrutable. I'm not buying it.' Hanili waved the nurse away. 'I'll deal with the menu later…same salty mess anyway,' she said.

Dele sat on the bed, facing Hanili. 'Your mum called the night we met Ambasi at the stadium. Ambasi took the call. His look…as if he'd seen his own ghost rising from the grave,' she said, playing with her fingers.

'You are not making sense,' said Hanili.

'It was Sandman who threatened Keli, for what you were doing in South Roko. But, but…the elder was Ambasi.'

'What did you say?' said Hanili.

'Ambasi, pastor…Keli went to see him.'

'And you expect me to believe this?' said Hanili. She swung her leg out from under the bed-tray and turned so that she could look Dele in the eye.

'I saw it…in code in his diary,' said Dele.

'He wrote this down?' said Hanili.

Dele nodded. 'He was writing an African Bible, but he had a diary of…issues, personal issues. The date at the top of each entry in his ledger corresponded to a Book of the Bible. If he put the 1st day of the month that was Genesis and so on. He told me about it the night before he dropped me off at medical school and went on about his Will. But I was so excited to be going away I didn't pay attention…'

'Ambasi, Ambasi…' said Hanili, with her chin cupped in her hands.

'With you in hospital, Mum and Dad gone, and Ambasi in hospital, Sandman free, I was on my own. I found this file in his wardrobe. He even had a little index and calendar just in case he lost his Bible.'

'Was he some aggrieved landowner or just a common-or-garden homophobic bigot?' said Hanili, with an angry wave of a hand.

'It was your populist policies-'

'He'd kill for a few speeches?' said Hanili, flicking her thumb with a little finger.

'There. You've just done it. The way you flick your finger reminded Ambasi of your mum, Tutu. Then he did his research.'

'You lost me completely now.'

'Your mum and Ambasi had a baby, before she left him…for England.'

Hanili threw herself back in the bed. 'No…no. When did you dream this one up?' said Hanili.

I wouldn't believe me either. 'A daughter. Adire. She died in England. Ambasi blames your mum.' Hanili searched Dele's eyes. Reality seemed to strike her. She thumped the orange bedside call button. No one came.

'I'm calling her now. Where's my phone. My phone. Get it for me. Nurse, nurse who's got my phone? Is this why mum never talked about Africa? I've burned my bridges she used to say.' Hanili hiccupped and started to shiver. She yanked the coverlet back on to the bed and pulled it over her shoulders. 'Now I know why.'

Dele got up to stretch her taut muscles and nerves. She walked round the end of the bed to open the door. The window curtains billowed into the room.

'So when *were* you going to tell me? After my first kidney packed up, or the second, or bits of my liver…with a message in my coffin?' said Hanili.

Dele pointed at a stray mug on the bedside cupboard. 'Should I ask the nurse to take this away?' she said.

'What do I care about fucking room service?' said Hanili, smashing her fist on the tray. An empty plastic bottle flipped on to the floor.

Dele picked the bottle up and leaned the door closed while Hanili, with her angry face in the fork of her hand, flicked crumbs off the top of the bedside tray. Hanili did not speak.

'Maybe I should go,' said Dele.

Hanili raised her head out of its rest and shook it. 'It's a lot to take in,' she said.

'Couldn't believe it myself. Burutu and Sandman picked up Keli on her way home after design class. If she didn't do what they told her family would suffer,' said Dele.

'Then she panicked, ran to Ambasi for help and he…he gave her this…so-called antidote. She thought she'd saved me. That's why she confessed. Poor thing. That's just plain wicked. The wicked invisible stepfather flies in on his septic broom. How could you even share the same space as that man?' said Hanili. She closed her eyes and shook her head.

Dele did not reply. A baby wailed in the floor below.

'Did he kill Keli too?' said Hanili.

Dele shook her head and rubbed her mother's ring. 'Sandman must have had Keli killed to cover *his* tracks, Burutu…' she said.

'I miss her desperately, she used to sing in the choir and make those kaftans, you remember the bright blue one I wore on TV on my birthday?' Hanili said with a sigh.

Poor Keli standing in the wrong queue without knowing it. The back of Dele's legs itched. She blushed and pretended to brush dust off the windowsill.

'What if Sandman had not got to Keli first?' said Hanili, raising her voice over the prattle outside the door. 'Would pastor have struck her down with a holy book? Do you all have this blind Roko gene for erosive and cross-generational fucking Old Testament revenge? Is that why you want to produce your cinematic floor show at the wedding? You can't help it if poor Ukwu and whoever else got hurt in the crossfire? Oh…I get it. They are your collateral. If you miss the ball, don't miss the man, as they say in rugby circles.'

Dele swung round. The ache in her chest turned with her. 'Depends on your point of view, doesn't it. I tried the warped Roko law…like it's my fault…anyway, this is priceless coming from miss life is so smoothie for me to see from the top of my ivory charity Christmas tree,' Dele said. She gripped Hanili's wrists and shook them. 'Those girls in the camp were not some WHO…UNESCO statistic. They were someone's little girls too, Hanili. The Haka, the inspector, Sandman, call him what you like, tucked his Arami and Lami in bed safe and sound, flew around the camps, the cockerel in the red fez…'

'I didn't mean-'

'Defenceless, orphaned, little girls reclassified as mad, for rehabilitation, and, and…my mum and me…in the camp on my birthday…I was thirteen…'

'Stop…stop,' said Hanili. Tears fanned down her cheeks. She gave Dele's face a clumsy wipe. 'Why didn't you tell me?'

'I loved you too much,' Dele said, burrowing into Hanili's warm morning smell. They wept.

'I've been meaning to tell you,' said Hanili as Dele came up for air. 'I wanted to in Olaf's helicopter. I had someone special…in London,' she said with a snivel and went quiet again.

Dele's face burned. *Is she dumping me?*

'We broke up, then I came here, deep down maybe to get away. We met up again when I went back…but it was finished. It's you I want,' said Hanili.

Dele squeezed Hanili tight. 'You know I will always love you,' she said. A radio jingle for a washing powder floated in from the next room and the evening shift of trolleys trundled past the door.

SIXTEEN

Dele opened the balcony blinds onto a sparkling day. For the third time that week since her visit to Hanili, she gave the orange seller a handsome tip, the look of delight and amazement on the little girl's face a treat in itself. *Was that selfish or exploitative because I enjoyed it too* she asked herself on her way back down the street with the morning paper.

'More? It's fresh?' Dele said, with a wave of the tea-pot. Mrs Lagbaja nodded. 'I really shouldn't, but what do those quacks know…denying an old woman life's simple pleasures,' she said.

Without going into detail Dele had asked Mrs Lagbaja what she should do with the tape.

'The deeply, deeply depraved man deserves what he gets. I'll never be able to replace my Comfy,' she said.

That makes it sort of 1-1 thought Dele. With ten days to go to the wedding of the century she still could not make up her mind what to do with the extract from Pumped Friction. What would Dad do now? she asked herself. Would revenge help find Dad? She didn't know. Would wielding this axe bring Mum back? Is it worth the collateral damage, "clatter and die image," as Mama Robi called it, or would it simply open another seam of revenge? She didn't know either. And what good had revenge done Ambasi except bring his life to a pointless end? And so she went on, like a rookie nurse in charge of a ward for terminal hypochondriacs, not knowing what to do for the best.

***

With ten days to go to the wedding Dele joined the crowd winding its way to Roko Park, the home of Sankara Hornets women's basketball club. Outside the stadium the famous Mama Fisi was doing a brisk trade in match programmes and her own range of replica T-shirts. Dele bought a programme and a steward in a luminescent yellow and silver striped jacket showed her to her seat on the edge of the second tier, next to Baba Funi.

'Thank you for coming. You can keep the programme…as an alibi,' said Dele.

'If anyone sees me they will think you and me are…doing something,' he said. A ridge of grey bristles spread along his jaw when he laughed.

'Seriously, Baba Funi I need some gist. Haka's wife, what's she like?' said Dele. She thought a mental picture of Sandman's wife would help make up her mind.

A roar went up. The Hornets had opened up a six point gap. Baba Funi waited for the swearing around him to die down.

'You mean Chief Lady Kamura? She used to work at HOSS, Hospital of South Sankara. Sandman got her the job. Her maiden name, Areje. Sandman saw her at bus-stop when she was sixteen. He would be about thirty at the time.'

'When did she leave HOSS?' said Dele.

'She is Dada's cousin, anyway let me finish. At the time Areje family is poor, some days even the gap in my back teeth see more bread than them. Sandman paid for her to finish school leaving certificate, then diploma for physical therapy. They have girl, Lami, then boy Arami, or is it boy then girl…'

They got up to let a glum supporter in a replica shirt squeeze pass.

'Have you met the woman?' said Dele.

Baba Funi tapped his nose. 'The woman can cut your wrist to make her own ends meet, overlap even. She is the one who put Mike in Sandman's trap.'

'Mike?'

'Don't rush me so. Mike is a Physio and good with computers. Anything to do with numbers or data Mike is your man. I think he is in charge of counting how long the patient is likely to be in hospital, how long since they went home, if they come back - that kind of thing, before the takeover.' Baba Funi lowered his voice. Dele leaned closer. 'One day they are on home visit, but maybe the patient is not in. Mike is checking Filuna the physio's electric socket with his screwdriver, if you read my meter, when Kamura…physical therapist…also arrives for home visit. She catches Mike and Filuna in middle of electric shock. Still follow my reading?'

Dele nodded.

Baba Funi smiled and carried on. 'Mike has wife, three pickin. Kamura told Sandman. Sandman pecked at Mike till Mike agree to work with Dada. As you know Dada is Kamura's cousin or whatever…that's all I know, God's truth.'

So that's how Dada got the discharge and expected length of stay data.

A supporter two rows down danced a jig, circling and looping one hand over the other until the cheering died down.

Baba Funi went on. 'Let me tell you another thing. She is a staunch juju woman. They say she make juju for her husband prick not to rise for any other woman. The juju man ask her three time is she sure that's what she wants, Kamura say yes three times. So the juju man did the medicine. They say that is why Sandman like all this carrying of small girls around, because the juju is only against women not girls. You get my jet?'

'Baba Funi, that's Type 7 watery bullshit,' said Dele, smacking her knee with her rolled up programme.

Baba Funi spread his arms with an air of injured feelings. 'Ah my friend, why you vex so…'

'Sorry Baba Funi, I should know by now that everything in South Roko has both a scientific and a jujugenic explanation,' said Dele.

***

Baba Funi's gossip still left her undecided. Then, during another sleepless night, with a week to go to the wedding, the scratch of her mum's ring against the mug of hot chocolate reminded her how the ornament came to be round her finger and not where her dad had put it on his wedding day. It reminded her that Sandman had scorned her, mocked her abused her and her mother and many others, destroyed her family and even dared her to do her worst. Do your worst. Do your worst. Those words rang through her mind as she prepared for her next move.

SEVENTEEN

Arami and Pupa's wedding reception was held in the banqueting auditorium of Zadunaria Central hotel, a hall so large that workers were said to exchange instructions by phone or loudhailer.

A security man in a red top and khaki trousers stopped Dele at the entrance. 'Show me your particulars,' he said.

How many times? thought Dele. The man looked at Dele's bogus identity card, then at Dele's face and back again. 'Your name? Take off your cap,' he said. Dele gulped, took off the peaked Beat Oven's roadie cap. Her short hair barely reached her ears, but she had kept her fringe long. 'Monica Harim,' she said, hoping the man would not see through the forgery.

'And your job here is what?' he said.

'I am design artist with the band. I play video to go with songs and with speeches from the VIP table,' she said, nodding over his shoulder at the main dais to her right.

The man looked at Dele's face then the card and back again. He lifted the card to the light like a cashier, flicked it like a playing card while Dele's heart drummed against her blouse.

'Ok,' said the man at last. 'Come,' he said, beckoning Dele through the mahogany doors. Inside, life-sized portraits of the couple in a heart-shaped halo smiled down from hundreds of glittering chandeliers. The man walked Dele up the sweep of white marble stairs and opened a waist-high gate to a first-floor aisle.

'This is where your band will be playing,' he said. He waved his wand around the aisle. 'When we start you must not pass this point or place without permission, understand?'

'Yes sir,' said Dele.

A roadie dropped a bag off behind the boxes of wind instruments and left. From where she would be sitting, next to the drummer, Dele could see over the aisle railings to the main VIP dais, but she saw with a flutter in her chest that the projectionist's cubicle on the floor above her, could only be reached by a separate staircase from outside. She put her identity card in the back pocket of her baggy light grey trousers, knelt down beside the set of drums to connect her projector: one set up for Ukwu's playlist and the other, to play the Pumped Friction tape. But when to play it she was not sure; before or after the speeches, or somewhere in between? And would there be time enough, and just the right element of surprise? Too much could go wrong. If Sandman or his men got her she was dead. But there was no going back. Now or never.

'What are you doing?' said the security man.

'My wire connections,' said Dele, jack-knifing on to her feet. 'It will take me thirty minutes, do you want to come back or…'

'I'll watch.' He pulled a scarf round his neck, swivelled round on the drummer's stool, his gaze on the box inside which Dele had strapped her data stick. She tried to drag the box towards her with a foot but it snagged on a cable and toppled over.

'What is in there?' said the man. He pointed at the box.

Dele's hands shook. She righted the box. 'You want me to open…only small decorations, it remains a small bit,' Dele said, pulling the sweaty shirt off her back and making a little gap between thumb and forefinger. She trampled over to a finger-thick cable, pretending to relay a connection.

The man flipped the box open and peered inside. Dele froze. 'Make quick, I want to inspect the-'

Just then the beanpole bandleader, Ukwu, leapt over the gate and tapped a yelp out of the microphone. 'Hey security, you want to join my band. If you don't know my tunes it's too late my brother,' said Ukwu.

'Some of us have better tings to do,' said the security man, checking his watch and straightening up. He gestured to Dele to put the lid back on the box. 'I am in charge here…of this band area. Anything you want, ask me. I told you no go areas until show start. Two hours to go. Hah some people arrived already, have they no food at home?' he said, pointing at a couple with three children in matching all-green outfits.

Ukwu waited for the man to leave. 'Dele, are you sick with Malaria or something? Tonight keep an eye on me at all times and you'll be fine. This is a big one for us. But your design is *soseyi*…man.' He blew a kiss. 'Our playlist. They are fine with it. Covers and one or two originals, but we cannot play controversial student tunes here.' He made a cutting motion across his Adam's Apple and tapped a microphone. 'Are you not going to get changed?' he said as he waltzed off stage.

'I am looking for a set of pliers,' she said.

Dele kneeled on the floor and set up her system to the right of the stage from where she could both watch the window of the projectionist's booth and reach Ukwu in a few strides. Peeping through the railings of the aisle she saw security men everywhere and decided not to risk walking around or even visiting the toilet, yet. After one last glance at the huge screen at the far end of the hall under which Sandman and the VIPS would sit, Dele lay her churning head on a bag and closed her eyes, wondering whether she should check her wires once more.

Band banter woke her up. She checked her phone. A few minutes to seven. Dele looked downstairs. The whole of South Roko society seemed to be squeezing in to the hall. She recognised at least ten Generals, but the Chinese ambassador seemed to have pride of place a few feet away from the VIP dais.

At seven thirty-five and to a fanfare the huge mahogany doors on the ground floor to Dele's right swung open. Each door seemed wide enough to take a pair of elephants standing nose to tail. Sandman strutted in. In a deep purple three-piece suit and golden shoes, he looked more like Kanye West than a Siroko cultural icon. His wife, Kamura, walked in beside him, her nose in the air like a seal's, whether the better to show the thick, diamond-studded chain round her neck, or to keep the purple damask *gela* on her crown, or to take in the awe in which she presumed she was held, Dele could not say.

Sandman took a seat next to the mother of the bride. Her red *gela* with its tips, spiky battlements, jabbed into his neck. From the main screen Dele could see the provenance of Puma's dental overhang and the dimple on her chin.

The four-course meal ended with a chocolate dessert. Flown in from Germany said the drummer. Dele took a few nervous mouthfuls and watched the green and red lights flashing on her black console. The bridegroom rose to his feet.

'I've waited so long for this day, the day my dad would grow up and give up playing with my toys so that I could leave home,' he said in reply to a special toast to the bridegroom.

The packed hall rose to applaud. YK the MC proposed a toast to the guests and opened the floor with a narrow woman in a lopsided headdress. Dele's heart stopped for a moment until she saw that she had got the correct set of graphics, images of ordinary Roko life, projected on the huge screens. On Ukwu's count to four the Beat Ovens set off with Fela's "Water No get Enemy." Dele knew it well and her display matched the faster tempo Ukwu wanted for a wedding. In a flash a kaleidoscopic collection of intricate headgears bobbed and swayed under the twinkling chandeliers. The women sang along with the gyrating Ukwu, now with hands waving in the air above their heads as if they had not a worldly care, now with fists clenched, held out in front and rocked back and forth together as if rowing a boat or kneading dough. Kamura, had changed from purple into a pink outfit, moved her head from side to side, her eyes half-closed and shaded by thick blue-black eye-lashes, shuffling on the spot with maniacal hula hoop wriggles of the hips, and rocking dainty white-gloved fists in time with the beat. A pot-bellied man in an embroidered white cap and green robes thrust his pelvis at her, his bulbous face screwed up in his bliss, sweat dripping on to his chest, and on her signal, a jut of the forehead or the flick of her brows, he peeled dollar bills off a thick wad of notes and pasted or tucked them wherever she wanted, neck, face, or down into the top of her cleavage. Sandman tapped the man on the shoulder. The man looked up, scarpered, gown gathered between his legs. Sandman shook his head at Kamura's shoes as if to ask how she could stay on her feet on such stilts. She laughed, turned round and waved her booty at his crotch. Dele felt sick.

Next came a calypso song. Sandman poured Puma's mother a drink, then waltzed through the dancing throng to talk to YK the MC. In a morning suit the MC looked like a cross between a whale and a penguin. The two men walked towards the lobby, YK a stride behind, arms behind his back.

On a signal from Ukwu, Ori the drummer closed the tune with a brief drum roll. Dele looked at her watch: half past eight. *What is Sandman going to do? Leave early? No, please no.* Her neck itched.

'Are you well?' said Ukwu.

'Just excited,' said Dele replacing her soaking ear muffs. She got up, felt faint, and sat down again. The MC tapped his microphone. 'Ladies and gentlemen a change to the programme. The Haka will be making his speech before the Ambassador.'

Dele glanced down at her programme. The security man walked into the enclosure. 'Come, we have problem with the link-up system and we can't find the technician. Did you hear me?'

'Sorry, did you mean my very self?' said Dele. *What if Sandman sees me?* On Ukwu's signal the band launched into a cover version of 'Ain't no stopping us now.' Dele nodded to the beat and turned away, hoping the security man would leave her alone. He tapped her on the shoulder, hard. 'After this number. I am waiting,' he said.

Dele watched the floor below in a daze. A woman in the bright yellow lace outfit, a uniform shared by all the bride's female relatives, grabbed Sandman, a flirtatious grin on her face. He smiled a polite decline, tugged the tip of his nose, twirled the woman round twice and stuffed some dollar notes into her hand. Kamura shuffled up, Puma's mother in tow. The other dancers gave the threesome room; ignoring their partners to take in the rare sight of Sandman, the Haka of Roko, without his fez in public. Dele wondered how many of them knew what their Haka had been up to. When Sandman executed a nimble pirouette and shuffle, like Usher in ultra-slow motion, Kamura clapped her hands to her cheeks in exaggerated surprise. Puma's mother clapped as well but Dele sensed a touch of envy to her pat on Kamura's back. The tune faded out. Sandman returned to his seat to empty a flute down his long throat. Dele's arms stretched, seized in a nervous yawn.

On the VIP dais, YK the MC thumped the microphone thrice without reply. The security man marched up to pull Dele up by the elbow. Dele's heart sagged because she had rather hoped that the man had forgotten or found someone else. In her anxiety she stumbled into the high hat. YK winced and raised a hand to his ear. 'The congas are drunk,' he said. 'And the drummer,' shouted someone from the floor, to loud laughter. YK thumped the mesh ball on the microphone. The microphone screeched and went dead. 'Order, order,' he said, trying to make himself heard. He handed the microphone to another man who blew on it thrice, giving it a quizzical look and handed it back. YK rolled his eyes. 'This thing is like woman.'

'We can't hear,' someone shouted.

'It's like man's thing, more off than on,' said a woman on a nearby table, tipping her head back with laughter and tapping her male companion on the chin. The man didn't look impressed and turned away from the leers on his table.

With her cap down over her face Dele followed the security man down the stairs, her heart thumping harder and harder with each step she took towards Sandman's dais. With a few meters to go to the High Table she heard a sharp sizzle from a loudspeaker. Seconds later YK's microphone screeched into life. YK raised the microphone to the ceiling or chandelier. 'Blessed to our golden couple.' He turned to the hall. 'You can hear?' he said.

'Yes,' came the reply from the floor.

The security man let go of Dele. 'You can return, but we may need you again,' he said.

Dele puffed her lips in relief. As she turned round a woman in a red frock reached out and pulled her cap off. 'Tell Ukwu to play Sweet Wife encore,' she said.

'Go and buy it in the shops,' Dele said. With a stare she snatched her cap back and raced back up the stairs. *You want to get me killed?*

Dele got back to her seat just as YK the MC took to the floor again. 'Do you all agree that we have all had the best time anybody could have ever had on this island?'

'Yes,' came the reply. 'Nah, on this world even. Nah, in the universe,' said a man sitting near the front in a glitzy yellow cap. More profuse murmurs of approval went up from a thousand throats.

YK beamed. 'I think you will all agree with me that Asiri Oniseme, Haka of Roko, needs no introduction. By his single hand, in fact with one black hand behind his back he solved many problems in white lands.'

He didn't. He got deported. But the facts seemed to have been lost on YK. Sandman didn't seem to mind either, rubbing his shiny forehead with mock embarrassment.

'...he has been to England. Old England. After he solved problems there he went to New England and did the same. But for South Roko you need both hands, both eyes-'

'And a biro,' shouted the man in the yellow cap.

'You are right sir. Without a biro, even a powerful minister like the Haka is just another pair of hands. Not so?' said YK.

'It is so,' said the man in the yellow cap.

Kneading her knees with sweaty hands, a nervous Dele rocked back and forth on her chair as laughter filled the hall once more, seeming to wind her gut even tighter round a hot spool. *Will the technician remember to switch me back on after YK?* Sandman leaned towards Kamura. He seemed to be whispering to her, his pose, with fingers curved under his nose and his eyes fixed on YK, perhaps suggesting that the MC was taking too long.

Dele's phone buzzed. It was Aanu. 'A problem. I'll get back to you,' read the text message but it was five minutes old. Dele guzzled from a lukewarm bottle of water. 'What problem do you mean?' she replied by text.

The murmurs died down and YK resumed. 'This man has done great things for our hospitals. He has kept our Roko currency strong. A dynamic man. Insatiable for success and restless for progress. Today he gained a daughter but tomorrow he will give a fortune away. A day to treasure. But I will not take any more of your time. Ladies and gentlemen I present to you the man himself, a diplomat, an elder, a minister, a father, husband, a wise man, prophet, visionary. Haka of Roko.' Cheers and applause rang out as Sandman took a few steps back and waited for a microphone.

'Please be seated. The heady notes from good wine, perfume and song have sweetened my friend YK's tongue.'

Laughter rippled from table four: 'YK, the man with wicked hips and tongue like sliced fork,' shouted someone.

'My most eminent and great MC, the honourable member for the most Southern tip of the most northern state of South Roko,' said Sandman in his reedy voice. He beckoned YK over to his side. YK rubbed his hands and smiled, but with eyes eager with obsequy and fear. 'Ah...please don't let them hear you address me like that. I beg. I am there by your grace, a humble-'

'YK. You care too much for me.'

It should be he "feared" too much thought Dele.

Sandman thanked everyone, his in-laws and the guests. He turned round to the screen. 'Slides please,' he said. The technician hurried up to the dais and handed Sandman a grey and black control. 'Sorry, sir.' The lights dimmed as the projectionist switched from Beat Ovens' to Sandman's presentation. Sandman scrolled through a bird's eye view of South Roko to show where he planned to build a library in honour of his late father. He clicked to the next slide. Someone at the back let out a gasp when an artist's view of the proposed Watawata development appeared on the screen. A woman started to clap. Sandman waved her down. 'Your dazzling beauty and jewellery are making my eyes water with joy,' he said, shielding his eyes with his palm. One man in a bright green cap laughed so much that he fell off his chair. Sandman took his bow. The audience got to its feet. They clapped on and on as if afraid to be the first to stop, like at a political party conference. YK waddled back up the stairs to stand next to Sandman. Beaming, Sandman clapped his hands to all corners of the hall. He excused the Chinese ambassador with two quick nods. The ambassador bowed, stopped clapping and sat down. His table and the rest of the hall soon followed.

A long queue snaked between the tables to congratulate Sandman. Sandman wriggled out of the two-handed grip of a white-haired old man and turned to greet the waiting Chinese ambassador. Dele checked her phone. No message from Aanu. What was that about? She checked her display. The screen said no signal. She wondered whether to go and find out whether the technician had gone to the toilet or for a drink or plain forgotten to switch her back on, but knew that she would run the risk of running into Sandman. And she could not send a member of the band because they had all gone on break. She wiped her soaking gloves on her knees again, rolled her shoulders and decided to wait.

The Chinese ambassador shook hands with Sandman. Sandman laughed at something the ambassador must have said. An amplifier screeched. The ambassador smiled, gave Sandman the thumbs-up, half-bowed and walked back to his table. Sandman waved back and was about to greet a man in a white hat when the microphone crackled. Dele's phone buzzed. 'Issues,' read the message from Aanu. Dele looked up at the technician's window, willing him to switch her back on. Ukwu returned to tap sparky protests from his microphone. YK stood at the far end of the hall, about to declare the floor open again. Dele went limp. Her chance had gone. The thought of watching Sandman waltz away unscathed once more brought the bitter taste of defeat to her throat. Ukwu raised a quizzical finger. Dele mimed to let him know that she did not have a signal yet. Ukwu shrugged and pointed at YK. 'We will have to play without your photos,' he said. Then out of the corner of her left eye Dele saw a thumb wag from the technician's booth. Her phone buzzed.

'Problem deprejudiced, sorry for delay, issues beyond my control,' read the text. *Can't he write in English?* Dele signalled with a raised finger for Ukwu to give her a moment. She took in a deep breath and, as practised perhaps at least a hundred times before, flicked a switch on her console and slotted in the data-stick. She pressed play and skipped to the microphone past a baffled Ukwu.

'Ladies and gentleman, Beat Oven presents the performance of the night. The parrot's opera - advice for new couples,' she said. She saw Sandman cast a searching glance at YK just before the lights went down.

'Dele what you are doing?' said Ukwu.

'It's an original composition,' said Dele.

The screen went blank for a second then lit up to show a parrot shrieking, thrashing about its cage. Feathers flew through the rails and fluttered round the room. Water dripped on to the floor.

"Fuck, fuck", screeched the parrot.

The audience laughed, pointing knowing fingers at the new couple. The shot zoomed out. Pupa's face loomed from the screen. The hall went quiet, the guests perhaps not sure what to think. Then they saw her stiff, bobbing jaw line and the veins standing out on her weeping neck, the trembling lips, the tears squeezing out of eyes clamped shut to roll down the side of her face and duck in and out of her ear. Gasps went up. A woman in a pillbox hat sobbed right under Dele's aisle.

But Dele knew what next to expect. She saw the jerky shot of Sandman' face, on the big screen, like that of a movie star, but as never seen in public, distorted by his explosive lift off, shooting from the hip, a shot so unexpected that he mistimed his forward guidance and his glistening black lozenge, dropped out of a coarsely creased sheath and into the light.

The hall fell silent, save for an amplified sniffle from the floor and a whimper from the two Pupas; the one present on the VIP dais and the one blown up on the white screen.

The lights came on.

No one moved, except first Arami who fled round the back of the dais. Then Kamura teetered over on high heels to her husband, stopped, then, with her jaw lower than the reach of her diamond necklace, kicked first one shoe off then the other turned and chased after her son. Pupa slumped into her dessert, holding her face as if it had been burned by acid. General Gironda tried to jump out of his chair, but aide-de-camps pulled him back. Dele could not see the General's wife.

Sandman's mouth dropped open wide. Speechless, he half closed it, but it dropped open again, as wide as a car's boot, his lower lip seemingly weighed down by the husks of spent clichés piling up in his jaw. Dele wondered what he would say. *It's not what it looks like, I can explain. You don't understand. It's a long and wrong story. It's before I knew who she was. A terrible mistaken identity.*

Well, ladies and gentlemen he's got history.

The band leader, Ukwu stood stock still, like a man struck blind. Dele led him to a chair and went to flip the microphone off its stand.

'Ladies and gentlemen Haka took many, even younger girls by force,' she said. 'Dada, his in-law used inside knowledge. He knew the diagnoses and how long patients would stay in hospital and so he hired some of their homes out for *mago mago*. The patients did not know, minister did not know…or maybe he did, we can ask him…he did not know that Dada had his own side-business, recording and selling on the black market. Maybe my friend disturbed them when she came home early and they left the camera running. Sadly, the doctor, Dada is no longer with us.' Dele looked round the hall. Her audience, sat silent, rapt. The Chinese ambassador, his august chin in one hand just sat and stared.

Out of the corner of her eye Dele saw Pupa raise her head off the table. Pupa swept the dainty bridal bouquet on to the floor, gathered her low-cut white gown and shuffled up to Sandman. One lady in the hall had her hands on her head. Another, in a bright orange dress raised her hands to her face in shock. Pupa took one of the microphones of the dais and started to speak. She sounded like a bird lamenting the loss to a hawk of her new-born chicks.

'He said he wanted to discuss a secret surprise for Arami with me. He forced me. I did not believe. What kind man is this? But I didn't know…what to do, to go back to go front, to turn right or to turn left or to fly or die…where am I to go?' She turned to her dad, who, tossing his head and throwing his arms in the grip of the men trying to restrain him, looked like a wild animal trapped in a cage. 'You had plans for us and business with the minister. I couldn't spoil…If I told you…'Her voice snapped, like a dry twig trampled underfoot. 'Sorry papa.' She dropped the microphone and ran out of the hall. Her mum gave bare-footed pursuit.

Dazed, Dele stumbled down the stairs, past the chief porter who had his mouth in his gloved hands as he backed out of the main doors. She saw the Chinese ambassador, at the diplomatic table, flip back his shock of dark hair and look at Sandman askance. *Now you know what he's like, you probably knew anyway but didn't care.* On table 4 a lively young woman in pink peered through the currency notes on her damp forehead, her dismay and surprise visible on what Dele could see of her face.

Not sure whether to crow or cry, an exultant chorus rose in her head nevertheless. It rang louder with each step she took towards the statuesque Sandman. Sandman turned to her, licking and chewing his lips. Dele drew herself up, whipped off her cap. 'I'm sure you remember me. You told me to do my worst.' Sandman's face sagged, life seemed to drain from his eyes and he staggered backwards, and fell back over a chair and into a stack of crated drinks.

'From the Veritys,' said Dele. She tossed the data-stick at her nemesis. 'Didn't Mr Dada tell you that I always make copies?' she said.

EIGHTEEN

Dele got back to Ambasi's flat at seven in the morning, her ears still ringing from sitting too close to the massive loudspeakers, the night's events whisked into a dizzying, thrilling, multi-coloured blur. The look on Sandman's face when the slide show started she would never forget. If this is what they meant by priceless they were right. She made a cup of tea and waited for Mrs Lagbaja to get up. Mrs Lagbaja sauntered into the kitchen at last at half past eight. 'I'll let you have this fancy new e-book reader someone gave me. Mills and Boon stories kept me up after Aanu dropped me off. Remind me never to travel in that bone wrecker again,' said Mrs Lagbaja. She wiped her eyes with her knuckles. 'Cup of tea would do, thank you.'

'Giradona's daughter must be cursing the day she set eyes on that family,' said Dele.

'You must read Knaves and Players,' said Mrs Lagbaja. 'Starts out like an adventure story but really about this girl who goes to Antarctica...not listening are you? That's the problem with you youngsters. No hinterland.'

***

Four days went like the wind, but the aching in Dele's heart, the fire she thought she had put out on that wedding night, seemed to have returned with compound interest. When Mrs Lagbaja went for a siesta or to read her book, Dele got dressed and went downstairs.

Outside, crenelated shadows lounged across the street. Dele wondered why the thrill she got from her revenge now also seemed to be in shadow and flat on its back. Revenge looked so great in "Once upon a Time in the West", so why did she feel like a child who had broken a long coveted toy on Christmas day? Perhaps Mum was right. Revenge was only a quick fix, like a squirt of Gtn to a failing heart; and not meant to be savoured like a multi-course meal or like vintage wine, or resonate for ages, like a classic work of art, but to be taken in, like a piece of tangy ice lolly, fig, or catchy tune, or a slap at a mosquito, and forgotten. After all, Sergio Leone didn't say how Harmonica felt after he killed his nemesis.

With the low evening sun in her eyes she sauntered up the street to tag on to the small group gathered round a man reading bafflegap from a glossy brochure.

'To town, miss?' said a taxi driver bringing his black and mustard taxi to a crawl. A tanker almost ran into him. Other impatient drivers sounded their horns. Dele shook her head. She needed to clear her head, not with a taxi driver in her ear. Two other cabs stopped. The driver of the second car had smiley eyes. Dele chose him because he reminded her of her dad. She got out at the central market.

'Be my lucky late customer, half price,' said a fruit seller, shooting a wilting mound of mango, guava and pineapple with water from a plastic toy gun. Dele caught a whiff of the woman's hairspray amongst the aromas clinging to the day's fag-end. Her phone rang.

'Will you have light tonight?' said Aanu.

'Who knows?' said Dele, wafting smoke from a roadside fire away from her face.

'You are too funny. Check YouTube. Sandman and Pupa show.'

'How did they get the tape? It's not fair to Pupa,' said Dele.

'Another thing though,' said Aanu. 'Sandman's men mobilised and commandeered ambulance that night. Maybe they used *Anjima* to make him disappear. The man is at large.'

She ducked under the loose coil of a passing cane basket. 'Not your magic again–'

'General Gironda's people are looking for him. They are more vexed than hungry lion, so don't stay late outside. Where did you say you were? If not for my jelly clutch I would pick you up. But I need to find Snakes Legs, oh.'

Dele closed the call. News that Sandman had escaped Gironda's wrath aggravated the ache in her chest. Her bus roared past, turned right into Libya street, taking the corner at speed, its bonnet steaming and side panels flapping like fish gills. Dele chased after it, but it did not stop. *Shit.*

'That stupid driver,' said a beggar from his throne which looked like a skateboard. He slapped his skeletal thighs in frustration.

Dele hailed a cab. It sped off. So did the next two. She decided to walk.

A young cyclist came up Libya Street in a "Free Universities" T-shirt. Nodding his giant "satellite dish" Afro to the reggae version of Fela's "Sorrow Tears and Blood" playing in the beer parlour, he pasted a "Release all Arimo" poster on a corrugated tin wall, stood back and grinned at his handiwork. Then he pushed his black bike up towards Dele and seemed to look for another spot for his poster. From behind Dele came the sharp sound of metal scraping the ground. She saw fruit sellers slither away and her unlucky beggar pull up and fold his flaccid legs in even closer, scuttling off, paddling furiously, it seemed, for his life. The young cyclist froze astride his bike.

Dele turned round. A green van tore down the street, its yellow hazard lights flashing, its exhaust pipe, hanging on by thin wires, clattering along behind it, protesting in orange sparks, loud farts and plumes of dense smoke. *Rokopats*. Screeching the van to a halt within inches of the young cyclist, the driver poked his head out of the window.

'What you are doing?' he said. Spit flecked his bearded face. He switched off the engine and a heavy tingling silence fell over the street, shattered in a beat by the sound of the tailgate exploding open and of a dozen heavy boot steps landing on baked red mud. Six men, in the dark green khaki uniforms of Giradona's Rokopats, ran over to the young cyclist, lifted him in the air and rammed his bottom down on to his seat post. 'What I done?' the young man cried. They tore the satchel off the man's back and threw it into the van. 'You are one of them? We'll show you chilli pepper,' said a squat, brutish man with green trousers rolled halfway up legs thick enough to support a flyover. 'Mumu, go get me drink,' he said. Mumu set off. Pub drinkers scattered as if hit by water cannon, clattering and overturning tables and chairs as they fled before the fresh-faced soldier. Dele flinched as well-aimed kicks to ankles felled the young man. She saw a dark column of blood spread down the back of his knees. He curled up, whimpering. But a soldier forced his head up and his arms apart, and, while another soldier held him down, they kicked and beat him, even with beer cans, till his Afro looked like an oversized red kitchen sponge. Somehow the man found the strength to writhe free and lift his head.

Don't do that thought Dele.

But it was too late. The man had his head snapped back with a kick. Dele heard a sickening click as the man's body jerked back as if he had been shot. She somehow expected the young man to fire shots at his assailants and roll out of danger like a movie star, or peep through his fingers like a footballer to see what concessions his team had won. Instead the man shuddered, and, like a victim of that final shocking retribution on Death Row, went limp, with foam dribbling from his mouth. Dele retched and almost blacked out and her ride in the back of the truck with Saro all those years ago flashed round her head. Desperate not to draw attention to herself, she grabbed on to a wobbly stall, willing rubbery legs not to let her down. *Should have turned back at Avenue de Ghana.*

The soldiers wiped their hands on the lifeless man's bloody T-shirt, picked up his headphones and cell phone, jumped into their van and squealed away in a cloud of dust and smoke: and with buffalo rampaging in her chest, Dele let out the breath she seemed to have for ever held in check.

A man with a goatee crept out of his lair to check the coast with a slow swivel of eye and head. 'He dead?' he said.

Another man went up to feel the cyclist's neck. He nodded. 'Just like that,' he said.

The first man shook his huge head and stooped to pick up a can of beer. 'Man's life cheaper than mosquito bite in this country.'

'At least mosquito enjoy drink first,' said a passing labourer and disappeared down a dark alley.

A vulture glided down from the top of an electric pylon to land a hop away from the body. 'Shoo, devil, let the man spirit get to heaven first,' said the barman, flapping his wrists and stamping his feet. The vulture cocked its bald head, seeming to consider its options, but must have thought better of a fight, and taxied away to resume its vigil from a table top a van's length away. In the dusty dusk it looked like a statue on a plinth.

'Only God can save us from these Rokopats,' said one man as another van squealed to a halt beside Dele. A dozen men, naked save for boots, the deerstalkers and khaki trousers held up by wide shiny belts, jumped out. 'Don't move don't move,' they said, firing guns into the air. 'Where are they?' said their boss, a man with shiny pectorals the size of wind turbines. He grabbed a passer-by and threw the poor man's spectacles into the gutter. 'Are you one of them?' he said.

'I'm civil servant. I just reach home. This is my only white shirt you've torn sir,' said the accosted man.

The man with the bulging pectorals put a gun to the civil servant's head. 'Who killed this boy?'

Dele pulled her cap down over her face and inched backwards. The civil servant dropped to his knees. He begged but got a slap on the face for his troubles. Dele heard gunshots up the street, looked up and saw the green Rokopat van reappear. Dele dived under a parked van, her ears rattling to the sound of even heavier gunfire. Hot grit and concrete pinged and sparked into metal, stung her face and arms. Guns spat at screams, snuffing them out. A man howled. The rear tyre on the van sank with a pop and a fizz and grazed Dele's left ankle. Jerking the ankle free, Dele wriggled further under the van. She saw three legs hobble past. A gun went off and the man with one leg fell, scrambled on to his foot. 'I beg, I beg,' he said, hopping along, but two shots followed and he fell again. Lighter treads came hurrying past him, it seemed in retreat. They fell too, the odd sputter from their guns drowned by the barrage from the other side. The van shuddered and Dele heard petrol tinkle on to the ground between her feet.

Must get away. She slid out, aiming for shelter between van and culvert, only to see the silhouette of an armed man in a beret crouched not much more than an arm's length away.

'I'm checking this side for them,' said the man.

Shivering with fright, Dele wriggled back under the van. She held her breath and tried to ignore the hairy insect legs stirring inside her ear as the man edged closer. The man hopped across the front of the van, banged the bonnet with his rifle and prodded the dead man.

'This one, ah na Moses. Come see, Moses.' The victors dragged Moses away. A gust of wind laden with cordite knifed through the gap he left. Trucks reversed up the street. It went quiet. Black spots danced before Dele's eyes. With her heart seeming to pound the spicy yams she had for lunch back into her mouth, Dele crawled out on her hands and bare feet into a jaundiced mist. She inched along amongst the smell of dust, blood and gun smoke, ducking with every glint from a tinfoil or discarded shell, the rustle of a hen flapping its wings or the click from a cooling car engine. A van's length from the end of the street she clambered over two dead bodies and one twitching arm, swerved round a whimpering cat, broke cover and ran.

***

'Where have you been, Syria?' said Mrs Lagbaja, lighting one candle with another as Dele stumbled in.

'It is war out there,' said Dele, sweeping sticky hair from her left eye.. Gasping for breath, she prayed for the guns rattling in her head to stop. 'Gironda's thugs killed a poor cyclist...he put a poster up about the Arimos. And they were pissed off about what happened to their boss's girl. That poor boy would still be alive if I hadn't started all this-'

'They don't need an excuse. Remember the Arimos demonstration.'

'I guess you're right. We nearly died from teargas that day…during the 2012 Olympics.'

'Was the curfew not meant to calm all down?' said Mrs Lagbaja. She settled back into the sofa. 'All it seems to have done is clear the streets for random killing.'

That boy was so brave. Perhaps his dad was missing too. I just watched.

Mrs Lagbaja tapped the radio on the stool beside her. 'Only reliable news is from abroad. BBC says Giradona is finished because of what happened…and that the culprit's at large makes him look weak. But he'll hang on till grim death. Nagati people say they will secede if Giradona is removed.' She leaned over to sip from her mug and dabbed her lips with a knuckle. 'I wish they'd stop referring to us as West Africa. It's deeply deeply offensive. We're Roko.'

'Same difference,' said Dele.

Mrs Lagbaja's replied with fricative grunt of dissent. 'They say a Chinese aircraft carrier the size of a village, is on its way. It's either that, or a UN resolution,' she said, one hand hovering over her mug.

'Bet on the carrier. The gun is mightier than a written instruction,' said Dele.

***

Dele showered and flopped into bed as exhausted as Pheidippides. But the day's event would not pile up neat and tidy, but kept bursting into her head in a wrinkled and untidy mess, dripping blood, wringing wet, tangled up with the sight of her headless mum, Jane, in the back of a van, with the thought of her sightless dad worked to death in some God-forsaken camp, of syringed air bubbling up Dada's veins, of Ambasi swinging by his neck, of Keli lying dead. Dele sat up. In the shifting shadows cast by the clouds as they wiped the moon's face, the standing fan in the corner seemed to segue into the head of the unfortunate Afro-haired cyclist, for whose fate Dele blamed herself. Then the cyclist's head changed into the face of a nameless girl, whose image put her in mind of rape and starvation as weapons of war and of the attacks by Boko Haram on Nigerian girls and the latest slaughter in the Central African Republic;

then popped into her head the fate of the South Sudan, a toddler barely weaned - would it too teeter after its elder siblings on the well-trodden slippery slope to perdition she wondered.

She looked at her phone. *Four-fifty*. Not from the teachers or the radio or her psychology lectures, nor from Ambasi or from the Bible or from the community leaders here or abroad of any faith, nor from reading abridged serious fiction and "classics for Roko" at school had she found an answer to the question: why are we humans made so wicked? The writers write about it, the artists draw and show it, my Prof "Freudyung" Olatunbosun of the Department of Psychology wrote many papers to explain it - oh he was jealous, or angry, or treated badly by his Dad and Mum or his teachers, or was bullied at school, or had a faulty gene, or did not think much of himself or others or she thought too much of herself. Some, like Sandman, have a racial, colonial or tribal, transgenerational, grudge - but why, Dele asked herself, are we set up to do evil, to be driven mad by jealousy, to be angry or sad or vengeful in the first place? Could we not have been designed to be happy, to rejoice even to find someone in the queue to sleep with our Hanilis?

She looked for a note pad on which to write down her questions. Is wickedness like long-sightedness? Is it in our genes? But if we were the first draft of an Almighty, All-seeing, All-knowing God, an experiment let us say, why did He not revise or rerun the trial, rub us out and start again? And if we were His best effort, the final draft; why did He have to publish us, and let all this misery unfold? Or is all this suffering here and abroad over the millennia, the pogroms, ethnic cleansings, industrial killings, chemical trimmings, final solutions - to Him like how she saw the impact of that last ditch long jump by Shobam on the girls of Freeman and Parker House, when she told them to get over it, it's only a game and made Rita cry? Does God say Verily Angel Gabriel or Jibril, I know they are devastated, but you and I know that nobody died, really, and those who come to me through my chosen ones can count on everlasting life?

NINETEEN

The lights dimmed. 'Electricity Board winking at us again,' said Mrs Lagbaja. She clunked her mug down on the coffee table.

'Good thing I bought these candles from Rusi's place,' said Dele, with an anxious glance at the flickering lightbulb.

Aanu swallowed his mouthful of beer. 'We'll have light because General Sajulo is on TV tonight,' he said, wiping his mouth with the back of his hand. 'Chinese dragged Giradona from the mangy sofa they gave him. Sajulo is new father of the nation. Two weeks, they don't waste time,' he said.

'Political chaos is bad for business,' said Dele.

Minutes later General Sajulo, a dapper forty year old officer from the minority Twi came on TV. 'I have no interest in grand titles. Traditional rulers and elders will be restored to their rightful place in our body politic. All decrees issued from the 1st January 2014 have been repealed with immediate effect. Ministers released under the wedding amnesty will be rearrested.'

'That was Sandman…in handcuffs?' said Mrs Lagbaja.

'Could be a library shot, though,' said Dele with a groan.

'They found him in the toilet in this woman's house…secretary or his wife's jeweller, who knows. But Sajulo is a master dribbler of political football. He knows that Nagati people will vex if Sandman is the biggest minister arrested. So he makes new laws. He sacked Banusi. Banusi is Kombo. Then he tells all the papers, cable TV channels, Sky, Fox, CNN that he, Sajulo, a new breed African leader had done something that has not happened before - sacked minister for corruption.'

'Banusi stole too much, even for Roko. Two mega-yachts with his name on them. Everyone saw the yachts during the F1 race in Monaco,' said Mrs Lagbaja, waving the paper under Dele's nose.

'Banusi sentenced to death because he is Kombo to balance the books with the Nagati. What do Kombo people think of this politically correct programme, equality at last, eh?' Dele said. 'I'll fill the kettle.'

'It is a capital offence to disrespect the general who gave you the licence to steal,' said Aanu.

'Quoted from the famous Rokopat Law Review,' said Dele.

'The press says what's all the fuss about when in Nigeria the minister could have claimed compensation for depreciation to his yacht caused by the adverse publicity,' said Mrs Lagbaja.

Dele's phone buzzed. She didn't recognise the number.

'Are you Dele Verity?' said the voice.

'Who wants to know?' said Dele.

'I'm *aide de camp* to the Head of State. Under new legal framework of the fusion of traditions, you are now first plaintiff in the case against the former Haka. His fate is in the hands of you and mama.'

'How do you mean?' said Dele.

'Mama's parrot is still missing. Haka will hang…but you decide.' He rang off before Dele could reply.

'Who was that?' said Mrs Lagbaja, dabbing her lips with a finger.

Dele told her.

'I'd have his head off in a second. For what he did, and to Comfy,' said Mrs Lagbaja.

'But it all seems so…so arbitrary, he seems to make it up as he goes along,' said Dele.

Aanu cracked open another can of beer. 'Why you talk as if you prefer manure to butter on your plate? Sajulo is dynamic. He ordered rice for us from China,' he said, giving his can of beer an inquiring shake in front of his ear.

'You are grateful because he bought rice…with your own money? Without your say? Why not salmon, or caviar?' Dele said.

'People don't want all this talk. They want food. When Haka and Banusi and all those henchmen quench and we eat cheap rice, Siroko people will be happy,' said Aanu.

'Happy? Or is that apathy with a painted smile?' Dele said. The kettle boiled. *To kill or free Sandman?* she thought. Then a frightening idea popped into her head. Sandwoman.

TWENTY

Dele got off the chair lift at the bottom of a mower-striped lawn. In the distance Sandman's white mansion stood on four fluted columns. Its shadow leaned away and to the east and cast the lawn in part shadow. In the Bay of Roko, a quarter of a mile away to Dele's left, peroxide waves leapt off the turquoise sea splashing foam at the jagged rock face below which Sandman's and Banusi's yachts once moored.

'Where do I meet her?' said Dele.

Her guide pointed to Kamura in conversation with a man in a purple surplice.

'Madam just finished Sunday morning service. He come to pray for the minister to be free,' he said.

The garden sprinklers juggling rainbows above the lawn stopped to let Dele pass. On the right a Golden Retriever frolicked in its own swimming pool beside an air-conditioned kennel.

'Go well,' said Kamura when she saw Dele, signalling with a surreptitious wave of her hand for a maid to hustle the pastor away. In a yellow kimono, Kamura had small round eyes and her lips looked primed with Botox or polyfilla and drooped at the margins like a child's. On her wrist, a watch the size of a small lighthouse shone in as many colours as the day has hours. In all but that item of jewellery, her bearing, arrogant, smug, mingled with a hint of malice and an air of overweening entitlement reminded Dele of Yourlot.

An aeroplane droned above. Kamura wiped her brow and shook her fist at the sun-bleached sky. 'When Asiri was there this cannot happen...flying plane over our airspace to disturb us on a Sunday, kai, this is an insult, infra- dig.'

A maid set out canned drinks, platters of seafood, sandwiches and cheeses and Kamura ushered Dele to a blue gazebo overlooked by a glass-stained window depicting an African Grey Parrot.

'Prawns or what?' said Kamura. She sat down.

Dele shook her head, but sat next to Kamura round the corner of the table. 'I'm taking part in an experiment…no food after breakfast. How is Pupa?'

Kamura cracked her high heel into the marble patio. 'Don't mention that girl's name,' she said, looking as if she'd been showered in a reptile's recycled mouthwash. How much did that man, Banusi, pay you?' she said.

'I came to say sorry…I tried to get your husband to tell me what happened to my dad, putting everything else aside-'

Kamura yelped, jerked up in her chair. The steel-coloured fascinator fell off her Naomi Campbell-inspired shoulder-length hair, but she did not seem to care. 'What are you doing here?' she said, slapping a maid about the head.

'Sorry ma,' said the maid, picking up her mistresses' hat and scurrying off in a crouch like a tennis ball girl.

Kamura turned to Dele. 'You disgrace me and my son in front of my friends, my family. My son on medication…I cannot see him.' She paused. The pupils of her eyes shone like spear tips. 'Banusi will pay tenfold, hundred fold for this.'

Ditto Sandman. 'I didn't come to…sorry I won't take any more of your time,' Dele said. She dipped a cotton wool-soft serviette in a glass of ice cold water, wiped her face and got up.

Kamura glared at Dele, her eyes burning with spite and fury. 'Where were all of you when Asiri tendered for contract and some illiterate copied his application and we nearly died of hunger.' With the yellow kimono falling down one arm, she waved the other arm at Dele like a sword. 'Where were you when Asiri tried to sue ministry and they lost the file, cracked the data-stick, adjourned and adjourned because the judge was in Mecca or Lourdes or in America? Where were you when they used to call my family "flies on a pile of shit"? Where were you when Asiri made investment and the market turned and the man ran away with his money and that woman, Daro, whose husband not travelled beyond her village is dressed like a fairy and I am in rags every day?'

'So your husband has no case to answer?' Dele said.

Kamura screamed. 'Don't come here to talk nonsense. Those *kelekele* aid workers from overseas put these words in your mouth...and Banusi paid you.' Her voice got louder. 'In America girls talk nonsense about their papa. How can this happen to us in Sankara?'

Dele smashed a can of cola on the patio. Kamura hopped away from the drink fizzing over her shiny stone floor. 'You are rude and too forward and you have no...training,' she said. Her voice had gone hoarse.

'Is that what Sandman calls what he does? Training. You deserve what you reap,' said Dele.

TWENTY ONE

AsoRoko Barracks at midnight; as dark as a blocked drain. The guardsman got out of the car and leant through the rear car window. Dele thought she saw a gun in his hand.

'Breeze not too strong miss?' he said.

Dele blinked grit from her eyes. 'It's ok,' she said. The man flipped his right wrist round to glance at his watch. Dele flinched, but the flash of metal in his hand came from a pen torch. He tucked it away.

'In an hour or so, it will all finish…kai, they're here,' he said. A pair of twinned bright headlamps ghosted up. Two uniformed men got out of the car. The shorter one lit a cigarette. Its spark and sweet fragrance reminded Dele of Ambasi. She heard footsteps. Seconds later a tall masked man appeared out of the dark, carrying a bag in his right arm.

'Welcome. You are Verity? Wait,' he said, trotting over to the other car. He jerked open the back door and pulled a man out. Bareheaded, in a white cassock, he had his hands tied behind his back. It was Sandman.

'Take him,' said the masked man, pointing to the other end of the field. In the distance, a noose hung from a crossbar in a shaft of steely moonlight. 'Let's go,' said the masked man, his voice terse, movements brisk, a beat short of impatient, like a man keen to get back to a new lover before her touch or mind turned cold.

'You okay?' said the masked man.

Dele nodded, but her legs seemed to have turned to lilies. She stumbled out of the car and leaned against the warm bonnet for a few moments to still the fluttering feathers in her chest. 'I'm ready,' she said, fastening the top button of her jeans jacket as she walked. She found Sandman standing on the crate with his hands tied behind his back and a noose round his neck. He had his eyes closed. *He's praying? For what? Satanic salvation?*

The masked man grunted and gestured at the crate. 'You've been to Goke they tell me...so you know what to do. You stand one leg inside like this...' he said, pointing to a faint white line in the sand.

'Yes,' she said. She did remember Goke Rocks. There also it was a young woman who struck the crucial blow.

'You want to ask him anything?' said the masked man.

'I don't beg the likes of her,' Sandman said.

'Ah. Ready?' said the masked man. Too angry to speak Dele could only nod. The masked man jumped off the platform, fished around in his bag and handed Dele a two-foot long axe. It shone and smelt new, of lubricant and wood preservative, had a handle four inches thick and weighed as much as her class teacher's wooden table. Contempt and defiance gave way to a flash of fear in Sandman's eyes. *Now you know what it's like.*

The wind seemed to whisper Sandman's real name, *Asiri, Asiri,* through the trees. The noose gave a leathery croak. Dele stepped over the white line. As she raised the axe above her head a tall thin man loped into view with a piece of paper fluttering in his hand.

'Wait,' said the masked man.

Dele put the axe down and stretched her fingers. *What now?*

'Excuse me sir, are you the Excu officer?'

The masked man grunted and took the new man aside. 'What are you saying?' he said.

'General Sajulo sent me to check. Is it for the parrot case that he is hanging?'

'Give me that,' said the masked man. He scanned the paper, tracing the words with the torch. 'Go,' he said. 'Not you, you come miss. Sorry. They have tried him for parrot and he is guilty but they have not tried him yet for the other matter-'

'What are you saying?' said Dele.

'Send him back...to wait for the second trial?' he said.

If Aanu was here he would say this was Sandman's juju working. 'You cannot be-'

Another motorbike coughed into view.

'Good evening or morning,' said a man in a pale jacket. He left the engine running and ran up to give the masked man a white envelope.

'It is from commander Sajulo,' he said.

The masked man handed Dele a torch and a piece of paper. It had the General's seal on its bottom right hand corner. Dele read the brief message twice. 'It seems the commander in chief has passed another clarification decree,' she said, turning to the masked man. 'It says here that as Sandman is already guilty of the parrot offence and as he cannot produce the parrot anyway while in detention over what he did to Ms Giradona, this bridging decree makes all possibility of appeal disappear - like a line of sugar thrown into the sea,' said Dele.

'Or cocaine.' The masked man paused.

Dele did not react.

'Let's get the show on the move,' the masked man said with a shrug. 'As I said, stand there, left foot over on his side of the line in the goal-mouth sand, side-on, not square, feet apart…that's it, now you are balanced,' said the masked man.

It's now or never. Dele raised the axe, reeling backwards under its weight. She swung the axe down. The crate splintered. Sandman dropped a foot, his head jerked back, feet crossed and pedalled the air and his eyes bulged as if in search of other orbits. Dele did not see the end.

***

'Where am I?' said Dele. She groaned and rubbed the back of her head.

'Hospital for check-up. Two minute you no wake,' the driver said.

Am I dead? Where is Sandman? Dele felt her sore nape and occiput. The yellow streetlamps and trees moonwalked past the car.

'Oh, oh, I remember now,' said Dele when the car stopped at a road sign five miles from central Sankara. 'Ha, I'm fine now Mr…what's your name, sir?' said Dele.

'Nagode. You landed on the back of your head,' said Mr Nagode.

He's gone, Mum, Dad, gone. 'Believe me my head has never felt much better,' said Dele, fingering the date-sized lump on her occiput.

TWENTY TWO

Aanu got off the kitchen chair. 'I can't stay. Just wanted to see how you were after…what happened, I'm off to meet Snake Legs. Soldiers beat him the other night.'

'Give him this,' said Dele. She gave Aanu a box of dates.

And Aanu dear, Dele was very brave…but could you please dissuade her from drawing these awful gallows.' Mrs Lagbaja passed a sketch to Aanu over the kitchen table. 'Here,' she said.

Aanu's looked at the drawing. For a second he looked bemused, then an amiable look crossed his face. 'Draw what you like if that's what grows your tubers,' he said, giving Dele a friendly punch on the shoulder.

'It's my phone. Mr Momoh the airport manager,' said Dele. Aanu unzipped his jacket and hovered.

'I hear Haka is no more,' said Mr Momoh.

I should know, seeing as I was there. 'Any news about the Arimos?' said Dele.

'Sorry. I have been calling pastor. No reply. I heard about his…how his time ended…only the other day. Accept my condolences.'

'Appreciate it,' said Dele.

If he's just heard about Ambasi I don't care much for his grapevine.

'Bisuyi, the blind man you saw at the airport has been released. I met him…but don't get your hopes up. He's not well.'

'Can I see him?' said Dele.

'It is hectic at the moment. We are airlifting Haka's thugs for trial. But I will speak to him and other released Arimos afterwards.'

'What about Burutu?' said Dele.

'I am working on him too, maybe he will want to cut another deal.' Aanu tapped Dele on the shoulder and signalled that he had to go. Dele closed the call.

'Mr Momoh may have some news,' she said.

314

'How can this...man get around so easily after a coup?' said Aanu.

'I'm afraid I agree with Aanu...I'm not saying don't accept his offer...but-'

'Check its sell by date,' said Aanu.

'Exactly,' said Mrs Lagbaja, gesturing for a top up of her mug of tea.

***

'I am coming, over the matter we discussed,' said the airport manager.

Mrs Lagbaja walked in to the living room. 'Who was that?' she said.

'I said Mr Momoh,' said Dele, tucking her phone into the pocket of her jeans.

'Same man who called last week?'

Dele nodded.

'Wouldn't trust him as far as I could dribble. I'm off to Igbobi to inspect this new aviary. I might be a while,' said Mrs Lagbaja, hauling a brown and orange bag off the sofa.

Dele had just closed the door after her lodger when Hanili called.

'Career change. I've applied to our Trade Section,' she said.

Her words sucked the life out of Dele's legs. 'You're not leaving?' said Dele, leaning against a chair.

'Gee heavens no. You won't get rid of unilateral kidney Hanili that easily. I'll, em, be working from here, monitoring the World Trade Organisation. Get the big ones to stop their unfair trade subsidies. Perhaps I'll save more lives that way than by digging boreholes, and I'll still have you.'

'I'd come over but the airport manager's coming to pick me up,' said Dele.

'I...don't like the sound of that,' said Hanili.

Dele scratched her ear. 'It's about Dad,' said Dele.

'Closure's not always what it's wrapped up to be. What are you going to do about Ambasi's book?' said Hanili.

'I decided that the world didn't need another divisive religious book,' said Dele.

'Says the Verily General Mugabe Mobutu Verity.'

'Someone at my door…'

A man in a light blue air force pilot's uniform knocked and marched straight in to Dele's flat.

'Almost twelve sharp, you are ready? Mr Momoh is downstairs,' he said, with a lubricious air.

Clown. Dele looked out of the window and waved. Mr Momoh waved back from beside a white Japanese SUV. In a red T-shirt, green chinos and white sneakers he looked like an overgrown schoolboy who had been dressed by his mum.

'I'll be right down,' Dele said. Dele let the man out, and waited by the window until he appeared outside. She called Hanili again. 'For what it's worth I'm texting you a photo of Mr Momoh's car,' she said.

'Love you, be careful,' said Hanili.

'Love you recklessly, endlessly,' said Dele. She blew a kiss into the phone. Dele put on her jeans jacket, swapped her stud for a pair of pendant earrings and went to stand in front of the bedroom mirror to practice jabbing them into the eye or ear of an imaginary assailant. *Better than nothing.*

'No cigarette stubs in this car?' said Dele, as she got in, patting the pocket of her jeans for the reassuring feel of her phone. The car smelt recent new, perhaps less than a year old.

Mr Momoh seemed to hesitate before he shook his head. 'This is the best time to go, now that the internal inquiry is concluded, before Sajulo changes the law again,' he said, blinking his syllables faster than usual. 'This last two weeks since we spoke is like they wrap us all in blanket of chewing gum. We cannot move, cannot breathe…one day they say one thing, the next they pass new decree. They say I can see Burutu, then say he is not reliable, so I only go by what Bisuyi the Arimo, told me.'

Whose car is this? thought Dele.

After an hour they came off the highway and on to a dirt-track.

'Can you stop after the bridge? I want to buy coconuts for Mrs Lagbaja,' said Dele.

Mr Momoh gave Dele a puzzled look but parked the car on the verge beside a cluster of waist-high mushroom-like plants.

'My lodger's favourite,' said Dele.

Mr Momoh sighed but didn't seem to mind the delay.

'Have you been to this...camp...before,' said Dele as she clambered back in armed with three hairy coconuts.

Mr Momoh shook his head. 'But I hear it is for stubborn cases.' He went quiet.

I hope Dad wasn't too stubborn.

They plunged into the forest. The dense canopy of treetops shivering like a giant sieve seemed to bounce spiky grains of golden sunlight off the windscreen. After four hours, they came to a bright clearing. A soldier appeared from behind a tree and shook the gun in his hand like a cruet. Mr Momoh stopped the car. Dele picked up her coconut, to crack heads with if things got sticky. The car rolled forward.

The soldier's hand went to his holster. 'Did you not hear me?' he said.

'Sorry it's...the automatic...handbrake, my mistake,' said Mr Momoh. With one hand holding his trousers up by the buckle the soldier leaned in to the car. 'What model?' he said, beaming at the green fluorescent display.

'Diesel 45sti,' said Mr Momoh. 'Proceed,' said the soldier, gesturing to the gateman. Dele belched her relief and dropped her dry and prickly grenade back under her seat. Mr Momoh steered the car in to a walled carpark. Dele waited for a serval with a rat in its mouth to saunter past first, got out of the car, stretched and yawned with fearful excitement, wondering what "closure" had in store. A soldier in a dark grey uniform murmured into a walkie-talkie as he marched up.

Mr Momoh saluted.

'You are Momoh. And you?' the soldier said.

'Dele Verity. Student.'

'She's here to find out about one of the accused,' said Mr Momoh.

The accused? Her legs trembled like a plucked guitar string. Mr Momoh propped her up by the elbow.

'That is what they call them here,' said Mr Momoh.

'Come, take, I am guess your size,' said the soldier. He clicked his heels and gave Dele and the manager hooded nylon jackets and a pair of boots each. Dele's pair felt as large as a baby elephant's.

'I nearly forget,' said the soldier. He unsheathed a machete.

Dele hopped backwards. A boot fell off her left foot.

'It's for cutting through bush,' said the soldier, handing a smaller cutlass to the manager.

'I'll have one too,' said Dele, reburying her foot.

'No, take this,' said the soldier.

Dele slipped the tiny penknife into the front pocket of her jeans and smoothed back her damp hair.

'Come,' said the soldier. He struck through a browning hedge with his machete. Dele slithered down the gentle slope after him into the humid gloom and, for the next fifteen minutes, thumped, brushed, clawed at by spindly twigs, by purple, paddle-shaped petals, flute-shaped white stems and vines a foot-wide, she clomped along, the head-high fronds springing to behind her like a sphincter, making her wonder how, if she had to, she would find her way back alone.

Then, through a bunch of brown seed pods, the forest gave way to an open field. Above, feathery snow-white clouds floated west in a dazzling sea-blue sky; and ahead lay rows and rows of tomato plants fenced in by high barbed wire. At the far end of the field stood half a dozen fat trees. They looked the wrong way up.

'South Roko Baobabs,' said Mr Momoh. Dele nodded, her eyes fixed on the largest tree on the end. It had a wide slit in its pitted brown trunk and about twenty paces to its left stood a borehole in front of which lay a hoe, a cutlass, a length of thick rope and other farming implements.

They had crossed half the field when the soldier stopped. 'Only two men remain. One die inside that tree last week. I think they removed him by now.' Dele's hopes stopped and panic gripped her neck.

The soldier stared at the largest of the baobab trees and clapped his hands, like an owner would at his dog's kennel. Nothing happened. 'Maybe he deaf,' he said. He sighed and pierced the silence with a two-fingered whistle. A flock of birds exploded from the trembling treetops, darted helter-skelter and fluttered down like cinders.

Dele wiped the cold sweat off her face and neck. They set off again, crunching caked mud underfoot. Mr Momoh wheezed. The soldier hummed. Then, with thirty or so paces from the Baobab trees, Dele thought she saw the glint of metal and a shadow move inside that largest tree trunk. Her step quickened and her eyes locked on to the tree as if, after hundreds of years, it would there and then up sticks and leaves. With ten or so rows of tomatoes between her and that same tree she stopped. She stopped because she thought she heard or felt a familiar cadence in that flip, flop, shuff, flip, flop, shuff, flip. She stopped because each slap of a slipper against the ground she thought she heard from within that tree quaked the earth beneath her own feet. She froze because for a moment she could not seem to see or breathe.

Then a ridged scalp ringed by curly grey flakes emerged from the dark through soft shadow into the sunlight. Hunched, in a baggy open-chested pale blue top and pair of trousers, the shapeless sort the judokas wear, the man shuffled forward in a wide leftward arc. With his feet in a large brown pair of slippers, his stubby toes looked like cocktail sausages in a sauce. He had a yellow bucket swinging behind him in his left hand and had his right fist clenched. This right hand shook as if tinkling a bell, its knuckles pointing where he was heading; and, like a man who had long learned to look and listen over his shoulder wherever he went, he held his head rigid and turned ever so slightly the other way. *Can he see?* thought Dele as knots of anxiety wrestled inside her pounding chest. The man paused, raised his head for a beat or two and resumed his weary way to the well. Then he turned away and coughed into an elbow.

At that Dele let out a strangled shriek. Bothering no longer to shake the soil or crawlies off her legs and with silent apologies for squashing the crops, she trampled weeds, fended off a bendy sapling, kicked a clump of soil, skipped over a rabbit hole and a moulting snake, hurdled a hollowed tree trunk, a rusting watering can, a rock, a snail, ducked under a trellis arch, swatted a fly, and flew towards her dad, crying 'it's me, Dele, it's me, daddy's little girl-girl in the world.' And some of those same heavy years seemed to fall off the man's bent back and neck and wrinkled face; and his dull dry eyes flashed into teary life and he stopped, smiled, dropped the yellow bucket and clasped to his bony chest his only child.

Sola Odemuyiwa is a cardiologist in Surrey and the author of Deadly Conception and The Pregnant Mule.